Eden Rise

Also by Robert J. Norrell

Up from History:
The Life of Booker T. Washington (2009)

The House I Live In:
Race in the American Century (2005)

The Alabama Journey:
State History and Geography (1998)

The Alabama Story:
State History and Geography (1993)

The Making of Modern Alabama:
State History and Geography (1993)

We Want Jobs! A Story of the Great Depression (1992)

Opening Doors: An Appraisal
of Contemporary American Race Relations (1991)

James Bowron:
The Autobiography of a New South Industrialist (1991)

A Promising Field:
Engineering at Alabama, 1837–1987 (1990)

Reaping the Whirlwind:
The Civil Rights Movement in Tuskegee (1985)

EDEN RISE

A novel by

ROBERT J. NORRELL

☙

NEWSOUTH BOOKS
Montgomery

NewSouth Books
105 S. Court Street
Montgomery, AL 36104

Copyright © 2012 by Robert J. Norrell
All rights reserved under International and Pan-American Copyright Conventions. Published in the United States by NewSouth Books, a division of NewSouth, Inc., Montgomery, Alabama.

Library of Congress Cataloging-in-Publication Data

Norrell, Robert J. (Robert Jefferson)
Eden rise : a novel / by Robert J. Norrell.
p. cm.
ISBN 978-1-58838-268-9 — ISBN 1-58838-268-0
1. Civil rights movements—Fiction. 2. Alabama—Race relations—Fiction. I. Title.
PS3614.O767E34 2012
813'.6—dc23

2012026219

Design by Randall Williams

Printed in the United States of America
by Maple Press

For Tracey

Contents

	Prologue, 1993 / 3
1	The Sound of Doom / 11
2	Smells of Death / 21
3	Shots in the Night / 32
4	Baby Gone Home / 39
5	The Man from Chicago / 44
6	Judge McKee / 48
7	Joe Black Pell for the Defense / 54
8	Barbershop Cuts / 66
9	Sacred Fire / 73
10	Truth in the Truck / 78
11	Gooch / 85
	Interlude I, 1993 / 95
12	One Word / 99
13	Gaineswood / 106
14	Revelation / 111
15	Big Tom / 118
16	Vietnam / 124
17	Heat and Combustion / 128
18	Negro Detection / 136
19	Get Lost / 143
20	Family Honor / 149
21	Midnight Hour / 155
22	Circling Crows / 159

23	Not Long / 165	
24	Nuclear Standoff / 171	
25	Dust on My Feet / 178	
26	Changed Men / 183	
	Interlude II, 1993 / 191	
27	Dixie / 194	
28	Negro History / 202	
29	Damn Champion / 210	
30	Surprise Witness / 214	
31	Latin and Celtic / 226	
32	God Knows / 232	
33	New Politics / 240	
34	The White-Haired Girl / 247	
35	Leaving / 259	
36	The Sparrow / 267	
	Postlude, Spring 1994 / 275	

Eden Rise

Prologue

1993

"You can make the difference, Tom," U.S. Attorney Randy Russell told me. "I know it's been years, but even now you can do us justice."

Russell's urging caused me to lose much of a night's sleep. I got up that Saturday morning and went to an AA meeting. *Let go of it, because you can't keep it from happening.* I hadn't known that AA lesson the awful summer I was nineteen, when the world seemed to cave in on me. And now Randy Russell was asking me to summon that dead world's ghosts. At 9 A.M., I called my sister and asked if she had time for a ride down home.

"I need some advice."

"Sure thing," said Cathy. "Telling my big brother what to do has always been my favorite pastime."

I picked her up and we headed southwest out of Birmingham, the midday sun behind us, pitching its yellow rays almost horizontal to the ground. It was the coolest light of the year, the friendliest and easiest to use, though it didn't last long. It brilliantly illuminated the hardwoods, which had all donned their saffron and auburn and crimson, though many had already shed their leaves.

Cathy eyed me carefully when I edged hard into a turn at Tuscaloosa. We rode due south on the gentle rise and fall of pavement through pine thickets around Moundville and Greensboro. The little towns had run down in the decades since I left, their concrete streets now broken and potted, many storefronts vacant. Three out of four houses begged for paint. Compared to our prosperous suburbs, with our ever-expanding shopping malls and our French-imitation mini-mansions and our very black asphalt streets, these little towns could show us nothing *new*. Nearly all had lost population since the 1960s. The prosperous whites—including Cathy and me, the remnants of our small-town clan—had departed for more manicured places. I wasn't sure where the blacks had gone, but most had abandoned that part of the world.

South of Greensboro the rolling of the land became gentler, the landscape more open. We had reached the Black Belt prairie, and soon our own little faded town rose up ahead. Eden Rise sits on the last ripple of that gently rolling prairie before it flattens out entirely. The Virginia planters built a village on the elevation when they gleefully moved to Alabama in the 1830s. They came to take advantage of the charcoal-colored soil that lay atop a great limestone formation. The Virginians expected this "self-liming" soil to combine with the hot sun and the big rains to make an Edenic paradise of cotton—having already worn out the garden soil in the Old Dominion. They brought along their large array of slaves, a fact I discovered when as a confused middle-aged man I decided to research the genealogy of my family. In looking for my ancestors I came across the massive property holdings—of both land and flesh—of the Randolphs, the Ruffins, the Cockes, the Withers, and the other first families of Virginia who were also the first families of this prairie garden. The thousands of Africans were the real cultivators of the new Eden. The owners of the land disappeared on Civil War battlefields, or if they survived, they left after the war for Birmingham or Atlanta or Mobile.

Other whites had soon presented themselves to take control, among them a Scots-Irishman named McKee who spawned my line. They all discovered what the first settlers knew—that, while the soil would indeed grow bumper crops of cotton, it turned into a glue-like mud with the first spring deluge, thus making harvesting the big crop a frenzy of work in the snatches of dry time between long periods when animals and equipment and Africans were stuck in the mud. Of course, by the time I was farming as a young man, improved drainage and wide-wheeled tractors mostly kept us from getting stuck.

The road into Eden Rise looked different from how it did in my childhood. The tin-roofed sharecropper houses had disappeared, and if they had been replaced, it was with a manufactured home, what we called a trailer-house when I was growing up—a rectangular box made of fiberboard and covered with beige aluminum. They were cleaner and nicer than the shacks they replaced, but like their inhabitants they sat unrooted on the land. Little in fact was now rooted in the Black Belt soil. I didn't know of anybody now growing cotton within thirty miles of where I grew up. Much of the land around Eden Rise, including parts of our own, was used for catfish farming.

Still even an old dirt farmer like me had to admit that the catfish ponds, which covered several acres each, often in groups of three or four, were beautiful on this bright day as the sunlight bounced off the water. I pulled off the road and parked in front of a pond that we owned—though its slimy inhabitants belonged to a corporation based in Mississippi. On the pond's bank, when most of the other flora had called it a season, lantana bloomed promiscuously. It lit the water's edge a fiery red.

Having gotten this close to home, I didn't really want to go into town and drive by our family home, or my grandmother's, or the courthouse, the scene of so much trouble back in 1965. These places would make me remember the injustice, now almost thirty years old, that Randy Russell wanted me to help him correct. I was happy to stop right here, amid the beauty of farmed fish. I got out of the car and stood looking at the water.

Cathy joined me. "So? Talk to me," she said.

RANDY RUSSELL, PRESIDENT CLINTON's recent appointee as U.S. attorney in the Northern District of Alabama, had asked me to meet him at John's Restaurant in downtown Birmingham. I had just dug into my snapper tails and coleslaw when he smiled tentatively and said he was going to file a criminal case for violation of civil rights in the 1965 Yancey County murder.

I jerked back hard from my food. I thought he had invited me to dinner because he was going to offer me a job on his staff. I had spent the previous evening pondering whether I wanted to give up teaching constitutional law at Cumberland law school.

"What?!"

"Yeah. I'm going to get a conviction this time."

I was having trouble swallowing my food.

Russell went on. "I just feel like I'm supposed to do something about it. Make up for old wrongs, correct past injustices."

I guess there had been a long silence at the table when he plunged ahead. "Tom, I'm going to need you to be a witness. You know, the main witness."

"That was a terrible time in my life. I'm not going back there."

He looked at me a long moment and then shrugged. "You're a lawyer, Tom, an officer of the court. You have an obligation as a material witness." When I didn't respond, he shrugged again. "I can subpoena you."

It sounded like a threat, coming from a thirty-something prosecutor who was still riding his Huffy when my best friend was murdered in 1965. I didn't like it. "I've forgotten most of what happened," I said.

He looked at me without blinking. "You can remember."

As she gazed at the shimmering water, Cathy tapped her can of Diet Coke. "I heard Russell has an idealistic streak. Son of a Methodist preacher, isn't he?"

My sister is good-looking at forty-five—tall and shapely in her Gap jeans and crisp Oxford shirt. Gray streaks add character to her thick, dark hair. She runs a usually profitable public relations firm, manages a mostly happy marriage to a busy surgeon, and has raised two generally well-adjusted teenagers. Her success as an adult, especially compared to my own irresolution, has earned my deference to her opinions about the big issues. But since that summer of 1965, I've also known she was something of a genius at human relations.

"You said you wouldn't do it. Why do you need advice?"

"You understand why I don't want to testify?"

"You're trying to avoid a hassle."

"So it's the right decision?" I said.

"I didn't say that. *You decided*, and it's your decision."

I looked over toward Eden Rise, hazy in the fall warmth. "What's the reason to do it? You understand that these trials are just a quick fix for liberal guilt?"

The idea, of course, was not original with Russell. In the last few years, several far more notorious civil rights murder cases—Medgar Evers in Mississippi, the four girls at the Sixteenth Street Baptist Church in Birmingham—had been reopened and old racists dragged into court before juries now including blacks. I had followed those proceedings with a distant skepticism, born partly of the assumption that whites didn't *ever* get convicted of such crimes and partly from my lawyerly doubts about the efficacy of old evidence—dead witnesses, lost documents, and such. But those killers did at last get convicted, which made people believe they could shut the door once and for all on the past.

I had shoved into the shadows of the past the face of my friend Jackie Herndon, dead now for twenty-eight years. There too were the angry eyes of my father, the lazy face of the prosecutor, the sneers of the attorney defending Jackie's killer, the contempt of townspeople who thought I had betrayed my birthright. The last thing I needed was to parade ghosts into a federal courtroom. The post-civil-rights-white-punishment-and-redemption trials became major media events. There wasn't enough whisky in Birmingham to get me through that.

I suspected the insincerity of people using the past for today's therapeutic needs. These trials were a way for blacks and whites to avoid dealing with the serious human relations problems we faced in the 1990s—failing schools and the indifference to them, drugs and crime, black kids growing up virtually without parenting, smug whites insulated in suburbs like mine. You had the conservatives who now used Martin Luther King's dream of a color-blind society as their authority for denouncing affirmative action and minority set-asides when they had not agreed with anything King said when he was alive. There were the neo-Confederates who insisted that the Civil War hadn't been about slavery so they could feel good about being Southern and create cover for their persistent white-supremacist instincts. And all the folks doing backflips to forgive George Wallace for fomenting hatred in the 1960s because later, when blacks had won the vote, he asked to be forgiven. *I* would never forgive George Wallace for how he tried to ruin my father in the summer of 1965.

The ones most willing to confuse forgiving with forgetting were black.

All right, forgive him if you want, but that doesn't undo what he did in the 1960s. We're still paying for that, with a lot of the payback going to blacks who remain so outraged at what happened back then that they refuse to acknowledge that history has moved on and some things have gotten better. Just a few months ago, I heard a black preacher declare to a big group that we still had slavery in Birmingham, and he got a rousing response.

People lie about the past so they can lie about the present. They become so selective about what they remember the truth gets lost. For me, the past just meant regret.

All this tumbled out as we communed with the catfish. Cathy nodded solemnly. "I see what you mean about the insincerity." She studied her Coke can. "But in the world of PR, you tell clients to figure the price of doing nothing. What's it cost you *not* to testify?"

I shrugged.

"Oh, come on, Tommy. You risk seeing yourself as a coward, somebody who lost the guts you showed as a nineteen-year-old."

"Courage is overrated."

"Bullshit. You *don't* believe that." She shook her head. "The guy subpoenas you, you'll tell the story like it happened. You're incapable of lying in court."

She picked up a rock and threw it far into the pond, setting off a frenzy just beneath the surface. She looked back at me. "Plus you might get something good out of testifying."

"Like what?"

"On Oprah they call it closure." Cathy has this way of arching one eyebrow when she is about to nail your dumb ass to the wall. "You've been beating yourself up your whole adult life over what happened."

She and I knew well the side effects of my lifelong recrimination. We called them the three Ds—divorce, drinking, depression.

"Who knows. In a new trial, you might find out you're not guilty after all." She flung another rock into the pond and picked a stem of scarlet lantana. "Let's go look around town."

We drove around the square. Everything looked a lot different. In 1965 it had bustled and shone, clean and bright. Now the Farmers and Merchants Bank bore the name and logo of a big Birmingham holding company. The windows of the barbershop, shoe store, and hardware store on the south side were boarded up with sheets of plywood. Pasted on them were posters for a rap concert in Selma that was now two months in the past. The grass on the square hadn't been mowed in a month, nor had the dead leaves under the magnolia been swept up. No flowers bloomed.

The Confederate statue had a six-pointed star spray-painted on its base. "Somebody in town embracing Judaism?" I wondered aloud.

"Gang symbol. See the pitchforks above it?" Cathy's teenagers kept her well informed.

We drove past the sprawling ranch house we had grown up in—where in the summer of 1965 I argued with my father and where, after Jackie's death, I was a virtual prisoner. The house now sported purple shutters. Cathy clucked her tongue. "At least they're painted." The shutters on the neighboring house were peeling and hanging askew.

We proceeded to the curved, tree-lined drive that rose to a columned mansion from the 1850s. Cathy knocked on the back door and told the live-in caretaker we were going to look around for a few minutes but wouldn't be coming inside. After a slow stroll around, I said it looked pretty good.

"Needs painting." She pointed to the upstairs windows.

We sat on the front porch in the ancient glider, once a bright aqua but now a dull, pale blue. It squeaked loudly; we couldn't glide.

"The Rose of Sharon still blooms." Just as I pointed that way, a sparrow chirped. "Here-kitty-kitty-kitty," my grandmother Bebe used to sing in mimicry of the songbird. As a three-year-old, Cathy had changed it to "Loove, Bebe, Bebe, Bebe."

When I began to hum an old hymn, Cathy cast a sweet smile my way. "I know you don't want to sell it. I don't really, either." She paused to let the sparrow have his say.

"You can't have it both ways, Tommy. You want to hold on to our past when it's the memory of Bebe, but then you repress the hard stuff."

On the way back to the car, she slipped her arm around my waist and leaned into me. "You know your decision is going to be the right one as far as I'm concerned. I'm just pointing out a couple of things to think about."

We stopped at Dreamland in Tuscaloosa and ate some ribs and watched the Crimson Tide play Mississippi State on television. On Monday I called Randy Russell. Late that afternoon I began to tell him what happened on the highway to Eden Rise on May 24, 1965.

1

THE SOUND OF DOOM

1965

Our freshman year at Duke University completed, Jackie Herndon and I met outside my dorm at 6 A.M. and loaded our stuff into the trunk of my Ford, a cherry-red 1963 Galaxie hardtop I'd inherited from my grandfather. We drove to the dorm where Alma Jones lived. We were picking her up and driving to Alabama to begin our summer break.

Alma's dorm door was locked. We tried all the doors, and all were locked. "You told her six o'clock, right?" I said.

Jackie shrugged. "Yeah, I told her twice to be packed and ready to go."

At 6:30, a girl came out the door dragging a big suitcase. I offered to carry her suitcase to her car if she would go tell Alma that her ride was waiting. She agreed. In a few minutes Alma appeared at the door.

"What's the damn hurry?" she grumbled.

"It's a long way to Alabama, at least twelve hours," I said.

She scowled. "All right, all right, I'll be down in a few minutes."

A grimace flashed across Jackie's face. "I'm sorry, man."

Jackie grabbed his basketball and began twirling it on his finger. He raised the ball high above his lean, six-foot-seven-inch frame. His unlined, mocha-colored face studied the spinning orb intently. I noticed again what I had observed when the two of us were studying in the cafeteria—Jackie's hands. His very long fingers wrapped effortlessly around a basketball. He had long, perfect fingernails and unblemished brown skin on the backs of his hands, but nearly white palms.

The fact that Negroes had white palms had fascinated me since I first noticed it as a five-year-old and had asked my grandmother's cook about it. "Orene, why your hands two colors? You wash 'em hard?"

She had smiled. "They just that way, Tommy." The mystery of Negro hands.

We waited an entire hour before Alma came down bearing two big suitcases. She looked over at Jackie. "Put those in the car." No "please," just a command. Not a word of apology about making us almost two hours late leaving.

Even angry at her, I was awed by Alma's presence. At six feet, she came closer to looking me in the eye than any girl I had ever known. Tight jeans accentuated her endless legs and the round butt perched atop them. Her skin was smooth and about the color brown of the Hershey's chocolate wrapper. She had a small gap in her flashing, proud grin. There was no question about why she started Jackie's engine. She started mine too, and watching her fold herself into the Ford's back seat, I felt for the first time desire for a black woman.

I was starved and desperate for a cup of coffee. At the drive-through window of a donut shop, I ordered a dozen donuts and coffee. Alma demanded milk. Still no "please," and no offer of money. Full of donuts and milk, she lay down in the seat as we pulled away.

I headed southwest down the North Carolina piedmont toward Charlotte. From there I would move through the South Carolina upcountry and the northern Georgia hills to Atlanta. There was no cloud in the sky, and the air was already warm. Jackie tuned the radio to Junior Walker and his All-Stars. He tapped time on the red leather seat between us as the saxophone trilled and the backups sang "Shotgun. Shoot 'em 'fore they run now. . . ."

"Damn it, turn that off!" Alma said in a shriek.

I should have stopped the car right then and had it out with her. But I was chickenshit. Jackie shook his head, either as intimidated by her as I was, or unwilling to offend the sexy woman with whom he was spending the summer. Jackie would have all summer to woo Alma or be terrified of her: she had persuaded him to help her teach at a "freedom school," a special school for black kids from segregated schools in a small Alabama town not that far from my home in Eden Rise. Alma was Duke's leading civil rights activist.

Jackie wanted me to join them at the freedom school, and I had said I would think about it, which was why she sat up in the back seat after two hours of sleep and said "Well, are you going to work with us or not?"

I shook my head. "I don't think so."

"Why not?" There was a challenge in her tone. "What you got better to do?"

"That's just not what I want to do." In fact I didn't know what I wanted to do that summer except to eat my mother's cooking and visit my sick grandmother. The idea of teaching at a freedom school made me nervous. Out of the corner of my eye, I caught the disappointment on Jackie's face.

"Anything's better than trying to help a few little niggers, huh?"

Jackie jerked around to face her. "Leave him alone or we'll be walking to Alabama."

Why was she so hostile to me? I hardly knew her and could count on one hand the number of sentences we had exchanged before our ride that morning. I had never said or done a contrary thing toward her. I figured she had to dislike me for what I was, a white Southerner, or what she assumed I was from my accent, my haircut, and my button-down shirt and penny loafers—a bigot in training.

When she fell asleep again, Jackie and I talked in low tones. "Is she always like this?"

Jackie groaned. "Man, I knew she liked to run things, but I thought that was because she was older, not 'cause she's a bitch. I dread being with her in that little-assed town."

"You could bail out too and go home with me."

Jackie squinted at me. "What about your parents?"

I said, acting my most confident, they would be fine with it. Jackie and I had never talked about my parents, and I wondered if he also thought I was a typical Alabama bigot like the ones who appeared in the newspaper jeering at black people marching for the right to vote.

"You sure?"

"Yeah, I'm sure." I was, of course, lying out my ass. Mama and Daddy would be startled that I brought home a colored guy, but Mama probably would recover quickly. If it turned out to be uncomfortable in Eden Rise, we'd just jump in the car and head back to Jackie's home in the Virginia tidewater. We could be longshoremen or paint ships, or something.

Jackie nodded. "Don't say nothin' till we get there."

It felt like a late July sun on the boring new interstate through the piedmont of South Carolina. The outcroppings of clay might have been heaps of hickory wood on fire, and the signs offering the premature peaches of the season—sadly enough, the most interesting sight in my vision on this ride—glared back at me in orange and black. The white rays boiled me the whole way, though some of the heat emanated from within, so intensely did I dread the scene I imagined would take place at the freedom school.

AFTER ATLANTA, SPINDLY PINES monopolized the roadside to Newnan, past LaGrange, and on into Alabama. As we drove on, the sun hovered over the horizon in front of us. It now cast a light much easier to use, and its angle threw multilateral shadows across the pastures that covered much of this part of the Alabama Black Belt. When I was no longer driving directly into the orange mass on the horizon, I could appreciate the delicate shades of white in the Queen Anne's lace and the brilliant yellow of the Brown-Eyed Susans that decorated the roadsides. But to remind you that these beautiful ladies didn't rule the roads unchallenged, sprinkled among them were the tall, prickly stems of the noxious rusty weed my daddy called "dock."

Herds of cattle had wandered away from the lonesome pecan trees and now they munched their supper of fescue and clover, swinging their tails to swat away the horseflies that tortured them. A yearling steer, the black and white scion of an Angus-Hereford intermarriage, had backed his rump against a cedar fence post and was scratching himself in a furious war against lice, sending shimmers for hundreds of feet down the barbed-wire fence line. The air had cooled off a lot, which always made it easier for me to appreciate the beauty of Alabama farmland—the jades and olives and emeralds among the crops and grass and leaves and of the accents of gold and ginger and bronze from the soil and trees and animals. The bitter odor of herbicides recently applied to the young crops of cotton and soybeans bore through the open car windows. But I also got the sweetness of honeysuckle and the fecund stink of cow manure.

I liked all the smells, even the cow shit, because they reminded me of Eden Rise and being a boy there who watched and helped things grow that I would harvest, knowing I had participated in a cycle of nature God had ordained. That cycle, I knew from my father and mother, was what we were here to partake of. I grew up in Eden Rise believing I knew why God made us and why He placed us here, as stewards of His soil.

I turned the radio up louder, needing the sound to keep me awake. I was listening to "1-2-3," in which Len Barry declared that finding love was as easy as taking candy from a baby. I didn't share his confidence. Love had *not* come easy for me this year at Duke, or ever. Beth, my college girlfriend for a time, had enticed me into the sweet excitement of sex and then cast me off like a wool cardigan in a heat wave. I was still smarting.

"I gotta go to the bathroom."

Alma could have said so in Montgomery, through which we had just passed and where there were plenty of gas stations and drive-ins with bathrooms. But now there was none in sight, and I stayed silent.

"I *said* I need to stop."

"You wanta go on the side of the road?"

"No, damn it, find a bathroom."

We were several miles farther down the barren county road when she pointed over the seat. "There's a gas station up there."

It was actually a country store, signaled by a faded sign and surrounded by three or four junk cars and two dilapidated outbuildings. I doubted that it had public bathrooms. But I stopped anyway just to shut her up. I pulled up to the gas pump, topped with a glass Esso sign. The store's unpainted plank walls were faded to a dull gray. Red tin signs advertising Pepsi-Cola and Prince Albert smoking tobacco looked like they had been new when Granddaddy was a boy. The screen-wire door hung partly open when I went inside to pay for the gas.

Empty boxes cluttered the tongue-and-groove pine floor, which needed sweeping. Dusty cans of Del Monte corn, Van Camp's pork-and-beans, and Possum sardines and faded boxes of saltines only partly filled the two rows of shelving. I inhaled dust and mold—there had to be a leak in the roof or a broken window somewhere. At the front of the store, adjacent to the pay counter, a glass case held a few loaves of Velveeta and some bright red tubes of baloney. A drink box was pushed against a nearby wall, and I went to it and fished out a bottle of Dr Pepper. I pulled a pack of Planters peanuts off a wire rack and approached the cash register, which rested on a counter that was serving as a landing field for a squadron of houseflies.

The heavyset white man at the cash register looked me over as if he'd never seen a customer before. He wore faded bib overalls, a stained tee shirt, and a straw hat. His potbelly made inoperable the waist buttons on the overalls, exposing dingy boxer shorts. Three days of white beard covered his face, and a large plug of tobacco distended his left cheek.

As he reached out to take my money, the old man looked out the window at the gas pump and frowned. He turned slowly back toward me. "What are you and them niggers doing here?"

I didn't look at the man and put my hands in my pockets. "We're just passing through."

"Y'all some them freedom riders?" I glanced over his shoulder at the double-barrel shotgun leaned against the wall. "No, sir," I said. "We're just passing through."

I eased myself out the door and stopped Jackie on his way into the store. "Not a good place to stop," I said. I jerked my head toward the store. "The guy's real hostile." I looked over at Alma, who was still in the backseat tying her sneakers, the car door open. "Tell her we need to go on, okay? I'll fill the car up as fast as I can."

Jackie went over to the car and talked to her in a low voice. "To hell with *that*," she said loudly. "I got a right to use the toilet." She pushed past Jackie and headed for the store.

For almost thirty years now, I have cursed myself for not shoving Alma back in the car, diving into the driver's seat, and peeling out of that particular acre of hell. It never occurred to me that I didn't *have to put the damn gas* in the car. *Five fucking dollars* worth of *twenty-five-fucking-cent-a-gallon* gas. But I had paid for it, and the limits of the nineteen-year-old mind kept me from fleeing immediately, gas or no gas.

Still, I had almost finished gassing up when I heard Alma shouting inside the store.

I looked through the dirty front window and saw her gesturing at the man. I couldn't make out everything, but I heard her say "bathroom." A pause. *"You can't run a damn Jim Crow store no longer!"* and *"Who you calling . . . "* and then *"What the hell..."*

I was behind the gas pumps, Jackie in front of them. He looked over his shoulder at me. "I better go get her." I let him go first, and surely I shouldn't have.

He moved quickly toward the door and I was following when Alma appeared in the door frame. "That motherfucker's *got a gun!*" Pure hatred, not fear, in her voice.

"Come on, Alma, let's get out of here." Jackie was half pleading, half ordering her.

She looked back in the store. *"Fuck you!"* Jackie got to her just then and started pulling her toward the car. Alma was shouting. *"Let go of me! I'm going to the bathroom! He can't do that shit no more."*

The old man appeared in the door with his gun in the crook of his left arm, his right hand cradling the barrel about halfway down. He was glaring at Alma as Jackie dragged her toward the car. I ran to crank the car so we could get the hell away from there. Just as the key slipped into the ignition, I heard a deafening boom. I knew that sound. I had heard it often from the time I started hunting quail and dove with Granddaddy. The boom came from about the same distance that I was taught hunters should stay apart from each other when shooting at birds—thirty feet. The storekeeper had the shotgun at his left shoulder.

I reflexively sprawled flat across the seat but then realized I had to rise and help. I was squirming from under the steering wheel when the second boom went off.

The ringing in my ear had just subsided when the man spoke. "You goddamn agitators. We orta killed every one of you sonsabitches."

I had a gun, too. Granddaddy's pistol.

I rolled out of the car and onto my knees outside. My hands were trembling so badly that I fumbled under the seat trying to jerk the pistol out of its holster. It was heavy and slippery, and it took three tries to get the safety catch off. Move, move, *move*. When I came around the back of the car, I saw Jackie lying motionless and silent on his side. Alma was on all fours. *"He shot me! He shot me!"* She had wet herself.

I heard a snap. The old man had reloaded the double-barrel. He looked at me and Alma.

"We shoulda killed all you bastards when you first started coming down here." He raised the shotgun again.

I lifted the pistol in the direction of the man and started firing. The first bullet shattered the window to the man's left. His eyes flicked at the crumbling glass. My second shot hit the door frame above his head. He jerked the shotgun up and aimed at me.

Shoot, shoot, a voice screamed in my ear. I aimed at the man and pulled the trigger. I pulled it again and then again. The man fired simultaneously with my last shots, but one of my bullets hit high in his right leg and his aim jerked. I felt a sting in my shoulder, but it was glass, not buckshot, from the shattered Esso sign above me.

I lowered my gun, deafened, stunned. The man had pitched forward on his belly and I saw him crawling toward his gun, which had fallen a few feet to his side. I ran over and stomped my foot on his outstretched left hand. With the pistol pointed at his head, I snatched the shotgun off the ground.

"You move," I said, "I swear I'll kill you." The man stared back at me with a look not of fear or hatred or pain but of blankness. His eyes were open wide but unfocused. It was as if there was no content to him, no recognition that he had tried to kill three people just because we happened by and two were Negroes. It was as if he had scratched an itch on his chin.

I knelt over Jackie and pulled him on his back. My hands went red. His torso was drenched in blood. I raised his tee shirt and saw mutilated skin and tissue down his right side. He was bleeding from several places on his neck. I wanted to howl at the horror of what I saw, at the mutilation of this beautiful body. I flashed back to the hog-killings I had witnessed as a boy—the gushes of pig blood as the teams of black men held steady a scalded Hampshire carcass and the strongest of them pulled a twelve-inch blade the full length of its belly.

My lunch rushed upward into my throat, and it took two deep swallows to get it back down. Jackie's eyes were wide but I wasn't sure that he could see me. His mouth was open and he was panting rapidly.

I yanked off my tee shirt and pressed it against the neck wounds leaking so much blood. "Hold on, buddy, we going to get outta here."

Jackie's eyes started to flick from side to side, as if he were looking urgently for something. I wiped some of the sweat off his forehead. I felt the clenched muscles of his brow.

Alma was screaming. *"That motherfucker tried to kill us!"*

"Are you hurt?"

"Yes!" She held out her left arm. I saw a lot of welts and small wounds from the shotgun but not much blood. She wasn't hurt badly.

"Call an ambulance!"

I knew we didn't have time for that. We were at least a half hour from a Montgomery hospital. Jackie needed to be at a hospital now. Getting an ambulance would take twice the time.

"Call an ambulance right now!"

My fear flashed into anger. I jumped toward her, opened my right hand, and slapped her as hard as I could. She staggered sideways. She was stunned into silence but only for a moment.

"You white *bastard!*"

"Shut the fuck up and help me get him in the car, or I swear I'll leave you right *here.*"

She started to say something but she stopped when I drew back my hand. I looked at Jackie, and she followed my gaze. His desperate condition channeled our anger into action. I lifted up his torso and put my arms around him and lifted. "Pick up his feet." She did.

I backed around the gas pump, slid into the backseat, and pulled Jackie in to lie lengthwise on it. Something told me that Jackie shouldn't lie flat. He needed pressure applied to those neck wounds. I told Alma to come and take my place, hold Jackie's torso up, and keep the tee shirt pressed against his neck. She was crying again now, but she did what I said. I threw the shotgun in the front seat, jumped behind the wheel, and made a sliding U-turn in the gravel beyond the gas pumps. As we pulled away, the old man was sitting up, his left hand clamped on his injured leg. He'd live, the sorry piece of shit.

The sun was gone now and dusk was fading to night. Fireflies blinked all around as if to switch off the light and spread the darkness. Crickets chirped incessantly, and a whippoorwill rang out a call that had always sounded like doom to me. The trouble it had summoned for so long had surely arrived.

I glanced at my watch. Almost 8:45. I had checked the time when we stopped at the store, because I had been trying to calculate when Jackie and I would get to Eden Rise. All this had happened in less than ten minutes. I didn't have a second to think about it, and I couldn't have known it anyway, but in that time—only enough to smoke a cigarette, or chew the sugar out of a piece of gun, or listen to a couple of good songs by the Supremes—I lost Eden Rise. I wouldn't get there that night, and when I did find my way, it wasn't the place I had left.

2

SMELLS OF DEATH

The tire noise on the rough pavement roared in our ears as I raced the Galaxie through the darkness. I kept looking to hit Highway 80, the big road to Montgomery, but we had gone farther down the county road than I remembered. As time slipped away, panic crept up the back of my neck. My naked back, sweaty from heat and fear and bloody from broken glass, stuck to the leather seat.

"Hang in there, Jackie." I glanced over my shoulder but it was too dark to see them. "Can you hear me, buddy?" I waited a moment. "Is he moving?"

"He moaned a minute ago. He's really hurt." At last she sounded scared.

"Are you keeping that shirt pressed on his neck?"

"It's soaked through now."

The smell of Jackie's blood and Alma's urine now overpowered the odor of the chemicals lately put on nearby fields. We *had* to stanch the bleeding. I slammed on the brakes, rushed to the trunk of the car, and rifled in my bag until I found two clean tee shirts. In the dim light of the car's dome bulb, I could see how sodden the shirt was. Jackie's eyes were half closed, and he wasn't moving. His right hand lay open on his thigh. A jagged smear of blood marked the white palm. Those beautiful hands.

I shoved one of the clean shirts at her. "Hold him up!" Panic filled my every membrane.

The shotgun lay propped against the front passenger seat. I had been taught to admire the beauty of shotguns. This one had been the object of loving kindness. It gleamed, its pewter-colored barrels bearing just the right sheen and odor from the recent caress of a chamois cloth lightly coated with gun oil, its cherry stock waxed and buffed. Its presence suddenly made my heart thump in my ear and my right hand shake uncontrollably.

I jumped out and slung the weapon as far as I could into the blackness.

I finally came to Highway 80, turned east, and pushed the accelerator to the floor. I held the car steady at 100 miles per hour, whizzing so fast by other cars that I could hardly make out their shape or color. My window was rolled down just far enough to create a loud whistle from the air rushing in. I had never driven so fast before, but the danger suited my panic. I felt like I was floating above the ground—and indeed the car did bounce at times on the uneven pavement. When the lights refocused their gaze on the highway, three times they caught the reflections of the eyes of possums and a skunk. Their tiny twin points of red glare made me think I wasn't the only scared creature on Highway 80.

Nothing slowed the big Ford until I got to the outskirts of Montgomery. I smelled the big stockyard, and as I approached a red light in front of it, I could see nothing coming from the other directions so I pinned the accelerator to the floor and ran it. At the next intersection, I got a green light and made a tire-squealing right turn onto Fairview Avenue. I ran another light and flew past the signs for dry cleaners and funeral parlors and package beer stores, all just smears of red and green and white. Jackie was making no sound that I could hear.

Finally ahead on the left was St. Jude's Hospital. I cut in front of a truck that braked hard not to hit me. When I shouted "emergency," a guard pointed me around to the side. I fell out of the car and scrambled inside, then stopped a short woman in a white uniform, and begged for help. She shouted over her shoulder toward the back of the emergency room as I rushed her to Jackie. Two orderlies appeared and lifted his limp body onto a gurney. She hurried them back through the door shouting.

"*Type this blood now!*"

The smells of Ajax and ether hit my face as I entered the hospital. Before I cold see where they were taking Jackie, I was hustled to little room lighted by a bright bulb hanging from a wire in the high ceiling. A nurse began to inspect my heaving chest and shoulders. Beatrice, she said her name was; she looked about my age. I studied the way her thick, black hair fell in long, shiny, clumpy strands and wondered what they felt like to touch.

For the first time my body started to hurt. "I'm cold."

"I'm going to get you a gown and a blanket in just a minute, honey, just soon as I get these little wounds dressed."

"He mostly missed me," I said. She nodded, smiling, but kept her focus on my injuries. She asked my name and how the accident had happened, if my family knew I was there. "Why did you come to St. Jude's?" she said.

"Because this is a colored hospital and my friend is colored. I've been here before. Sister Carol is a friend of my grandmother." Sister Carol was the nun who headed the hospital.

I lay back on the examining table and closed my eyes, wondering where Jackie was, what the doctors were doing to him. Maybe he would need surgery to get the shot out. Beatrice covered me with a blanket and I soon fell into an edgy sleep. I awakened to the soft voices of two people, one of them Sister Carol, the other a black male doctor in a long white coat. The doctor began to pick out pieces of glass. I asked about Jackie.

The doctor glanced at Sister Carol. "Tom, Jackie's lost a lot of blood," she said.

"We tried to stop the bleeding, but it wouldn't stop. *We really tried.*"

She took my trembling right hand. "We know that, dear." She smiled. "Your grandmother is on her way here."

"Bebe shouldn't come. She's sick."

WHEN THEY LEFT, I drifted back into the strange sleep. I awakened when I felt someone stroking my arm. As I sat up on the examining table, I saw my grandmother's pale, shocked face. She cast her eyes from my bloody face to the smears across my chest. "Look at you, Tommy," she said. She turned away and found a cloth, which she wet and used to wash my face.

"Does anything hurt you, dear?"

"You're so thin, Bebe. How you feeling?"

The worry on her face deepened the hollows of her cheeks, framed by the thin strands of white hair that had fallen out of the bun at the back of her neck. "Do you hurt badly?" she said again.

"No. I'm just so tired. What time is it?"

"Almost midnight."

"Where's Jackie?"

William Addison, Bebe's house man and driver, slipped into the room, his broad face creased with concern. "Here, son." He handed me a Coca-Cola. "Your mama and daddy are on their way."

Sister Carol appeared at the door and asked me to go with her to another room, and she nodded at Bebe to come along. I followed warily, and saw Alma sitting on a straight-backed chair. Her arms were covered with small bandages, and her bloodshot eyes were locked on the black doctor beside her. Sister Carol told us to sit down. Her eyes swept from Alma to me.

"I'm afraid I've got bad news. Jackie has died."

There was a long moment of silence. "Are you sure?" Alma said the very words on my tongue. They were sure. The wounds were so bad, and he lost so much blood.

I looked at Bebe, who held my shaking hand and gazed at me. Her eyes had become sunken into her head by disease. Her dry lips quivered slightly, perhaps in preparation to offering me words of comfort, but she was interrupted.

I turned to Alma. "You made this happen." I hadn't been thinking that—it just came out. I had stopped breathing. My heart thumped loudly in my ears. The fringes of my vision turned red, and little white stars floated in and around my line of sight. I doubled both fists. She needed to pay for this. "We didn't have to stop there. We didn't have to stay there, except you made us."

I rose. I wanted to hit her again, but harder.

But then I felt Bebe wrap her bony hand, its livid veins barely obscured by her translucent skin, around my wrist and stroke the forearm above with her other hand. I breathed.

Alma gasped and then sobbed. "I want to go home!" She told Sister Carol she came from California, and the nun said she would try to arrange to get her there.

"We have to tell Jackie's mother," I said. Sister Carol nodded. "We'll take care of that. You need not worry." Bebe took my hand. "Come on, precious, let's go home."

But standing outside were two tall men in gray uniforms, black jackboots, and wide-brimmed gray felt hats bearing the Confederate battle flag on their crowns. In my experience, no men of martial authority were more impressively turned out than Alabama State Troopers. "Are you a family member?" one said to Bebe. He nodded at her reply and turned back to me. "Mr. McKee, you're under arrest. We're going to detain you until the Yancey County sheriff gets here to take you to his jail."

I lost whatever breath I had left. "Oh, please, no," Bebe said.

"I'm sorry, ma'am, but that's what they're going to do."

"What is the charge against my grandson?"

"Assault with intent to kill, ma'am."

"And whom do you say he assaulted?"

"He shot a man named Buford Kyle at a store in Yancey County."

She stared at the trooper. I had no words. The silence had extended at least a half minute when William Addison stepped forward. William was short and light brown, heavy around the middle, though his girth was disguised somewhat by charcoal wool pants worn high. His countenance, as usual, was sober.

"Miss Brigid, we've got to get Tommy cleaned up before he can go anywhere. And, *Miss Brigid*, we've got to find him some clothes."

Being addressed as "Miss Brigid" apparently had William's desired effect of shaking Bebe out of her shock. He usually did not show her such deference.

Her shoulders rose. "Officer, give us a while to get my grandson cleaned up and dressed."

The trooper frowned. He studied her, looked at me, and said he would wait a few minutes. They withdrew to the entrance at the end of the hall where they could watch us.

William led us into the examining room. "Missy, we need Joe Black down here—*now*." He walked her to the pay phone in the hall and gave her a dime. Hearing her words made the nightmare more real to me.

She stepped back into the room and leaned close to me. "Tommy, you must say absolutely nothing to these police."

Exactly twelve minutes later, after I had donned a green surgical shirt and again lay on the examining table, a man I had never seen before suddenly appeared in the room. He wore khaki pants, a golf shirt, deck shoes, and a crimson-colored cap with an insignia "A" on it. He was not quite five feet, six inches tall, weighed less than 140 pounds, with a horseshoe-shaped fringe of white hair wrapped around his otherwise bald head. He smelled of Old Spice and cigars. He only raised his bushy white eyebrows at me, but when he looked at my grandmother, a smile of sweet love spread across his wrinkled old face. "There's my beautiful Brigid McCarthy." His voice was rich and gravelly.

"Oh, Joe." She stood unsteadily, and they hugged. "Will you help Tommy?"

"*Absolutely*. Son, I'm Joe Black Pell." His eyes flicked to the open door to the hallway and then returned to me. "I need to know what happened, and I'm going to ask you a few questions. You answer 'yes,' 'no,' or 'I don't know.' Once I've finished, some police"—he pronounced it PO-leese—"are going to ask lotta questions. Don't say anything, not one word, 'cept for yo' name and home address, unless I say you can answer. You follow me, son?"

I tensed and nodded.

"Did you shoot first at this man?"

I shook my head.

"So, he shot at you and you fired back in self-defense, ain't that right? Answer out loud."

"Yes, sir." *But Jackie was still dead even though I tried to defend him.*

"Is it yo' gun, son?"

"Well, it was Granddaddy's gun." He had died suddenly last August, and Bebe had given me his car to drive back to school after Christmas. After Beth and I had a passionate reunion in the backseat, she whispered to me she hadn't found her panties. Looking for them later, I groped granddaddy's holstered pistol strapped to the underwire of the driver's seat. The race troubles in 1963 and 1964 must have made him think he needed a gun in his car.

"Son, that's more than yes or no. It was in your possession, right?"

"Yes, sir."

"Then it was yo' gun. Did you take that gun in that store to try to start some trouble?"

"No!"

"Did you git that gun after this fella starting shootin' at you?"

"Yes, sir."

"Son, did you drive into Yancey County trying to stir up some trouble over civil rights?"

"No, we were just—"

Joe Black Pell was holding up both hands, palms facing me. "Yes or no, son."

"No."

"Brigid, I'm going to go out here and talk to these troopers. Y'all stay put till I get back, and *do not* answer any questions if they sneak their way past me."

Joe Black had been gone only a minute when Mama and Daddy rushed into the examining room. She took one look at me and hugged me, pressing my face into the graying blonde of her hair. I could smell her perfume and taste her tears. "Oh, thank God. *Thank God.*" Then she pushed me to arms' length and inspected my shoulder and chest. "How bad are you hurt?"

"Not much. But Jackie, my friend—he died."

Mama pulled me tight for at least a minute. I could feel her crying.

Daddy then moved close to me. I smelled the cigarettes that Mama had been trying to get him to quit. He had aged since Christmas—his hair was grayer and there were pouches under his eyes. He was six-three, almost as tall as I was, but his shoulders looked weighted toward the ground. He was massaging the knuckles of his right hand as he studied me, his brow knotted. "You all right, Tommy?" I nodded. He gave a relieved half-smile.

He looked at Bebe. "Why is Joe Black Pell out in the waiting room?"

"Tommy needed a lawyer, and Joe Black was johnny-on-the-spot. Did you see the state troopers?"

"Mama, you know Daddy hated Pell. I'm going to call Harv Foster and get him over here."

She shook her head and gave him a hard look. "Buddy, your daddy is dead. It doesn't matter now what he thinks, or thought. Joe is a smart and tough lawyer, and he's here."

My father grimaced. "Oh, Mama, Pell is just an ambulance chaser. You know that."

She shook her head. "I know no such thing. He's always been a great friend to me. Tommy needs help *now*. It would take hours to get Harv Foster over here—*that is*, if he took his fat rear end to bed sober, which I doubt." She lowered her voice. "They say the Yancey County sheriff is on his way."

Joe Black reentered. "Hey, Buddy, how you doin', son?" he said to my father, who only nodded as Joe Black shook his hand. The lawyer turned to Bebe and reported he had been on the phone to the state attorney general. "Richmond Flowers is calling the judge down there to ask him to release Tommy to you, Buddy, so he won't have to spend any time in their jail. 'Course, you'll have to make bond."

Bebe gave Daddy an I-told-you-so nod.

The little man looked up at Daddy. "I'll go down there with you." He read my father's chilly reaction. "If you want me to."

Daddy shook his head at Bebe, who was looking at him rather than at the lawyer when she said, "Joe Black, that would be very kind. We need you to do that."

At 4 A.M. two Yancey County deputies appeared at the hospital. When they put my hands behind my back, I felt myself step away from my own body again. They put me in the back of a patrol car. With my hands shackled behind, I had to sit leaning forward for the forty-five minute ride to the jail. The only break from the panic of losing the use of my arms was the pain shooting up my cramping back. In the Yancey County sheriff's office, time dragged. Mama, Daddy, and I were too exhausted to talk. A clerk took my fingerprints. As dawn broke, a parade of people traipsed through, and it took a while for me to realize they were coming by to look at the boy who had shot one of their neighbors.

Buford Kyle, I overheard, was in the hospital, shot up but surviving. Maybe when he was bandaged up they would haul him in for killing Jackie, and his neighbors would have someone else to stare at. I locked my eyes on the floor.

The justice of the peace read the charge against me: assault with a deadly weapon. When I heard him say, "including the possibility of ten years in jail," I started to shake all over. Joe Black put his hand on my shoulder.

"Ain't no way you going to get the maximum, son," he said in a voice only I could hear. "Listen here, don't even think about that. We going to do ever' damn thing to make this trouble go away." Then he stuck his right index finger into Daddy's chest. "They ain't going to be pushin' us around down here, I guaran-damn-tee you that, Buddy." Daddy just looked at him.

ON THE WAY TO Eden Rise, Mama sat between Daddy and me and held my hand. "It wasn't anything you did, Tommy. Just a tragic accident."

I saw the clenched muscles on Daddy's forehead. He didn't wait long to get to the point. "Tommy, why were you driving these people down here anyway?"

"I just wanted company for the long drive, and he was my really good friend."

He kept his eyes on the highway. "Son, don't you know that was just asking for trouble? These counties are just crawling with nigger agitators, and people are really upset about it."

Mama turned sideways in her seat. "*Buddy—*"

I interrupted her. "Jackie is not a 'nigger agitator.'"

Daddy plunged ahead. "Tommy, ever since all the trouble at Selma, these damn people have been going around stirring up the colored to try to register to vote. The Klan has been meeting all around the Black Belt and threatening to hurt these agitators."

"Daddy, I was just trying to get my friend where he wanted to go.

We were almost there and this girl had to go to the bathroom and we stopped at this store."

"You shoulda known better than to stop with an integrated group at a country store in the Black Belt." His voice and mouth were tight.

"I've been going into stores with colored people all my life. I didn't think about this being different. I was tired and just trying to get where we needed go."

"Well, you shoulda known it was different with agitators from up North."

"Daddy, Jackie was *not* an agitator—"

"Why didn't you just give 'em bus fare? It woulda ended up costing a lot less."

Mama's face reddened. "*Buddy*! You *shut* up, you hear? It's not Tommy's fault."

Daddy was blaming me. But racist though he was, he was right. I didn't think about the danger, and I should have known. Jackie was dead because of my stupidity.

Suddenly I was choking. The warm wind that came through the window of Mama's station wagon drove my breath back down my throat. Sweat oozed from every pore of my body, which itched. I stank from thirty hours of sweat. The sky should have been blue but the mid-day sun had washed out nearly all color, leaving it a dirty white. On the right, rows of young cotton plants wilted in the furnace. On the left, a herd of cows huddled in a thicket of willows by a stagnant stream. I caught the stench of decaying flesh just at that moment and saw two buzzards picking at carrion—it was a baby calf—outside the cluster of cows.

Then I looked forward and realized we were approaching the old store ahead on the left. I raised an index finger and pointed. Mama looked at me and then jerked her head forward.

"That's the place?" Daddy said.

I nodded and he slowed the car as we went past. The bleached walls and the faded signs and the shattered gas pumps were now scorched by a sun that felt like it hovered only a few hundred feet above ground at noon. I trembled all over. I saw the man aiming the shotgun. I saw Jackie lying bloody in the gravel.

"Stop."

Both my parents frowned and shook their heads.

"*Stop!*"

Daddy eased to the side of the road a hundred yards past the store. I opened the door before the car came fully to a stop and rushed into the weeds that lay between the pavement and a cotton field. I bent over and puked.

I stood up, and the sunlight blinded me. Then the gag reflex jerked much harder and I fell on all fours. Bile burned my throat from the bottom up like a garden hose was spewing acid from my guts. The sun scalded the back of my neck. I thought I was through after the third time, but my stomach kept wrenching my insides. My torso convulsed. I began to sob. By the time Mama got me to my feet and back in the car, by the time she wiped my greasy, stinking face with Daddy's handkerchief and pulled my trembling head down to her shoulder, I didn't think I would live through this torture. Nor was I sure I wanted to.

3

SHOTS IN THE NIGHT

I awoke at 6:30 that evening and found Mama at the stove, stirring a pot and talking on the phone. She was frowning. "No, we have no comment. No, there won't be any interviews." She rolled her eyes at Daddy, who was standing across the kitchen, drinking a Budweiser and smoking a cigarette. "Sorry." She hung up the phone and shrugged. "*Newsweek*."

Immediately the phone rang, and Daddy answered. He listened a moment, and scowled. "You chickenshit bastards, you ain't running anybody off, *you hear*?" He slammed the phone down.

Mama looked at him tentatively. "What did they say?"

He looked down at the kitchen tile. "'It's time for y'all to git on up North where there's a lot of niggers to love,'" he repeated in a flat voice.

"Don't people have *any* decency?" She took the receiver off the hook. It lay on the counter like a venomous snake.

My sister Cathy stood by the kitchen table, her arms swinging, her knees jerking up in rhythm. She was practicing her cheerleader routines. She shrugged at me. "The phone's been ringing all afternoon."

The afternoon newspaper lay spread on the breakfast table. There were pictures of Jackie and me under a huge headline, "Negro Student Killed in Yancey Shootout." Jackie was pictured in his Duke basketball uniform. Next to him was my senior yearbook picture. The article said an "altercation" had left "the college basketball star mortally wounded" and "storekeeper Buford Kyle in serious but stable condition" at a local hospital. I was described as an "armed member of the Student Nonviolent Coordinating Committee originally from Eden Rise."

"*Oh God.* Look at this! We gotta correct this! I'm not a member of anything. It was Granddaddy's gun. They make out like I came down here hunting somebody to shoot."

Daddy was rubbing his right hand. "Well, that's how it looks."

"That's a lie. Next reporter calls, I'm talking to him."

"The *hell* you will. Lyin' bastards will write whatever they want to make us look bad."

"Well, they'll have to straighten it out."

"You stay away from them."

I turned to face my father. "You just want to sit here and let them lie about me?"

He took a deep drag on his Pall Mall. "I'm telling you to sit here and keep your mouth shut and don't cause any more trouble. We've got a plenty already."

"*Go to Hell.*" Whatever vessel it was that pumped my adrenaline had suddenly fired, and words came out automatically.

I tried to explain. "I didn't make that happen. I just tried to keep that sonuvabitch from killing my friend. Anybody ought to be able to ride through Alabama without getting killed."

Daddy's eyes were wide and his cheeks started to color. He stepped toward me, but he didn't get far before Mama stood directly in front of him.

"*Stop*. Right now, Buddy. Stop. You shut up." She jerked around toward me, her eyes afire. "*You* shut up too. You don't talk like that in my house ever again, you hear me?"

We ate supper in silence until I asked what was going to happen to Jackie's body. Daddy wore no expression when he told me William Addison was going to fly up to Virginia with it.

"I want to go."

"That's just asking for more trouble. You going to stay here, out of sight."

I couldn't abandon Jackie now. "Daddy, he was a good friend. I should go with the body, out of respect."

"You need to be thinking about 'out of trouble.'"

Mama gave him a hard look. "Buddy, if Tommy's up to it, he should go. I'm going to go."

Daddy pushed away from the table. "Tommy, I don't understand what happened to you up there at Duke. Don't you see how all these agitators have come into Alabama and just stirred everything up?"

"Been in all the newspapers," I said.

"I bet it was." My father's eyes narrowed. "It's just so damn ridiculous. The blacks around here have been treated well—especially here in Eden Rise. They haven't been hung or beat up or anything like that. We never had any trouble all the time I was growing up. Honestly, I don't remember a cross word between any white and any nigger. The blacks need to back off or we'll have a damn race war."

I took a deep breath. "Daddy, the whites here have asked for a lot of this trouble. I saw pictures of that beating on the bridge in Selma. There was no cause for that."

"King just looks for places to get headlines," my father shot back. "He doesn't give a good goddamn about those niggers in Selma. He's just playing to the cameras to raise money and get the federal government down here."

My anger rose again to meet his. "King's speeches are a lot easier to take than all the cussing of nigger agitators I been hearing around here my whole life. No wonder people around the country listen to him. No wonder they think Jim Clark and George Wallace are the hand of the devil. He's right and they're wrong."

Daddy's chest was heaving. "And I'm wrong too, boy?"

I nodded, knowing that what I said next would bring wrath. "Yeah, I think you are, Daddy, if you support what they been doing."

Daddy's face had turned a deep red and he was gripping the table. He exhaled, shook his head, and shifted his gaze from me to Mama. "Betty June, what did I pay to have our son go up to North Carolina and get turned into a nigger lover?"

As she stood up, Mama shoved her chair back from the table so fast it tipped over and slammed against the tile floor. She extended her arm and pointed her right index finger at Daddy.

"You'll shut your nasty mouth, Buddy McKee, if you know what's good for you. You won't talk to Tommy like that in my presence."

He stared at her. "Well, Goddamnit, I said he's not going to that funeral and that's the end of it." He got up and we heard him slam his way out of the house.

MAMA AND I STARED at each other for a long time. Cathy kept eating, her eyes on her plate. Mama came back and sat down. "Tommy, try not to let your daddy get you down. *I'm* going to take you to the funeral." I couldn't make a reply. "You have a headache, don't you? I can see it in your eyes." She brought me three aspirin and smiled sweetly as she handed them to me. She reached out and brushed my limp blond hair off my face. Her fingers were thick and the nails short, but their touch was gentle.

"Your Daddy's better than what he just said, and you know it." Daddy had been under a lot of pressure since he became probate judge the previous fall, she said, after my grandfather, Judge Tom McKee, had dropped dead in the courthouse just days before I left for college. Daddy had been appointed his successor. He wore the job like a scratchy new suit, Mama told me. Cathy nodded at that. Daddy had spent his life farming our family's six thousand acres.

"Tommy, everybody in Eden Rise is just so scared. You wouldn't believe what these men want your father to do."

"Mama, he's so hateful. You know what a racist he is."

My parents had argued about race and politics since I was about fourteen, with George Wallace the first lightning rod. I'd been disgusted by him the moment I heard him speak at Boy's State in June 1963—a bantam rooster at the podium, shifting from one leg to another to throw his chest out to the audience, waving his fist and denouncing one federal official after another, promising a "barbed-wire enema" to his old law-school buddy, Judge Frank Johnson. When the other boys cheered and rose to their feet, I felt scared. But Daddy had voted for him, much to my mother's fury. He was a "dangerous little dictator," she said. Not half as dangerous as "that troublemaker King" or "those goddamn Kennedys," Daddy had shot back.

Mama had forbidden me from taking her side, but Daddy knew what I thought of his politics even before this awful night. The alienation between us had troubled me throughout my teenaged years. I wanted to return to the earlier time, when he would pick me up and toss me in the air, his big face entirely taken over by a wide smile and laughing eyes. We would go on long rambles around the farm when he identified plants and trees and animals and told me about those things in the natural world that we had to watch out for: weather and bugs and weeds. We were lucky to live in the prettiest place on earth, he told me.

THAT EVENING OF THE day after Jackie died, every time we put the telephone receiver back on the cradle the crank calls resumed. Finally Daddy phoned the sheriff to come over. Beneath Mac McCallister's crew cut his big square face often wore a look of amusement that could instantly turn into a smirk. His spare tire made it hard to imagine that McCallister had been the great left-handed pitcher and quarterback at Eden Rise High that Daddy remembered.

"Buddy, ain't much we can do. Ain't got no equipment to trace calls. It'll ease up, I bet."

Neither of my parents were happy with McCallister's indifference. As soon as he left, Mama turned to Daddy. "Buddy, all those phone calls weren't coming all the way from Yancey County. That's long distance. Some were local, and I think McCallister knows more than he's letting on."

Mama was right about McCallister. When George Wallace had appointed him after the old sheriff died, Granddaddy had said it was dangerous to let people like McCallister—the son of a drunk who operated a pool hall—have such an important job.

I was still tossing in my bed that night when I heard a thunderous crash, then loud shouts on the street and a vehicle roaring off. I ran down the hall and followed Daddy into the living room. I watched his eyes locate the bullet holes in the wall. For the second time that night, he summoned the sheriff, but this time the chief deputy came. He stayed only a minute but stationed two men in front of the house. Daddy's farm foreman, Junior Jackson, soon showed up with one of the hands, Sam Ford. I helped them tape plastic over the window holes, relieved to be able to fix at least one broken thing, while Daddy paced in front of the house with his shotgun.

We were drinking coffee at four o'clock in the morning, not saying much, when the phone rang. I grabbed it. A young man said: "We told you nigger lovers to leave. You stay and we'll burn that house down with you in it. You stay and we'll get the boy." *The boy* was me.

I repeated what I heard. Junior broke the long silence that followed. "Maybe y'all *better* go a while. We guard the house."

Junior was "much of a man," as the colored people said. He was six-six and weighed more than three hundred pounds. His shoulders were wider, his chest deeper, and his arms bigger around than any human being's I had ever seen. His skin was almost true black, and his voice registered at the lowest human octave I'd heard. A thick mustache and a wide mouth set off his full, round face. He smiled easily, talked a lot, and liked to joke around, but he wasn't joking now.

"Shit, Junior. I can't let some damn rednecks run me outta my *house*. We're okay while the deputies are outside," Daddy said.

Mama had gone to the front door and now she called. "They're gone, and there's a strange truck parked down the street."

Junior drew a pistol. He led Daddy and Sam out the back door to slip around the side of the house to get a look at the truck. I was following when Mama grabbed my arm. "Unh-unh. You stay here."

The truck suddenly roared away. It was red, but we didn't get its make. Junior and Daddy were about to give chase but found that their truck tires had been slashed. When they were back inside, Mama looked at Daddy. "You think the sheriff is looking after us? I'm telling you, his people are behind some of this." He didn't answer.

Junior studied Daddy. "Buddy, if y'all stay, you going to have to find some protection."

"You mean bodyguards?" Mama's brow was furrowed.

"I mean a rough mother—" he caught himself and glanced at Mama "—a guy who going to shoot a few rounds if he need to."

Daddy shook his head. "Where we going to find somebody like that, Junior?"

He studied Daddy. "You care what color they are?"

Daddy didn't answer, but Mama shook her head at Junior. "We don't care."

Junior turned to Sam and gave a quick nod. Sam Ford was about sixty-five, a heavyset man wearing thick-lensed, horn-rimmed glasses. He was the husband of Orene, my grandmother's cook. Sam spoke slowly—with the enunciation and diction of an old Negro who had never lived outside the Alabama Black Belt.

"I know 'bout this boy up in Chicago." He paused, nodded slowly, and then settled his eyes on Daddy. "Some say he be the meanest nigger in Illinois."

4

Baby Gone Home

At the funeral home in Norfolk, Virginia, the solemn undertaker led my mother, William, and me into a small, dimly lit room furnished with a few straight chairs and a sofa bearing a design of deep red flowers and olive-colored leaves and vines. Someone in the room was wearing a musky perfume, which made the air feel even stuffier than its eighty degrees. The undertaker introduced us to Mrs. Herndon and Lena, Jackie's fourteen-year-old sister. His mother was almost six feet, and wide in the hips and shoulders, which made her look strong, not fat. Jackie had strongly resembled his mother, but her features were thicker and fleshier. Her brow was furrowed and her mouth fixed tightly, the big brown centers of her eyes ringed in pink. Mrs. Herndon's was the saddest face I had ever seen.

I hung back, grasping for words and trying to find the breath to say them, but Mama went straight to Mrs. Herndon and hugged her. The two mothers sat side-by-side and talked quietly, holding hands and passing a box of tissues back and forth. Mrs. Herndon's hands dwarfed Mama's, but like hers they revealed themselves as instruments of hard labor. Jackie had said she worked in a laundry.

Soon Mrs. Herndon raised her eyes and beckoned me over. I felt my knees go weak. "Jackie always said good things about you." Her face was still perfectly sober.

"He was my good friend," I said.

"Tell me what happened to him at the store that night." Her voice was sharp, even angry.

I wanted to loosen my necktie so I could talk better, but it didn't seem appropriate. I just started in, haltingly. I tried to keep my words even and measured. I told her about Alma—who had gone back to California the day after Jackie died, I'd read in the newspaper. I told about the storekeeper shooting at us and how I shot back—too late—and our desperate drive to the hospital.

"Have they charged this Buford Kyle with murder?" she asked.

"Ma'am, they just charged manslaughter."

She frowned. "What is wrong with you white folks? What made this man think it was okay to start shooting my baby?"

You white folks. I shivered. I had lived most of my life alongside black people. I didn't want to be herded into the same pen with Buford Kyle or George Wallace, or even my father.

At that moment, a tall black man strode directly to Mrs. Herndon. He spoke to her in a deep voice, glared at me, and then turned back to her. "This who got Jackie killed?"

I cringed. She shook her head in disgust, then looked at Mama. "I'm sorry, Mrs. McKee. This man is Jackie's father." She turned back to the man. "I ain't taking your mess now, Melvin. Don't come in here drunk, *as usual*, and expect me to take it."

Jackie had told me that he hardly knew his father, that he had never lived with the family. I caught a strong whiff of liquor as the man leaned toward me.

"Is you the white man that took my boy to Alabama and got him killed?"

I thought he was going to hit me, and I doubled my fists. But Mrs. Herndon rose and called out for the undertaker, who hurried over with a man so big his suit looked ready to tear at the seams. They hustled Jackie's father away from us.

"Goddamn. Treated like shit at my own boy's funeral," he snarled. He gave me a last brutal look on his way out. "I'm sorry, Tom," Mrs. Herndon said. Somehow Melvin's anger had dissipated her own, and she just wanted to talk to me about Jackie. She was proud of his interest in science. I told her how Jackie had helped me pass a geology course the past spring. He had told her he was going to the freedom school to teach science. I decided not to say that Jackie had changed his mind about that, which would have required saying more about Alma and her angry demands.

I blamed Alma for Jackie's death but I didn't want to go into that now.

The undertaker returned to escort Mrs. Herndon to see Jackie. She stood, took Lena's hand, and then looked back at Mama and me. "You come along," she said. I froze. I'd been dreading this for the entire last day. I had never seen a dead body. Bebe had insisted on keeping Granddaddy's casket closed. I especially didn't want to see Jackie. I looked at Mama, hoping she would see my fear, but she nodded firmly toward Mrs. Herndon. I had no choice but to go.

Large sprays of roses, carnations, and gladiolas were crowded around the steel-gray casket, which gave the dimly lit parlor the cloying smell of a greenhouse. Mama took my hand and led me to a place discreetly behind Mrs. Herndon and Lena. They whispered quietly to one another as they leaned over the coffin. Finally they stepped aside and Mama pulled me forward.

He looked like a painted doll. The features were recognizably Jackie's, except his eyes were closed. His skin was so uniformly creamy brown and smooth that it didn't seem at all real. I had never seen Jackie in a suit, but his body was dressed in a black one with a maroon tie. A red rose lay across his chest. The only thing truly familiar to me was Jackie's hands, folded on his chest. Now they were perfectly cleansed of the blood that had covered them when I last saw them. But now they looked as if they were chiseled from marble. Strange as it sounds, I would have liked it better if they had been holding a basketball.

I looked as long as I could bear, and then I took another breath and fixed my eyes on a pink gladiola just beyond the top of the coffin. Finally Mama turned us away and we faced Mrs. Herndon.

Mama dried her eyes. "He is so beautiful."

Mrs. Herndon smiled disconsolately. "Thank you for bringing Jackie back to me." She looked away for a moment. When she returned her gaze to us, her big eyes were wet again. "Today's May thirtieth. Jackie's birthday. He was eighteen today."

Her words sucked all the air out of my lungs and yanked me back to a memory of Jackie telling me how he got his name.

The Duke freshman team, of which Jackie was instantly the star despite being the youngest member, had played in South Carolina but he had been thrown out of the game—a shock to me given his even temper. He took a swing at a guy who had been pulling the hair on his legs and calling him nigger. He told me later how his coach had taken him aside, reminded him about Jackie Robinson, how whites screamed racist abuse when he started with the Dodgers but how Robinson held his temper and beat the other teams with his bat and his base running, not his fists. Jackie and I were shooting baskets outside my dorm, when he told me this.

"My full name is Jackie Robinson Herndon. Mama was real pregnant with me when he went into the majors in 1947. So, when I was born, she named me for him." Jackie's eyes had twinkled. "She always told me if Branch Rickey hadn't started Jackie with the Dodgers that year, I would have been named for her next favorite Negro, Cab Calloway." He gave me a half-smile. "*Cab* don't sound much like a ballplayer, does it?"

Jackie Robinson Herndon. Breathe, I told myself. Breathe.

ON THE DAY OF Jackie's funeral, charcoal-colored clouds dumped rain on the little Baptist church with the fury of a hundred firehoses. But the bad weather didn't keep away mourners. The church was almost of full of elderly women, who studied me intently as Mama, William, and I entered the church and sat two pews behind the family. "Tha's him." The loud whisper of an old woman. "White boy drove him down there."

The small choir sang plaintive spirituals—"Go Down, Moses" and "Baby Gone Home"—that were punctuated by claps of thunder and Mrs. Herndon's wails. She kept crying out Jackie's name and a single word she seemed to be addressing to God: *Why?* Her shouts and the cracking thunder made me start trembling.

The preacher's words put me in hell. "They killed Emmett Till and tied him to a fan and threw him in the river . . ."

"They *did!*"

"They shot Medgar Evers and he died at the feet of his crying babies . . ."

"They *evil!*"

"They bombed to death those four little girls in the Birmingham Sunday school..."

"Help me, *Lord*."

"They shot and buried Chaney, Schwerner, and Goodman under a mountain of dirt."

"Oh, God."

"They shot our Jackie..."

The mourners' responses grew louder with the mention of each martyr and turned into a angry shout with Jackie's name. My arms and legs shook, my stomach churned, and my ears roared from some inner racket. The lights in the little church glared through my eyelids even when I clenched them shut.

In the awful moments when Jackie was shot, there were things I had to do, actions I had to take that were directed from some deep survival instinct. But now I was trapped in that little church, unable to move. Mama's firm hand took mine. She leaned in to me. "Breathe, precious. Breathe slow."

5

The Man from Chicago

From the airport William drove to Bebe's home, where we found her chatting with a light-skinned colored man. A little over six feet tall, he wore a black suit, a tight black knit shirt that revealed a muscular torso, and black boots. He had a goatee like some kind of a black beatnik and large gray eyes, partly hooded by drooping eyelids that made him look both suspicious and sleepy. What was this guy doing with my grandmother?

William cleared his throat. "Tom, Betty June, I want you to meet Marvin Whitfield."

"Tommy," Bebe said, "Marvin is here to provide you protection."

The bodyguard. He seemed too cool to have earned the reputation for meanness. He looked more like a musician. I guessed about twenty-five but found out later he was just past thirty. Blacks always look younger to me than they are. There had to be meaner-*looking* Negroes in Illinois. Now, confronting him, I doubted I needed someone to protect me. I should just lie low for a while. But, of course, no one had asked me if I wanted a bodyguard. Whitfield looked me over as if assessing whether I was worth saving.

Bebe offered us beer. "I'd like a smoke," Marvin said in a slow, matter-of-fact voice.

He and I moved to Bebe's front porch where we drank Budweiser, he smoked Kools, and we eyed each other. He took a switchblade from his pants pocket, pared his fingernails, and cut back his cuticles. His slim fingers flicked the parings away. The nails shone with clear polish. I had never seen that on a man. He took a pistol from the back of his waist and placed it on the glass-topped garden table next to the glider where we sat.

When he crossed his legs, he exposed another, smaller pistol strapped to his ankle. The porch light was attracting mosquitoes, so I turned it off, and we sat in the darkness. His cigarette competed with a nearby gardenia's rich, sweet perfume to scent the muggy air. Cicadas were making a racket interrupted only by the periodic call of a whippoorwill.

"Tell me how all this shit got started," Marvin said, exhaling smoke, not looking at me.

I briefly recounted what had happened at the store and the harassment since then.

"This nigger who got killed . . ."

A reflexive anger flashed. "Don't refer to him as a nigger. I'm sick of that shit. *Jackie Herndon.* His name was Jackie Herndon. He was my college friend."

He regarded me out of the corner of his eye. Finally he broke the tense pause. "This . . . boy, he do anything to piss off the old cracker?"

"Nothing. Just tried to get this girl out of there."

"Did this bitch start the trouble?"

"Well, yeah. I mean, she sure aggravated it."

"Were you trying to kill this old man?"

"I was just trying to make him quit shooting at us."

"Well, you did that, didn't you?"

"Yeah. I would have killed him if I was any better shot."

"We can work on that."

I asked how people in Eden Rise knew about him. In that same languid voice, he told me his grandmother was originally from Demopolis, about twenty miles from Eden Rise. I knew of the Demopolis Whitfields, but they were all rich and white. Marvin's ancestors probably were slaves of the white Whitfields. When William called him two days ago, Marvin caught a plane to Birmingham.

We sat in silence for several minutes. Then, in a nonchalant tone, he said, "Since I got out of prison, I been giving protection."

"Protection to who?"

"Some connected-up people. And the Nation of Islam."

I was dumbfounded. "You mean like Malcolm X's Black Muslims?"

"Not for him. For the honorable Elijah Muhammad. They kicked Malcolm out and then some guys killed him."

"Yeah, I heard about that. Saw some of his people in Harlem."

I felt his full gaze on me for the first time. "What *you* doing in Harlem?"

"Just visiting with a friend." My college girlfriend's father.

"Get yo' white ass killed in Harlem."

"I almost got my white ass killed in Alabama."

He chuckled. "I guess you did. Ain't no place safe, is it? I guess that fact is good for me, huh?"

"You work for mobsters?"

"Yeah. Drug dealers, pimps, loan sharks, mafia guys. Bad people. *Very* bad people." I made out his grin in the dim light. "I ain't never had to babysit before, though."

I swallowed his insult, because I was really interested now. I asked why he was in prison, and he replied that he had shot two boys in a gang fight. But he served only two and a half years in prison because he was under eighteen and had a good lawyer that William Addison had found.

"I'm obligated to William. So when he called and said he needed some help, I was going to come immediately."

"How do you know William?"

"He and my grandmother were good friends. He helped look after me after she died."

"Your grandmother and William, were they more than friends?" It was hard to imagine William ever was young and had a life outside Bebe's house.

"My mama, before she died, she told me that William had been in love with Grandmama and she should have married him. But she didn't love him in that real womanish way."

"Wonder why she didn't have it for William?"

"Damn, how old are you, boy, 'bout ten? She had it for somebody else."

I felt stupid. "Was the other guy your grandfather?"

The pause seemed especially long in the dark. "Sure was," he said—and nothing else. The evening temperature didn't drop, but the porch felt suddenly colder. Marvin kept rocking in the glider, smoke curling around his face. I could make out a scowl in the dim light. I decided I didn't like him, and I didn't want to have him around. And so I sat there in the black midnight, the buzz of cicadas filling my ears, and cursed my continuing bad fortune.

6

Judge McKee

Daddy was reading the newspaper when I entered the kitchen the next morning. "I told you not to talk to reporters," he muttered without looking up. "Buncha goddamn agitators." When I didn't reply, he said more loudly and sharply, "You heard me. Why did you do it?"

I flinched. Reporters had pelted me with questions when I left the church after Jackie's funeral. Mama and William had tried to hurry me past them, but I resisted and spoke up.

"I wanted to correct that stuff about me being in SNCC. That's all I said."

"No, you said more than that. They've got you condemning this man Kyle."

"Daddy, he killed my friend. Of course I'm going to condemn him."

Daddy rose from the kitchen table. "Well, now they're all over this gun and why you had it. If you had kept your mouth shut, like I told you to, none of this would have been spread all over the paper."

That was wrong. "You think none of this would have been in the paper if I hadn't answered a few questions?"

Mama entered the kitchen. "Buddy, just stop. It's done."

"Goddamnit, I'll decide when I'll shut up."

She shook her head. Her tic was jumping. "I wish you could hear yourself, Buddy. Tommy's not the problem around here. He's the one who was wronged."

At that moment Marvin sauntered in. Mama greeted him warmly and introduced him to Daddy, who looked him over without expression except a nod, didn't offer to shake hands, and then left.

"Marvin," Mama said, "I apologize for my husband not being more polite. He's upset about what all this trouble is doing to us."

Marvin just nodded. What in the world could this dangerous thug from the Chicago ghetto think of a white Alabama woman defending her contemptuous husband? Probably that she was ridiculous, but he didn't let on.

Cathy rushed into the kitchen. My sister was a strikingly beautiful girl. Her long neck, framed by heavy, dark hair, made her look taller than she was at five-nine. A thin summer nightgown revealed the outline of her lean figure. Her almond-shaped brown eyes took in the scene. At some point I had seen an old photo of Bebe and realized that Cathy bore a striking resemblance around the eyes to my grandmother in her youth. Cathy's were still cloudy from sleep as she focused on Marvin—she didn't realize at first who he was, but when she did, she turned around and left abruptly. Seconds later she came back in her housecoat.

As Mama introduced them, Marvin's eyes swept up and down my sister and then landed on her face. He half-smiled and extended his hand. "Good morning, Miss McKee." Again he scanned her from head to toe.

She blushed and reached up to smooth her hair. "Hi, Marvin. Welcome to Alabama."

They held a gaze for a moment and then she turned to the coffee pot. She spoke over her shoulder. "Y'all talkin' 'bout Daddy?" She sat down at the table and looked at Marvin, then me. "Tommy, he's really changed since he became probate judge." I had the feeling she was saying this for Marvin's benefit more than mine.

"What you mean, Baby Sister?" Marvin said. His tone was seductive, and a half grin slipped onto his face. Cathy smiled at Marvin's immediate familiarity, but then she quickly averted her eyes. My hands curled on their own into fists. The black sonuvabitch was flirting with my sister. I couldn't stand that. Especially since she seemed to like it.

"I mean Daddy's just not like Granddaddy. He's just not comfortable being the judge. Do you know what I mean, Tommy?"

My anger distracted me and I didn't hear the question. When she repeated herself, I focused on her words and knew exactly what she meant. When people called Daddy "Judge McKee," my first impulse was to look around for my late Granddaddy, the *real* Judge McKee.

While I was growing up, Daddy was working so hard at farming the family's six thousand acres that Granddaddy led me on many of the adventures that fathers often have with sons. Granddaddy and I had gone on fishing trips up and down the Warrior River in his old green flat-bottomed boat. We went to Denny Stadium in Tuscaloosa to see the Crimson Tide play football. Granddaddy seemed to know everybody in the stands, and he introduced me to Justice Lawson of the state Supreme Court and Dr. Carmichael of the University and Governor Persons and Mr. Martin of the Power Company. I had followed a safe five steps behind him on the dove hunts that the affable Sam Engelhardt, state head of the White Citizens' Council, put on at his big plantation. And we went to the Dollarhide Hunting Club, where Granddaddy and I would wait all day in a deer stand hoping to get a clear shot or two, and then go back to the lodge and eat T-bone steaks grilled by old colored men who constantly answered "Yessuh!" Not until Duke did I realize I'd grown up the entitled prince of my small town, that people—especially black people—bowed and smiled at me because of who my Grandddady was, who my family was. Now I squirmed at the memories.

But I was grateful for Granddaddy because he was a man of the world and made sure I rubbed shoulders with the world, too, at least as he knew it. Mama and Daddy had showed me how to work, and Bebe had taught me to read good books and "elocute" properly when I spoke, but it was Granddaddy who had educated me about politics and history and sports, about business and the economy and foreign relations. Because I was so often sitting right beside Granddaddy when he had a serious conversation about the state of the world with some other man of high social rank, I heard complex opinions put forth that I later had to ask Granddaddy to explain. I realized from an early age that Granddaddy did love to explain to me how the world worked. And so he assessed for me why Eisenhower beat Stevenson in 1956, explained what the Suez crisis was about, told why *Sputnik* mattered, speculated on what had caused the recession of 1958, and analyzed why Bear Bryant was a good football coach and Ears Whitworth had been a lousy one.

Years later, long past the summer of 1965, I realized that from watching Granddaddy in social situations I learned how one man influenced the thinking of another. He smiled quickly but never so long as to make one think he was overly accommodating; spoke to people by name and remembered something personal about each one; interjected an old joke here and there and a witty remark frequently, but never made fun of anyone, at least not any white folks from Alabama; never openly contradicted a wrong opinion, even when he went on to demolish the very idea; and remembered any shrewd thing ever said by the person to whom he was talking.

"But, you know, Tommy," Cathy went on, her eyes still on Marvin, "if Granddaddy had lived, he would have been just as upset as Daddy has been the past few months. He might not have showed anger like Daddy but he wouldn't have liked it a bit."

She bobbed her eyebrows. "You remember what he used to say all the time?" She tucked her chin, put a frown on her brow, and lowered her voice to sound like a man. "'We let the little white chillun go to school with the nigguhs, they'll grow up and wanta get married.'"

"Cathy!" I cringed and shot a look at Marvin.

"Cathy, please." Mama was embarrassed too.

Marvin burst out laughing. He looked at me. "I'm interested in the one they called Big Tom."

"That was our great-grandfather," I said. "He was dead before Cathy and I were born. How'd you know about him?"

Marvin shrugged. "From William."

I turned to Mama, who had a puzzled look on her face. Finally she spoke.

"He filled the room when he was in it. You should ask Brigid about Big Tom."

Cathy sat down with Marvin and began quizzing him about Chicago. Marvin was responsive enough but kept it general and didn't mention anything about prisons, mobsters, or pistols, which was fine with me. Cathy would have been even more dazzled if he had. Feeling unnecessary, I went outside with my basketball to the hoop beside our paved driveway and began shooting baskets, something I had often done when

I needed to think through things or just get the hell away from the people inside my house.

Marvin followed me out and stood between the goal and the street, surveying up and down. I asked him if he wanted to shoot with me, but he shook his head as he was lighting a cigarette. Here was another strange thing about the guy—I'd never known a male who wouldn't shoot basketball when the opportunity presented itself. Weren't all black guys devoted to basketball?

In a few minutes Mama came out to tell me that it was time to get ready for church. I hadn't even realized it was Sunday. "I'm not going." Church was the last place I wanted to be.

Mama started to speak but stopped and gave me a skeptical look. I shook my head at her slowly. She nodded solemnly. I could see her deciding against making an issue of it. But Mama was a powerful believer. "Next week."

I shrugged. If she pushed, I'd have to tell her just what a doubter I was these days. God didn't save Jackie. Therefore God must not exist.

A FAMILIAR CAR STOPPED in front of our house, and I felt myself smile in relief. This Ford Falcon belonged to Bobby Ray Shoemaker. "Shoe" was my closest pal since the first grade. Short and wiry with a narrow mouth and a perennial buzz haircut, Shoe had been the best guard on all our school basketball teams—a good ball handler and passer with a deadly set shot if he was left wide open. We had been active in the Methodist Youth Fellowship and the Future Farmers together—his daddy was a part-time farmer and the town's fire chief, indeed the only paid fireman in the county. We had double-dated to the prom both junior and senior years and spent lots of time just talking, and sometimes not talking, while we shot baskets on my driveway.

"Wha' ya say, Tommy?"

I bounced him the ball and he stopped, took aim, and fired off a twenty-footer. Net. "Still the deadeye, Shoe."

He laughed and we shook hands. He glanced over at Marvin, who stood a discreet ten yards closer to the street. Shoe looked back at me and frowned, asking silently who Marvin was. "Bodyguard," I said very low.

"Fuckin' A," Shoe said.

"Didn't you hear about somebody shooting up our house?"

He frowned again. "Well, I guess . . . I mean . . . I heard somethin' but I don't know if it was right." The Shoemakers lived five houses down, and his daddy worked closely with the sheriff's office. In a place the size of Eden Rise, everybody knew all there was to know about something like that. There was no way he didn't know.

"You talked to Diane?" he said. Diane Maxwell had been my high school girl friend.

I shook my head. "She around?"

He said she wasn't in Eden Rise.

I threw Shoe the ball and studied him a minute. Shoe wasn't looking at me, even when he didn't have the basketball. He was by nature a talkative guy and we were the best of friends. I asked about his first year at the University of Alabama, who he was dating, what his summer job was. He was friendly enough, but he didn't ask any questions in return. I felt like an old-maid aunt extracting information from a nephew late for a hot date.

I bounced him the ball but he let it fall on the driveway. "Hey, Tommy, it was great to see you, but I gotta get on to church." We shook hands again, and he finally looked me in the eye. "You okay, buddy?"

"Yeah, I'm all right, Shoe. Good to see you."

He turned, glanced at Marvin, and stepped quickly toward the Falcon.

A rush of anger came over me. "Hey, Shoe, just a second." He looked back over his open door as I trotted toward him. I stopped just on the outside of the open door.

"Shoe, you know who shot up my house?"

His eyes bugged momentarily before he looked to the side. When he looked back toward me, he was shaking his head, the corners of his mouth turned down. "Unh-uh."

I nodded, and he quickly slipped inside the car and pulled the door to. He drove off without another word, and he and I both knew his silence was a goddamn lie.

7

Joe Black Pell for the Defense

I had come with my father to Bebe's for lunch. Joe Black Pell was due to arrive any minute. "Mama, it's a mistake to use Pell to defend Tommy," my father said. "I've talked to Harve Foster and he's willing to help. Pell doesn't have any principles."

Bebe frowned. "Buddy, you're just parroting your father, and he never liked Joe Black's politics. Joe Black is very smart, tough as they come, and he's loyal. If Harvey Foster took the case and some big shot said 'boo' to him, he'd drop Tommy in a second."

"You don't know that."

"I think I do, and you know why? Harvey never uttered a cross word to your daddy, and a good lawyer will take his client on when he needs to."

"A good lawyer does what his client wants."

"Look, Buddy, Joe Black has already started defending Tommy. He jumped right in that night at the hospital, and we should be thankful to have him."

Daddy sat back and scowled. "Well, I just don't like the sonuvabitch."

She winced as she leaned forward in her easy chair, her legs still propped on the ottoman. She pointed a bony finger at Daddy. "You know, Buddy, you may be forty-seven years old, and I may be about to die, but it's still not all right for you to cuss in front of me." They glared at each other for a moment before she spoke again. "Besides, it's going to be expensive and I'm the one with the money to pay out for a lawyer."

She had played her two trump cards—the fact of her advancing cancer, and her control over the McKee finances. As if that settled it, she turned and looked out the window. Fury filled Daddy's eyes, and he suddenly pushed out of his chair and stomped from the room. I squirmed in discomfort as Bebe stared at the door that closed behind him.

The effect of disease on her appearance was profound. She had been a beautiful woman—willowy with high cheekbones and black-Irish coloring—and she had remained so until the past few months. Once when Cathy and I were examining a 1920s-era photograph of her in a family album, we agreed Bebe looked very like Audrey Hepburn. When Bebe and I were at the Elite Café in Montgomery once, an old man in a linen suit and white buck shoes had stopped at our table for a reunion with her. As he was leaving, he said to me, "You take good care of this girl, you hear, son? The old boys in Montgomery still say Brigid McCarthy is the rarest beauty of them all."

I wanted to say something, anything, to reassure her about her decision on Joe Black. "Bebe, I think Mr. Pell is a very colorful character."

A smile slowly came on her thin, gray face. "'Colorful' hardly captures Joe Black's character. Colorful like Blackbeard the pirate." She looked away for a moment and then returned my gaze with a twinkle in her dark eyes. "Actually, the more apt analogy would be to Huckleberry Finn."

They had gone to Catholic school together in Montgomery, Bebe explained, and the young Joe Black was mischievous, funny, but also very smart. He always insisted he wanted to marry Bebe, but his family didn't have much money and by the time he had worked his way through college and law school and established a law practice, she was already married to Granddaddy. Much later Joe Black married a nice but rather plain Methodist, Bebe told me, but they didn't have children. Joe Black was active in the "loyalist" wing of the Democratic Party, the group that supported the national Democrats and opposed the more conservative Dixiecrats, a faction in which Granddaddy had been a prime mover. Because Granddaddy didn't approve of Joe Black, Bebe went years without seeing him, but after Granddaddy died, she asked Joe Black to help with her business.

"I did what my husband wanted for almost fifty years," she said, "and that strikes me as abundant wifely submission. I thought I needed an adviser who wouldn't always be telling me what 'the Judge' would have wanted." The confusion must have been apparent on my face, but she didn't explain further except to say, "Joe Black has been very attentive over the recent months."

HE ARRIVED AND WE had lunch. Daddy didn't come back, and his absence shadowed the table. Bebe called for Orene. "Since Buddy's not here, let's seat Marvin at that place." When Marvin appeared and was introduced, Joe Black said, "Chicago! Son, that's 'bout my favorite city." Marvin looked curiously at the little, old man and nodded with almost a smile.

When Joe Black took the last bite of his chess pie, he smiled up at Orene. "You outdid yourself, darlin', with this effort. What's yo' secret?"

"Good buttermilk and fresh lard for the crust." Orene leaned over and kissed the little man's bald head. "I'm going to put the rest in a box for you to take home."

"God *bless* you."

Bebe asked Joe Black what he knew about the charges against me. The court had set Buford Kyle's trial for the second week in August, and I would testify then. I felt myself shiver a bit at the very idea of it.

"Brigid," Joe Black said as he pushed away from the table, "the circuit solicitor told me this morning that he could see Tommy and me this afternoon to talk over the situation. We oughta go on down there and see can we talk some sense into this prosecutor, Cal Taliaferro. By the way, where is Buddy?"

She shrugged and glanced over at me. "I think you must go on without Buddy. You and Marvin can look after Tommy for me." Joe Black smiled widely at the vote of confidence.

WE HAD JUST DRIVEN out of Eden Rise when Joe Black asked what career interested me. It took a minute to respond because I was distracted by all that he was doing while he steered his Buick down the road. He took a cigar knife out of his pants pocket, carefully sliced the closed end of a large cigar, and then punched the thin rod up its center. He licked the twelve-inch cylinder all the way around twice, took out a box of matches, burned the cigar end for ten seconds, and finally put it in his mouth and puffed three times. While accomplishing these tasks mainly with his right hand, his left had been engaged in navigating past two trucks and a tractor on the narrow road, adjusting his outside mirror, and tapping time on the steering wheel to "King of the Road" playing on the radio. I had never seen such manual dexterity, and it was a good thing or we'd have been dead in the ditch.

I glanced over the seat at Marvin, who was shaking his head in disgust. I guessed that country novelty songs weren't big in the Chicago ghetto.

"I like that Roger Miller, don't you, son?" Joe Black said. "I kinda identify with that, drivin' like I do from one courthouse to the next." He puffed a couple of times. "I'm sorry, son. I interrupted you telling me about what kinda work you wanna do."

"Well, Mr. Pell—"

"Son, call me Joe Black. I'll let you know when I get old enough to have that 'Mister.'"

"All right. I guess I might be interested in being a lawyer, although I'm not sure."

"It's a good profession if you willing to work hard. 'Course I worked hard a long time before I made any real money." I asked if he defended many people charged with crimes. "I don't do this kinda work anymore, except in this case as a favor to your grandmother. I mostly sue insurance companies and corporations"—he pronounced it *caw-pra-shuns*. "Lotta cases don't go nowhere, but every now and then one pays well. I love being in the courtroom, trying to persuade twelve jurors to see the situation my way. I love getting money outa big companies."

CAL TALIAFERRO, THE CIRCUIT solicitor, was seated at a beat-up desk piled high with files in an office glaring with mid-afternoon sunlight bouncing off brassy honorary plaques when he received us. The solicitor was a stocky, red-faced man with strawberry blond hair glued down with Brylcreem. His voice made me think he'd been on the Camels for a long time, and the blood vessels on his face suggested a similar close relationship with Jack Daniels. He was the kind of man who could put a smile on his face and hold it well past the point at which you understood it represented not friendliness or mirth but only a politician's habit.

Joe Black slapped Taliaferro on the back and made jokes about prosecutors. He asked Taliaferro if he expected opposition in next year's elections. "Oh, there's a little lawyer over in Selma, pretty wet behind the ears, who's making some noise about going against me." The smile widened. "Don't think he'll be too strong."

"Now, Cal, you let me know if it gets serious," Joe Black said. "I been known to put a little money behind good public servants, and I got a good many friends who'll do the same if I squeeze just a little."

"Well, I appreciate that, Joe Black, and I'll sure remember it." He pointed Joe Black and me to the two chairs across from him. Joe Black settled back into a chair with cracked leather upholstery and motioned me into its twin, which left Marvin standing at the door, unacknowledged by Taliaferro, who looked at me. "Tom, I'm real sorry about what happened down here, and I'm hopin' we going to be able to get this matter taken care of without too much trouble in your life."

I thanked him and looked over to Joe Black, who forged ahead. "Now, Cal, are you really going to have to go to trial in this case? Realistically, you ain't going to get a conviction."

I was startled to hear my lawyer make the suggestion that the man who killed Jackie should not even be prosecuted. Buford Kyle needed to be in prison for a long time. I knew I had to shut my mouth, but I could feel Taliaferro stiffen, suddenly wary in a whole new way.

"Well, Joe Black, as you know, this Kyle fellow is white trash and should be in the penitentiary for killing the nigger boy, but I agree with you ain't no jury in Yancey County going to send him there." Taliaferro shook his head perfunctorily. "But I've already heard from the Attorney General that I gotta prosecute Kyle."

Joe Black nodded. "All right, I understand that situation, but assuming a Yancey County jury acquits Kyle, this whole business oughta be over. No point in prosecuting this boy here for defending himself once the man who *killed* an innocent colored boy has been let go."

Taliaferro's smile twitched. "Well, we going to have to see. Folks here don't think the Herndon boy was innocent—he was an agitator and Kyle was defending himself."

This was too wrong to ignore. "But Mr. Taliaferro, I was defending *myself*. He was trying to kill us all." Taliaferro started in surprise, and Joe Black shot me a warning look, then moved in. "Cal, just because they some hotheads around who mad at Tommy here, that doesn't mean you gotta go along with 'em. You bigger than that."

There was no smile now, not the least remnant of one. Taliaferro gazed at Joe Black but wouldn't look my way. "We just going to have to see about that." He busied himself with a bunch of scribbled notes. "Now, Mr. McKee, if we could go over some of the questions I'll be asking you on the witness stand—what happened at the store, why you were going through Yancey County that day."

Joe Black raised his hand. "I'll get the boy ready, Cal. Don't you worry."

Taliaferro shrugged and we left. I felt the eyes of the solicitor's office workers boring into my back as we left and went out into the hall.

JOE BLACK WAS UNCHARACTERISTICALLY silent on the drive back to Eden Rise. At one point I looked over the back seat at Marvin, who shrugged at me as if to say, "What shut him up?"

"Taliaferro's going to try to get me," I said.

Joe Black's voice lacked all its normal geniality. "Taliaferro best be sure he's on solid ground, because by God he'll have some nasty enemies if he keeps after you."

"Well, it sounded like you promised to help him get re-elected."

"*Shit, boy*"—he spat the words at me—"I was just telling him I'm going to be paying attention to his political future. He don't do right by you, that boy from Selma going to have the best-funded damn circuit solicitor campaign we ever saw in Alabama, and I don't even know his damn name yet. I raise $25,000 for Mr. X 'fore Cal Taliaferro gets his ass wiped from tomorrow morning's crap. You understan'?" His face was hard and still but for the flexing jaw muscle as he chewed the stub of a cigar.

His courtly way returned when he reported the unhappy outcome of our meeting to Bebe. Was there any possibility, she asked, that the

Alabama attorney general might overrule Taliaferro?

"I don't think so, darlin'. Richmond Flowers says the dove-shoot of nigras in Alabama is over. We going to stop people from killing 'em just 'cause they feel like it. Richmond said it was 'morally and politically impossible' when I made the suggestion they drop it." He shrugged. "Wouldn't even listen to some incentives I was about to propose to him."

Bebe looked a little startled. "Joe Black, do you mean a bribe?"

"Certainly not. I mean a five-figure donation, in cash, to his campaign for governor next year, and much more from other friends of mine. But like I say, he wasn't listening."

"Joe, why does Taliaferro want to keep after Tommy?"

"Pressure from the segregationists. They trying to jerk a young nigger lover in line. Taliaferro's being real political. Because the AG's office is pressuring him to go after Kyle, he's trying to cover hisself with the local folks by equating Tommy shooting Kyle with the death of Jackie Herndon. I explained how they weren't equivalent, but he couldn't be told."

She flinched. I couldn't tell if it was physical pain or a response to what Joe Black had just said. "If Tommy's tried, a white jury might convict him."

"It's quite possible."

They discussed my fate with such matter-of-factness that my gut twisted in fear and I wanted to run out of the room—run out of Eden Rise forever. But I tried to keep my voice as steady as theirs. "What exactly will happen if I'm convicted?"

"We get you bonded out while I negotiate a reasonable penalty."

"What you mean, 'reasonable penalty?' The law says up to 10 years." Now my voice was quavering.

"A little incarceration, or better, no jail and some probation."

"Incarceration" sounded like the second-worst word in the world. "What do you guess about jail time?"

"You're under twenty-one, no previous convictions for anything. Could be six months or a year."

"Where would he serve it?" Bebe said, her voice soft.

"Crucial thing is to get somewhere other than 'hard-case' prisons like Atmore."

IMAGES OF KNIFE FIGHTS and homosexual rapes were flashing through my mind and I was trying to swallow my fear when Joe Black led me out to the front porch so we could start getting ready for the trials. He said the issue in Kyle's trial would be his motive, what provoked him to shoot. There might only be two witnesses, Kyle and me. When I asked about Alma, he said Taliaferro hadn't located her. "Which is good. I mean, I would find her if I thought it'd help, even if I had had to hire that Jew who found Eichmann. But she puts a face on the outside agitator defense they going to use. From what you've said, she probably be a terrible witness."

His look was sober. "*You*, on the other hand, going to be a good witness. You going to tell the truth, but I want you to tell the 'lean truth.' I mean not everything you know but what is most relevant to the question. Ya understan'?"

I wasn't sure but I nodded like I did.

"So, Tommy, now tell me, you and this boy Jackie, how'd y'all get to be friends, or were y'all *really* friends?"

I then told him about Jackie, beginning with the first week of school when I was shooting baskets on the courts behind the dorm and was surprised when this very tall colored boy suddenly appeared. He had close-cropped hair that accentuated the delicate shape of his head. Jackie had asked politely if he could shoot with me. The first time I bounced him the ball he took three dribbles and then went up for a jump shot higher than anyone I had ever seen. He caught the ball on the first bounce and leaped again, this time twisting around in mid-air and laying the ball high against the backboard with a reverse spin. During the next week Jackie and I fell into the habit of playing pick-up basketball games every afternoon. We chose the teams, deciding after a while it would be more fun to be on opposite sides and guard each other. After two hard hours of running and jumping, we would go sweatily to the cafeteria. Jackie was a favorite of the black women who worked on the cafeteria line. They always asked how he was feeling and didn't he want a little more mashed potatoes or an extra piece of cornbread. As Jackie's constant supper companion, I got their favor, too: "Tommy, let me put this other chicken leg on top for you, honey."

Joe Black was nodding. "Aw right. So y'all big friends from the basketball court. That's good. Playground friends. Now, Tommy, the circuit solicitor going to ask you why you were driving through Yancey County that evening. What would you say to that?"

The true answer went back to my failed relationship with Beth Kaplan, whom I had dated through the fall and into the winter. My dorm mate Jeffrey, Beth's childhood friend from Long Island, had introduced us. Short and buxom with a wild mop of kinky black hair, Beth kept up a steady flow of nosy questions, sharp opinions, and witty barbs on our first date to a Duke football game—she had asked me out—and then she bedded me that same night. I was taken aback and delighted. We dated all that fall, but after Christmas she began to withdraw and then she dumped me. She said she was tired of it. I was angry, hurt, and made to feel boring. I told her I loved her. "You're not in love," she retorted. "Just in heat." I was devastated.

Her rejection made me look hard at who I was. I had gone to college thinking everyone would be like me—the best people from their hometown, learning and having fun together. But it wasn't like that. Instead of a collection of high school stars like I'd been in Eden Rise, each one was unique—and in one way or another, superior to me. Compared to Jackie's, my athletic skills were pitiful. Kids in every class were much smarter, and my grades reflected my mediocrity—mostly Cs. I couldn't crack jokes or make funny comebacks the way Jeffrey and Beth did. I was a star in Eden Rise, but in the major leagues of Duke, I was barely even on the bench. I thought for a time I would stand out by becoming a party guy in a fraternity. The Sigma Nu house was full of good-looking, wealthy Southern boys who had grown up fishing, hunting, and watching football—a perfect fit for me, I thought. But I discovered I couldn't conform to what they wanted. I knew it as soon as one of them said Beth's last name, "Kaplan," in a derisive snicker to her face. Worse, being Jackie's friend made me as welcome in the frat as Martin Luther King. On a pledge workday when I was mopping the party room floor and several brothers were hazing pledges, Frank Strother, a senior from Birmingham who had rushed me very hard, had sneered at me. "McKee, you mop good. Just like a nigger."

Strother's face dared me to say something, but I didn't. "But you ought to be good with a mop, McKee, being a nigger lover like you are." My hands tightened on the mop. "You hang around with that nigger all the time in the cafeteria. White folks not good enough for you?"

I charged him but the other so-called brothers pulled me away. After that day, I began to drift away from Sigma Nu, and maybe because of that, I'd had drifted into involvement with civil rights protest. I didn't do it out of any great moral commitment. It was more that I hated the Frank Strothers of the world. And I needed Jackie's friendship, especially after losing everybody else's.

All this ran through my mind as I sat before Joe Black, but I couldn't speak. How would this old man understand this convoluted story? It wouldn't make sense to anybody else. So Joe Black plunged ahead on his own. "As I understand it, you were giving two friends a ride to their summer job. It's what folks in Ruffin County are taught is the polite thing—give somebody a ride if they ask. Period. You follow me?"

I nodded. The lean truth.

"He's going to ask you if you ever participated in any civil rights protests." When I didn't answer right away, Joe Black waited a moment. "Son, if you did, I need to know now. It'll come out anyway."

Alma Jones had stopped Jackie in the cafeteria and demanded that he participate in a march at the Durham town square in sympathy with the Selma voting protests. Jackie had gazed down at his sneakers. "Oh, come on, boy!" she had said angrily. "Last night they showed on TV how those Alabama police just beat hell outa those poor folks on a bridge. You gotta help!" She shot me a hard stare. "You too."

I had seen the beating on the Sigma Nu television—my last time at the fraternity house—and listened to comments from Strother and others about "niggers getting what they deserved." I was thinking of that when Alma demanded that I march, too. In downtown Durham the next afternoon, Jackie and I had joined about fifty people walking slowly down a commercial block. Alma spotted us and came over with a placard that read: "Selma: Let the Negroes Vote." Jackie and I walked side-by-side up and down the block. There were more police and reporters than there were protesters. The next morning the student newspaper ran a story with pictures of the protest. There Jackie and I were in the background of one picture.

When I recounted this to Joe Black, he nodded. "Aw right, aw right. Let's move on. The circuit solicitor's going to ask why you took Kyle's shotgun." I just stared blankly at Joe Black for a while.

"You didn't wanta take the chance of him start shooting at you again. Then he's going to ask why you threw it away. You probably threw it away 'cause it wasn't yours and you didn't want some policeman to see it and keep you from getting this boy to the hospital. Ya understan'?"

Those were pretty good answers—better than the truth, because I didn't really know why I did some of what I did.

"See, son, in this Kyle trial, your testimony is going to be a kinda dry run for when you get tried. You going to tell yo' story in such a convincing way that some of those jurors going to believe you, even though they don't want to." He smiled. "Word going to get around the county the boy is telling the truth, and then they going to *acquit* you two weeks later in your trial. You hear me?"

I wanted to believe Joe Black, but I knew I was simply too scared to be a good witness. I couldn't say that, though, because the little man with the big smile on his craggy face was willing me to think something else about myself.

WHEN WE FINALLY WENT back inside, Bebe was dozing in her chair. Joe Black and I were tiptoeing through the den when she raised her head.

"Joe, dear, don't go yet. I have one more bit of business to ask you about. Tommy, will you go get that pie from Orene and put it in Joe Black's car so that it won't spill?"

When I came back, Joe Black was sitting on the ottoman, leaning in toward Bebe, talking in a very low voice. I could make out only a few words of what he was saying: "two ex-wives . . . goes to Las Vegas . . . circuit solicitors don't make that kind of money." Bebe arched her eyebrows. "Must have some powerful good credit."

As I walked Joe Black to his car, I said something about appreciating his work on my behalf. "I really don't know why you're taking on all this trouble."

He pulled a pure white handkerchief from his back pocket, bowed his head, and coughed into it. When he looked at me again, he wore a wistful smile and his cloudy blue eyes were wet. He leaned his head toward Bebe's den and nodded slowly at me. "Son, I been in love with that girl in there since I was eight years old. I do anything in the world for her before she goes. Ya understan'? Anything."

8

Barbershop Cuts

Marvin and I went into Eden Rise on the first Saturday morning after Jackie's funeral for the simple reason that I needed a haircut. Crepe myrtles lined the four sides of the town square. A few water oaks, several dogwoods, and a big magnolia were scattered on lush Bermuda grass. Some azaleas clustered here and there, but their flowering days were almost over for this year. The local garden club had made sure that pink roses and yellow day lilies and some red cannas colored this June morning, along with a multi-colored bed of marigolds in the open area near the center of the square. The square's man-made improvements were a couple of long benches and a monument to the Confederate soldier, armed and facing northward—awaiting as always the return of General Wilson's raiders.

The day was rousing itself. Lining the square were shoe and clothing shops just opening the doors, our family's Farmers and Merchants Bank, the courthouse (also ours most of the time), the café, and the offices of the lawyer Harvey Foster and his accountant brother. The streets leading off the square went more or less in the cardinal directions—south to Demopolis, east to Selma, north to Tuscaloosa, and west into the "nice" residential neighborhood where I lived, its homes an eclectic mixture of steamboat-gothic frame houses, brick English cottages, and newer, sprawling ranchers like the one I grew up in. Bebe's columned brick house sat on the tip of the rise just outside the town's western edge. Along the main roads leading to other towns were arranged the businesses that needed more room: the car and tractor dealerships, the grocery stores, Western Auto, Bill's Dollar Store, the feed and seed co-op, and two funeral homes—one for whites and one for blacks, the latter owned by William Addison's brother. The McKee cotton gin and warehouse was a block off the square on the Demopolis road.

The air felt fresher that morning than usual for early June. It had rained the night before and a little cool front had come in behind the rain. The temperature at noon barely topped 80—absolutely balmy for that time of the year. The oaks rattled gently and the light dappled beneath them on the just-watered turf. Some fluffy clouds were easing across the sky and breaking up the glare. Weather like this had always lifted my spirits—when it was warm enough to be in shirtsleeves and bright enough to buoy your spirits but not hot enough to put you in mind of your proximity to hell.

The barbershop on the town square was crowded, and I was hungry—I'd missed breakfast because I had slept late after being up half the night after a bad dream I couldn't chase away: Jackie dying, then alive, then dying again—so we headed for the Eden Rise Café for a hamburger. They made a greasy burger with lots of onions and mustard.

Marvin had already eaten a big breakfast and said he'd keep an eye on me from outside. Just as well, it turned out. At every place at the counter was a card that read "We Reserve The Right To Deny Service To Anyone." The half-dozen tables in the café had the same card, a warning to blacks that they weren't going to get served here, regardless of the Civil Rights Act that had passed the summer before.

Or at least they wouldn't be served inside. There was a window across the café where occasionally a black person would appear and place an order. Why had I not questioned any of this earlier? Segregation, I could see with my new eyes, was alive and well in the Eden Rise Café. I chose to ignore the fact that eating this hamburger effectively preserved Jim Crow. I didn't want to think about race trouble anymore, because that's all I had thought about the past few days, and it had left me with a terrible ache all over my body. I was going to treat my ailment with a greasy burger and try to forget about it.

The sole waitress, a dumpy woman with dyed red hair, looked me up and down and took my order wordlessly. As I bit into the burger, she raised her voice to a man at the end of the counter.

"They's going to be a nigger invasion in Eden Rise schools in the fall." Lyndon Johnson was forcing "all the niggers" to transfer, she said, which meant her daughter would end up sitting by "some smelly coon" in fifth grade.

"Bobbie, what you going to do?" It was the other man at the counter. "What *can* you do?"

"Well, we need to get our butts in gear and organize us a private school before fall." She knew everyone in the diner was listening—but there was *one* person in the café she wanted to hear her diatribe, and that was me.

A man across the diner spoke loudly. "You lead the way, hon, and we'll foller."

"I won't have to. Folks with more time and money than I got is going to do it."

It was like watching an elementary-school skit, full of racist clichés, pitched loudly enough for deaf people.

I saw Bobbie whispering to the loud man. They were both looking at me while they consulted. I quickly looked away, but then Bobbie suddenly appeared in front of me.

"What do you think? Do you think we should have a private school, or do you think the children should go to school with niggers?"

She was tapping the counter with a pencil in her left hand, a kind of drum roll leading to my answer—or to the diners' denunciation of me. I wanted to slap the living shit out of her.

I glanced at her, and then I looked through the opening in the wall behind her. There standing and looking out was a middle-aged black man wearing the white apron and white hat of a cook. A toothpick dangled from the corner of his mouth. His dark brown skin glistened with sweat inspired by the griddle over which he hovered. His eyes were big, almost bulging, and the whites were stained yellow. I watched him for several minutes in my effort to avoid looking at any of the other diners, and I noted that he never looked at anyone directly, not me, not even Bobbie when, put out with my silence, she turned away from me and handed him an order. I wondered if it was a strategy to make us all go away—if he never looked at us, we weren't there. It made sense to me. The man had to have heard the recent exchange, and he probably stood there in the heat and grease of his griddle and heard this crap day after day, even when I wasn't there to be the integrationist special of the day. Maybe he'd been standing there in the same white cap and apron hearing it for ten or fifteen years without anybody ever wondering what he thought about it. Or maybe people made their racist pronouncements as a kind of dare to the man—say anything contrary to us, nigger, and you're fired, regardless of how good you cook those damn burgers.

Bobbie turned back to me. "So? What do you say? Should the government be able to make my daughter play jump rope and share a toilet with a buncha nasty blacks?"

I wanted out of there before I yielded to my impulse to rearrange this woman's ugly mouth. But I was also ashamed that I didn't object to her bigotry, because haters like her get along because nobody objects, everyone agrees or stays silent in our cowardice.

"I just don't know, ma'am," I said. "How much do I owe?"

I walked back toward the barbershop with an eye on Marvin, who was leaning against my car. He was studying the front of McCallister's pool hall, which sat between the sheriff's department and the barbershop. He glanced at me without acknowledgment and returned his focus to the pool hall. Two young guys walked out of the pool hall and stood for a moment in front of a red pick-up. They wore jeans and cheap, button-up cotton shirts with short sleeves folded up a turn. Their hair was oiled into a perfect duck's ass. A Confederate flag covered the back window of the pickup.

They stared at Marvin, who accepted their gaze and returned it blankly. They got in the truck and revved the engine as loud as possible, as if it was saying for them, "Fuck you, nigger." Marvin didn't move, nor did he avert his eyes the way the café cook did. No "git-back" in Marvin.

Inside the barbershop I took a seat. There were two barbers working and five other customers waiting. I figured I would have to wait thirty minutes, forty-five at the most.

Harry Dean, the shop owner, a round fellow with almost no hair himself, had given me my first haircut when I was two years old. He had placed a board across the armrests of his barber chair and pumped the chair up to maximum height, thus elevating me to the level that "Mr.

Harry" could clip my platinum locks. Granddaddy laughed at the expressions on my face as Harry snipped around my ears. When he finished, Mr. Harry handed me a penny for the gumball machine.

Growing up, I had loved going to the barbershop to listen to the men talk to my grandfather. They wanted to hear what the county's richest and most powerful man had to say, and some of them wanted the biggest man to hear their views. It was there that I heard why Harry Truman was a traitor to the Democratic Party with his "so-called civil rights platform." There it was explained why Governor Big Jim Folsom, the liberal who drank too much and consorted with organized labor, was unsafe on the segregation question. Granddaddy had been in Harry's chair one Saturday in 1954 when he declared that Earl Warren and Hugo Black were going to have to be impeached if the Constitution was to survive. But I had been in the chair in 1960 when a local farmer took issue with the Judge on whether Alabama Democrats ought to throw their weight behind Harry Byrd, the segregationist Virginia senator, on the ballot of a splinter party, or stay loyal to the national party and support John Kennedy and Lyndon Johnson. "That Kennedy's dangerous," Granddaddy had answered, with a stern look at the farmer, "and Johnson betrayed the South on that civil rights bill in 1957. The nigras just have too much influence with Kennedy and Nixon."

It was a rare thing to see Granddaddy contradicted, and if a vote had been taken that day in the shop, I guessed that the McKee influence would have prevailed overwhelmingly. It was soon after that I started going to the barbershop on my own, and coincidentally I thought, about the time that my own views began to veer, ever so slightly, away from Granddaddy's. I had been shocked at about age fourteen with the news report of an old black yard man in Montgomery who got snatched off the street and castrated by Klansmen—for no reason other than they wanted to do it and could get away with it. When I asked my grandfather to explain why it had happened, he started talking about how the sit-ins created "nigra trouble." Much as I loved and admired Granddaddy, I didn't see how college students sitting in at Woolworth's justified cutting off an old man's balls. After that, I just nodded silently when Granddaddy held forth on politics and race.

Even without Granddaddy present during my visits to the shop during my teenaged years, Harry Dean had stayed just as friendly and attentive to me, especially when I was the captain of the Eden Rise basketball team. Harry replayed every game Eden Rise won as he cut my hair and solicited my opinions on why the team was doing so well.

But today as I sat down Harry didn't even say hello. He chatted with everyone in the shop but me, though he kept looking at me as he talked to others. All right, I thought, just give me a haircut.

I opened a copy of *Esquire*. "Harry, you think the nigger vote bill is going to pass?" It came from a skinny, sixtyish man sitting next to me who I knew from the farmer's co-op where he worked.

It was the café all over again.

"Elvin, it looks more like it ever' day," Harry said. "That damn Johnson ain't going to be happy till we're all taking orders from Sapphire and the Kingfish." There were chuckles around the shop at that, which inspired Harry Dean to keep going. "Niggers get control, you know the first thing they going to do, Elvin? Start raising the property taxes. Niggers don't own no property, so what do they care if the taxes go up a hundred percent? Hell, a thousand percent! Hey, it won't hurt me too much—I just got my house, but these farmers with lots of land, they'll suffer something terrible with a nigger tax assessor."

I kept my eyes glued to the *Esquire*, but I wasn't stupid. They wanted me to feel uncomfortable. Harry was talking to me when he mentioned big farmers with lots of land. I had once asked Granddaddy how much property tax he had to pay every year, and when I was told $19,000, I had been amazed at how much money that was. Now I realized that it was only about three dollars an acre per year. Of course a colored tax assessor would raise taxes if they were that low. They should be raised. But the white landowners in this county wouldn't agree.

Elvin was just getting warmed up. "And you know, Harry, those Washington, D.C., senators we got, Sparkman and Hill, they too old to fight hard against the nigger vote bill, and they too liberal anyway. They live in Washington—what do they care if the niggers take over in Alabama? We need a fightin' sonuvabitch up there."

Harry stopped cutting, held his clippers up in his left hand, and pointed them at Elvin. "We need George Wallace up there worse'n we need him down here now."

"You mighty right about that, Harry. That rascal, he'd make them Washington liberals think twice about lettin' the niggers just take over Alabama."

Elvin had a gleam in his eye, which I knew was something George Wallace managed to put on many an Alabamian at that time, so powerful was his hold on the feelings of people who wanted to believe, against evidence and reason, that this little man with slicked-back dark hair and an upward curl in his top lip was going to save white supremacy and take away their fear.

"What do you say, Alton?" Elvin shouted, as a heavyset middle-aged man in khaki pants and shirt entered the barbershop. Alton Parrish was a local farmer I knew from church. Harry Dean's voice was all mock seriousness. "Alton, don't enter my shop without speaking to President Kennedy!" Alton grinned, and I saw him fix his eyes on something on the floor—a Kennedy half-dollar that had been glued there. He stepped within a few feet and then spat a long stream of tobacco juice that hit squarely on top of the coin. I felt myself flinch. *"Bull's-eye!"* Elvin whooped. "Alton, you a regular Lee Harvey Oswald!"

Harry Dean laughed loudest. Stropping his razor, he looked at me and then away. "Come on, Alton. You next."

I watched him for a few seconds before I spoke. "Mr. Dean, I believe I was next."

Harry Dean walked deliberately over to where the tobacco spit lay and sprinkled sawdust from a bucket over it. He kicked it around a little with his shoe to cover it, then he took three steps toward me and looked down. "Naw, McKee, Alton is next. It ain't your turn."

Harry Dean had never called me anything but Tommy during the scores of times I had been in his shop. I held his gaze until he turned away, but there was nothing to say, because I couldn't make the sonuvabitch cut my hair. I headed for the door. It was never going to be the same for me in Eden Rise.

9

SACRED FIRE

Jackie was pulling on the barrel of Buford Kyle's shotgun, which kept firing over and over. Another nightmare had awakened me, and at 2 A.M. I was standing in the kitchen, eating pie and drinking milk in the hope a full stomach would send me back to sleep, when the phone rang.

"Y'all fixin' to burn up like that nigger church is doin' right now," said a low, hard voice. Then he hung up.

I expected Mama and Daddy to wake up and come ask about the call, but they didn't, and I held the dead phone in my hand, not sure what to do. Marvin suddenly appeared. When I told him what I heard, he fetched his weapons and his shoes.

"I'm going to walk around outside. You stay at the back door and listen if I call."

At first I heard only crickets, but then in the distance came the sound of a siren. Soon it was multiplied at least twice. In five minutes Marvin returned, shaking his head. He hadn't seen anything. "But all them sirens sounds like Chicago on Saturday night. *Somethin' happenin.*"

"You wanta go look?" I asked.

When he nodded, I got dressed, slipped the phone off the hook, and pointed my car in the southerly direction that the sirens had seemed to go. It only took a minute before we saw the flashing lights of fire trucks and police cars on an unpaved street in the all-black southern section of Eden Rise. As I crept toward the lights, black people sprinted by the car in the same direction. I parked a hundred yards from the trucks and we walked toward them.

Zion Baptist was a white frame church of a style often found in rural Alabama. At the front corners of a fifty by thirty foot rectangle were two turrets that were actually tall square boxes with flat tops—no steeples.

The double front doors were set back between the two corner boxes. The church was old. At that moment the front of the church looked exactly as it would under normal circumstances, but the rear of the building was burning.

Marvin and I dashed around to the side of the church to see the orange flames crawling up the side of the building. Several men in fireman jackets were watching close up, their arms at their sides.

"Heart pine . . . !"

"Like kindlin' . . . !"

"We need water!"

"Ain't no hydrant down here!"

People around us were running up with five-gallon buckets of water drawn from house spigots. The town's water system didn't reach into black areas.

Marvin shook his head. "That ain't going to do no good. Need lot more water'n that."

That remark connected a circuit in my head, and I starting running to the car, Marvin in pursuit. "Where we going?" he called after me.

Our herbicide truck had a five hundred-gallon water tank that we used to dilute the chemicals before spraying them. I had filled that tank dozens of times at the warehouse and driven the truck to fields where Junior was applying poison. At the warehouse I hit the tank with a plank to hear whether there was water in it—it was almost full—and we hopped in, gunned the engine, and roared back toward the church. The street was blocked now, with a few cars and dozens of gawkers on foot. I honked the horn but the people and the drivers paid little attention. Marvin suddenly jumped out, whipped out a pistol, and fired into the air three times. People jumped and screamed.

"Out of the way, motherfuckers. We got water!"

That opened a way through the crowd, and I steered the truck on the grass down the side of the burning church and backed it as close as I dared. I turned on the hydraulic pump, jumped on the back truck of the truck, and starting aiming the water nozzle at the fire.

What a miraculous substance water is. When the leaping orange shoots instantly turned to gray smoke at the places I hit, my adrenaline surged. In little more than a minute, the water seemed to have obliterated the fire in a large part of the back of the church. But when I lowered the hose, my arms trembling and aching, I saw it had moved forward toward the front turrets.

I shouted down toward Marvin and pointed. "Pull back and point it that way!"

He shrugged. "Don't know how to do no stick shift."

I was crawling down when Sam Ford stepped out of the crowd, shouting. "I move you, Tommy."

Sam got me in the right spot. The roar of the fire was deafening, like the world's largest waterfall. Fire Chief Jack Shoemaker, Bobby Ray's father, shouted to me to spray on the roof. I did that for the next five minutes, wrestling with the wriggling snake of hose, and then felt the hose start to go limp in my hands. The water was starting to run out. I jumped off the back of the truck and ran around to the cab, ready to go re-fill the tank, but Mr. Shoemaker blocked my way. Bobby Ray, also wearing a fireman's coat, stood beside his father.

"It's no use, son. The floor joists are lit. It's a goner."

"You sure?"

"Yeah. Eighty-year-old pine. Dry as a bone. You coulda set it with a paper match." And somebody probably did, I thought.

Marvin, Sam, and I watched the fire get onto every floorboard, siding plank, and roof beam of that dignified little church. We watched it metamorphose from a cool white box to a blistering, orange gas explosion and then to a mound of gray and white ashes over which hung acrid yellow smoke.

The transition had mesmerized me for an hour when Orene came rushing up. "Oh, no. *Nooooooo!*" Sobbing, she looked at me, but I could think of absolutely nothing comforting to say. "Tommy, they done burned down my church."

"Baby, I told you to stay home." Sam had taken his wife by the elbow.

I hugged her and she leaned into my chest.

All my life I've heard whites profess their affection for blacks who worked in their homes, a lot of which is pure bullshit to make them feel better about their culpability in the mistreatment of blacks. But I can say, without fear of Godly retribution, that when these events took place in 1965, only my mother, Bebe, and Cathy were dearer to me than Orene Ford among all women in the world. It was agonizing to see her in such pain.

I looked over Orene's weeping head at a cluster of young white men standing fifty yards behind us, away from the ashes of the church. They watched us intently, rocking back and forth on their heels, and I saw a couple of them work to swallow triumphant grins. I glanced to the side. A group of black people—folks from this street, I guessed—were watching the white men and seeing what I was seeing. One of the young black men shouted toward the whites.

"Them cracker churches burn, too, motherfucker!"

Shoe also was watching the white guys. I went to where he and his father stood and asked what had caused the fire. Jack Shoemaker looked not at me but at the ashes. "Lit kerosene. Set at the back."

"Who did it?"

He shrugged. "Your guess good as mine." He still wouldn't look at me, but I caught Bobby Ray's eye for minute. I looked around. "Sheriff here?"

"Was. Gone now."

"Gone. Just like the church, huh?"

Now Jack Shoemaker did look at me, nodded slightly, and walked toward his firetruck, sitting shiny red and useless near where the brick church steps rose to nothing but ruin.

When I returned to Marvin and Sam, I saw a young black man, short and stocky, facing Orene, her hands in his. I couldn't hear much of what he was saying, but I could tell he was praying, just for Orene, who was still near hysterics. When he finished, Orene turned to me. She coughed her throat clear. "Tommy, this Reverend Banks, my minister."

We shook hands and he nodded. "Brother McKee."

"I sure am sorry, Reverend."

"Thank you. We just going to be praying for the Lord to help us rebuild."

"Yes, sir." I looked at Sam. "Fireman said it was set."

Sam had his arm around Orene. "We know." He looked at Banks.

Banks nodded and spoke to me, because, I later realized, Sam and Orene, and even Marvin somehow, already knew what he had to say.

"I held a meeting of the Southern Christian Leadership Conference here two weeks ago. A voter registration meeting. There were some white men outside watchin' when the meeting was over."

We all looked over at the clutch of white boys I had observed earlier. None of us standing there said anything, but silently we handed down the indictment.

The only thing I witnessed that summer as shameful and senseless as Jackie's murder was the burning of Zion Baptist. I felt my own murderous anger at the white men loitering nearby and a sickening despair at the finality of their arson. That night in 1965, I started learning that white Southerners, no doubt most of them professing Christians, have had a longstanding compulsion to burn down black churches. It started during Reconstruction, when freed slaves first built their own churches and used them for schools and political meetings. Now I was witnessing, helplessly, our sacred pyromania. Of course, white Southerners have condemned it as *unpardonable*, but what you notice after you study it a while is that the outrage is really empty. Nobody ever has to be pardoned because almost nobody is ever caught. I dare say half of Ruffin County had a good idea who burned down Zion Baptist that night, and I believe I was looking at them, but in the weeks to come nobody was ever charged, tried, or as far as I know even questioned about it.

The good thing about it was the unforeseen consequences of that fire. Like lots of infernos, it went out of control—well after the smoke had cleared the next morning.

10

Truth in the Truck

The next morning, when we went to the warehouse to return the water truck, Junior said Marvin and I could help him return a big truck that a seed supplier in Mobile had lent us to haul soybean seed to Eden Rise. Junior wanted us to follow him to Mobile and bring him back. I was sick of hanging around the house, spending too much time replaying in my mind Jackie's death, avoiding my father's tightlipped presence, and worrying about whether I would end up in prison. The idea of actually doing something was a relief. "Marvin, you need to see more of the *great state* of Alabama," Junior said.

Marvin answered with a grimace. "Fuck Alabama."

I thought: *No, fuck you. The sooner you're gone, the better.* Marvin was a constant reminder of how my life had careened into a ditch.

Junior led us westward to Demopolis, where we picked up Highway 43, which took us south through Linden and Thomasville and Grove Hill, small towns I knew from having played basketball in their gyms. The Linden teams weren't very good and the Grove Hill boys played dirty—stepping on your feet under the goal when going for a rebound. The country boys from Thomasville weren't very tall but they could shoot the eyes out from twenty feet.

The farther south we went, the fewer crops we saw and the further we removed ourselves from the natural beauty of Eden Rise. The rolling land was covered with loblolly pines and kudzu, vegetation I thought of as pestilent, ugly and fast-breeding. A yellow pine forest has always struck me as lacking all character when compared to hardwoods or fruit trees, and kudzu chokes everything around it to death. A generation back all this land had been farmed, but since the 1930s the cotton fields the first settlers cut into the red clay had returned to monochromatic forest, too thick to see into, most of it owned by paper manufacturers. I still wonder where all the people went.

In Grove Hill, they were building a new school, not out of brick the way the public schools traditionally were, but out of pre-fabricated sheet steel, a rectangular box with a flat roof. It looked more like a warehouse than a school, but the sign outside read "Future Home of Clarke Academy." It was one of the private segregation academies being set up in anticipation of public school integration. This was what the people in Eden Rise Café wanted for our community.

Marvin asked how far it was to Mobile, and when I told him it was three hours, he groaned. "Shit, man. Why we have to do this?"

"We didn't have anything better to do, and it needs doing," I said in a no-nonsense voice.

He shook his head. "I could have found something better than riding down this boring-ass road."

I was happy to be out of Eden Rise, even if Highway 43 wasn't Alabama's most scenic.

The radio was playing "Eight Days a Week." Marvin reached over to the dial. "That shit stinks, man." He stopped when he found James Brown's "Papa's Got a Brand New Bag."

"You like that?" he asked. I shrugged. The godfather of soul didn't do much for me. "Better'n that Beatle shit," Marvin declared. We were silent for a long while as James Brown gave way to Fontella Bass. I liked "Rescue Me."

A welcome silence followed but it didn't last. "What I'm going to do for pussy down here?" I could only shrug at his resigned look. "Up there at college, man, you get any pussy?"

"Not much. Well, I did for a while, but then she dumped me."

"Why she dump you?"

"Said I was boring."

"*The fuck* kind of reason is that? Tell me about her. You really like her?"

"Yeah, I did. A girl from New York."

He asked her name and when he heard it he screwed up his face. "She a Jew? Be careful them damn Jews."

"What does that mean?"

"Jews are bloodsuckers. Fuck you over in a second."

"That's bullshit."

"Ain't bullshit. It's the truth, man."

"No, it's *complete* bullshit."

He looked surprised. "Why you think that?"

I kept my eyes on the highway. "Because you're saying the same kind of hateful, racist stuff that people say about Negroes, only you're saying it against a Jew. That's fucked up."

"Man, you don't know shit about how them Jews in the ghetto treat us. High prices for bad stuff, high rents, won't give us no jobs."

"I *do* know something about that. Jewish merchants getting their stores burned and looted because the people are mad at the cops. Some of 'em lost everything."

He was scowling. "How you know this?"

"This girl's father took me to Harlem and showed me around. He told me about it. He liked the people who lived there, but he showed me how tough it was for the merchants."

"That don't mean he wouldn't fuck over a nigger if he had a chance."

"You know, things this guy said to me made me believe he was more sympathetic to colored people than anybody I'd ever met. Jews aren't the problem for y'all."

Marvin jutted out his jaw. "The Nation of Islam teaches that Jews are the worst of the white devils."

"Anything that teaches that all of one group is evil is just screwed up. That's what's so wrong around here with whites telling each other that all blacks are inferior."

Marvin stared at me angrily, and it scared me. I was thinking about how I could get him back to Chicago when he spoke again.

"That Jew pussy must be *good!* Gotta *get* me some of that." He cackled. Before I could react, he went on. "Hey, I been wanting to ask you: That girl who was with y'all when your friend got killed, what'd she look like?"

"She was tall, good-looking."

"How light was she?"

"She was dark."

"Didn't you want some of that?"

"No." But then I thought about Alma a moment. "I coulda been interested if she had acted normal toward me."

"You think colored girls are attractive?"

"Same with white girls—some of 'em. You like white girls?"

"I *love* me some white pussy. Had a good bit of it, too."

I was shocked. I was nineteen and it was 1965; I took it as an act of racial aggression for Marvin to want white women. The rape myth about black men and white women had been planted firmly in me. At that moment I imagined that his white women were whores and sleazes in Chicago, or innocent women he took advantage of, but I didn't ask.

He smiled. "That Baby Sister, she a spectacular jewel. I'd like to have me some of that."

My heartbeat raced and my right hand started to shake. I started to pull the truck over, but I couldn't lose sight of Junior up ahead or we'd be lost.

"You leave her the hell alone." I could feel my teeth grinding.

He laughed. "You white men all the same."

"I'm warning you. She's sixteen years old."

"What? *You* going to keep me away from her? *Shit.*"

I jammed the gas pedal and let the acceleration slam Marvin back into his seat. I had to get rid of him as soon as we got back to Eden Rise. All I would have to do was repeat this conversation to Daddy, and Marvin would be on the next bus back to Chicago.

AFTER WE DELIVERED THE big truck at the Mobile docks, Junior climbed in with us and announced the ride had made him hungry. He knew of a good café nearby. I was the only white in the place. Junior flirted shamelessly with the waitress, a chubby girl about my age. "What's yo name, sweetie? Carnell? Ain't that pretty! Pretty as you! This here my nephew Tommy. Sho is. He my sister baby." Only when Junior let go his rumbling laugh did Carnell start to giggle. We ate collard greens and sweet potatoes, backbone and pork chops, and even some chitlins, which were new to me, greasy and chewy but tasty. Junior drank two tall Colt 45s, and when he found out that Marvin couldn't drive the truck's stick shift, he let him have a malt liquor, too. He gestured with his chin at Marvin sipping his Colt 45. "Sorry-assed town niggers." I couldn't tell if he was joking but I surely agreed with the "sorry-assed" part. When Carnell brought the check, Junior's face showed outrage. "'Leven dollars! We ain't got no 'leven dollars. My nephew going to wash y'all dishes this afternoon." Carnell looked afraid, but then Junior's laugh boomed.

In the truck Junior pulled a silver half-pint flask out of his coverall pockets. His hands were as big as baseball mitts, the flask a cigarette lighter in comparison. He took a quick sip. "It's my knee medicine, you understand." He winked at me. He had hurt the knee playing sandlot football when he lived in Chicago during World War II, he told me. "Chicago a fun place to be. Great parties and clubs. Ain't that right, Marvin?"

"Whole lot better'n this fuckin' Alabama," Marvin said. "Can't figure why you came back."

Junior told us why. In 1948 his daddy had died, and after the funeral, his mother had begged him not to go back to Chicago, and she had put my daddy up to offering him a job farming. Junior said Daddy turned out to be a good guy to work for. He respected Junior, asked his advice, and took it most of the time. Daddy had sold him eight acres for a home site and then co-signed for the loan. For the last ten years, Junior had been the farm foreman.

"Daddy seems under a lot of strain," I said, testing Junior a little.

Junior sipped from the flask. "He don't like this judge thing too much, but he think he gotta do it. Miss Brigid, she think Buddy can keep peace better than some others could. Buddy don't know for sho' he can, but he going to try."

"Only ones causing any trouble in Eden Rise are the ones burning churches," I said.

"Well, Tommy, this civil rights business, like they having over in Selma, could blow up in Ruffin County very easy."

"Any niggers vote now?" Marvin asked.

"Used to be just William Addison and his brother Robert, the undertaker. You know, the high-toned brothers, ones with money. Rest us old farm niggers, we get killed if we try to vote."

Junior saw my frown at his remark about William. "That shock you, boy? Don't get me wrong. William all right—his only problem is he ain't going to get far from Miss Brigid's apron string." He let go a rumbling laugh. "William brother got his nose up in the air. Robert Addison, he don't seem to care nothin' 'bout no po' folks." Junior took a drink. "My daddy always say, 'ain't much more useless than a rich nigger.'"

He took another pull on the whiskey. "Buddy maybe can let some colored get registered to vote without having a big fight in town."

My daddy, the keeper of racial harmony? That was not what I heard at home. "You really think Daddy can keep trouble from Eden Rise?"

"Well, I don't know for sho' he can, but I believe he come closer'n anybody else. Somebody else in charge, we going to have some trouble."

"Well, I get the idea Daddy doesn't want things to change too much."

"He probably don't, but he smart enough to know it *going to* change, 'cause things changin' fast already. Buddy know we wanta vote. He made sho' I got to vote."

In 1956 Junior had hinted to Daddy that he wanted to vote in the presidential election. Without announcing what he was doing, Daddy stopped off one day at the courthouse and led Junior to the board of registrars. He told the registrar he vouched that Junior had property and could read and write. A black had to have a white sponsor, which almost none had.

"Well, the registrars, they thinks if Buddy wants me to vote the Judge must be wanting me to vote. Ain't *nobody* going to cross the Judge, you know that, Tommy. So, zip-zap, I'm registered, been going to the polls ever since."

"Did my grandfather approve of you getting to vote?"

"*Naw*. But he wadn't going to go against Buddy too much, and he probably knew I wadn't going to abuse the privilege."

"What do you mean?"

"Well, he knew I wadn't going to bring a big bunch of colored down there to try to vote."

Marvin scowled. "Niggers always be afraid down here."

"Fuck you. You registered to vote in Chicago?"

"They won't let convicted felons vote." Marvin pursed his lips.

"Well then, nigger, don't come down here criticizing *me* for what I ain't done when you got yo' sorry ass fixed up where you *can't* vote."

They made me nervous arguing. "Junior, what do you think is going to happen about the voting?"

"Tommy, I think this votin' bill they talkin' 'bout now going to get a lot of colored registered. But it might get lotta people hurt if it ain't done right. More the whites fight, more the colored going to fight back. Burnin' down that church, that make folk mad."

He paused a moment. "Pull over, Tommy. I gotta see a man 'bout a coon dog." In the waning minutes of dusk, the three of us were taking a leak on the truck tires when Marvin asked how much farther it was. We were almost to Demopolis. Junior reminded Marvin that his folks came from Demopolis.

"You know Big Tom McKee?" Marvin said to Junior.

"Well, sho, 'round him a lot. My daddy was Big Tom's man. Sorta ran things like I do a little bit now. Big Tom a heavy-faced man. Rough-talking." He curled his lip and pitched his voice with a twang to imitate Big Tom. "'Nigger, git over here. Nigger, do that or I kick yo' goddamn ass.'"

I felt my face go red. "The colored people musta hated Big Tom."

"Well, most of 'em 'fraid of him. Course, whites just as scared as colored. Big Tom didn't talk to me or Daddy like he would to others. Walter Jackson, he didn't let nobody say much about Big Tom around him. He was Big Tom's man."

Junior draped an arm around Marvin as he let go a rumbling laugh. "Daddy used to say that he only ever saw one somebody who wadn't afraid of Big Tom McKee, and that was a colored girl."

There was neither sound nor movement in the dark truck.

"Who was that?" I finally said.

"Better not get into that now, Tommy boy. We almost home."

I looked over at them, but it was too dim to make out anything on either face.

11

Gooch

When I got up from a late afternoon nap, something I needed these days because of my difficulty sleeping at night, I found Cathy and Marvin playing cards at the kitchen table.

Cathy looked up at me, delighted. "Did you see that, Tommy? You cheated, Marvin. That's how you beat me. What kind of low person cheats at gin rummy?"

"'Course I cheated. Tryin' to tough you up, Baby Sister. You need to know how men really are. Most of us ain't nice like your brother." He smiled wickedly at her.

She scowled back, but it was half a smile, too. "You are such a criminal, Marvin."

"Baby, you don't know half of it."

Since the trip to Mobile, I had been trying to figure out the best way to get rid of Marvin. I was going to ask either Daddy or Bebe to fire him. Mama seemed to like Marvin, and she was totally convinced I needed a bodyguard. I was still hoping that things would stay calm, but with Buford Kyle's trial only five weeks away, I knew that emotions could get stirred up again and I'd be at risk. But maybe we could hire some retired state trooper or prison guard if I needed someone to ride shotgun for me.

Marvin shuffled the cards rapidly. He used each hand alternately to perform the overhand and the hindu and the weave. "How'd you get so good with cards?" I said.

"In the slam. Plenty time to get good there."

Cathy watched him intently. "You left-handed, Marvin?"

"Ambidextrous with cards and most things. Throw baseball right-handed, bat better on the left." When he picked up his hand, he looked over the cards at Cathy. "You not a bad dealer yourself, Baby Sister."

"Granddaddy taught me. He was left-handed and tried to get me do it that way, but I'm too much a righty."

I remembered Granddaddy playing cards with Cathy. He so loved to get the cards in his hands that he'd play Old Maids for hours with Cathy. Once I watched an all-night poker game at a hunting club where Granddaddy won over a thousand dollars. A fat Birmingham lawyer shook his head the next morning: "Hell, Lefty, you done got all our money."

Cathy picked up her cards, sorted them, and shot a hard look at Marvin. "I'm going to beat ya this time, you lyin', cheatin', miserable thing."

"Hell you will." Marvin leaned back in his chair and smiled over his cards at me. "Ain't I taught her good?"

Cathy won the next two hands and announced that she wanted to watch American Bandstand. We went in the den, and she was soon dancing in front of the television. My sister had studied piano since she was seven and was damn good. Her delicate, long fingers could fly over the keyboard like hummingbirds. She sang well, had near perfect pitch, listened constantly to the radio, and watched "Bandstand," "Shindig," and "Hullaballoo" on TV.

"See that girl." She was at the television pointing to a particular place. "She's doing the Swim." Cathy demonstrated that to us, and then she moved on to the Jerk and the Mashed Potato as the show concluded its half hour. Marvin smiled at her, but he was just barely tolerating the music. Finally, he said, "Baby Sister, you need to learn some soul steps."

"Oh, please, Marvin, teach me."

No, don't, Cathy, I said to myself. She tuned the radio to a rhythm and blues station from Selma and, as I sat there and steamed, she pulled him up to dance. I didn't want to stay and watch but felt I couldn't leave the room either. Over the next hour he demonstrated how to do the Stroll, the Boogaloo, and the Shingaling. She quickly learned each dance, getting more and more excited as the afternoon progressed. Finally she pulled me to my feet and in spite of my protests got me up to step with her, and while I wasn't very good, it was fun. When the R&B station played a commercial, she flipped to WBAM in Montgomery just in time to get the Righteous Brothers. She grabbed Marvin, pulled him close to dance, and stared into his eyes as she sang that she had lost that loving feeling. My heartbeat picked up speed, and I felt pressure in my right temple. This dancing was getting out of hand, not only because Marvin liked my sister but, to my disbelief, because my little sister liked him back.

I was thinking about how to stop it when Daddy suddenly stood in the door of the den. Her arms still draped around Marvin's shoulders, her torso flat against his, Cathy said, "Hey, Daddy. We been having our own *Bandstand*." Marvin nudged Cathy away, and I started leaning toward the door. Daddy glared at Marvin but didn't speak to him. "Cut that shit off, Cathy." She did as instructed. I led Marvin out to the patio. To his credit, Daddy didn't call in the KKK. But the look on his face told me that Marvin would soon be on his way.

THE NEXT MORNING THE fields beckoned me from my tense home. Sitting at the wheel of a tractor put me inside a happy paradox: my senses were assaulted with bitter smell of hot petroleum, the vibrations the huge engine sent through a ten-ton steel apparatus, and the constant roar of the unmuffled combustion, but there was also the inspiration you got sitting above the expanse of green plants and the profound comfort from feeling like you were the master of something vital, the one insuring that the mass of growing things would survive the summer in good health and provide a great bounty in the fall. In that place, nothing could bother you as long as you put the International Harvester on a precise path. At the end of ten or twelve hours, you could stand up on your massive red-and-black machine, grimy and tired and sun-burnt, and enjoy how much you had improved this luxuriant garden.

I told Marvin I was going to start plowing cotton and soybeans. He didn't like it, because he knew he'd have to go along. Maybe if I made him sweat in the field he'd quit and go back to Chicago of his own accord, and beat Daddy to firing him.

I was soon steering carefully down half-mile-long rows of six-inch-high cotton plants. Marvin was perched above me on the fender of the huge back wheels, a pistol tucked into the back of his jeans. It was clear he'd rather be anyplace else in the world, probably even prison. After about an hour, he shouted that he wanted to get off. I shut the tractor off, and we climbed down into the dusty field. "Goddamn. My ears ringin'. That noise going to drive me crazy."

But to my dismay, he adapted. I showed him how to adjust the "feet" on the cultivator—the shiny, silver, v-shaped steel blades that broke the soil near the plants and plowed up the morning glories and crabgrass that had invaded the field. He drove a few rows just to prove he could do it, and then he returned to the fender, satisfied in his achievement.

I could steer precisely without concentrating on the task, and so I had always daydreamed wildly while plowing. Before I went to college I had been able to conjure up scenarios of great success as an adult—of wealth and fame and romantic love. Now that Jackie had been murdered, I discovered that I had lost the ability to imagine a successful future, except for the one musing which sent me off on a flight visualizing Beth Kaplan's sudden appearance at the end of the row, and my dropping her in the moist soil and fucking her. I hoped Marvin didn't see my erection.

About mid-afternoon I was turning the tractor at the end of a row, lost in the mist of my daydreams, when Marvin grabbed my shoulder. "Stop it and get off."

I jammed my left foot down on the clutch and the tractor jerked to a stop. I jumped off the back of the tractor, leaving Marvin in the driver's seat looking to the right. A truck was coming up the dirt path toward us. "You know them?" he said.

"Let me look."

"Keep your damn head down."

I stood on the cultivator and peeped over the fender at the old, blue Dodge truck. "I don't know that truck."

"That ain't Junior or Sam or none of them?" When I shook my head, Marvin got off the tractor. "Stand up there at the front of the tractor. Keep it between you and whoever this is."

The truck came to a stop about fifty feet from where Marvin stood beside the cultivator. Three young white men got out. They all looked to be in their late teens and wore blue jeans and tee shirts. Two had dirty blond hair and were skinny, and one was heavyset with dark hair. They strode toward where Marvin stood, each one holding something down by their legs.

"What can I do for you gentlemen?" Marvin said. I had never heard such politeness from him. "We're looking for Tom McKee." It was one of the blond ones. He had very bad teeth.

"What may I ask is your business?" Marvin smiled.

The big one stepped forward. "Nigger, that ain't none of yore business. I believe I see him right over yonder."

He was looking around the tractor toward me and didn't see Marvin move at him.

Marvin swung his leg toward the big man's shin, and when it connected, the man shrieked and lurched forward into the cultivator. Marvin drove a hard kick into his side. As he screamed, Marvin whirled toward the other two, now with both his .38 and his switchblade drawn. They crouched as if to fight him, revealing their weapons—crowbars. Marvin fired the pistol, missing them both, but they were so startled that he had the opening to leap forward. He slugged one of them in the mouth with the blunt edge of his knife. I saw blood and a tooth fly as the boy flopped to the ground.

Marvin pointed the pistol at the one still standing. "Move, motherfucker, and you're dead."

The boy raised his arms as if in surrender.

"Get down on all fours."

When he did, Marvin dropped both his knees in the boy's back, flattening him in the dirt with a resonating grunt. He grabbed the boy's hair, snapped his head back, put the pistol against his right ear and fired a bullet in the dirt. I could hear the echo and the boy's wail. Marvin switched the pistol to his other hand and shot again into the dirt beside his other ear. The boy was screaming and crying, holding his head. Marvin turned back to the one he had hit in the mouth. I wanted to call out and tell Marvin not to kill him but somehow knew I had to trust him. He pinned that one on his back and jammed the pistol far down his throat. Then he took the knife in his other hand, raised his left arm high, and brought it down hard, jamming the blunt end of the knife into the boy's ribs. He repeated this three times, and then switched the gun and the knife between hands and did it again. The boy screamed with each strike.

Marvin moved back to the big, dark-haired one lying by the cultivator, took aim, and kicked him twice between the legs. Then he took the pistol, held it between the big man's legs and fired twice. The man screamed and I almost did too, both of us thinking he was shot *in* the crotch. The quickness and brutality of Marvin's actions was startling.

When I edged around the tractor, he was regarding the three of them with total calm, as if he'd just awakened from a nap. "I'm going to go on and kill these cracker motherfuckers," he said in an eerily even voice. I panicked. "No, don't." No more death.

"Why not? They'da killed us if they could."

"I just don't want to. You beat 'em up good enough."

He shook his head in disgust. "Should go on and kill 'em." He stared at me for a long moment. "Then help me get 'em in the back of they truck."

We had to carry them, and I took their legs. "They stink."

"You scared you going to die, you shit your pants."

"What we going to do?"

"Get 'em outa here. Take 'em where they come from." He went over to the one holding his crotch and moaning. "Where you sorry motherfuckers from?" When there was no answer, Marvin whipped out his backup pistol—the other one was now empty—and jammed the short barrel directly into the right eye of the man.

"Gooch." Marvin looked at me.

"It's a crossroads in Yancey County."

"Okay. You lead, but don't go through no towns. Back roads."

Marvin looked back at the three men, all lying curled up on the floor of the truck bed. "Anybody try to get outa the truck 'fore I do," he announced to them in a loud voice, "y'all going to be the three deadest crackers in Alabama this afternoon."

I got in our truck and led Marvin on dirt roads to circumvent Eden Rise and then on country roads around and beyond Selma. It was a slow lead at first because Marvin had to figure out how to operate the clutch, but he got the hang of it. Forty-five minutes later, I parked near a store at

Gooch. Marvin rode past me, through the intersection, and down about a mile until he pulled off on a dirt side road. When I caught up, Marvin was leaning over the truck bed.

"You tell Mr. Kyle and all his friends 'bout meetin' me this afternoon, and that I was nice enough not to kill y'all," he was saying to them. "But tell 'em this too: If anybody that looks like y'all, talks like y'all, or smells like y'all shows up looking for Tom McKee, I won't be sweet and nice like I was with y'all this afternoon. Anybody from around here even says the name Tom McKee, them motherfuckers will die a slow and painful death." His face went even harder. "Now, do y'all understand what I'm sayin'?"

Two of them moaned. "Okay."

Marvin walked quickly to my truck. "Move over, I'm going to drive. Gotta practice. Show me a different way back."

I tuned the radio to the Big Bam, where Herman's Hermits were singing about Mrs. Brown and her lovely daughter. Marvin grimaced at the sounds of the British and reached for the dial. "Man, I can't take that shit." He found Fontella Bass on the Selma soul station, whence came her plea to be rescued from loneliness. "Now that's some motherfuckin' music right there." He gave me a challenging look. I nodded; the truth was I liked the sound and somehow I identified with the sentiment.

"Your hands all right from the—?" I gestured behind us, back at Gooch.

"Yeah, man, they fine. I look after my hands." He held them up one at a time to show me their fronts and backs. Because his skin was light, the color contrast between his palms and the backs of his hands was not nearly as stark as Jackie's.

"I mostly use weapons. Use your fists, you going to get hurt, probably break your hand. I used to have some knucks, but they heavy to tote around, take a minute to get on. Guy up in the projects sold me my first knife, showed me about using the butt like a fist. Works every time."

"Why did you fire that gun beside that guy's ears?"

"It's very painful, makes you where you can't fight, but it don't leave no mark. Same with the kicks in the balls and the knife butt in the ribs. That big one won't be able to raise up for a couple of days but he probably won't even go to the doctor. I probably broke three or four ribs on the other one but didn't break the skin. All three of them going to hurt for a long time but what they got to show that they got bad beat up? They ain't got shit."

Marvin drove along silently for a couple of minutes. "Probably a good idea you didn't want me to kill them guys. We woulda had cops everywhere, more trouble than we got already. Way it is now, word going to get around among them crackers you got some protection." The understatement of the afternoon. Marvin shook his head. "But them guys wadn't much, Tom. I could tell the way they charged up to me—they didn't know what they was doing. Smart guys woulda laid back, tried to pick me off."

"What would you have done?"

"Killed 'em quick as I could." He studied the road ahead solemnly. "The next guys who come may be better and I *will* kill 'em and you won't talk me out of it." More cause for dread.

"You be thinking about some place we could put some bodies. Deep hole we could cover up be best. Mafia guys always say the key to their success was disappearing the body. You almost never going to get caught if they don't find the body." I thought immediately of several abandoned sharecropper shacks on our land, each of which had a well somewhere nearby. Marvin looked away. "'Course, if we do have to ice a few, word'll get around that folk who came after you just vanished—shhh-zamm!—and there won't be no more motherfuckers come lookin.'"

This frightened me, not only for the likelihood that my life remained in great danger, but also that in protecting myself, I participated in mayhem and possibly murder. But the foiled attack put faces on the danger lurking for me. It was no longer just a voice on the telephone. I had *seen* people who wanted to hurt me—who probably would kill me if they got the chance. Just average-looking guys, like the ones I had grown up with. It made me see that I had to have Marvin—he was what separated me from a violent death. I just had to put up with all his bad opinions and keep him off Cathy.

And maybe I had to get out—get away from Eden Rise, far away, where thugs from Gooch would not pursue me. When we got home, I said nothing about what happened in that field, but I'm pretty sure Marvin told William, and he in turn had instructed Orene to send lunches to the field to keep Marvin and me from riding around Eden Rise and risking trouble. I felt more under siege than ever.

A FEW DAYS LATER, in 93-degree heat, we were sitting under a pecan tree at the edge of a soybean field. The still air carried the scent of drying grass and dust. We needed a rain. Orene's chicken and dumplings had left us sleepy.

But Marvin wanted to talk. "You think a lot about Jackie?"

"Every hour of every day I'm awake. Dream about him most nights."

"I guess I can understand that." He was quiet a while. "I've killed three people. Two of 'em I don't worry about. Coupla niggers who woulda killed me if I hadn't got them." He paused again. "But the other one, I feel real bad about. Nobody knows it was me who killed him."

As Marvin told it to me, there had been a gang rumble when he was fourteen. He shot wild and hit a kid, a friend. He knew he was the one who killed the boy, but everybody said it was the other gang. "I've felt terrible about it ever since. Didn't mean to do it but that don't do him no good." I said I didn't understand about gangs. "Group protection. Mama not payin' me no attention. Strung out all the time. Living on the Southside, you got mean real fast to survive. When you tough, people respect you, think you somebody. Turned out I was good at fighting, especially with weapons."

"What 'bout your daddy?"

"I know who Mama *said* he was. He didn't come around much, and Grandmama didn't like him. She wouldn't let him around after I was bigger. He's in prison now, I think."

"You don't really have much family."

Marvin chuckled darkly. "No daddy, not much of a mama, no brothers or sisters. Only strong person my grandmama. That's why William paid attention. Felt sorry."

He swallowed the last of his pie. "You havin' a hard time now, but you got a lotta folk that care about you—your mama and grandma and your sister. I wish I had a sister."

"You wanta keep being a bodyguard?"

"Naw. I like this here, but I don't want to do it in Chicago no more. Get killed if I do."

"You like this now?"

"Well, it's gettin' more interesting."

He grinned wickedly. I flashed back to his complaint about the absence of women in Alabama and then to the image of his dancing with Cathy. Then I remembered the blood and the flying teeth and the screams of pain from the Gooch boys, and I wondered if that was what had made Marvin warm to Alabama. Whichever it was, I felt threatened, and I became more convinced that I needed to get away from Eden Rise.

Interlude I

1993

The sports news I was reading was about to spoil my eggs and bacon and biscuits when Wayne sat down across the table from me at our favorite breakfast diner.

"I bet that damn Auburn coach is behind this investigation," Wayne said to me, tapping my newspaper. The news had just broken that a star player at the University of Alabama had secretly signed a contract with a sports agent the night that the team won the national championship in the Sugar Bowl.

"Well, maybe," I said, "but if Gene Stallings knew about it and didn't stop it, which is how it looks, Alabama deserves to get penalized for being stupid. Or arrogant."

"Damn, Tom, you can't turn off that overdeveloped skepticism of yours even when the Crimson Tide is under attack." Wayne scowled, then let a smile turn up the right side of his mouth. "Guy on the radio yesterday said he was so torqued up about the trouble he couldn't eat anything but baby food, but you seem to be eating just fine."

Then his little, pale blue eyes twinkled. I asked if he wanted to use my tickets for Saturday's game in Tuscaloosa.

"Shit, I wish I could. I can't afford it, not with all the shopping therapy my wife needs. She's a very sick woman." Wayne made a good living as a securities lawyer.

Our waitress refilled our coffee cups and we went on to talk about the recent court decision, *Shaw v. Reno*, that said you couldn't use race to make voting districts. I'd been discussing it with my students in my civil rights law course, explaining that it was going to get harder for blacks to get elected. Wayne frowned. "Hell, I'm not sure that's a bad decision. Might stop all this packing blacks in the same district. That just elects

Republicans." Wayne was a Yellow Dog, a Democrat so true he would vote for said canine if it was on the party ticket, and he hated the current Republican tide that was turning the white South solidly against his party.

"Well, the black leadership wants black faces in office, and I can understand that. It's been slow coming—a lot slower than people thought it should be." I knew the arguments—indeed, had made them in court—but I was not convinced of the long-term wisdom for blacks of any policy that perpetuated a racialized electorate. When I voiced this doubt, Wayne smirked.

"Your problem is you know too much to be a liberal. 'Course, you know too much to be a conservative."

"But enough to be a mushy moderate."

"You said it, buddy. Be more comfortable one way or the other, wouldn't it?"

He was right, of course, about my evolving political agnosticism, my growing alienation from his party's leaders, and my middle-aged mindset that issues were too muddled and politicians too self-serving to earn my loyalty. On the other hand, the self-righteous right-wingers infuriated me. I was a lot surer about what I was against than what I was for.

"We've had this conversation before and you know the answer," I said. "I need to spend my time on self-improvement, not saving the world."

Wayne asked how my interviews were going with Randy Russell, the district attorney. I had met with him twice. He had gotten the crucial evidence out of me in the first twenty minutes of the first conversation, but we had talked for two hours because he was so curious about what had occurred later that summer, and beyond. He treated me like an ancient artifact. Still, I thought his curiosity was mostly sincere.

"What I meant was, how you handling it? How do you feel after you talk to him?"

What he meant was: does this resurrection of the past throw you into a deep funk, as it has done periodically since 1965, spinning you into the kind of depression that resulted in bouts of drinking, the end of a marriage, and a change of career? Wayne had been my AA sponsor for fifteen years, and he knew all about what had haunted me since 1965.

After the first talk with Russell, I was mostly okay—I think because the reconstruction of those events required a kind of oral narrative that I hadn't attempted since 1965. I had just quit talking about it then and had never started back. A guy in an AA group, a World War II vet, said he had a lengthy visit in hell at Okinawa in 1945, and he had chosen never to tell anybody about it. I had been like that about my summer of 1965. So it was a new experience to recount it now.

But the second conversation, on the day before my breakfast meeting with Wayne, was less a chronological account than an analysis of what happened and why. And as I answered Russell's increasingly penetrating questions—he was by no means a stupid guy—I slowly began to slide downward into the pit of self-doubt and self-recrimination.

"You just pitched yourself a good ol' dry drunk, didn't you?" Wayne said, with an edge of sympathy and amusement.

"Guess I did. But I didn't drink."

"Good. I didn't think you did. I would have known. But what did you do?"

I had moped around, gone for a walk, and watched TV. "I'm just real anxious about having to testify." The trial was set for the spring.

Wayne smiled at me. "You can handle the courtroom. Hell, you're great in the courtroom. No, the real problem is letting go of your bad feelings about yourself."

"I've paid a lot already," I said. "I don't want to have to keep on paying. Or find I owe debts more than the ones I have. Plus, it pisses me off the way people like to assign all blame to the bad guys of history—the Hitlers and the Bull Connors and the Richard Nixons—so they can avoid acknowledging that nearly everybody was in on the evil."

"Well, Tom, I reckon more than ninety-nine percent of the human race is less interested in such complexity, in the ambiguous nature of the human experience, than you are." He punctuated the lecture point with a nod, to which I just shrugged.

"Now what you going to do after your next talk with Russell? I mean, besides meet with me."

I had to think. "I'll find some of my women and get something to eat."

He nodded. He knew about my women—Cathy, my mother, my shrink. It seems odd now that it never occurred to anyone in 1965 that I should be seeing a shrink to deal with the trauma that I experienced. I go every two weeks now, and it used to be weekly, but when I was nineteen I coped on my own. Well, not really on my own, but without professional help. People then thought psychiatrists were for when you had really lost your mind—like when you had been committed to Bryce, the state mental hospital in Tuscaloosa. Back then people assumed that the solution to personal tragedy or trauma was religion. When something terrible happened, you embraced your faith more tightly and held on till you were comforted or you died.

"What you going to talk 'bout with these women?"

"Food. Football. Kids."

"Good boy. Issues you can't be ambivalent about." He smiled widely and knocked on the table with his knuckles. "You going to be *fine*."

12

ONE WORD

The next Saturday night Mama announced, looking at me, that we would be going to church the next day. I suppose she said it just in case I had somehow acquired the mistaken notion that what Bebe called "all this trouble" had canceled our commitment to Christianity.

Mama had read me Bible stories from the time I would sit still in her lap. She would explain many natural phenomena as what God wanted—he made the lightning and thunder and rain. When our dog died, she told me that Sportcoat had gone to be with God and Jesus in heaven, which allowed me a vision of the afterlife that included not just canines but cows and mosquitoes I slapped flat. In Sunday school the teachers had required me to recite all the books of the Bible in order and to memorize innumerable passages of scripture I can summon up to this day, and which might have influenced my life more than I know: *Blessed are the meek. . . . For God so loved the world. . . . Jesus wept.* I had learned several of the Psalms by heart, and Bebe had given me ten dollars and a slice of peach pie for memorizing the Sermon on the Mount and then reciting it to her. When I became a teenager, I joined in the activities of the Methodist Youth Fellowship, which offered me a place to be godly and to hang out with girls.

But I did all this without thinking very seriously about what I believed about God or the Trinity or salvation. Damnation I understood as the direct result of sinning. I just assumed that what I had been taught was true, and that I would never be quite sinful enough to go to hell.

Jackie's death prompted me to think more than I ever had about what I really believed. I lay in bed for hours going over and over what possible reason God could have for allowing it. Did I really believe that

God could have a larger purpose in letting Jackie be killed? If there was no good to be realized from his death, then how could you believe that God was in control? Maybe there was no God at all. If there was no God, then bad things happened in the world because people were bad—or because they were just as likely to be evil and violent and hateful as they were to be good and loving. Night after night of thought yielded only sweat and frustration.

But maybe I just needed my Christianity refreshed and things would clear up. So when Mama decreed our attendance at the Eden Rise Methodist Church on the following morning, I put on my seersucker jacket and dark blue necktie willingly, my expectations higher than usual.

My father leading the way, impassive as ever, as a family we climbed the steps of the church, an impressive brick structure with bright, white columns set high off the ground. Because Marvin now went everywhere with me, he walked silently beside me, but well before we got to the top step, three men emerged from behind the columns and stood in front, between us and the door. I knew them all—one was the farmer with the bull's-eye aim at the barbershop. None spoke to us. They just stared hard.

Daddy stopped short and looked at the men. Recognition suddenly came over him, and he turned to Marvin. "We'll be okay from here. Just wait in the car."

Marvin's hooded eyes moved from Daddy to the three men and then back to Daddy without a word. With a faint smirk he watched us move to the church door, then he met my helpless gaze. There was nothing I could do but be pissed off.

Over the strains of "Holy, Holy, Holy," I looked at Cathy, thinking about what what we had seen on the church steps. "They thought Marvin was a demonstrator," she whispered. "These civil rights people have been going around to white churches trying to get in on Sunday morning, and the men in the churches have been standing in the door to keep them out." She bugged her eyes at me. "It's the only Christian thing to do." She looked forward at the altar and then leaned into me again. "I wonder if Sam and Orene had a place to go today."

I listened for something to be said that day in the Eden Rise Methodist

Church about the disaster that had happened to our fellow Christians at Zion Baptist. Not one word. The ruling ethic of white Christians was to ignore such injustice against blacks, or to blame the blacks themselves for the bad that came their way. If the lie was told in church, especially if it was a silent lie, it was sanctified.

The liturgy of the Methodist Church was so familiar that I followed it thoughtlessly, speaking and singing at the appropriate time. It turned out that God didn't descend from the stained glass that morning and explain to me His system of justice. So I began glancing around the sanctuary, counting people I knew. I saw Shoe and his parents and noted that he hadn't stopped to shoot basketball since the previous Sunday morning. There was Sheriff McCallister, his fifty-two-inch torso oozing out of his cheap forty-four-regular suit, his clip-on tie a luminescent red. Harry Dean's bald head shined almost as bright a few pews in front of us.

Finally I spotted Diane Maxwell, my high school girlfriend. Diane was pretty—long blond hair turned up at the ends, light blue eyes, fuller-figured than most of the girls her age. I let myself drift back to the night just before I left for Duke, when we had gone to our favorite parking place. We kissed wetly for several minutes, and then I began to massage her soft breasts. When I fumbled behind for the hook of her bra, she sat up and quickly removed it. When she lay back down on the seat, she pulled up her skirt and spread her legs, and I wriggled on top of her. She started to moan as I rocked against her pelvis and sucked her nipples. When I slipped my hand between her legs, I found that her cotton panties were wet.

"Tom, wait." We had been practicing this kind of heavy petting for the past six months, and this was where she always had stopped me. "What are your plans?"

My plan is to fuck you, I thought, but I said, "What do you mean?"

"I mean what are your plans about college? Tommy, you could still come to Tuscaloosa. Think of all we could do together."

Now, sitting in the church, I wilted again at her words. I thought how much better my life would be if I had said the magic word. *Tuscaloosa—*

that melodic name derived from the Mississippian Indian chieftain and which now represented the excitement of our coolest college town, where Alabama kids learned to be stylish, sexual, and decadent.

Would she have reached down and pulled my hard dick out of my pants and jerked those wet panties to the side and guided me into her? Diane just might have done that.

Now, of course, it was obvious I should have said the word. And there I would have been, in Tuscaloosa, safely ignorant of the existence of Beth Kaplan and the Sigma Nus, who somehow begat Alma Jones, which led to the death of Jackie Herndon, and then to the godawfulness I was going through now. Instead of uttering that one powerful word, *Tuscaloosa*, and having Diane open herself to me, I completely fucked up my life by saying something else.

Sure, I wanted to think that at some point I would have dealt with the racism that seemed to foul everything in my home place, but I could have faced that as an adult, on my own time, in some safer, happier future and not in the torturous present.

"I'm flying to North Carolina on Monday," I had said with my pelvis as hard against hers as I could make it. Instantly she began to squirm away from me in that steamy car and rearrange her clothes. She sat up, put on her shoes, and turned the rearview mirror to examine her makeup. "You're making a mistake," she said to her reflection, too angry to look my way.

I looked across the sanctuary at Diane. What if I went up to her after church and told her now that I was ready to go to Tuscaloosa and could we make up for lost time?

THIS WAS THE ONE Sunday of the month that the Methodist church offered communion, and the congregation was slowly, pew by pew, moving to the altar at the front of the church. I knelt by Cathy and the minister passed our way the plate of crackers and the tray holding little glasses of grape juice.

"This is the body and the blood of Jesus," he said in a whisper.

Diane had been served at the other end of the altar, and we passed right by each other on the way back to our respective pews. She never looked my way.

I began to notice the furtive looks my family was getting. Maybe it's my imagination, I thought at first. But standing for the doxology, I knew it was real. I leaned toward Cathy. "They're eyeballing the hell out of us."

"I thought maybe I forgot to put on my blouse," she whispered back. "But they won't look us in the eyes."

The usher who passed the collection plate was my high-school vocational agriculture teacher, Mr. Dooley. I had been a mainstay in the Future Farmers of America throughout high school, one of Mr. Dooley's star students. But when Mr. Dooley handed me the plate, he looked over my head.

The closing hymn was "A Mighty Fortress Is Our God":

And though this world, with devils filled, should threaten to undo us,
We will not fear, for God hath willed his truth to triumph through us:
The Prince of Darkness grim, we tremble not for him;
His rage we can endure, for lo, his doom is sure,
One little word shall fell him.

But Lord God above, what was the word? What was the word if you had lost Faith? If you had no hope of Peace? If you were too angry to believe in Justice? The one word that might have saved me was *Tuscaloosa*, and now it was too late for it.

As we edged toward the church door, no one came over to greet my family. Only two or three people were willing to nod my way. I felt a rush of heat inside my shirt as my fury rose at the collective ostracism of all my good friends in the Methodist fellowship. Had it been pure horseshit all along, this idea of a communal worship among Christians, or had it just suddenly turned to that? How could at least some of the people of my church not be sympathetic to me for what had happened?

At the door the minister shook our hands and leaned toward to me. "I'm praying for you, son," he whispered. Maybe he didn't want anyone to know that he deemed me worthy of prayer.

And what did his words mean? Was he praying that I find comfort and acceptance of the murder of my friend, or was he praying that I mend my evil, nigger-loving ways?

On the way to the car, Cathy gave me a look that meant, "Uh-oh, look out for an explosion." She nodded toward Mama, whose face was like stone. I wasn't the only one who was mad.

Marvin was standing outside the car watching us move his way, one hand tucked behind him, the other in his left pants pocket.

Just before we got to the car, Virginia McKee intercepted us, with Daddy's younger brother Bill, trailing behind her. A short woman, Virginia tried to hide her potbelly with loose dresses. On most days, her blue straw hat with feathers would have drawn attention away from her overly rouged cheeks except today that face was bursting with such distress that diversion from it was not possible. She was crying and talking in a loud voice. "Buddy, you have got to do something!"

Daddy stopped as she got very close to him. "What do you mean, Virginia?"

"I mean this trouble with Tommy is ruining us, Buddy. Nobody in there"—she angled her hat toward the church—"would talk to me. The whole town thinks we're a bunch of nigger lovers." She gave a quick glance at Marvin. "You even bring this nigger bodyguard to church."

Mama stepped in and grabbed Virginia's hand. "You calm down. That's not Tommy's fault. You watch your mouth around my family." Uncle Bill, his jowls covered with sweat, was shaking his head at his wife. "Come on, Virginia," he said. "This is making a scene. We can't do anything about it here." Aunt Virginia allowed herself to be pulled away but she turned and glared at me. "You should think about other people before you do something that stupid."

Mama was almost hyperventilating, but she remained silent on the short drive home. When Daddy put the car into park in the driveway, she glared at him and spoke through clenched teeth. "I expect you to do a better job than that of defending your son."

He looked straight ahead. "There was a lot of truth in what Virginia said."

Mama's mouth had dropped partly open. "What is wrong with you?"

I had a hard time believing what happened next, because nothing remotely like it had ever happened before. Mama raised her arm in front of her, swung her purse at Daddy, and hit the side of his face. The purse snapped open and flung its contents all around the car. Cathy, who was sitting between Marvin and me in the backseat, lunged forward and grabbed Mama's wrists, and held them.

"Mama. *Mama, stop.*"

Mama slumped down in the seat and began to sob. Daddy got out, slammed the door, and headed toward his truck.

Would a loving God allow us all to live like this, in such turmoil? At that moment, I surely did not think so.

13

GAINESWOOD

"I'm sorry about what my aunt said." I still sat in the car, paralyzed by what had happened over the last hour. Marvin stood nearby lighting a cigarette. "Fuck I care she calls me a nigger bodyguard? What I am." His face was completely blank, his eyelids only half-drawn. A picture of relaxation.

"She's just real society conscious, mostly concerned with what her friends think." Then I told Marvin what happened in church.

He shook his head. "You mean the white people wouldn't talk to your mama and daddy, and they the richest folk in town, just 'cause some cracker tried to kill you?"

I looked out into the mid-day glare. "Lotta pressure among whites to support segregation, keep things the way they are. I guess people have just decided we're nigger lovers, and they don't want anything to do with us."

Marvin nodded, took a long drag on his Kool, and looked away for a moment. "Very, very interesting. Niggers care 'bout what other niggers think too, you know? We always tryin' to find out what the other one saying 'bout us. But we also gotta care 'bout what the whites think." He frowned. "But whites don't have to give a shit what niggers think."

"I guess that's right, but it's changing. Whites are fixing to have to care a whole lot about what the colored think."

Marvin nodded solemnly. "Hey, man, you religious?"

I shrugged. "You?"

"Shit. Church would fall down if I walked in."

Cathy came out of the house and reported that Mama wanted to be alone and that the three of us should go to Demopolis and get something for lunch. "I'm driving," Cathy announced. "There's something I want to go look at." She knew something, probably from Bebe, that I didn't.

She drove down the bumpy street to the site of Zion Church. Beside the charred rubble a large green tent had been put up, and inside it were rows of wooden folding chairs filled with people in the midst of worship. She eased the car to a stop and we rolled down the windows. A choir was humming, a piano was yielding tinny notes, and an alto soloist was issuing a slow, irregular melody.

> *Sometimes I feel like a motherless child*
> *Sometimes I feel like a motherless child*
> *Sometimes I feel like freedom is near*
> *Sometimes I feel like freedom is near*
> *But we're so far away sometimes, sometimes, sometimes*
> *So far, so far, so far, so far, Mama, from you, so far*

If the emotion of the spiritual had not been enough to torture me, if the stark contrast between the poor burned-out black Christians under the army-surplus canvas and the rich, hateful white ones we had just left in their fireproof cathedral—if all that had been insufficient to blacken my already dark mood and convince me of the diabolical cruelty of my universe, then what we saw next grabbed my throat and strangled me until I could not speak or swallow.

William and Orene were each gripping one of Bebe's elbows, partly holding her up and partly guiding her to their car, Sam creeping behind to position an umbrella over her and save her from the blistering sun. She must have been leaving early, taking in all she could before she needed to go. Her light gray linen suit swallowed her wasted frame. Beneath her maroon straw hat, Bebe's emaciated face, its skin like cracked porcelain on the verge of falling onto the sawdust at her feet, showed how excruciating the few steps were.

I shuddered. "Oh, God."

Cathy took my hand and grimly drove us away.

WE WERE EATING FOOT-LONG hotdogs and drinking milkshakes at the Dairy Queen drive-in at Demopolis when the Toys' "Lover's Concerto" came on WBAM. Cathy began to sing it, complete with hand motions and moony eyes made at Marvin. She seemed determined to arouse Marvin.

But Marvin ignored her. His mind was elsewhere. "Why didn't he hit her back? If a nigger woman hit her man, he's going to knock the shit outa *her*."

Cathy and I glanced at each other. "He's not mad at *her*," I said. "He's mad at me. I'm the one he wants to hit for causing all this trouble."

Cathy shook her head. "I don't know. I think maybe he didn't do anything back because he knows, deep down, she's right about him and he's ashamed."

"That's bullshit," I said. "He thinks he's right to be a racist and I'm a traitor."

"I don't think that's it."

"Y'all want to hear my theory?" Marvin asked.

"Sure. We need all viewpoints on this shitty subject."

"I bet he knew if he did anything back he'd have a fight on his hands from the backseat."

Cathy looked at me and nodded.

We sat silently as long as Cathy could stand it. "Did y'all hear about the two Yankees who were passing through Demopolis and got curious about how you pronounce the name of this town?" Marvin obliged her by saying we hadn't heard. "Well, they stopped at this very drive-in and went up to that window over there and said in their very Yankee accent, 'Miss, please pronounce the name of this place and say it very slowly so we can understand you.'" Cathy had picked up the Brooklyn accent she mimicked from watching interviews on the teen dance shows.

"Well," Cathy said, back in her narrator's voice, "that little girl over there—you know they got some rednecks over here in Demopolis—she says"—now in a third accent—"'Yes, sir, I be real proud to do that.'" Cathy took a deep breath and gave Marvin her most innocent little-girl look.

"'DAY-REEE QUEEEN!'"

Pleased at our laughter, she turned to face the steering wheel. "Mama said don't hang around any place too long."

She drove us to Gaineswood, the white Whitfields' ancestral home in

Demopolis. It bore little resemblance to the conventional Greek revival houses like Bebe's scattered across that part of Alabama. Gaineswood looked like an Italian villa—a low, sprawling house finished in yellow stucco. It was designed to look small rather than to impose the idea of wealth and power through sheer size in the way that the typical columned mansion did.

Cathy asked if we wanted to take the tour. I didn't. "Somebody might recognize us and ask a lot of questions."

Marvin nodded. "And then I'd have to kill 'em."

"Oh, Lawdy Mercy." Cathy mimicked Aunt Virginia after her second gin-and-tonic. "That might leave a stain on the Puh-shun rug that Gret-Granddaddy Whitfield brought back from Noo Wawlins the yee-uh befo' the Waw started."

So we sat in the car and viewed Gaineswood. Cathy got excited when a new song from a new English group came on the radio. She already knew the words to "Satisfaction."

It was, Marvin remarked, "better'n most white music. Them boys been listenin' to niggers."

Cathy nodded. "Elvis told 'em to do that."

Marvin was contemplating Gaineswood. "When niggers take over Alabama, I 'speck I be living there. Either that, or I'm going to tear it down, move it to Chicago."

Cathy looked shocked and reverted to Aunt Virginia-speak. "Oh, don't do that. It's our heh-itage. Just live there with yo' wife."

"Okay, her and both my girlfriends."

"And all three sets of pickaninnies?" she said with her eyebrow arched.

"What pickaninnies? They all be pretty little High Yellows. My women all be white."

"You *kinda* yellow yourself, Marvin."

"That's why I'm so pretty."

She grimaced and turned the drawl up two notches. "Unh-unh. Not *fo' me*. I like my men *dawrk*-uh."

Marvin's head fell back on the seat as he cackled. "*Damn*, Baby Sister. You *somethin'*."

Three earlier generations of Thomas McKees would have shuddered in unison if they'd heard Cathy's words. At some level I knew it was *only* a performance, a teenaged girl flouting convention in a safe place for the innocent (mostly) entertainment of two older guys. She was trying to distract me, and I appreciated that. But she was also shocking me. Obviously I would have to give her a talking-to.

14

REVELATION

The next morning I helped Sam service the herbicide sprayer. Marvin kept wandering to the side and sitting down. This annoyed Sam. "Boy, it won't strain yo' back to get up here and help us get this done."

"Fuck that. I didn't come down here to be no goddamn farm worker."

Sorry piece of shit. I thought it but didn't say it. Then Sam answered for himself. "Well, that's what we do is farm work, and while you here you can get *off* yo' triflin' ghetto ass and lend us a hand." Sam was somewhat less intimidated by Marvin than I was. There was a work ethic among farm people: If somebody was working nearby, you were obligated to pitch in or you looked unneighborly and lazy. People would talk in most unflattering terms if you showed any hesitance to get your hands dirty. Daddy was always quick to take the least pleasant task when several of us were working together. Whites labeled a black a "no 'count nigger" if he showed any reluctance to work, and Sam was the older, conservative type who had no tolerance for idleness among his race because it made all blacks look bad.

We had worked silently for a while when Sam paused and looked at me. "Son, I hope this trouble ain't going to scare you off from coming back here and farmin' with us."

"Well, I don't know, but it sure is making things hard right now."

"This going to pass. You too good a farmer to let somebody scare you off from here."

I remembered the times Daddy had yelled at me for screwing up. "Well," I said to Sam, "I never thought I was any good at it."

"Sho' you is. Since you a little bitty boy, you pitch in there and try to work like you a man. Didn't never have to tell you but once when you got something wrong. Never did complain 'bout gettin' hot and dirty. Seemed just happy as any of us to eat Vi-eena sausages and sardines for lunch out in the field. Shame you don't come on back here and use that talent."

It felt good that somebody thought I had the ability to do something right with my life, but I had no intention of ever again living in Eden Rise—and I couldn't quite imagine why anyone would want to be there now.

"Sam, if I was colored, I know I wouldn't stay around here. I'd go some place where they wouldn't burn down my church."

He nodded. "Uh-huh. I thought 'bout leavin'. But I never wanted to go too bad. I went up to Chicago once, Detroit another time. I didn't like them big crowds. Plus it be so *cold* up there in the winter." I put a wrench on a pipe so he could unscrew a nozzle. "Farming's 'bout all I know," he said. "Orene always been happy working for Miss Brigid. I'd think about it more when the whites would kill some colored fella. But that hadn't happened too much 'round here."

"But, really, you must have gotten tired of the way whites have mistreated the colored."

Sam shrugged. "Well, Tommy, we didn't really know nothin' else. It was just how things was. I never thought about going into some white restaurant. I was a little curious 'bout politics, but we just knew that white folks was going to keep that they business."

"I mean, do you care about the whole civil rights thing now?"

"Oh, I'm for it all. It'll be better for us. It's mo' fairer." He looked up and across the warehouse then back down at the nozzle he was about to mount. "But it ain't going to be easy, son. White folk ain't going to just turn over the keys to everythin' real polite-like."

DADDY HAD SUDDENLY APPEARED in the shop. "Let me show you what I got in the mail today," he said, striding toward me. His voice was cold as he pointed toward the warehouse office. When Marvin followed, Daddy turned to him. "You stay out here."

He pitched an envelope toward me, and I grabbed it and pulled out a photostatic copy of a newspaper article that had a picture of Jackie and me standing behind some other people holding signs. It was a story about the Selma sympathy march in Durham.

"Where did it come from?" I asked.

"Just came in the mail, anonymous. Had a note. Said, 'He better not testify.'"

I kept silent.

"Well, what do you say about it?"

"Not much *to* say. I marched. For less than an hour. Nothing happened, no trouble." I kept my voice flat, even. He wasn't going to get me on this one.

"Why'd you do it?"

"I was pissed off about how they beat up those people on the bridge."

"Shit, you were six hundred miles away. You didn't know what happened."

"I think I did."

"That may be the single stupidest thing you ever did." His scowl got worse. "I still can't understand what makes a white boy from Alabama drive two agitators down here. No, I guess *that's* the stupidest thing."

I felt like I had been stabbed. His face reddened as he moved in closer.

"Goddamnit, you gotta forget about testifyin'."

I thought he was going to hit me. But he took a deep breath, turned, and took the time to light a Pall Mall. He started massaging his right wrist. "Look, this whole thing has gotten way out of hand. We gotta put a stop to it."

"How we going to do that?"

"We just tell the circuit solicitor you don't want to participate in the trial."

"He can make me—subpoena me."

"If his main witness—hell, his only witness—is not cooperative, he may give up. If he doesn't have to try Kyle, then he won't try you, and all this shit is over."

"Kyle oughta to be tried for killing Jackie."

"Well, son, 'ought to' is easy to say, but the fact is he ain't going to be convicted."

"If the jury doesn't convict the man, that's their decision, but it's my obligation to Jackie to testify."

He shook his head. "Well, that's a mistake. It's just going to keep everything stirred up." I just looked at him. "Come on. We gotta go up to Mama's. I'm going to put a stop to this." He told Marvin to stay at the shop.

We found Joe Black Pell seated in Bebe's den with her and William. The lawyer's presence clearly angered Daddy even more than he already was. Bebe announced that Joe Black had been helping her with estate matters, and since we happened to drop in, it was a good time for him to explain them to Daddy. Very carefully the lawyer began to report that he was working on the sale of Farmers and Merchants Bank. A business broker thought the bank was worth two and a half million dollars, and he had a couple of prospective buyers.

"Tell him to get busy, Joe," Bebe said. "I know I don't have time to fool around."

Daddy looked incredulous. "You mean, you did all this and never asked me or Bill about any of it? Daddy wouldn't have wanted this."

Bebe's mouth formed a determined line. "Buddy, it was my decision to make, and I've made it." She looked over at William, who solemnly returned her gaze. "You will recall, please, that your father never consulted you about any business except farming. If he wanted it different, he shoulda put it in his will. It apparently never occurred to him that he would die."

The coldness in her voice worried me, but it was somehow consistent with the awful changes in her appearance wrought by cancer. If you didn't know how sick she was, you might have guessed that it was the face of a bitter woman or maybe a drinker. Why hadn't she talked it over with Daddy and Uncle Bill? In their place, I would have wanted to know.

Joe Black broke in. "Buddy, we going to get top dollar."

"Honey," Bebe said softly, "you get all the farmland. Nothing will change for you."

Daddy was shaking his head back and forth. "I can't believe you're just selling the bank out from under Bill. That is so thoughtless."

"Buddy, Bill will get the proceeds of the bank sale. It's a good time to get out. The economy is booming right now."

"According to you," Daddy said bitterly, "and to hell with what Bill thinks."

"It will be best for Bill, I believe. He hasn't done much with the bank the last ten years."

Daddy's hand shook as he lit a cigarette. "Why've you done this?"

She arched an eyebrow. "It should be obvious. I'm dying and want it settled before I go."

He shook his head again. "Mama, Daddy would *not* have wanted this."

"Buddy, your daddy is dead and you don't *know* what he would have wanted. But it doesn't change the fact that I have little time left, and I'm going to use what I have to bring about a peaceful end to the McKee empire."

"I'm goddamned if I can understand you."

Daddy's anger at Bebe troubled me, but I understood his resentment at having his position undermined. I had assumed that one day it would be my choice to take over that empire, to be the richest and most powerful man in the county. I knew now I didn't want to spend my life in Eden Rise, but deep down was the old expectation that I could choose to be lord of it all.

Bebe stared out the window. "We've got to let go." She turned and looked at Joe Black and then at William and finally at her son. "That's what I'm trying to do—let go. Buddy, you must also, for your own good."

She cocked her head at me. "Where's Marvin? You didn't leave him outside to perspire in the car, did you?"

Daddy gave her an angry frown. "That's another thing. Mama, I need to tell you—this thing with the bodyguard is not working out. We need to get rid of him."

She frowned. "Why do you say that?"

"Having a colored bodyguard just antagonizes people in town. You should have seen how they looked at us at church." He didn't tell her about seeing Marvin and Cathy dancing.

Bebe looked at me. "So, what do you say?"

I really didn't want Marvin around, but I went ahead and told them the story of the visitors from Gooch and how Marvin had dispatched them. That whole episode had scared me. "Well, unless y'all just let me leave here—"

Joe Black interrupted. "Can't leave. Your bond says you gotta stay in Ruffin County."

"Then I guess Marvin should stay," I said. "He's strange, but he does look after me."

Daddy glared at me and then turned to Bebe. "Mama, he needs to go. I don't trust him around Cathy." Bebe turned toward William, and I followed her. We both saw anger flare in his eyes. He cast a hard look at Daddy. "Cathy has nothing to fear from Marvin," William said.

Daddy and I shared a deep prejudice about black men consorting with white women. But I knew two things: Marvin did lust after Cathy, which made it more than a racist myth, and she had provoked a lot of Marvin's interest, even if she did it for fun.

Daddy glowered at William. "How do you enter into this? "

At Daddy's words a light went on in my head. William was a chauffeur and now mostly a nurse, but he and Bebe were also *very* close friends. Suddenly exposed was Daddy's umbrage at Bebe's relationship with William. It turned out, however, to be one of those moments in life when an important exposure is made virtually irrelevant because another, more startling disclosure suddenly overruns it.

Bebe settled an intense gaze on Daddy. "Do you know who he is, Buddy? Don't you know who Marvin Whitfield is?"

"Some criminal from Chicago."

Bebe's voice fell very soft. "Buddy, his mother was Big Tom's child by his colored girlfriend, Callie Whitfield. Marvin is Big Tom's grandson . . . your daddy's nephew . . . your first cousin." She almost smiled. "Far as I know, the only first cousin you have."

I flashed back to the cryptic conversation between Junior and Marvin on the way back from Mobile, the only somebody who wasn't afraid of Big Tom McKee. *Holy shit.*

"What did you say?" I had never seen the look on Daddy's face.

Bebe nodded once. "That's right. Your first cousin."

Amazement was turning to anger in Daddy. "Why am I just now hearing about this?"

"Well, your daddy just didn't want it talked about, thought it would have caused unnecessary anxiety and too many questions. I didn't really agree but of course when he was alive, I did mostly what he said."

His eyes were starting to catch fire. "For God's sake, why did you bring him back here now?"

"Well, all this trouble with Tommy came up, and I had heard from William over the years about what kind of person Marvin is, and I just thought it was something I ought to take care of. Let's get the family secrets out and maybe we can live better in the future." Daddy's mouth was still open but he said nothing else. "Marvin works for me, Buddy, and he's staying as long as I can keep him or as long as I'm alive. You understand?"

Daddy left Bebe's without another word. I followed, and while I wasn't angry like Daddy, I was equally astonished by what I had just heard.

15

BIG TOM

"All right, I just heard the story." I had found Marvin, Junior, and Sam eating tomato sandwiches in the warehouse office. "Well, did everybody know but Daddy and me?" I looked at Sam. Sam knew what I was talking about right away. After a moment he nodded. "All the colored do. Buddy didn't know?"

"No. He was more shocked than I am."

Junior nodded at Marvin. "I told you he didn't." He looked back at me. "What he say?"

"Nothing. Couldn't get any words out." I considered Sam and Junior good friends to Daddy and me, and yet neither had told us about Marvin, about his relation to us, about this fundamental truth about ourselves. My throat was constricting. It was getting to be too much.

"Y'all come on. I have a right to know."

Marvin went to the refrigerator, got out a Coke, and brought it to me. "Niggers just ain't supposed to give whites bad news," Marvin said. "You know that. Wadn't our place."

They looked back and forth at each other until Sam spoke. "Go on, Junior. Tell the boy the story." Junior shrugged his huge shoulders and took a long swig of his grape Ne-hi. "Well, your great-grandma was real religious and not much to look at, and here come this young girl, 'bout twenty years younger than Big Tom and they just got theyselves a hot thing. Man and a woman git goin' and they got to do it." He let out his big bass chuckle. "Don't matter too much what color they are onct they get that thang goin'. You know."

I guess I did know, didn't I? It was hard to imagine a man like Big Tom feeling what I had felt in that first flush of lust for Beth Kaplan, but he must have.

"Big Tom, he used to slip over to her house way back off the Selma road in the late afternoon. Daddy wouldn't let us talk about it, but my aunt said Callie took the same train when Big Tom went to Chicago on business. He get a Pullman berth, pay them colored porters to look out." Junior told the rest of the tale as he'd heard it—that when Callie got pregnant they figured it was too big a problem for her to be around Eden Rise with an almost-white baby that looked like Big Tom.

I nodded at Marvin to tell him it was his turn. His eyes grew a little wistful. "Mama was real pretty—straight hair, blue eyes, nice build—until she got strung out on dope. They somethin' 'bout Baby Sister that looks like her." He studied me intently. "But I ain't down here in Alabama just to tell you stuff. What I want to know about is Big Tom."

Marvin was right. He was owed some information, and so was I.

BEBE WAS DOZING IN the den when we got there, but she started awake when we spoke to William. She gazed over at William, and he nodded back to her. "Like I told you, you opened a can of worms," he said. She shrugged. I told her Marvin and I both deserved to know about Big Tom.

"Well, all right. Big Tom was about the most powerful man and big too, a lot like Buddy in stature though not as handsome in the face. But he was so dominating in his thinking and talking and how he looked at you that it made you think you just couldn't challenge Big Tom McKee." In painfully drawn-out breaths she sketched his history for us. Big Tom had been born poor but made money farming and with a mercantile store. He had taken over the bank just before World War One, and it gave him much personal influence because so many people were in his debt, plus it provided the chance to take over the property of people in financial trouble. That was how he got most of the McKee farmland. He stockpiled cotton heavily in 1915 and 1916 on the hunch that it would go up because of the war. In late 1918 the price went to forty-two cents a pound and he had two thousand bales to sell—worth about $400,000. Big Tom knew that it was a once in a lifetime situation, so instead of doing what most farmers would have done, buy more land and plant more cotton, he put that money into stock—General Electric, Montgomery

Ward, and RCA, new companies that went through the roof in the 1920s. But he was shrewd about that too. He got a bad feeling about the market in the summer of 1929 and sold everything."

"But Bebe, I can't tell whether you liked Big Tom."

"Liked him? Well, I can't say that. Certainly I respected his talents as a businessman."

"Well, what did you *not* like about him?"

"Oh, you don't want to know my bad opinions about a man who's been dead twenty years."

Marvin wasn't having that. "Sure we do. I need to know."

She smiled. "Of course you do, dear." She sighed deeply. "Okay. He was coarse. He was little interested in the things that I cared about—books, music. He had no curiosity about the world except as a place to build an empire. He wasn't respectful of women."

"But he was respectful to you." William said to her. Then, to me, "He adored Missy. Thought she was the perfect one."

Bebe smiled at William. "Well, he listened to me, especially after I told him his two grandsons weren't going to grow up in a lynching town."

She told us how she and a college friend were riding home to Montgomery from the university and came upon a great crowd at a rural crossroads. As they inched through the crowd, it pulled back for them to reveal a black boy hanging from a tree in the yard of an old country store, a fire blazing under him. The scene had sent her to bed for a week.

"Well, this was about ten years later. They said the sheriff had a colored man in the Eden Rise jail who had beaten up this man Watson, a loudmouthed farmer. The colored man was his tenant, and everybody knew Watson made a practice of cheating his tenants any way he could—as so many landlords did at that time. Well, this colored fellow just had enough one day and beat the living daylights out of Watson. Then the talk started that the local boys were going to get the colored man out of the jail and kill him. So I went to see Big Tom, with Bill on my hip and Buddy straggling along behind me, and that's when"—she shrugged—"I told him my boys weren't going to live in any lynching town."

Big Tom didn't challenge her. He knew a lynching would unsettle the local colored people and probably send a bunch of them to Chicago or Detroit. So he went to the jail and got up close to the sheriff. "Big Tom was a big, intimidating man, and he knew it," Bebe said, "and he told that sheriff something like, 'Ain't *no* nigger going to get lynched in Ruffin County anymore, you understand?' The sheriff said, 'Well, Mr. McKee, I ain't going to get killed protecting some nigger.' And Big Tom says, 'Well, it's like this: You turn that man over to me now, and you get to be sheriff as long as you want. You let him get killed, I'm going to run yo' ass outa Alabama. *Go git 'im.*' The sheriff did as instructed, and Big Tom took the man to Walter Jackson, Junior's father, who delivered the man and his family to the Birmingham train station and got them all to Detroit. And that was the end of it. Nobody ever challenged Big Tom, white or colored."

We stayed quiet for a while, absorbing all this.

"Granddaddy was not at all like you describe Big Tom," I said.

"No, honey, my Tom wanted to be smoother, more urbane than his daddy, and he was—he'd been to college and had the advantage of a little culture." She stared away from us for a moment and then fixed her gaze on William. "Of course, that didn't make my Tom any more open-minded, did it?" William smiled faintly and shook his head.

During the Depression, she said, she and William had distributed a lot of food. Then after World War II, they tried to help folks get healthcare and some of the smart black children a better education. "I felt obligated to use some of the McKee money to help those who needed it. Big Tom agreed to it, but my Tom sometimes got furious when I told him what I had done. Of course, everybody in town thought he was this great philanthropist."

"I never thought of Granddaddy as greedy."

"No, Tommy, but you never had any idea about how much he had, and I did. I believe God put me on earth to pay penance for the McKees' greed for money and power." I didn't like what I was hearing about Granddaddy.

He had always been a part of the Black Belt group that controlled the legislature and the Democratic Party. He didn't want anything to upset that, but Bebe did things he thought undermined his power. She joined a group of women who pressured sheriffs and judges to be fair to colored men charged with crimes. In 1952 she and three women from Montgomery sat through a big murder trial in Hayneville just so the judge and the prosecutor would know that a few whites were watching if they railroaded a retarded colored man to the electric chair. That had infuriated Granddaddy.

"Tommy, your grandfather was smart enough to see the stupidity that lay behind white prejudice, and he had plenty of money to have stood against it without suffering any. But he cared a lot less about doing right than getting patted on the back by his white friends. The poor whites counted on people like him to keep the system fixed so any low-down white man was better in society's eyes than the most honorable colored man." She closed her eyes beneath her knotted forehead. "I told him that a couple of times. He'd growl at me about it, but I saw in his eyes that he knew it was the truth. And it made him keep his distance."

She was tired but I needed to know more. "Maybe y'all should have gotten a divorce," I said.

"Tommy, people of our generation didn't get divorced unless there was some scandal. I hadn't run around with another man, so he couldn't get rid of me without looking bad himself."

"Miz McKee," Marvin said, "why you different from most whites—why do you like colored people?"

"Oh, dear, it's not that I *particularly* like colored people. It's just that all my life I've seen people just uphold the most racist viewpoint because that was what people expected. That's what the men enforced, and I hated that." She winced in pain and her head fell back. William was going to her when she raised up again. "It was easier for a woman to resist it in small ways, as I did, than it is for a man." Her voice was weak and quavering. "The men could just dismiss a woman like me as stupid and soft-hearted. But a man who did that, they'd run him out of town."

William was shaking his head. "Yes, Missy, but there aren't many women like you."

She shrugged. "Well, I was from Montgomery and didn't always fit in with the local women. I stayed a Catholic. That made me different. Nobody was trying to make me a good segregationist over morning coffee." She looked at William. "My best friend has always been Will, and he educated me to another point of view. The average white person didn't have that."

She gazed at me, though I didn't think she really saw me. Then her head jerked a bit and she looked at me more intently. "I'm sorry, Tommy, I shouldn't sully your memory of your grandfather. I wouldn't do it now if I weren't dying."

I shivered at her starkness, but I realized something. "All my trouble has brought this out. If Jackie hadn't been killed we'd still have secrets."

Bebe studied me a moment. "Well, precious, I'm too close to the end to prefer ignorance over truth." Her voice had found new strength. "I think we need to know it all, and I believe that these revelations are the hand of God."

The rest of us might be confused and off balance, but my grandmother had never been more sure of herself.

16

VIETNAM

I reported the day's revelations to Cathy. She listened with her dark eyes wide, her head shaking. "Oh, my God" she said time and again. She turned to Marvin and pulled him up, into a tight hug. Then she leaned back and studied his face a moment. He was smiling, tentatively, but she wasn't hesitant. She planted a kiss on his cheek. "Now I know why I loved you from the start."

She looked away for a moment. "Tommy, I'm worried about Mama and Daddy. They're not talking. He goes to bed after she does." We need to support Mama, she said. The county commission was giving her an award for her years of sponsorship of the Key Club at the high school at that night's meeting. Cathy commanded that we all go and lend her our moral support.

MARVIN AND I EASED unseen into the courtroom balcony after the meeting had started. I peered over the railing at Daddy, who as probate judge was also chairman of the commission. He was presiding, facing the audience behind a table with two commissioners on either side of him. The commission was hearing requests for funding, and Mac McCallister was asking for three additional deputies for the sheriff's department. Daddy asked the sheriff where he would get the money required, which would be at least $30,000. At that point Commissioner Clem Brown, a fiftyish man with silver strands of hair combed over his bald head, said the money would come from savings in the school appropriation. I had heard from Mama that Brown and another commissioner, Joe DeShields, were trying to hurt the schools.

Daddy watched Brown warily and then turned to McCallister. "Mac, do you really need any more deputies? Are we having a crime wave in the county?" Joe DeShields interrupted. "Mac, let me answer that. McKee, I don't know where your attention has been the last few months"—he looked out at the audience with a smirk—"but we're being overrun with outside agitators in the Black Belt, and it's only a matter of time before we have trouble in Ruffin County. We've got to get prepared better."

Daddy glared at DeShields before he responded. "I know exactly what is going on in this county, commissioner, and I believe the sheriff has adequate staff to protect the county. No trouble has come up so far." There were grumblings and even a catcall from across the room—"You don't know nothin', McKee."

Daddy was visibly angry when he turned back to Clem Brown and asked what he wanted to cut out of the school budget. Money for foreign-language and art instruction was the answer. The motion to hire three new deputies passed four-to-one. Mama later explained to me that in the past two commissioners supported Daddy, but now they were siding with Brown and DeShields because they believed it would help them get reelected.

Daddy then offered a motion for a small salary increase for his staff. He passed around a sheet showing that the additional money would come from an increase in probate fee collections.

Looking out at the audience, not at Daddy, Clem Brown said: "Well, why should your pet employees get a raise when nobody else in the courthouse is getting one?"

Daddy's face flushed. "You know good and well, commissioner, that individual offices in the courthouse give raises as they deem appropriate if they have the money. Tax assessor's office got one approved last meeting." Daddy's motion was defeated.

Clem Brown introduced the county's state representative, Lee Cantrell, who announced that he had gotten a bill passed in the legislature to change how the Ruffin County Commission was elected. Now, instead of each of the four commissioners running in a specific district, Cantrell explained, all four would run countywide.

The two districts that served the south half of the county were about 75 percent black. If the blacks were all registered to vote, they would easily be able to elect black commissioners. But with the change to at-large elections, the northern half of the county, which was mostly white, could help keep whites in control in the southern districts.

Daddy was stunned—Cantrell and the commissioners had ambushed him. He ignored the raised hands of Brown and DeShields. "Lee, let me understand this," he said. "With this change, the folks up in the far north end of the county get to choose the commissioner who tends the roads on the far south end of the county, forty miles away." Cantrell said that was right. "Well, why didn't you let those good people up in Birmingham vote on who runs Ruffin County? How 'bout the folks in Detroit? Don't they need a say in this?" Catcalls came at Daddy from around the room. Cantrell shrugged and sat down. He had been close to Granddaddy politically, but like everyone in the room that night, he knew that power had shifted in a new direction, away from the McKees.

After all that, Mama had to go up and get her award. She couldn't even make herself smile and look appreciative. The whole thing was ruined for her.

DADDY CAME IN THE house, got a beer, and lit a Pall Mall. He kept rubbing his right hand. "The arthritis acting up?" Mama asked. She brought him aspirin. "Honey, the way they acted toward you was awful."

"I hate how they go behind my back," he said.

"Well, I hate how they're robbing the public schools."

Daddy shrugged. "If they don't start a private school this fall, it'll be next year. I don't really care now that Cathy's almost out of it."

She cocked her head to the side. "I'm not out of it. I teach in the public school every day."

He held up a hand. "I know, I know, BJ. But, hell, I can't see the whites around here accepting an integrated school." He sighed deeply. "What we'll get is two poor school systems. They're going to make a new private school into a holy crusade."

He lit another cigarette. Exhaustion made his voice hollow. "My daddy made it all look so easy. He never had this kind of trouble."

He looked at me, his face slack, devoid of the anger I'd been seeing.

"You didn't mean for this to happen, I know, but all your trouble helped it turn out this way."

"Then let me leave here," I said.

"You aren't going anywhere," Mama shot back.

I took a stand. "It would be easier on everybody if I just slipped out of Eden Rise. I'll come back for the trials, and then I'll be gone again. If I get off."

Cathy asked where I would go, and I said maybe North Carolina. Daddy shook his head. "Not North Carolina. You're through with that place. No more Duke." He spat out the last word like rotten fruit.

Mama frowned. "Buddy, that's unreasonable. Duke is where he needs to be when this is over."

"Not going to happen. He can go to Tuscaloosa." His scowl was defiant. "Or Tommy can go in the army."

Mama's voice suddenly rose. "And go to Vietnam?" Lyndon Johnson had just called up three hundred thousand troops.

"Might be good for him, fightin' Communists and not the people he grew up with."

Mama gasped, and her eyes popped out. "What is wrong with you?" Her voice rose to almost a shriek. "Get the hell away from me!"

I shivered as Cathy said, "Mama!"

"Shit, this family is falling apart," Daddy said as he left.

Mama exploded into crying. She gasped at me. "You going to be in college. You hear me? You hear me?" Cathy had her arms around Mama and was steering her out of the kitchen.

"He didn't mean it, he didn't mean it," Cathy was saying. "Tommy's going to be in college."

Cathy was no longer Mama's little girl but her protector, because in our crisis Daddy was part of what she needed protecting from, and I was too busy getting protected myself.

Cathy frowned at me and nodded toward Mama.

"You're right, Mama. I'm going to be in college."

I said it to calm her but it wasn't the truth. But one thing was true: They'd have to catch me before I'd go to Vietnam.

17

HEAT AND COMBUSTION

By now it was mid-July. It felt like someone had turned the oven on five hundred degrees and left it there when they skedaddled to Canada. Since the middle of June, the relentless sun baked everything. The air smelled like dust and smoke. Giant tree roaches looking for moisture invaded our house at night.

The morning after civil war erupted in our house, I found Mama in the backyard, watering her garden. For most white women in Eden Rise, gardening meant tending to a few flower beds. Mama did that and also put in vegetables in the open space behind our clothesline. She planted corn, a half-dozen varieties of beans and peppers, a row each of tomatoes, cucumbers, squash, okra, and whatever else she could squeeze in. She bought one of the first rotary tillers in Eden Rise, and she had plowed the garden herself until I got big enough to do it for her. We picked the beans, snapped or shelled them, cut the okra, pulled the corn and shucked it, and then she would go into marathon bouts of freezing and canning vegetables. Mama was a workhorse if there ever was one, and she expected Cathy and me to be right beside her unless there was farm work that took precedence for me. One day when she was eight, Cathy had tearfully asked Mama why we had to work so hard during the summer. "I'm sorry, honey," Mama said. "We just have to. That's how I was raised—to make a garden."

Today she was fretting over her impatiens. They had not bloomed to her satisfaction. "I let 'em get dry. Stupid." She handed me the water hose as she knelt among the impatiens, pinching dead blossoms. "Water those petunias and begonias. At least I haven't killed them yet."

After a bit she stood by me. "Tommy, don't make too much out of last night. Buddy didn't mean it." Last night she wanted to shoot him, but today all was forgiven. Unbelievable.

"He sure showed how little he cares for what happens to me," I said.

"He loves you dearly. He's just in a very bad way right now."

"He's mean—to me, to you, to everybody."

She frowned. "The government is going to send in these voting registrars, and he's all bent out of shape." Lyndon Johnson was about to sign the Voting Rights Act, which would take away all the means whites used to deny blacks the vote. No more literacy tests. Federal registrars would go into southern counties with a history of denying blacks the vote. Daddy expected to hear any day that federal registrars would begin signing up blacks en masse in Ruffin County.

"Plus Buddy's real mad at Brigid over her will."

"I know—I saw that—but it's still not an excuse."

Before Mama could answer we heard a musical "yoo-hoo." It was Aunt Virginia, coming around the side of the house. Mama rolled her eyes but offered her sister-in-law a cup of coffee and led her into the kitchen. I took the *Montgomery Advertiser* into the den.

Virginia's voice was always loud—as if she had to turn up the volume so you were aware of her determination to elongate all the vowels and drop all the 'r's in what she thought was her "evuh so cultuhd Black Belt voy-iss." She got even louder when she got excited.

"B. J., I'm sorry about what happened at church. I shouldn't have said all that."

"It's done." Mama's tone could not have been more flat.

"This is just so upsetting and unfair for the family." She went on to list the various women who had snubbed her in the aftermath of "all Tommy's trouble." She had missed out on bridge parties and shopping trips to Birmingham on which she should have been included. Nobody told her about the change in the meeting place for the garden club. "Some of the girls have been so unfair" was her refrain. If Aunt Virginia was officially commiserating with Mama and me, what we heard mostly was her misery.

"B. J., what are y'all going to do about Tommy? I mean, have you punished him?"

"No, Virginia. He hasn't done anything wrong."

"Oh, well, if you say so." The tone of indignation was aimed at someone so blind that she wouldn't see. Mama didn't reply, and it kept coming.

"Well, all this nigger trouble has just about ruined the nicest place in the world to live. The girls say this trouble really isn't going to be over until we've just shut down the public schools." Mama had long ago pointed out that Virginia assigned responsibility to "the other girls" in Eden Rise when she didn't have the nerve to own up to the thoughts herself. "That's really why I came by, to say that it would save poor Tommy the grief and danger if he left town. The girls say it really would be better if he didn't stay, B. J. His presence just creates problems."

In the next room I heard Mama's deep intake of breath as she tried to control her anger. "Virginia, I don't care what they think. You can tell the girls that, you hear?" Virginia said nothing. "Now, I have a headache and there's a world of things I need to be doing."

You had to admire Mama. Virginia was a manipulative sneak and mostly got away with it. I came into the kitchen as the back door closed. Mama looked at me and shook her head. "You okay?" I said.

She nodded. "I need to get out of the house. I'm going to the grocery store."

Marvin and I went with her because he needed cigarettes. After shopping, she was pulling away from the curb when a sheriff's car sidled in behind her with its lights flashing. She stopped, and a deputy ambled up to her door and asked to see her driver's license.

"What's this about, Deputy"—she read his nametag—"Jones?"

"We're just keepin' an eye on y'all, that's all."

"You don't need to follow me, Mr. Jones. I'm all right. You need to be looking for the people who shot up my house."

"Woman, you got a smart mouth. Get outa the car." Jones opened the driver's door. Mama was shaking her head and muttering as she stepped out of the car. When she leaned back inside to get her wallet, the deputy took hold of her arm.

"Get your damn hands off me." She tried to push him away.

"Hey, I don't care who you are, you won't cuss me and get away with it."

I leaped out of the front passenger seat and started around the car. I was reaching for the deputy when Marvin grabbed me from behind.

"Don't." He gripped me hard.

By then, Jones had drawn his pistol and trained it on Marvin and me. "Move and I'll shoot, either one of you."

Mac McCallister drove up then. He told Jones to put up the gun. "She's resisting my order and cussing me," Jones said. McCallister nodded but repeated his order.

"Well, Betty June, what do you say?" Mama was too mad to talk at first but she finally got out a few words. "Y'all are trying to intimidate me and my family."

"Naw, y'all making y'own trouble. The sooner you see that, better off you going to be."

She gave him a hard look. "What do you recommend we do, Mac?"

He gave her a wide and menacing smile. "You a smart girl, Betty June, prob'ly a lot smarter than them high-falutin' in-laws you got. I bet you can figger out what'd be best." She glared at him, shaking her head.

McCallister looked at Marvin. "Who's that?" Mama's face went blank. "Mister Whitfield." The sheriff studied Marvin. "Well, you and *Mister* Whitfield, y'all git on now."

Mama looked at Mac and then at Jones. "Get in the car, Tom." Marvin led me back to the passenger door. Mama got in the back seat. "You drive, Marvin."

I couldn't stop trembling. I saw Buford Kyle all over again, and Jackie rushing to protect Alma. I still expected gunshots.

"Are you okay, Mama?" I made my voice as even as I could.

"I'm all right, just mad as hell." She shook her head. "And completely sick of this."

We were quiet for a moment and then Mama thanked Marvin for his restraint.

Not me. "I wish you had hurt that bastard," I said.

"I coulda shot him, but he woulda got at least one of us, probably you. Can't take no chance on that. Special rules with cops, Tom. Gangs, mafia—they very careful with cops. Hurt one and they come at you with more power than you can ever handle. Even with these little cracker sheriff deputies, we gotta be real careful."

MAMA WANTED TO GO to Bebe's house. I should have known, what with Mama willing to leave groceries in the car in the summer, that the shit was about to hit the fan. She charged into the den where Bebe and William sat reading. "I need to talk to you, Brigid."

"What about dear? You look upset."

"I just got threatened by one of McCallister's deputies at the grocery store." Mama took two deep breaths. "He's sending us a message, Brigid, and I think it's time we heeded it."

"What message?" Bebe looked over at me.

"That the McKees are finished here. That Tommy's troubles are the ammunition to ruin us politically and ruin our family. We already *are* ruined, really, and we just as well admit it."

"What does Buddy say about this trouble with the deputy?"

"I haven't told him. I may not. Anyway, Buddy's blaming Tommy for everything and I don't trust his reaction."

"Oh, for goodness sake, B. J. He'll be outraged at this."

"Maybe. But he's not outraged at what has happened to his son." She glared steadily at Bebe. "And you're to blame for a lot of this, Brigid." Bebe's eyes opened wider. I wondered if Mama had ever talked to her like this. "Buddy didn't want to be probate judge and you forced him into it, and now he's become just as hateful as the other men around here."

"Oh, dear, Buddy hasn't done that." Bebe started to cough.

"Oh, yes, he has," Mama said, tears rolling down her cheeks. "I'm sorry to have to talk to you this way in your condition, but it needs to be said. When the Judge died, you became just like him—so sure you knew best about everything. Only you didn't think enough about what was best for Buddy. You caught him when he was feeling lost about the Judge's death, and he felt obligated to do what you wanted. And now he's ugly and cowardly and afraid of the colored people, just like the rednecks around here."

Bebe's mouth had fallen open. She blinked her eyes rapidly and looked away. I strove to think of some way to defend her, to share the blame.

"Mama, Bebe is sick. She—"

"Shush, Tommy. Brigid, then you go and start selling everything without even telling Buddy and Bill. You could have at least told them first—listened to them. You wouldn't have had to give in to his objections, and he might not have cared a bit. They're men, Brigid, grown men, except you treated them like little boys who need their hands washed for dinner." Mama shook her head. "Buddy can't express his anger at you because you're his mama and you're dying. So he takes it out on Tommy and on me, and he starts hating the blacks in a way he never did before." She took a deep breath. "Now there's not much power left in this family, thank goodness, but what is left you have and I want you to use it to try to turn Buddy around before something even worse happens. Do you understand? He's gotta get out of the judge's office."

Bebe looked at Mama a long time and then finally nodded. Mama turned around and left. I stayed, figuring Bebe needed me more than Mama did. Bebe stared into space for a minute and then regarded me. Tears rolled over her translucent skin. I gave her a soft look, desperately wanting to make her feel better.

MAMA WAS RIGHT THAT Daddy never wanted to be probate judge. When Granddaddy died and the family was receiving sympathy calls in Bebe's parlor, a short, round-faced man had appeared, introduced himself as Walter Fagan from Governor Wallace's office. Bebe hated George Wallace and was never more animated or agitated than when she was talking about him, and yet she was extremely cordial to Fagan, who was instructed to find out what the McKees wanted the governor to do about filling the judgeship. "My hope is that he will appoint my son Buddy here," Bebe had told Fagan. I remember the surprise in my father's eyes. After Fagan was gone, Daddy protested that he didn't want the job, that he liked farming. "Dear, you're the logical one, the eldest. People respect you."

With Daddy still looking grim and resistant, she played her trump card. "You know as well as I do that your father wanted you to succeed him."

Daddy had frowned at her. "When did you get so concerned about local politics?"

"When you told me yesterday that your daddy had died. A lot is going to happen in the time ahead, and this town can't have weak men in the lead."

So Daddy was caught between Bebe and Mama, two women whom he loved but who wanted him to do diametrically different things—one wanted him to acquire power in order to impose justice on the community, the other demanded that he relinquish it to protect his family. Plus, of course, Daddy had a whole set of other influences—the overwhelming segregationist sentiment of the white community and the certain knowledge of what his father would have done in the situation. They pushed him in a third direction—to fight to preserve the status quo.

I didn't know what I would have done in his place. Not the third choice, I'm pretty sure. But between the competing desires of Bebe and Mama for what Daddy was to do, I didn't know. Both were legitimate. Bebe's old eyes saw to the horizon. Mama was the lioness, looking down at her brood. Daddy's was an awful dilemma.

When I told Cathy what happened that morning with Aunt Virginia, at the grocery store, and between Mama and Bebe, she shook her head. "The poor thing."

"Which poor thing? Mama? Bebe? Aunt Virginia?"

"Mama. You need to understand about her, Tommy. She never has felt real comfortable in Eden Rise, and your trouble has made it much worse." She had grown up in Guntersville, a town nestled among mountains alongside the Tennessee River in northern Alabama. I barely remembered my maternal grandparents, Albert and Florence Lawson. He was the county farm extension agent, she the home demonstration agent. Mama and Daddy met in college at Auburn. When Daddy brought Mama to Eden Rise, she was nervous about the McKees' wealth. She had never known anyone who had a full-time cook and chauffeur. Daddy said it wouldn't make any difference because they loved each other so much. But Mama told Cathy that had it not been for her children and her school teaching, she would have been very unhappy.

"Do you think they'll be enemies after today?" I asked Cathy.

"I don't think Bebe will be mad at Mama for pointing out the truth." She paused and looked away. "But Bebe's not going to stop running things till she dies. And maybe not even then."

18

NEGRO DETECTION

"I wish we knew exactly what McCallister is up to," I said. Marvin and I were sitting with Bebe and William in her den the next afternoon. I'd come over to to see how she felt about her quarrel with Mama. I felt like I had to do something.

"I'd like to know too, Tommy," Bebe said. "Will, don't you think this might be a matter for a little Negro detection?"

William smiled back. "Could be, Missy. Could be."

"What y'all talkin' about?" Marvin said.

She chuckled. "That's what Will and I always called it—Negro detection. What that means is colored people always know everything that whites are doing, but whites know very little about what the colored people are doing. Negro detection can find out lots of things for whites, about other whites, by going through the colored people." She winked at me. "It's an irony I find delightful—that the people who have all the power often have only a small portion of the information."

"That's why white people act so stupid so much of the time," William said, his face deadpan.

"I knew it must be some explanation," Marvin said.

"You know, Tommy," Bebe said, "who is the master of Negro detection, don't you?"

I nodded toward William.

"Oh, yes," she said. "A veritable Sherlock Holmes of all things dark and secret in Ruffin County."

"Okay then, William," I said. "Find out what McCallister is doing to hurt Daddy."

Two days later Bebe summoned me to hear William's report. "I feel like sitting out on the porch," she said. "It's not too hot this morning." She patted a place beside her on the glider, and I caught a whiff of her gardenia bathwater. She looked better—she wore rouge and lipstick. White light bathed a bed of daylilies flowering with persistence just in front of the porch. A tall Rose of Sharon with pink flowers stood near the porch, shading the garden furniture from the rising morning sun, which by now had silenced the larks and mourning doves but not a nest of sparrows in the hibiscus. Bebe pointed to the little gray bird with the red and brown head. It whistled a high note and then trilled three lower ones.

"Tommy, do you remember what we used to say the sparrow's song was?"

I tried to sing it. "Looove, Bebe, Bebe, Bebe."

I always associated the sweet, familiar tune of her laughter with the front porch on summer mornings, and it did me more good than it did her to hear it then. We sat considering the sparrow for a short while. Then she cocked her head at William. Eden Rise's Sherlock, she told me, had first chatted with Orene, and then he made a series of phone calls. For an hour after that he took calls. The next morning, he went out for several hours. Late that afternoon, an elderly black man in a blue service uniform knocked at the back door and talked with William under a hackberry tree.

William nodded at me. "McCallister wants to be probate judge. That means conspiring to hurt the McKees with his two main allies on the county commission, DeShields and Clem Brown. He's going to give them goodies when he's in charge."

"A genuine Machiavelli, sounds like," Bebe said. "Will, how reliable is this information?"

"Pretty good. That man who came by at supper last night, he's worked at the county equipment shop for years. Never opens his mouth and the crackers up there who drive the road graders and gravel trucks talk in front of him like he's Helen Keller. DeShields likes to brag to his men about what's going to happen—to show how tuned in he is—and he starts talking as soon as he gets his orders from Clem Brown. Then it just spreads through the shop, and Helen Keller gets it all sooner or later."

"So why did this man give all this information to you, William?" Bebe said.

"He owed us a favor. You remember way back, his wife was the one with infected gums—couldn't eat, sleep, or wear dentures. You got her to see a gum dentist up at at the university hospital in Birmingham. Remember we took her there?"

"Oh yes," Bebe said, a smile flickering as she remembered. "She got well, got her dentures, and now she's up to about two hundred and fifty pounds."

"He told me some other things too," William said. "About the church burning and the shots at Buddy's house."

The scuttlebutt was that the arson and the shots were done by a group of young men who hung around the poolroom that McCallister's father runs. I asked if he got names of these guys.

A woman named Charity Foscue was trying to find that out, William said. Three years ago, Charity got word that her only daughter had been shot by her husband in Chicago. Bebe and William rushed Charity to Birmingham and got her on a plane. Charity brought her daughter back to Eden Rise. "She thinks you saved her life," William said.

"Which is ridiculous," Bebe said.

William shrugged. "But that's how she sees it. McCallister's maid happens to be Charity's sister-in-law. Turns out this lady serves breakfast to the sheriff and Clem Brown in the sheriff's kitchen a couple of times a week, and that sure enough what they've been talking about over their eggs and grits has been how to destroy Buddy. The sister-in-law says they've been real excited since the shooting in Yancey County, 'cause they think that's going to turn all the white folk against Buddy."

"She say who doin' the shootin' in the house?" Marvin was less interested in the politics than in the gunfire.

"She said McCallister kept talking about how 'the boys' were putting the fear of God into the McKees," William said, "but she didn't get any clear idea of who these boys were. They talk about what to do about the schools. They're planning to get all the white kids out into a private one as soon as possible. They discuss how to get a school built fast, where to get the teachers, how to steal as much equipment out of the public schools as they can without getting caught."

"What low-down scoundrels!" Bebe said. "How can they do that?"

"Well, Missy, they've been talking about closing the public schools in Alabama since 1954. You know that. The Judge used to talk about it a lot."

William looked at Marvin. "Another thing: The sheriff and Clem Brown spent a while talking this morning about this boy here. They're trying to figure out exactly who you are. Charity's sister-in-law said McCallister even asked her if she knew anything about a colored Whitfield boy staying with the McKees." William chuckled. "She played the Sambo—you know, 'Nah-suh, Mr. Mac, I don't know nothin' 'bout nobody with that name.' Of course, few colored people above the age of thirty in this county don't know about Marvin."

Marvin smiled brightly. "For real? Is that true?"

"They know the story of your lineage, even if they couldn't recognize you on the street."

William grinned wickedly at Bebe. "I told Charity to tell her sister-in-law about Marvin's career in Chicago working for the Mafia and the Black Muslims. She'll be passing that on to the sheriff."

A smile spread over Bebe's thin face. "Tommy, I told you—this Negro detection is a wonderful thing."

I thought Daddy ought to know what William had found out, so Marvin and I went to his office. Daddy was meeting with someone, and so we waited until he was free. In a few minutes the door to his office opened, and a short, bespectacled man in a gray seersucker suit came out. The man headed my way and was holding out his hand to introduce himself to me when I heard Daddy call my name. When I looked over at him, he was vigorously shaking his head.

"Tom!" the man said. "I'm Al Payton from the *Washington Post*, and I'd like to ask you a few questions about this trial." Daddy descended on him. "Payton, I told you he wasn't available for an interview."

"Judge, Tom is the real hero in this story. People outside Alabama need to know about his courage and why he acted."

"That's bullshit."

"What do you want to know?" I said.

Daddy was glaring at me. "Be quiet, Tommy." He turned to Payton. "Leave him alone or I'll have you removed from this office."

Payton addressed me anyway. "I just want to know why you think the man killed Jackie Herndon, and did y'all give him any provocation to shoot y'all." Daddy turned to one of the clerks. "Get the sheriff's office on the phone and tell them to send three deputies over here."

I nodded to Payton. "We didn't do anything but ask to go to the bathroom, and Buford Kyle started calling us agitators and freedom riders. Then he started shooting."

"Shut up, Tommy."

"All right, Judge, all right. I'm leaving." Payton stepped out of the office.

Daddy watched him until he shut the door behind him. Then he turned to me. "Don't ever come to this office without calling first, you hear?" I nodded, abashed but a little pleased with myself. "Reporters call or come by every day. Aggravating as hell."

"He didn't seem like a bad guy. Reporters from where?"

"All over—Birmingham, Montgomery, New York, Washington. There's a guy from the *New York Times* who calls damn near every day. They just want to keep stirring the shit."

"What do you tell 'em?"

"Told 'em to leave you alone."

"And I don't have any say in it at all?"

"God gave you a mouth to eat with, not to talk to reporters." I glared at him but didn't respond. I wanted to tell my side of the story, and I resolved that I would if I got the chance. Finally he asked why we had come there. I was angry, about to leave, when Marvin nodded toward Daddy's office. "Go on. Tell him."

We followed him into his office, where I recounted what William had found out. "Daddy, what happened with Kyle and Jackie has made your job a lot harder, but I think you should fight these guys. They're terrible, and you try to do the right thing." I was trying to get him to be my partner in this. "Our family has been the leader here for a long time. These rednecks shouldn't just take over."

Daddy looked like he'd lost a bucket of blood over the last week. "I don't know," he said. "That shit the other night at the commission, that never would have happened to my daddy. Wouldna snuck around on him. That legislator never would have put a local bill in without my Daddy's approval. They just don't respect me."

I jumped when Marvin spoke. "'Course they don't respect you. But it ain't personal, really. They want your power. You gotta fight those motherfuckers to keep it."

I leaped in. "Daddy, how about all these colored people they say are going to get to vote soon? They would support you over McCallister or Clem Brown."

He grimaced. "Hell, I won't get their support and I don't want it. We're all about to get run over by these damn federal registrars, telling us who can and can't vote. There won't be any local government anymore. Lyndon Johnson will pick which nigger runs this county and every county in the Black Belt."

"Well, they should be able to vote," I said. "I'd rather some of them be votin' than these rednecks behind McCallister and Clem Brown. The bastards burning down churches."

"Well, boy, if you going to side with the federal government against us we ain't got much to talk about. You talk about how our family has been influential in local politics for a long time—we ain't going to have any say when federal bureaucrats are in charge."

"The niggers ain't going to be expectin' you to do everything they want," Marvin said. "They just be lookin' for somebody who'll listen."

Daddy gazed at Marvin and then at me with a smirk on his face. His hand shook as he lit a Pall Mall. "All I need—two more liberal experts to tell me what to do."

My adrenaline started to rise. I had to tell him what a stupid, bigoted man he was. I had cleared my throat to declare exactly that when Marvin suddenly stood up. "Time for us to go, Tom." He looked ready to yank me up by my hair. We'd made it almost to the door when my hot blood got the best of me. I turned back.

"You can dismiss what I said, and what Marvin said"—my voice started to break—"but you oughta listen to Mama or Bebe and do what one or the other wants. You do anything else, you're no better than McCallister or Clem Brown."

Marvin twisted my bicep in his fist, and by the time I spat out the names of the two nasty bastards after my daddy, he was dragging me out of the office. He didn't let go of my arm until we got on the sidewalk outside the courthouse, where he threw it away like a burnt match. "Y'all all determined to end up hatin' each other." He looked back at the corner of the courthouse where Daddy's office was. "Should be fuckin' thankful you got a father."

I felt stung and betrayed.

He shook his head. "Y'all bad as a buncha ghetto niggers."

19

Get Lost

A few days later Marvin and I lay sprawled under a big cedar tree that was throttled by Virginia creeper. The cedar's fresh scent hung leisurely in the heavy air that had been warmed almost to 100 degrees at noon. It was one of a column of cedars that walled the graveyard that surrounded the tiny, gothic Episcopal church in Gallion, a thinly populated village a few miles south of Eden Rise to which we had wandered out of the boredom that, along with the moments of confrontation and anger, infused that summer. My imagination bent toward death that summer, but the main graveyard in Eden Rise was too close for comfortable contemplation.

The cypress siding of the church was stained an improbable red, as if to brighten the day of the legion of Collinses buried there. To be sure, the Collins family had allowed in the odd Spencer and Steele and Avery, though I guessed they were cousins or in-laws to the ruling clan. I noted how few had been put to rest there in my lifetime. You could have gotten the idea from the Gallion cemetery that dying had been a nineteenth-century practice, mostly since abandoned. Of course, if one of the first Collinses had been resurrected that day and walked around his old neighborhood, he might have concluded that living was a nineteenth-century pursuit, so scarce have the twentieth-century inhabitants become.

Marvin and I weren't talking much. I didn't exactly feel kindly toward him since he'd ambushed me with his tirade about Daddy and me. But we were stuck with each other, and especially after the episode at the grocery store I wasn't about to go out on my own and risk getting myself shot in the back of the head. We had been sitting a while watching a mockingbird dive-bomb a squirrel playing around a headstone when Marvin looked up from a plate of Orene's turnip greens, pinto beans, ham hocks, and corn bread and said, "You worried about this trial?" It was the first thing he'd asked me in four days.

"Yeah, both of them. I'm scared shitless about the whole thing."

"What worries you about it?"

"Everything. Seeing Kyle. Having to answer a lot of questions without pissing in my pants. Somebody may kill me."

"That's where I come in. That part ain't going to happen."

"I have to testify and then stand trial myself." I swallowed some cornbread. "I'm most afraid about going to prison." I had been having nightmares about prison—about getting killed or beaten in a dark cell by a gang of muscular men. After this nightmare, I stayed awake.

"You think I could survive in prison?" I said.

"Yeah, man, you could survive. Keep to yourself, don't act scared but don't get in nobody's way. Figure out who is the meanest nigger in there and give him lotta cigarettes."

I laughed, but Marvin shook his head. "I'm not kidding, that's the trick."

The closer it came to my trial, the more certain I was that I just couldn't go to prison. I happened to read in *Time* magazine an article about American boys going to Canada. LBJ's massive troop call-ups for Vietnam had spurred a sudden movement of draft-age men northward across the border. The story said that guys just quietly slipped out of their hometowns, traveled to large Canadian cities, and tried to live anonymous lives. The Canadians didn't do much to stop them, and once the boys were there, the U.S. government couldn't do much to bring them back. As I read the story, I grew intensely interested in it, and at first I couldn't understand what so intrigued me but then it dawned on me. That could be me. I could go to Canada and escape the torture of prison.

"You were going to skip the country, where would you go?"

Marvin gave me a skeptical look. I told him about the magazine article.

"Canada cold. Been there. Snowy, flat."

"How about Mexico? It's warm."

"They don't speak English."

"You can learn a language. I heard it's real cheap to live there."

Marvin considered this. "Good many Mexicans in Chicago. I was in prison with some of 'em. They said that about Mexico—it was cheap."

"What did you think about them?"

"They wadn't bad unless you give 'em shit. Some of 'em real good with a knife. Main problem is they women ain't too good-looking."

"Bound to be some good-looking ones."

Marvin dipped his cornbread in the turnip greens' pot likker. "You not goin' nowhere before the trial, are you? No point goin' if you don't have to."

"I'm thinking about it afterward if I'm convicted."

Marvin nodded. "Be easier just to go to some big American city and change your name, what you look like. I know a guy who'd get you ID, social security, a driver's license."

"How would I change what I look like?"

"Easy for white folk. Dye your hair, grow a beard, get some fake glasses."

He looked off at the graves. "You know what you could do? Grow your hair real long and go out to California where all them freaky people live—San Francisco. Just blend in with them." He raised a finger toward me. "But gotta be careful, don't get arrested for nothin'."

"You go with me?"

He shrugged. "Kinda curious about California."

Suddenly I had a moment of hope, almost the first one since Jackie died. It would be okay living anonymously in a big city if I had someone to help out a little at first. Objectionable as he was as, Marvin could help get me settled. I could make myself into a whole new person. Maybe I'd find a California surfer girl, like the ones the Beach Boys always kept coming across. The more I thought about that, the more I liked the idea.

THAT AFTERNOON MARVIN, CATHY, and I went to Demopolis, my sister for the milkshake, and me, unbeknownst to her, to read up on life in California at the public library. I dug up old *Newsweek* articles about the student rebellion and the beat culture in California, and while a lot of it was full of adults tsk-tsking it all, there was a booming population of young people who were joining in. Perfect, I thought, for a guy who needed to get lost.

While I was contemplating life on the run, Cathy and Marvin were reading up on "Marvin's people"—the Whitfields. He was grinning widely when they rejoined me. "I found out Baby Sister going to be mine after all." Cathy gave me her most serious look. "Tommy, it turns out that back in the 1700s and 1800s the Whitfield men usually married their first cousins—not sometimes, most of the time. And not only that, they preferred their cousins from the paternal line—you know, other Whitfields." She bobbed her eyebrows. "They might as well have made the family motto"—she turned on her deep-voiced, exaggerated drawl—"'If she don't look like Daddy, leave her alone.'"

I blushed. Marvin reached over and put his arm around Cathy. "Baby Sister be my first cousin on the paternal side, you see." He looked at her and made a broad sweep of his lips with his tongue. "Meet the first Mrs. Marvin Whitfield."

When we laughed out loud, the old librarian rapped her desk with a ruler. She had frowned continuously at Marvin since we came in. There was no one else in the library; we weren't disturbing anybody. I looked at Marvin. "Won't it be nice to be away from all the race shit?"

Marvin shrugged. "Race shit everywhere, man. Be some of it wherever we go."

Cathy frowned. "What do you mean 'wherever we go'?"

I stiffened and gave Marvin a shut-up look.

"Tommy, tell me what is going on." She stared at me sternly. "Tommy."

"No."

"Yes."

"Cat, I can't go to prison. If I'm convicted, I'm going to just disappear. I'll get killed in prison. Or if I end up in the army, I'll get killed in Vietnam."

She spooked like a cat at what I said about prison. "You don't know either one of those things is going to happen. Either one is the worst case." She looked at Marvin. "What do you think?"

"I think he could make it through prison, but he's right to be afraid of it. Don't know enough about the army to say."

Cathy stared at me, perplexed. "Where would you go?"

"Probably California, sorta go underground. Or maybe Canada."

Marvin looked serious. "What we going to do to support ourselves out there?"

"Work construction, tend bar. We'll find something. I have some money to get us out there and keep us going a while."

For once I had shut Cathy up. She was silent as we drove back to Eden Rise, but when Marvin stopped the car in our driveway, she leaned forward from the backseat. "Tommy, this is a very bad idea you have. Will you promise me you won't leave?" She was really pleading.

"Look, Cat, it's not you facing prison. I don't know what I'm going to do if I'm convicted."

Her forehead was knotted. "Tommy, think of who it will hurt if you go into hiding somewhere. Bebe will die without you, probably won't even know where you are. It will kill Mama. You're her pride, and you'll be lost to her in the way that a mother wants her son. We'll all suffer." She was starting to cry, and her words punctured me. "It will cancel out all the courage you've shown. You can deal with what happens, and we're all going to stick with you." She was sobbing. "Please. *Please*."

I cringed. "Okay. Okay."

"Promise?"

"Yeah." But I knew I would still go. I just wouldn't leave while Bebe was alive and I wouldn't tell her I was going.

But she read my mind. "You better not be lyin' to me!"

She turned her glare on Marvin, who had stayed silent through her inquisition. "If you let him do something stupid, I will kick your black ass back to Chicago."

She got out of the car, grabbed the door with both hands, and slung it shut as hard as her 120 pounds could propel it. Who knew Ford made doors that didn't fall off under such abuse.

"Thanks for all the help," I said to Marvin.

"Fight for you but ain't going to lie for you. At least not to her."

THE NEXT DAY JOE Black summoned me to Montgomery for trial preparation. Kyle would be tried first, but Joe Black now assumed that I would be tried just afterward, and we had to get ready for that. "They going to put Buford Kyle on the stand first as the chief witness against you. So Taliaferro will just get him to tell his story. Then when he's through with Kyle, I'm going to be all over that SOB." A smile suddenly lit his creased old face. "My investigators rounded up a lotta shit on him."

Then the smile faded. "But now, Tommy, don't you do anything silly. If you skip the country, or anything like that, it'll ruin your life, son." Cathy must have gone straight to the phone and called Joe Black. That was the real reason he sent for me.

"Even if you get convicted, everybody's going to know it was an injustice and it won't be held against you in the long run. If you become a fugitive, everybody going to assume you're guilty and you'll never live it down." He looked stern. "Plus it'll cost your family a fortune if you forfeit bond." I hadn't thought about that.

"But listen here, son. Don't put on the stripes yet. You a fine boy, and that jury's going to believe you over Kyle. You trust me on that."

Joe Black leaned back in his big leather chair and pulled two big puffs on a cigar that looked half as a big as a baseball bat. Then amid a cloud of smoke he rubbed one hand across his bald head, spit in the nearby trash can, and turned the smile back on.

"Plus, you musta heard what a tricky little sonuvabitch I am."

20

FAMILY HONOR

Mama asked us to pick up Cathy at cheerleader camp in Demopolis. "It's usually fun," she said, "but it is so blessed hot today I know they are burning up over there." The end of July had brought eight straight days over 100 degrees. She told us to come afterward to Bebe's to celebrate my grandmother's seventieth birthday. I was relieved to hear that Mama's anger at Bebe wouldn't prevent her from directing the normal family rituals.

We stopped at the Dairy Queen and then took our milkshakes to the parking lot of the high school football field to wait for Cathy to finish. Various groups of girls in shorts and tee shirts were doing cheers. I spotted the Eden Rise cheerleaders and pointed them out to Marvin.

We tapped along to the Temptations' "Sugar Pie, Honey Bunch."

Marvin pointed. "See that tall girl in the green shorts? One with the big butt? She might be my honey bunch." I agreed that it was a good choice if you liked that body type.

"Y'all white folk all fucked up 'bout a lotta things, but y'all main problem—y'all ain't got no ass. Now Sugar Pie over there in the green shorts, she got some ass on her."

"Why do you say *y'all*?" I said. "You got almost as much white blood as black."

"Like they say, you can take the nigger out of the country, but you still got a nigger."

"You sound like the men at my old barbershop."

I was burning up in the car. "Man, it's way over a hundred degrees out there on that football field."

"Niggers got more sense than be practicing anything in this weather."

We had been there long enough to finish our shakes when Marvin pointed to one group of girls. "What's going on out there now?" I looked and saw a crowd form a kind of circle. I heard shrieks and then other groups started to run in that direction. I leaned my head out the window to get a better look and heard a girl shout "Fight! Fight!" We went to the fence around the football field and watched for a few seconds.

"That over where Baby Sister was a minute ago," Marvin said.

Panic sent me trotting down the fence line until I got to the gate and then I started running toward the crowd. When I got there, I couldn't see anything because of the crowd. I asked a sweaty cheerleader what was happening. "Two girls *fightin' like hell!*" I asked who it was. "Cindy Butler and that McKee girl from Eden Rise."

I started into the crowd when it suddenly parted because the fighters had lunged into the onlookers. I pushed forward in time to see my sister roll on top of a shorter, thicker girl, who had just been on top of her. I almost didn't recognize Cathy because her thick, mahogany-colored hair, which usually fell straight to her shoulders, was now sticking out wildly in all directions. Her face was the color of half-ripe strawberries.

"Cathy!" I yelled but she couldn't or wouldn't hear me. Her fists were flying so fast they were a blur. She was swinging hard with both arms as she sat astride the other girl, who was on her back kicking her legs. The girl was trying to buck Cathy off but couldn't.

I had never seen Cathy with her fists doubled, much less witnessed her punch in anger. I was totally mesmerized by her prowess in combat. She started slapping the girl back and forth. The girl had stopped resisting.

"You—take—it—back—*bitch!*" Cathy uttered her warning in a rhythm that punctuated the blows she was raining on the girl's head. I had never heard the loud, raspish tone my sister's voice carried at that moment. It was different from when she had yelled at me about running away, more urgent, more hysterical. Nor had I heard her use some of the words that were now coming out of her mouth.

The girl somehow pushed sideways, pitched Cathy off her, and started to get off the ground. Lying on her side, Cathy kicked the girl in the knee, which dropped her back to the ground. Cathy lunged on top of her again.

"*You goddamn bitch!* I'm telling you to *take it back.*"

I tried to rush in but the girls spun away from me. Cathy grabbed the other girl by the hair and started shaking her head back and forth. Then she slammed the girl's head against the hard ground. *"Take it back! Take it back!"*

Marvin pushed past my shoulder. "She 'bout to hurt her bad. We got to stop this."

When Cathy grabbed the girl's hair again and pulled her head up in preparation for slamming on the hard ground again, Marvin pushed me forward. I stepped to Cathy, wrapped my arm around her waist, and jerked her up and away from the girl. As I lifted her off the ground, her arms were flailing, her feet kicking, and her fists holding handfuls of the girl's blond hair. She didn't know who had her and tried to fight me off. She let out a guttural scream, another sound the likes of which I had never heard her emit.

"You whore, you take that back!"

I spoke quietly into her ear. "Cat, Cat, it's Tommy, it's me." Marvin moved in close. "Baby Sister, Baby Sister, it's us. Shush. It's okay."

Her eyes were bugged out, and she seemed unable to focus for a few seconds. Then she recognized me and threw her arms around my neck. She smelled of sweat and dust. Snot ran out of her nose and smeared across my shirt. She started to sob as feverishly as she thrown her fists. "Oh, *Tommy!*" I pushed her away just a little and examined her face. There were several places on her cheek where the girl had scratched off Cathy's skin. She had been hit hard at the corner of her right eye. It would be swollen soon and then black.

Marvin gave me his all-business look and jerked his head toward the car. "Let's go. *Now.*"

There were people on the ground ministering to the other girl. Two overweight men ran up, one of them the Demopolis basketball coach. "What in the world has happened here?" he said. "Is that Cindy Butler down there?"

I was hustling Cathy away when the coach spoke in a stern voice. "Where y'all think you're going? We're gittin' the sheriff. Y'all stop *right* where you at."

Marvin spoke under his breath. "Keep walkin.'"

"Hey, nigger, I'm talking to you. I said stay here."

Marvin turned and went back within two steps of the coach.

"Now, mister, *I'm* going to talk to *you*," Marvin hissed. "We goin.'" The coach looked down at Marvin's left hand hanging with the unopened knife in it. Marvin closed the gap between himself and the coach. "Another word to me, you going to end up worse off"—Marvin nodded toward the moaning girl—"than her."

They held each other's eyes for a long moment, and when the man didn't speak, Marvin turned and took Cathy's other arm.

When we were safely out of Demopolis and Cathy's sobbing had slowed to an occasional hiccup, I asked what had started it. "The girl said something real ugly to me, and then she said it again, and I just lost my temper." She started sobbing again.

I asked her what the girl said. She didn't answer. Then it hit me what had happened.

"The girl said something about me, didn't she?" Cathy looked at me and shook her head. She wasn't disagreeing but indicating she didn't want to tell me.

"Tell me what she said." She shook her head again. "Tell me, Cat."

She buried her head in my shoulder and talked into my shirt. "She asked me where was my nigger-loving brother these days. Then, in front of all the cheerleaders, she said was my nigger-loving brother still dating that nigger at college. That's when I went for her. When she starting scratching me, it just made me madder."

She let out a loud sob. "I'm sorry! I know it was embarrassing."

Marvin whistled from the front seat. "Hell, it wadn't embarrassing. We was proud of you. I ain't seen a beatin' that good since I got out of the Illinois State Penitentiary."

She cried louder. "Oh, Tommy, I'm so ashamed. I'm going to get in so much trouble. They expel people for stuff like this." She was right about that. They had expelled people regularly at Eden Rise for getting in fights at football and basketball games. I said she might have to stay home a couple of days but that would be okay.

"Tommy, I've never heard of a girl getting expelled for fighting." Nor had I.

"Daddy will be furious."

Bebe's birthday celebration was over as soon as we arrived and I explained what had happened. Mama took Cathy to the bathroom to inspect her face. When they came out, Marvin called Mama over. "Them folk in Demopolis was threatening the sheriff. They may have swore out a warrant against her." Mama looked at him, not comprehending immediately, but then she did. "If we stay here, they might arrest her."

"That's right, and you can't go home. They may be there waiting."

Marvin and I were each finishing a big piece of white birthday cake in silence and Bebe was dozing in her chair when Daddy suddenly appeared in the door. Two men in uniforms stood behind him. When he asked for Cathy, Bebe started awake.

"They've gone, Buddy. Have some birthday cake. Offer some to your friends."

He frowned at her. "They go home? They weren't there a minute ago."

"They didn't say where they were going."

Daddy looked at me. "You know where they went?" I shook my head. He turned to the men in uniform. "I don't know what to say. I don't know where they are." The one standing closest to Daddy spoke. "Well, Judge, I've got a warrant. Folks in Demopolis are pretty stirred up. Your daughter closed both of the Butler girl's eyes, broke her nose, knocked out three or four teeth, and pulled out 'bout half her hair. Gave her a concussion. The girl's a pitiful mess." Daddy just shook his head. "You gotta bring her in, all right?"

When the deputies were gone, Daddy turned to me. "What *in the hell* happened?" I repeated what Cathy told us. "You think she really hurt the girl that bad?"

"It was the finest ass-whippin' I ever saw without no weapons," Marvin said. "Did it all with her fists." He demonstrated Cathy's haymakers. Smiling widely, he held up both fists. "Made me proud."

Daddy stared down at the floor. "This family is fallin' apart."

Then he looked at me. He didn't say anything, but he didn't have to.

I knew he was blaming me for this catastrophe too. "*Where'd* they go?"

Bebe was the only one of us who looked at him. "We didn't ask."

The anger on his face collapsed.

I think he was at that moment feeling the helplessness I did when the deputy accosted Mama at the grocery store. We could not protect our women any longer from the great jeopardy that had arisen in our lives.

Connected to the feeling of impotence was guilt that somehow we men had caused this danger, or at least that in our neglect we had allowed it. I felt sorry for myself, and sorry for the old man.

21

Midnight Hour

After a glum supper of birthday leftovers at Bebe's, Marvin and I went to the porch. There was a full moon, which meant we could see trees and the flowerbeds that were sprinkled across her yard. A little breeze from the west brought the fruity scent of honeysuckle. The cicadas provided the soundtrack for what was mostly a silent wake for the family I was destroying, until Marvin fetched a radio out on the porch, and over the next three hours we heard, at least a half dozen times, Wilson Pickett's plans for his girl at midnight. We each drank a beer that with the heat and the awful events of the day led to another and then another. By the time that big moon was high above us, near the midnight hour, I had put down eight Budweisers. I didn't know then that alcohol would be a problem for me. That night it seemed a comfort—at least until Marvin asked me again about my college girlfriend. He was trying to get my mind off the catastrophe of my family, or he had sex on his mind and he wanted a good story.

"Why don't you call her? I can tell you still like her. Maybe she changed her mind."

"Fuck her. I hate her." I was a nineteen-year-old nasty drunk.

"Naw, man, you don't hate her. You sad you lost her. Call her up and tell her that. She prob'ly feelin' shitty how she treated you."

"Fuck you know."

"I don't, but she may be thinking she did. What you got to lose, man? You *drunk* anyway. Say what you think, and then call her back tomorrow tell her you was drunk, sorry you said whatever shitty thing you say. Easy as pie, man."

I sat there silently for a while, my ears buzzing from the beer and the crickets. Then an animal must have moved in the dark because the crickets suddenly paused. Just then a bird sang.

My grandmother's sparrow somehow turned my emotions and my memory toward a moment with Beth. I staggered to the phone.

When I told Beth's mother who I was, she asked why I was calling so late. I apologized and composed myself enough to say I'd call back another time. But then her dad came on.

"Tom, this is Arthur. We've been so worried. Are you okay?"

"Yes, sir."

Arthur and I had hit it off when I visited her house on Long Island the previous Thanksgiving. "I'll have to call you Mr. McKee if you keep calling me Mr. Kaplan." A thin, stooped man, he had taken me to Harlem, where his father had been a storeowner and where he had accounting clients, all Jewish merchants. He had given me a tutorial on race relations in the ghetto, including the terrible fallout from the Harlem riot the summer of 1964. And yet Arthur was deeply attached to the people of Harlem and strongly committed to civil rights. He gave money to the NAACP—a common practice, he said, among New York Jews who sympathized with other victims of injustice. On Amsterdam Avenue, we had walked past a young black man in a black suit and a black bowtie selling a newspaper. A few steps beyond, Arthur had leaned into me. "That right there is the cause of a lot of the anger up here." He explained that the bowtied man was a Black Muslim and a follower of Malcolm X. He asked if I had heard of Malcolm X. I hadn't at that point. "You will. Malcolm X and the Muslims preach hate for all whites, especially Jews."

Beth came on the phone. "Tom, I've been so worried about you. Are you okay?" The husky voice—Beth smoked—prompted memories of certain moments with her. "I'm all right. Little drunk tonight, but okay." If I was slurring words, or if she was surprised to hear from me, she ignored it. "I'm so sorry about Jackie. I can't believe that happened. It must have been awful."

I flashed to Jackie's funeral a moment. "How did you know about it?"

"Tom, it's been all over the papers. There was a story in the *Times* about the shooting, and then a couple of days later a longer story about the funeral. Had your picture in it."

"My picture in the *New York Times*?"

"Yeah. Jeffrey and I wanted to come to the funeral, but it was too complicated getting off work. It must have been sad." Jeffrey lived on my hall at Duke—he was Beth's high school friend. "Jackie was a sweet, good guy."

At first I couldn't get out a word. "It was real sad," I finally responded. My mind fragmented for a moment. "His mother was real upset."

"I can imagine." We hovered in a long few seconds of uncomfortable silence. "Well, how are you doing with it, Tommy? Are you real depressed?"

"I'm responsible for what happened." I stopped for a moment to swallow hard—I was about to cry. "It's torn my family up."

"Tom, I wrote you a letter but I didn't mail it yet." Another awkward pause. "So now I'm going to mail the letter, okay?" I said sure. "And I'll see you in Durham this fall, right?"

There wasn't much point in lying. I explained about the trials, but I stopped short of describing my likely autumn matriculation at an Alabama state prison. "Lots of sadness about Duke for me."

"Yeah, I guess so. Hey, if it's okay, I'll call you the next time, Dixie."

Dixie. Beth called me that at intimate moments.

I wandered back to Marvin, who asked how the call had gone. "She was concerned."

"*Good.* Concern, *tha's good.* You know how you spell *concern*, don't ya? P-U-S-S-Y."

"Marvin, shut up."

"I'm just sayin.'"

All that night I ached again from the end of the sensuality with Beth, from the lost thrill of romantic love. I had fallen hard for her on our first date. We had had dinner after a Duke football game and then ended up in my dorm room. I had delighted in the olive cast of her skin and her thick bush with the little trail of dark hair that ran up to her belly button. Her breasts poured out of her bra, which once removed revealed almost black, hard nipples. Padded hips, a rounded tummy that folded twice when she bent over the bed to kiss me, but she still had a well-defined waist. A full, jiggly butt but not too fat. Thick, kinky, wild hair that tickled my face when she mounted me. It didn't take her long to figure out I was a virgin, but she was sweet and patient even as she was desirous and urgent. She alternately whispered and screamed, and while I didn't meet her every need, she insisted the next morning that she was completely satisfied.

After I walked her to the bus stop, I sat on a bench outside my dorm. It was windy and cool as the sun-dappled brightness on the mostly shaded bluegrass beneath the hardwoods on the quad. A dove cooed somewhere in the trees. I stared up at my room for a long while and then let my head fall all the way back. I kept flashing back to the wet look in her eyes when I was on top of her. As I examined again the Gothic stone buildings of the Duke campus, I decided that the world looked different from the day before. And I was a completely new person.

22

CIRCLING CROWS

I awoke the next morning with a dry mouth and a banging head, which I treated with coffee on the patio outside our kitchen. The heavy air pressed against my forehead. It also demoralized the birds, which were silent except for the bobwhite. It was over 90 degrees at 8 A.M.

Marvin joined me. "Damn. Hot as hell." He studied me. "You okay?"

"Just thinking about my fucked-up life."

"You worried about Cathy?"

"I have no idea where they are."

"They just went off somewhere. They all right. Them women smart. We going to drive that damn tractor today?" He was trying to point me in another direction.

I winced at the idea, but fortunately the crops were now laid by—they were too big to plow. In the next few weeks, I explained to Marvin, we would hire crop dusters to spray poison to kill boll weevils and after that the same planes would spread defoliant on the cotton to knock the leaves off. Marvin asked why we wanted the leaves off, and I explained that it made it easier for the cotton-picking machines to get to the cotton bolls.

Marvin had told me he had never been fishing. We got cane poles, tackle, and a shovel and drove twenty miles to the Warrior River. I dug some worms, and we found a shady place on the bank to relax while we watched our red-and-white bobbers sit undisturbed on the water's surface. We didn't get even a nibble for two hours. "Probably too hot for any sane fish to bite," I said. Marvin shrugged. "Maybe them fish ain't got no taste for worms. I could believe that." A little store back up the road a couple of miles would have some cheese for bait, I said. Marvin thought a grape Nehi would help with the heat.

The store seemed empty when I went in, but when the door slammed after me, I was surprised to see Jimmy Oliver, a guy I knew from my high school class, emerge from the back. Jimmy was about five-eight and slight with a thick head of orange, curly hair and a million freckles on his face and arms. I never liked Jimmy; he'd compensated for being ordinary and mostly insignificant in every way by being a loudmouth in big groups of kids. He was occasionally funny and saw himself as a big cutup, but more often his words bullied people weaker than he was. I'd always kept my hostility toward Jimmy to myself until the day President Kennedy was shot. I had secretly liked John Kennedy—the unusual speech, the cool manner, his writing—and at basketball practice when they announced he had died, I had been stunned, sad, and angry. Then Jimmy had announced, "I guess the nigger lover got his." I was outraged. In the scrimmage a while later, I drove an elbow into Jimmy's face, which caused a gush of blood. I felt avenged at the time, but later I knew it was a chicken-shit thing to do.

"Hey, Jimmy," I said now. "Didn't know you ran this place."

"My mama got it last year. Guess you been off at college." Jimmy had a kind of half smile on his face. He knew exactly what had happened to me.

"I want a half pound of Velveeta and two drinks and these peanuts."

Jimmy got the cheese out of the refrigerator, took a butcher knife in his left hand, and cut off a chunk. He wrapped it in white paper. While I was handing him money, I noticed Marvin standing on the step on the other side of the screen front door.

"You know, Cindy Butler is my cousin." Jimmy said it and then waited, looking for something on my face. "Cathy better watch out."

Was he warning me or threatening me? Jimmy had never been much of a tough guy.

Marvin, it turned out, had no doubt about Jimmy's meaning. He stuck his head in the door. "Mister, I need to see you out here about this gas pump." I was confused. We hadn't bought gas.

Jimmy hurried out the door—then suddenly disappeared. There was a loud bang.

Jimmy was lying about fifteen feet from the door, at the base of a three-hundred-gallon steel tank of kerosene, with Marvin bent over him, about to jerk him off the ground. Marvin lifted Jimmy and then bent him backward on the silver tank. This tank already had absorbed five hours of sunlight to get its temperature way above the danger-to-touch level.

"What you say you going to do to Cathy? Open yo' mouth and say it to me, motherfucker!"

"I'm not going to do nothin' to her!"

Marvin snatched the big nozzle hanging on top of the tank and slammed it against the side of Jimmy's head. When Jimmy screamed, Marvin pulled the trigger on the nozzle, spraying Jimmy's face with kerosene. He was trying to push the nozzle into Jimmy's mouth when the boy had the presence of mind to pitch hard to one side and fall off the tank. When he hit the ground, he scrambled up and ran around the back of the store.

This was not the cool, detached professional I'd seen dispatch the Gooch boys. Marvin was in a red rage. I ran to follow them and saw Jimmy, blinded by the kerosene, trip and fall. Marvin caught up and grabbed him again. "No, you ain't going to bother her." He spoke in a low voice, like he was talking to himself. "You ain't going to be able to hurt her at all."

I tried to pull Marvin off of him, but he shoved me back with one arm and put his other arm around Jimmy's waist and picked him up, the boy coughing and retching at the same time. There was a red Chevrolet truck, about a 1955 model, parked to the side of the store. Marvin took three quick steps and then slammed Jimmy into the grill of the truck, as if the boy's head was a battering ram. I grabbed at Marvin's shoulders, trying to get him to stop, but he backed up and did it again, this time driving Jimmy's head into one of the truck headlights, which shattered. Jimmy let out a wail. He tried to cover his head with his arms. Blood streamed from his scalp.

"Marvin, that's enough. You fixin' to hurt him *bad*." That was what he had said to me to get me to pull Cathy off Cindy Butler.

Marvin jerked his head around at me, his face the picture of extreme malice. "Motherfucker, what you think I'm *tryin' to do*?" He dragged Jimmy to a five-gallon bucket and jammed his head down into the bucket.

"Marvin, stop."

When he yanked Jimmy's head up, it was a dark, shiny mess. The bucket held used motor oil. Jimmy was screaming and puking.

Marvin flung him on the ground. "Let's see you run, motherfucker. *Run.*"

"Marvin, *you have to stop.*"

Marvin kicked Jimmy. "*Run, goddamnit.*" Jimmy got up and stumbled toward a field of head-high corn. Marvin walked determinedly after him. I ran to catch up. "Please, Marvin, *please.*"

Marvin kept walking. "That white sonuvabitch won't be threatening nobody *no more.*"

A little distance into the corn, Marvin caught up with Jimmy, knocked him down, and drove the boy's face into the warm, loose dirt. He pressed both his hands onto the back of Jimmy's head and held it in the soil.

"Marvin, *stop.* Don't kill him. It doesn't matter what he said. He won't hurt Cat."

Marvin jerked Jimmy's head and flung him on his back. I thought Jimmy was dead but then he coughed. Marvin had opened his knife and was waving it at Jimmy with his left hand.

"See, boy, I'm going to make sure you don't bother her 'cause you fixin to be some little chunks of lunch meat for them crows up there." It was true. Crows were circling over the corn in slow arcs. Their caws came faster, as if they were commenting excitedly on the quality of the work their kinsman was performing below, already savoring a meaty lunch.

I fell down on the ground next to Marvin just as he laid his knife at Jimmy's hairline. With his right hand he held the boy's slippery red hair. I thought for sure he was going to scalp Jimmy. Instead, in one long swatch he hacked the hair off the top of Jimmy's head. Jimmy and I both thought Marvin had scalped him but there was no blood.

"Please, Marvin, I'm begging you, *stop.*"

He met my eyes. Then he looked back at Jimmy. "Jimmy, can you hear me?" he said. He sounded almost polite. He said it again when Jimmy didn't answer. Jimmy's eyes were squinted shut and there was dirt caked on his lids. Finally the boy whispered that he could.

"Jimmy, can you remember this? If anybody causes any trouble for Cathy McKee, I'll be back for you. Can you remember that? Anybody try to hurt Cathy, Jimmy, *you* going to pay for it. So you think about yo' dick and balls gettin' ate up by them big black birds."

Jimmy nodded slightly. Marvin rose quickly and headed toward my car. He was examining his hands when he suddenly detoured into the store and came out with a bottle of dishwashing liquid. He went to a water faucet on the side of the building and very carefully soaped and rinsed his hands. They were not only clean but perfectly still.

"I'll drive. Lemme have my drink."

He turned up his Nehi and poured it down his throat. Mayhem made him thirsty. As we pulled away from the store, he took another long swig and turned to me. "I been seein' that thing around." He nodded toward the red Chevy truck.

I knew I had seen it somewhere else too, but I couldn't place it.

"Parked by the barbershop. Front of the pool hall," Marvin said. "It belong to Jimmy?"

"Don't know."

"We have to find out."

Back to the riverbank, my anger rose. Another country store, nearly another killing.

"You didn't have to do all that," I said. Marvin glared at me. "Once you sprayed kerosene on him, he was done. You didn't have to beat him that bad. You scared the shit outa me."

"You need to get used to it. I heard the motherfucker threaten Cathy."

"You enjoyed what you did to him." He turned away. For once I'd shut him up.

He had studied his cane pole for an hour. "Don't you tell Baby Sister none of what happened back yonder, you hear? Y'all close, but she don't need to know about that. You hear?"

I finally nodded. I didn't know whether Marvin wanted to keep Jimmy's implied threat from Cathy or if he didn't want her to know about the astonishing brutality that an enraged Marvin Whitfield could visit on another human being. Either way, I wasn't saying anything.

I prayed that summer that it wouldn't happen again. He had heard my plea. Once Marvin did that to Jimmy Oliver, once he had allowed his rage unleashed, he put it away for the moment. But I knew it was still there, like a sabre tucked way in the closet—you don't think about much and you never see it, but you know it's still back there somewhere and if he ever fetched it out, somebody else would have hell to pay.

23

NOT LONG

Beth's letter made me feel better. "Last winter, when you told me you loved me, I said you didn't, that you were just saying that to keep us together. I knew you were sincere. I did a horrible thing—the worst thing I ever did to anybody." She wasn't bored, but she was scared that getting so involved with me would keep her from succeeding in a career and leave her like the miserable, complaining housewives of her Long Island town. "Jewish women are intense—as you may have noticed." She had always had a problem with depression, and she got depressed about how our relationship complicated her career ambitions. "I should have tried to explain all this to you at the time, but I wasn't sure I could. I just felt like the only way out was to end it with you. Stupid and selfish." She said she still cared about me. "I wish I could kiss your pretty blond head."

The letter raised questions. Would we get together if I went back to Duke? If she wanted me back and I got convicted, that would make going to jail all the harder. I couldn't grasp any idea of what my future could be. The letter also made me see the chain of past events. When we were in the middle of romance, Beth and I had talked about going to Europe together this summer—two lovers doing the Grand Tour on the cheap. I had been thrilled at that prospect. Instead of driving Jackie to Alabama, I might have been reclining with Beth in a Venetian gondola. Those things were connected in a way, and they gave me pause about starting over with her. I couldn't forget how flatly she had smashed my feelings.

She called and asked what I thought about the letter. "Interesting" was all I could get out.

"But do you forgive me? That's the question."

"Sure, I forgive you, but I don't know that changes things."

"Well, I'd like a second chance with you."

I told her I'd think about second chances. We talked for over an hour that night. She wanted details about what had happened that summer and what I had found out in the course of things. "Damn, Dix, your life is screwed up, but it's the most interesting screwed-up life I've ever heard about." Afterward I felt almost cleansed of tension, but then a while later the stress gushed again and drowned my hopefulness. All Beth could give me right now were reminders of sweet times that were now past.

While Mama and Cathy were gone, Marvin and I spent a lot of time at Bebe's—partly to be close to Orene's kitchen, but also because I wanted to spend more time with my grandmother. As much as I wanted to deny it, she was failing quickly, and being with her now felt as precious and transitory as a sunset. I told her I'd taken a class at Duke called "Race and Region in Modern American Literature," and she insisted that I start teaching her what I had learned. The class had been taught by Professor Kensington, a diminutive sixty-year-old in a bow tie and tweed jacket who pronounced about as "aboot" and talked with his teeth clenched on his pipe. "We will study a great flowering of literature in the South after about 1920," he had announced at the first class, at the end of which he declared, "Come to my class prepared—or risk the fate of a top Duroc at a southside Virginia hog-killing." I foolishly forgot about that image and was unprepared the day he called on me to profile the protagonist in *Look Homeward, Angel*. Kensington eviscerated me, finally yanking out my liver when I couldn't even name the mountain town whence Thomas Wolfe came. "My, oh, my, Mr. McKee," he'd said. "You appear to know even less about geography than literature."

Now, as I sat with my grandmother on the front porch as the summer heat swelled on that July morning, I told her the books I'd read with Kensington. She stopped me at Flannery O'Connor. "A good Catholic girl," she said.

I read "The Artificial Nigger" aloud. When I finished, Bebe said, "She wants us to be in awe of the power of God, don't you think, Tommy?"

Sitting next to my dying grandmother, my best friend dead for no reason at all, I faced a trial and probably prison. "Her awe of the power of God doesn't do much for me right now."

"No, dear, I can see that it wouldn't. It has to be hard to grasp faith in the Almighty in the face of such circumstances."

I was thinking about that when William went to answer a knock at the back door and returned with the young minister I had met when Zion Baptist was burning. Reverend Banks gave me a serious look. "Young man, our congregation is praying for your strength and deliverance from injustice." He bowed his head to Bebe. "Sister Brigid, the whole congregation is lifting you up. We are asking for relief and healing."

"Let's emphasize relief, Reverend. I'm ready to go, or will be shortly."

When Orene brought a tray of coffee and cake, Banks greeted "Sister Orene" and inquired after her "blood," which was reported to have sugar counts still too high. Orene sat down with us, something she otherwise never did.

Banks turned to me. "Son, when our church burned, your grandmother, without being asked, contributed many thousands of dollars to rebuild."

"Reverend, I asked her," Orene said. "Sho' did."

Bebe laughed. "Reverend, I can refuse anybody, maybe the Lord himself, but not Orene Ford." She got serious. "Tell me, Reverend, what the colored people are thinking about politics."

"Sister Brigid, once we get a good many folk on the voting roll, we'll think about elections."

"When that time comes, and it won't be long, I hope you'll give some serious thought to running for office. I think you'd make a good probate judge or sheriff."

I had not given up on the idea that Daddy might still prevail in the courthouse. And it hadn't really occurred to me that a black man might hold any such office. Bebe was way ahead of me in thinking about the future. Ironic, given how little future she had.

Banks took out his Bible and read a long passage to Bebe, and then he prayed a long while. After he left, I remarked on what a likable guy he was, and Bebe agreed.

"And he's smart. He's taught me a lot about the Bible, as a matter of fact. You know, Tommy, Baptists put a lot more stock in the Bible than Catholics do." I didn't know that. "Yes, he's ministered to me quite attentively since he heard I was sick." She raised one eyebrow. "Whereas the Methodist preacher has not been here once." Although she had never joined the Methodist church, she had usually attended with Granddaddy. "I threaten him, I suppose, because of my racial attitudes. Of course, he quit getting his monthly check from this house once Tom died." She shrugged and smiled.

Joe Black and Daddy were coming over for lunch that day. As Bebe dozed, I went out and waylaid Joe Black at his car. I needed to tell him something that I didn't want Daddy to hear. He eyed me, then pulled a cigar from his pocket. "Let's sit here under this pecan tree and I'll smoke while you talk, son."

Joe Black had already quizzed me about any civil rights demonstrations I had participated in, but I hadn't told him about this one thing I did. By coincidence, on my drive home for spring break the car radio brought reports of the civil rights march from Selma to Montgomery that would end that day. I got curious. At the columned and domed state capitol, surrounded by other Greek-revival buildings which seemed to compete to see which could be the whitest, reporters and television cameras waited for the marchers. Soon I spotted the approaching throng, mostly blacks but many whites, too. When they got close, I stepped into the street and was swept forward along the edge of the crowd, becoming part of the joyful mass. The long chants of "Freedom! Freedom!" were thrilling. Various people, black and white, smiled at me, and I realized I stood out as a young white guy in an open-necked summer shirt. The crowd halted, accumulating in the street directly in front of the capitol. I felt almost an electrical shock in my neck and arms when I saw a compact, strong-jawed black man mount the back of a flatbed trailer parked in the street before the capitol steps. I realized it was Martin Luther King Jr. He began to speak in a slow manner, his face somber. At first, every sentence he uttered brought shouts and applause, as he recounted the hardships of the first efforts at civil rights. I had never seen a speaker hold an audience so rapt. After a while, his delivery sped up and the crowd ceased interrupting him so much. He reminded them of the years of protest that had begun with a bus boycott in Montgomery a decade before, and he talked about the violent treatment of civil rights workers that occurred in the "colossus of segregation," Birmingham, in 1963. Selma had brought together this interracial throng. He told the crowd that the work of this movement was not completed, that they had to keep marching against discrimination. He began to talk about how long it would take until prejudice had been conquered. "How long?" he said, and then he offered a series of reasons why he could say, "Not long." Because, he said, "no lie can live forever." Because "truth pressed to earth will rise again." Because, he said, God was just and he would prevail in bringing justice to the victims of prejudice. "Glory, Glory, Hallelujah," he shouted several times at the end.

I felt his words in the adrenaline that rose within me with each declaiming phrase. If I, as a mere observer, felt the power of his words, then people around me were shouting and crying and smiling with joy as the speech reached its crescendo. After King descended from the truck and was absorbed by the throng, many people around me remained transfixed, watching the place where he had stood.

I told all this to Joe Black, and heard my voice grow more fervent as I recounted some of the words and spirit of that day. He nodded. "Tommy, I'm glad you told me. Don't worry. If it comes up, you just knew it was a big moment in history and you wanted to be there to see it."

He smiled widely as he wiped his mouth with his handkerchief. "Hell, I canceled a big deposition so I could be there."

"You were there?!"

"Sure was. That fella's a helluva talker, ain't he?" He was smiling and shaking his head.

AT LUNCH DADDY BARELY participated in the conversation. Bebe asked Joe Black what it would be like for me at Buford Kyle's trial. He said the circuit solicitor would ask what happened that day, my reasons for being in Yancey County. Then Kyle's lawyer, Hubert Brophy, would attack me.

Joe Black had known Brophy, a labor and plaintiffs' lawyer in Birmingham, for forty years.

"We used to always be on the same side in politics. But now he's gone way over there with the reactionaries in Birmingham. Defending the Klan like they're religious martyrs." He clipped the end of a huge cigar. "He'll shout in your face. Taliaferro may try to protect you and he may not." He punched up the cigar. "Judge McKinley was an old friend of your granddaddy. He's going to retire after this term, and he shouldn't put up with much foolishness."

Bebe spoke lightly. "I'll be there to remind Judge McKinley that we know who he is."

"Wait, now, Mama," Daddy said. "You aren't up to that."

"Don't you tell me what I not going to do, Buddy. I'll be there. Abner's providing me with pain medicine." Abner McGehee Hill, another childhood friend, was Bebe's doctor.

Daddy looked at Joe Black. "Tell her that's not necessary."

The little lawyer was shaking his head as he licked the cigar from one end to the other. "Can't do it, Buddy. She needs to be there. But just while Tommy testifies."

She smiled triumphantly. "Now, Buddy, you and Tommy run on. I'm going to take Joe out on the porch and let him smoke that nasty cigar he's been making love to for the last hour."

I'D THOUGHT MANY TIMES during the summer that Bebe would never live to the trial. Several times I had found her with her head lying back with her mouth open and her eyes closed. Each time I was gripped with fear. Her bony face and sunken eyes made her look almost dead when she was awake. I flinched when she suddenly grimaced with the pain.

Before the summer of 1965, I knew nothing of the intimate relationship between life and death. When Jackie died, it was as if someone flipped a light switch, and life went to death like a room falls instantly dark. But Bebe's life was dimming slowly, like a midsummer dusk under a clear, Eden Rise sky. Watching her die by degrees, with such great intention, I learned how life and death could merge in time.

24

Nuclear Standoff

"Tommy, my eyes too bad to see just right under there," Sam said to me one day when I was in the farm garage helping him service the combine in preparation for the fall soybean harvest. He pointed beneath the steel housing that covered the sprockets and cogs that made the big machine function. "You mind pumpin' some grease in there?" I scooted under the machine to look for the grease nipples. Then I heard Sam say, "I need mo' grease for these guns." Sam had made a simple declarative statement, but he meant it as an order to Marvin, who was sitting nearby on an overturned five-gallon bucket, smoking a Kool. Marvin didn't move, but Sam didn't have to upbraid him this time because the heavy steps of Junior Jackson's brogans were a brief prelude to the boom of his bass voice.

"Nigger, get *off* yo' goddamn sorry ass and get him a bucket of grease."

"Fuck you. Git it y'self." I was glad to be safely under the ten-ton machine.

"Marvin, you put them guns on the floor and step this way and we'll see who's going to make who do what."

"Junior, I don't lay my damn guns down for nobody."

But I heard the click of leather heels on the concrete floor as Marvin stepped across the warehouse to fetch the grease. By the time I had finished my task under the combine, Junior seemed to have forgotten about the tiff. He had brought ribs and beans for lunch.

"We talked to Reverend Banks about the voting situation," I said. I wanted to hear Junior's views on the local blacks and politics.

"Yeah? What'd you think, Tommy?"

"Seemed like a pretty smart guy."

"Did?" He shrugged. "Maybe."

Junior seemed not to want to talk about Banks.

"Junior a Church of God," Sam said. "Ain't got time for no Baptist." Sam was a deacon at Zion.

Junior was shaking his head. "Don't have nothin' to do with him being a Baptist. Most folk is Baptist. I just don't think we oughta let somebody be in charge just 'cause they a preacher. Some of the rest of us got sense, too. Plus, Banks a little too friendly with them house niggers like William Addison."

"What you mean house niggers?" Marvin didn't like criticism of William.

"William mighty close to Brigid McKee. He going to do somethin' she don't want?" Junior shook his head again.

Sam leaned back in his chair. "My wife a house nigger, Junior?" Junior didn't answer. "Banks a good man," Sam said.

"Seemed like it to me," I said.

"When the church burned down, Banks didn't get wild. He was good, got the job done."

Junior scowled. "What I mean is, we shouldn't just follow the preachers. Need to think for ourselves. We may be some old field niggers but we ain't stupid." Sam was shaking his head. "Junior, you just need to come on out and say what you mean. You believe you good as anybody to lead the colored. You may be right. Lotta people do like you."

Marvin shook his head. "I ain't one of 'em."

It was a revealing conversation and a preface to the future of Ruffin County, I realized later.

AFTER LUNCH, MARVIN AND I plowed the perimeters of several fields to make it easier to turn the cotton pickers and the combines around when the fields were harvested. In the late afternoon, my tractor started to misfire, and then it stalled out completely. Junior brought Sam to work on the fuel line, but it was near dusk before we restarted the machine. On the way back to the warehouse, a sheriff's car pulled up close behind our truck and flashed his lights. Sam stopped, and two deputies approached it, one on either side. Neither was more than twenty-five. I didn't recognize them. The one on the driver's side spoke to Sam. "Which one of y'all is Whitfield?"

I tensed. I figured Jimmy Oliver had told the sheriff what had happened to him, and McCallister had put two and two together on Marvin.

The other deputy suddenly opened the door on the passenger side. "Y'all get out."

Up ahead, Junior had pulled the tractor off the road and was walking back to the truck when the first deputy looked at Marvin. "You Whitfield?" Marvin nodded. "We going to take you to the sheriff's office for questioning."

Junior reached the group at that point. "What this about?"

"I already said. We going to take Whitfield in for some questioning."

"Am I under arrest?" Marvin said.

"No, we just want to talk to you."

Junior spoke very slowly. "Now, deputy, why would he want to go with you if he ain't done nothing wrong and you already said you ain't here to arrest him?"

I realized that Junior had his left hand in his coverall pocket, that Sam had his right hand in his bib overall pocket, and that Marvin's right hand was behind his back. Marvin probably already had the knife in his left hand. I was the only unarmed man out there.

"Because we're the law around here, and we ain't puttin' up with a bunch of smartass niggers defying our orders."

"*Smartass niggers?*" Junior's booming voice startled me. "What smartass niggers? We're just plain old farm workers at the end of a hard day, on our way home. We may be niggers"—he looked at me—"most of us anyway, but, deputy, ain't nothin' smartass about us."

The other deputy had gone to his car, talked on his radio, and now returned and gave a quick nod to his partner.

"But we ain't no stupid-assed niggers neither. Ain't nobody going to the sheriff's office with y'all, and them damn thugs that hang around there, unlessen' we have to. And we don't have to without y'all arrest somebody for some crime. And we ain't committed no crime."

We endured a full half-minute of silence that was broken only by the sound of a siren. In a few seconds, two more sheriffs' cars pulled up in front of us.

Marvin spoke to me in a low voice. "Tom, get back in the truck."

"Boy, stay where you at!" ordered the talkative deputy.

I looked at the deputy, said nothing, and moved to the truck's passenger door. I was about to get in when I saw the rifle that Marvin had put on the rack behind the seat. I took the rifle and jumped into the truck bed. I laid the rifle on top of the cab and peeped over it.

Marvin glanced up at me and frowned. "Keep your damn head down." He returned his gaze to the deputies. "Sam, slip 'round the truck, stand by the side." Marvin moved backward so that he hugged the truck grill. "Junior, you take a few steps back into that ditch behind you and get ready to drop on your belly. You hear?" Junior grunted.

The deputies' eyes started to get big as they realized what Marvin was doing. Four other deputies trotted up to the truck, unaware of how tense the situation had become. The first to arrive was almost out of breath. "What's happening, Randy?"

When the deputies' attention had momentarily moved to the new arrivals, Marvin squatted and put a gun in each hand.

The deputy named Randy swung his head back toward Marvin. "This nigger ain't cooperating about coming in for questioning. We going to have to make him go."

Marvin slipped just behind the fender of the truck. He laid his armed left hand on the truck's hood and kept his armed right hand at his side. Sam stood just a few feet behind him, his left hand now supporting the wrist of his right hand, which held his pistol. Junior was hunkered down in the ditch, his pistol swinging in front of him.

"I don't believe you going to do that, cracker," Marvin said slowly. "I ain't bothering y'all or nobody else, and I ain't going to no sheriff's office tonight. You can either load back up in your cars and leave or you can deal with us right here."

All you heard were crickets. For a full minute the six deputies stayed frozen. They now understood that they were facing four men with drawn guns who stood behind some cover. Five sets of vehicle lights were shining in various directions in the now black night, throwing shafts of brightness in several directions but also forming creepy shadows with any movement. I could see all our potential targets, but we were at least partly hidden in the shadows.

One of the recent arrivals spoke up. "I don't know about this, Randy. This could be rough. Are you sure you know what you're doing?"

"Shut the fuck up, Bubba."

Bubba Johnson I knew. When the ninth-grade civics teacher upbraided him for not learning about the three branches of government, Bubba had uttered what became a famous line at Eden Rise High: "Mr. Green, I don't care what kinda gubmint we have as long as I can keep gittin' plenty that good ol' pussy."

Marvin spoke as if he were asking Bebe to pass the gravy. "I'm going to take out the master of ceremonies here." He waved his gun at Randy. "Sam, you blow the head off his partner. Junior, you shoot Bubba." He paused a moment. "Tom, you git them two others. Nobody stop 'till I tell you to."

At that moment I almost pissed in my pants. But I put one of them in my sights.

There was only a short silence before Bubba broke and ran to his car and squealed off.

"Stupid fuck," Randy said.

"Naw, he be the smartest cracker out here," Marvin said. He let everyone listen to the sound of the fleeing car die out. "Any one of y'all draws a gun, the fun begins."

The standoff had lasted only a few more moments when another vehicle drove up. Mac McCallister got slowly out of the car and walked up to the group. He surveyed his five deputies.

"What's going on here, boys?" There was no immediate response. "Randy?"

"We're trying to get Whitfield to come to the office but he refuses to come."

"That right, Whitfield?"

"Absolutely correct, sheriff."

"Why not?"

"I ain't done nothin'. I don't trust you to treat me with brotherly love."

"Brotherly love. *Shit*," McCallister said.

Junior sat up. "Mac, why don't you say what y'all wanta ask Marvin."

McCallister looked over at Junior. "All right, Junior, since you asked so nice. He's been around town for a while now, and we make it our business to keep up with dangerous niggers—dangerous people—who show up in Ruffin County. We checked around and found out he has a long criminal record, has killed people in Chicago, and is associated with them radical Muslim niggers. We don't need them kinda people here, Junior, and we just want a chance to tell Whitfield that to his face."

Junior was now standing with his gun down to his side. "Well, Mac, you just done told him. You heard the sheriff, didn't you, Marvin?"

Marvin looked at Junior but didn't say anything.

"He heard you, Mac. Sho' did. But he ain't going to go to no sheriff office tonight, and he ain't never going to go by hisself. You understand that, sheriff?" McCallister made no response.

"And if you try to force him to go, it's going to be a mess out here tonight, Mac. You understand that, don't you? These little boys you got out here in way over they head. I'll get one of you. Sam over there, he get one of you. Tommy may get one." Junior paused a moment to let his prediction sink in. "And Marvin, he is a dang'ous nigger, just like you say, sheriff. He'll kill the other three, four of you quicker'n you can say Chicago, and enjoy every minute of it."

There was another pause, which Junior again interrupted. "You get that, Mac?"

McCallister looked at the deputies, then at Junior, and finally he stared off into the black night for several seconds. "All right, boys, load up. Git back to the office."

Without another word they drove off. When their lights and engine noise faded, we stood quietly in the black, broken only in front of us by our truck lights. It was just the crickets and us. The air held the odor of automobile exhaust and Marvin's cigarette.

"That was a nice little speech, Junior," Sam said.

"Yeah," I said. "It was."

"Thank ya. Anybody give a good speech when they got somebody to back 'em up."

"Tha's right." Sam let the crickets have their say. "Marvin, I'll say this: you ain't wuf a shit workin' on a farm but you come in real handy 'round a buncha crackers."

Junior let loose a deep roll of laughter and slapped Sam on the back. "Good to know these town niggers ain't plumb worthless, ain't it?" He looked up at the big tractor. "I believe we'll come get that thing in the morning, Sam."

I went home feeling pumped up, strong. Daddy looked at me oddly, and I could see him deciding not to say anything. But that night in bed, I started shuddering, thinking of what might have happened on that dark road that night. If one of those deputies had even pulled a gun, there would have been a massacre. What would happen to us if we had killed all those men? Would Marvin have wanted to "disappear" the bodies? We could never have gotten away with it. Junior and Marvin knew that, which gave rise to Junior's speech to end the standoff.

I worried that there might be other attempts to round up Marvin, perhaps when Sam and Junior weren't around. The sheriff's deputies were unlikely just to forget an incident in which they had to back down from three armed blacks. But at least Mac McCallister knew that from now on he wouldn't have his way in Eden Rise against Negroes without being challenged.

As I thought about the tense encounter along the roadside, I marveled at how little violence there had been so far as a result of civil rights. To be sure, too many had already been martyred and I knew there would be others. Martin Luther King Jr., for example, was constantly threatened. But most whites expected a race war, and none had come to pass. There had been almost no black retribution for the wrongs done over the centuries. Maybe that was because Negroes just wanted to prove the whites wrong on that score, too. But it also may have been that blacks were no longer afraid, and whites knew it. It was like the nuclear standoff of the Cold War. If you shoot first, no telling how it will all end.

25

Dust on My Feet

The next morning Mama called to say she was serving lunch at home at noon. I examined Cathy's scratches and the black eye and pronounced that she was healing nicely, but actually I was appalled at how purple and swollen her hands remained. She was nervous. I was on the verge of asking questions about where they had been, when Daddy arrived and the atmosphere grew tense. When we sat down, Mama said, "We've been to Birmingham."

"Did you go shopping?" I said.

"We did," she said casually, "for a new school for Cathy." When I looked at Cathy, her eyes were fixed on her plate.

Daddy stopped eating. "Why?"

Mama didn't look up from the sandwich she was inspecting. "Because she's going to school in Birmingham this coming year."

"You just decided that?"

Mama gave him a quick glance. "She and I decided."

"Which school?" I wanted to keep the conversation moving.

"Probably a private girl's school. If not there, a public high school."

"You just did this without talking to me?"

"I'm talking to you now, Buddy." She nailed him with a hard look. "You keep saying this family is falling apart, and I'm doing what's gotta be done to protect my kids."

Cathy's eyes were filling up. "Daddy, I can't go back. I'm going to get punished, bad. That Butler girl's got nasty cousins at our school. I'd end up fighting all the time."

Marvin's stern look at me said *you keep your damn mouth shut*. I imagined for a moment what Eden Rise High School would be like if it was integrated. The previous night's showdown might be a regular occurrence among schoolboys—a frightening prospect.

"What about your teaching, Mama?"

"I went by the school board a little while ago and resigned."

Daddy's jaw dropped. "You're kidding."

She laughed bitterly. "Never been more serious in my life. Put down a deposit to rent a house. Cathy and I will move there as soon as this trial is over and Tommy's gone back to Duke."

I was dumbstruck. Daddy looked like he'd been clubbed. Leave Eden Rise? Mama's face had a hardness on it, but when I checked to see if her tic was jumping—a sure sign of her nervousness—there was not a twitch. "I'm shaking the dust of this place off my feet."

One person's garden is another's briar patch. Until that lunchtime, I had never seriously entertained the possibility that my parents' bond might be breached, that they might actually split up. Having to contemplate the actual destruction of my family shot panic through me—real pain in my bowels. It was like what I felt when I was given the unthinkable information that Jackie had died.

DADDY ROSE AND LEFT the kitchen. Cathy withdrew to her room, Marvin to the back yard to smoke. I helped Mama clear the dishes. I wanted to be with her. I asked if I could help with the garden. "Oh, Tommy, I hate to go out there. I've neglected the garden so this summer."

"Well, let's see what we can do."

The first thing we did was to pull off the tomatoes that had rotted on the vine and cut the okra pods that had gotten too big and tough. She got a hoe, I started the rotary tiller, and we attacked the weeds that had taken over the middles of the rows. After that we picked a basket full of Kentucky Wonder beans that were only a little past done. After two hours, we stopped for ice water. She patted my shoulder. Her smile was wan. "This has been a terrible summer, and one of the worst parts of it has been not being able really to enjoy having you around."

"I know. It's been completely screwed up. Let's hope there's never another one like it."

"There won't be." She forced a brighter smile, put down her glass, and picked up her hoe.

"Mama, I wish you really didn't have to go through with this Birmingham thing."

She squinted into the glare. "Tommy, we don't have much choice. Cathy couldn't go back to high school here. I'm so alienated from everything that I don't talk to anyone but Cathy."

"Well, what about this house?"

"Oh, we'll keep it. Buddy's so confused that he probably will want to stay right here. Even if he does go, there's not much reason to sell it now."

"This scares me about you and Daddy. Don't y'all split up." I couldn't say *divorce*.

"Your daddy's going to have to get some peace with things. He's in a bad place, and he's not lettin' anybody help him." She shrugged. "Anger's a terrible thing. Not to say he doesn't have good reason to be angry. Lord knows I'm so mad I don't know what to do."

"Tell me."

"Oh, you know. The politics, the church, my in-laws, the way Buddy's acting. Not to mention the God-awful things done to you."

"Mama, I'm so sorry I caused—"

"Tommy, stop. No more apologies."

She started to tear up. "But anger is really destructive—it hurts me the most. I've got to let go of it somehow. There's nobody here to talk to. I push too much of it off on Cathy. No sixteen-year-old should have to be her mother's psychiatrist."

I put my glass down and pulled her to me. She sobbed for a few moments and then sighed deeply. She pushed away and then looked up at me. "Let's look forward. We're going to get through this summer, some of us are going to Birmingham, and you're going back to college."

"Going back to college is still a pretty big if, Mama."

"Well, if this legal stuff works out right, you're going back to college, right? To Duke."

"I have thought about maybe going to Tuscaloosa, but I don't know. I haven't really planned on going back to Duke, either."

"Well, I want you to go back up there. You need to be away from all this mess here, and Tuscaloosa isn't far enough."

I thought about that for the first time—what it would be like to be a new student in Tuscaloosa after a summer of civil rights trials—and suddenly I knew she was right. I would never get away from the aftermath of Jackie's death. But then I was pretty sure I wouldn't do that at Duke either. I expected to be on the other side of the country living in a big city apartment, hanging out in coffee shops and bookstores at night.

"You know, you're right. Tuscaloosa would be too close."

She smiled, pleased. I had a pang of guilt about letting her assume that the return to Duke was now settled. But she was blocking out the possibility that I would be sentenced to prison.

She said she had talked to Jackie's mother the previous night. I felt a heavy gloom descend as I flashed back to the distraught woman at her son's funeral. She was holding on, working, looking after her daughter. Mama had offered to fly her down for Buford Kyle's trial but she said she couldn't.

"She probably doesn't want to come where they killed her son. I wouldn't, in her place."

"Well, I'd want to clap eyes on the one who killed my child. I intend to kill Buford Kyle with my eyes when I see him. Unlike your daddy, I think you should testify. It's the right thing."

"Yeah, and then they'll convict me, and I'll end up in prison." I wanted her to know how frightened I was, so she would understand when I disappeared.

"I have faith that's not going to happen, Sweetie. I really do."

I studied my mother for a moment. "Mama, you say I should testify, stand up for what's right. But you don't want to stay here and try to make it work."

She looked at me and then smiled sheepishly. "You're too smart for your mama's good, Tommy. You're right, it's inconsistent." She thought for a moment. "I divide things into past and future. I think you should testify to try to set the record straight on a terrible injustice. But for the future, I can't see my family being happy here. I won't be able to do any good for anybody here. I don't think Buddy can. In a new place, maybe we can help ourselves and somebody else. All that's going to be here for us in Eden Rise is bitterness and suspicion."

She turned and trudged toward a tangled row of cucumber vines. She bent over, pulled a rotten cucumber and flung it into the weeds at the back of the garden, then reached for another.

26

CHANGED MEN

I waited for the teller to count out the $800 I was withdrawing from my savings account. Travel money. My plan was to make four small withdrawals over the next few weeks until I had my $3,000 of savings in cash, stashed away for when I needed to go. If I took it all at once, Uncle Bill might notice and tell Daddy.

I was folding the envelope to put the cash in my pocket when Uncle Bill appeared. "Tommy, can you come in my office for a minute?" I was caught, but there was no way around going with him. "Sit down, son. I want to talk to you about something." Bill appeared surprisingly nervous for a man about to rat me out. "Tommy, I wanta apologize 'bout what happened at church the other Sunday. Virginia had no call to tear into you. She and I both know you are really an innocent victim in what happened. She just gets all worked up when she thinks people are mad at her. I don't want you to think we don't care a whole lot about you. We do."

I thanked him. He and I had always been friendly in a superficial way. We never had talked seriously about anything, and I had wondered if Bill thought seriously about anything.

"I guess you heard I'll be soon leaving the banking business," he said next.

I didn't know what to say, but I had to say something. "I know Daddy was upset that Bebe sorta pulled the rug out from under y'all without telling you."

"Tommy, I'm real happy to be gettin' out. I mean, it was one of those things I hadn't thought about, 'cause I hadn't imagined what else I'd do, but when Mama said she'd sold the bank, I felt this great feeling come over me, like I had never felt before. I could do something completely new and different with my life." A smile covered his heavy, square face.

"Like the man said, 'Free at last, free at last.'" Bill laughed.

"Well, what are you going to do, Uncle Bill?"

"We're moving to the beach—Gulf Shores, Alabama. I've bought a marina, and I'm going into that business on January first, next year."

The exodus from Eden Rise seemed to be contagious. I was pretty sure he didn't know about Mama's decision to leave. I decided I'd let my parents break that news. "That sounds like so much fun, Uncle Bill. Is Aunt Virginia okay with it?"

"Oh, yeah, she's thrilled. She loves the beach. Virginia's bothered by all the nigger trouble. She's ready to get away from here. There's not much race problem down at the beach."

I realized that the few times I had been to the beaches in Alabama and Florida I hadn't seen many colored people. No black people meant no race trouble. That was how everyone thought—if there was only one race around you, then there was only one race anywhere.

"Did you tell Daddy yet?"

"Yeah, he's sad to see us leave. He's havin' a rough time. All the change has him upset. And he thinks he's got to hold on trying to run things, just like our daddy did, or some of these rednecks out here will really screw things up. Or the niggers will."

"Do you need power that way, Uncle Bill?"

"Naw, son, I don't. I hate making personnel decisions in the bank. Some men are born with the need to boss, and some of us weren't." He shrugged. "I just wanta get along. It was always easy when Daddy was here. I just did what he told me to do."

"I guess everybody did."

"Well, son, that's my point. Buddy didn't really do what our daddy wanted. Everybody knew he was Daddy's favorite—he was the smartest, the best-looking, a good athlete, a natural leader." Uncle Bill shook his head. "You know, I coulda been resentful 'bout Daddy's partiality, but Buddy was so good to me, always protectin' and lookin' out for me, I didn't mind."

Bill smiled as if he were telling me something that was on the masthead of the *Montgomery Advertiser* every day. In fact, I knew little about

Daddy's relationship with his father. "Your granddaddy wanted Buddy to use the family position to go high up in politics, but all Buddy wanted to do was farm. The Judge thought farmin' was what you did if you were too dumb for anything else." Bill let out a quiet laugh. "Told me it was a waste of talent for Buddy to spend his time drivin' a tractor. Buddy knew Daddy felt like that but he farmed anyway. Then when Daddy dropped dead, Buddy felt like he let Daddy down. He's trying to make up for it."

"Well, what should Daddy do?"

"Finish his term and get out. No future for him in politics. Never wanted it anyhow. Buddy just ain't like our Daddy. Neither am I." Bill gave me a kind smile. "Neither are you, Tommy. Times change, people change, and we've just got to see it and move on."

I CAME OUT OF the bank distracted, trying to reconcile the notion I had of my father with the picture of him that Bill had given me. Marvin was leaning against the adjoining building, studying the front of the courthouse.

"What's all them folk going in the courthouse for?" he said, pointing with his chin. A line of black people extended out the door and onto the sidewalk. It took me a moment before I realized that today was the first day the new federal voting registrars were receiving applicants.

Marvin and I slipped in a side door and observed the mass of people standing in the hall and on the stairs up to the second floor where the board of registrars office was located. It was an orderly, subdued gathering—as if these several hundred people had signed an oath to be on their best behavior because someone was watching to judge their respectability and worth not just as a registered voters but as human beings. A black woman and her ten-year-old son were moving up and down the line selling Cokes and bags of peanuts. They were doing a good business, because the air wasn't stirring in the courthouse and the line seemed not to be moving at all.

Daddy was watching outside the probate office. Just then two men in suits came into the courthouse and walked up to Daddy. Several others in short sleeves milled about them. I could tell something serious was happening, so I eased over to get within earshot. "Judge

McKee," one of the suited men was saying, "we are here on behalf of the Justice Department to request the use of the large courtroom upstairs for the registrars." He had the same accent as Beth's father. The short-sleeved men were writing down what the man was saying. Reporters.

Daddy looked at him. "The courtroom is not used for registration."

"Is the courtroom in use today?"

"Well, not today, but there are proceedings scheduled for tomorrow."

"We formally request use of the courtroom today and every day for the next two weeks."

"Request denied."

The New York man folded his mouth into a smirk. "Have it your way, Judge. If you let us make an example of a belligerent Southern official, all this will go more smoothly in the months ahead." He turned to his colleague. "Call the office and get them started on a contempt proceeding." He looked back at Daddy. "A subpoena for you to appear before a federal magistrate tomorrow will be here shortly, Judge. We'll see you in Montgomery in the morning."

Daddy shook his head, a deep crease on his brow. He and the suited man stared at each other for a long moment. "All right, take the courtroom," my father said. The two men quickly headed up the stairs, the reporters scurrying along behind.

I didn't know what to say—he wouldn't want to hear me tell him I thought he had done the right thing. "He didn't leave you any choice, Daddy," I said. He looked at me as if I were a complete stranger. He hadn't realized I witnessed the confrontation.

"You shouldn't be here. Y'all go on."

Before I could say any more, I heard Junior Jackson's distinctive bass voice. He was coming in the courthouse door shouting greetings, laughing loudly, slapping men's backs, and kissing some of the women waiting in the line. He headed toward us. "What's happening?"

"This is what's happening." Daddy waived his arm at the crowd on the stairs, and then looked back at Junior. "World's going to hell."

Junior jerked his head to the side and squinted at Daddy. "World goin' to hell 'cause some colored wanta vote? That what you think?" Daddy had triggered Junior's temper.

Daddy met Junior's eyes. "I don't like the way it's being shoved down our throat."

"Ain't bein' shoved down my throat. When I swaller, it goes down real smooth."

"It didn't have to happen like this."

"Don't know how it mighta happened, but the way it has is okay. Gettin' the job done."

"Well, we going to have hell to pay."

"Buddy, look at them people goin up them steps. Most of 'em been payin' hell all they lives. You know that." His voice had tightened. A vein throbbed at his temple.

"Junior, lotta these folks are illiterate. Somebody's telling them what to do."

"Just 'cause somebody can read don't make 'em smart. You got plenty college, Buddy. But you done quit thinkin' for yourself. You lettin' these crackers on the commission tell you what to think about everything. You startin' to sound like that goddamn sheriff."

What Junior was saying wasn't all true, he knew it, but his anger was doing the talking.

"Junior," I said, "Daddy—"

"I ain't buyin' that bullshit about illiterate niggers. People can't read, most time not they fault. Never got to go to school. Out there pickin' some white man's cotton. Ain't that true?"

The question hung in the courthouse humidity, a threatening dare. Junior was taunting Daddy to contradict him. Daddy just stared at Junior, who went on. "Lotta them folk in that line got plenty sense enough to know right from wrong. That makes 'em good enough to vote, I think. Plenty white folks can read, they don't know nothin' 'bout right and wrong."

Daddy still didn't say anything, which further fueled Junior's anger. He edged his gigantic frame a few inches closer to Daddy, who at six-three and 230 pounds, shrank in comparison. "Buddy, you think Sam Ford a smart guy?"

"Sure."

"Sam make all them tractors run. Fix that fuckin' combine every time one of us fills it up with rocks. Tear that cottonpicker apart and put it back together in twenty-four hours if we ask him to. You think he smart?"

"No question."

"Sam can't read, can't write nothin but his name. He smart enough to vote, Buddy?"

"Yeah, Sam's got plenty 'nough sense to vote."

"Well, he *don't* vote, 'cause he knew they wouldn't let him 'cause he can't read." I was scared. I thought Junior might hit or push Daddy.

"Well, he oughta come on down here now."

"Why don't you tell him that, Buddy? It would mean a lot. You shoulda helped him do it a long time ago."

My father looked beaten, intimidated, and incredibly sad. I knew he would rather be on the moon than trapped here by Junior's huge, angry presence. All he could do was to stare at Junior, and to Daddy's credit he held Junior's fierce gaze.

Junior's temples were throbbing, and spittle was punctuating his words. "You don't like me tellin' you what to do, do you, Buddy?"

"No, I don't, Junior." My father's voice was flat, almost sleepy.

"All right, I ain't going to tell you what to do but I will say this: If there's any trouble down here while these folk trying to get registered, I won't offer you no advice. Won't say a goddamn thing. But don't be looking for me, or Sam Ford, or any other nigger in this county, when it's time to pick that three thousand acres of cotton you got fixin' to open out there. Same goes for gettin them two thousand acres of soybeans out the field. You'll just have to call on all . . . yo' . . . many . . . white . . . *friends* around here."

I was silently pleading for Junior to stop. Marvin was braver. "Junior, that's enough."

Junior jerked his head around at Marvin. "Nigger, *I'll* decide when I've said enough." He turned back to Daddy. "Or you can ask that fine boy of yours"—he waved his arm at me—"who they say you won't even talk to no more. *Goddamn it*, you lucky to have him. Some no-good cracker motherfucker tries to kill him and you ain't down on yo' knees thankin' God he's alive. I didn't get no boy, Buddy. If he was mine, I'd treat him better than that."

Junior stopped to swallow and catch his breath. "You a mighty smart guy, Buddy, but you clean forgot who yo' friends really are."

With that, Junior suddenly pivoted on his heel and strode out of the courthouse.

When the confrontation started, I thought Daddy had it coming. Junior told him what he should have heard long before. Daddy had deceived Junior—he led Junior to believe he was more sympathetic to black concerns than he actually was. But the crisis of the past few months, centered on Selma, had shown Junior that Daddy was cold to their cause. But why did Junior challenge him now—and try to humiliate him here?

Maybe because now that a power was coming down greater than what Daddy had, Junior could afford to speak the truth. I could see that Daddy just happened to be the guy in charge when the rules were changed. Is any human being really prepared to renounce immediately all that he had been taught to believe and then to accept gracefully and sincerely a contrary set of beliefs?

After Junior walked away and everyone had taken a couple of deep breaths, Daddy focused again on me. "Son, what the hell are you doing here? Y'all need to get out of here." I could hear the deep fatigue in his voice.

"We're leaving right now." But I had to say one thing. "It looks like all the registering is taking place without any trouble, Daddy." I wanted to tell him just to let it happen, to relax somehow, and I wanted to say I knew Junior's harsh and public words hurt. But that was all I could find to utter.

Daddy looked over at the line. "Yeah, so far. The folks are being real polite and orderly."

Clem Brown suddenly appeared in front of us. "Buddy, you need to have that nigger selling them peanuts arrested. This ain't the goddamn county fair in here."

"She's not causing any trouble." Daddy looked away from Brown. "It's hot and people are having to wait a long time."

"Shit, Buddy, you're just making it easy on these agitators. You going to bring in lounge chairs for 'em? Maybe serve 'em up a bait of chitlins?"

I wanted to slug Clem. Marvin knew; he put his hand on my elbow. Daddy scowled at Brown but said nothing, and then Brown went on. "We can get Mac in here and run a few of these agitators in the jail. Then the rest of 'em will scatter."

Daddy seemed to rouse himself. He glared at Clem. "*We* ain't got nothing to do with it, Clem. *I* run the courthouse, and you and McCallister know that. Anybody who starts harassing these people will end up in the federal pen. I ain't going to prison over this. Besides, it won't stop the registration for five minutes—probably speed it up. That woman with the peanuts ain't causin' any problem, you hear?"

"You're chickenshit, McKee."

"Your opinion, Clem. Your opinion."

Brown stalked off. Daddy watched him go and then turned to me and shook his head. "Shitass." I nodded my total agreement. He waved at Marvin and me. "Y'all get outa here."

Outside, Marvin shook his head, frowning. "Junior Jackson a goddamn bully. Just 'cause he bigger'n everybody else, he think he can tell everybody what to think."

"Doesn't mean he isn't right."

"He wadn't right 'bout everything. Somebody come in that courthouse and start some shit, that ain't Buddy's fault. Junior don't know all that other mess Buddy dealin' with—them federal men and that cracker—Shitass Brown." He looked away. "Junior right about some of it, but that don't mean that somebody shouldn't whip his fat black ass all the way to Detroit."

I had to laugh. "And who's going to do that?"

Marvin finally smiled. "Nobody I know."

Interlude II

1993

"Tommy, I didn't expect you to give up your Saturday morning to do yard work for me," said my mother, her spine as straight as ever, her hair cottony in the light autumn wind. Her blue eyes scanned me. "Aren't you going to the game?"

I had awakened that morning knowing that my mind was too unsettled to focus enjoyably for three hours on a football game—not to mention the hours to get to the stadium and back. That fall's scandal over a Crimson Tide player's contract with an agent had mushroomed into Watergate proportions, at least among my circle of friends, who had more important things to think about than Hillary Clinton's national health-insurance plan. In silent protest against behavior that sullied the memory of the previous year's national championship, I didn't even give my tickets away.

"Decided I'd rather clean gutters and enjoy the weather," I said.

The 60-degree air carried the faint scent of burning leaves, the work of some libertarian Birmingham suburbanite with a keen sense of how late November should smell, regardless of town ordinances. The morning light was yellow and subtle—plenty brilliant to highlight the glory of the auburn leaves on Mama's two backyard maples, but not bright enough to illuminate the monkey grass beneath them. Here and there across the sprawling back yard, patches of mums and carnations—yellow, purple, white—along with the never-say-die impatiens in red and lavender, broke the deep green of the zoysia.

I fetched a ladder and went to work, and Mama—as always unable to stay inside when work proceeded outdoors—positioned her gardening stool beneath me in front of a bed of coral and red snapdragons and began sending weeds to the great beyond.

She pointed her trowel across the yard. "Do you like the purple mums?"

"Yeah, I guess. I mean, it seems like they should be yellow or white, but they're interesting."

"You are such the traditionalist, Tommy. You don't like change, not even in the garden."

She smiled up at me as I pushed a wheelbarrow of gutter refuse past her. As she pointed to the compost pile against her back fence, I noticed the multiple shades of gray, white, and blonde in her bob cut. The lines on her neck told her age, but she still radiated natural beauty, especially when she was digging in the dirt.

"I could offer to make you my new chocolate cream cheese pie recipe, but I bet you want the same-old-same-old for your yardman's pay."

"You got it. I'll help whip the meringue."

My mother liked the idea that I cooked—and better than my sister the businesswoman.

When we had the pie in the oven and she had poured me a cup of coffee, she asked how things were going. I said fine and then paused, which elicited from her a long, silent gaze. She knew me well enough to know what my pauses meant. "Well, I been talking to this prosecutor." Randy Russell had spent most of the previous afternoon in my office.

I told her we were just about ready for the trial. "He had the transcripts of the original trial and we read through a lot of that. He told me what he was going to ask me when I get on the witness stand."

She sat regarding her hands, pondering this. I didn't know where she was in her thinking. Finally I asked. "Mama, how much do you think about 1965?"

"Very little."

"Do you try not to think about it?"

"No, it's just not that relevant now. I think about you and Cathy, the grandkids, my yard, my church work—what's important to me now."

She looked up at me and must have seen the skepticism evident on my face. She shook her head. "Really, that was an amazing time, a turning point in our lives, I know that. But I don't dwell on it now, and haven't in years."

"But it was so crucial to who we are."

"Not so much to me. To you, your daddy obviously, but not to me." She nodded and her eyes took on a distant look. "I see it as a blessing in many ways."

I met her eyes. "You have any regrets about leaving Eden Rise?"

"Best thing that ever happened to me." She responded to the question on my face. "I've lived a wonderful, peaceful life here. Good friends. Rewarding volunteer work. The thrill of seeing my grandkids grow up."

"You don't resent Eden Rise?"

"Well, I did at the time. But once I got away from that time, I let go."

"Some of those days in 1965 seem like yesterday to me."

She gave me the look of maternal love that could brighten my life when everything else around was dark as midnight.

"It was different for you men. That time was about power. Deciding which way the future was going to go. But not for me or Cathy and it wasn't that way for Brigid except she was dying and angry about the past and trying to correct it." She pushed back her chair and went to the stove.

Mama had a kind of fatalism, or faith: history happened to her, but it was beyond her control, and if at some level she knew that it shaped her present, it was about as relevant to her as yesterday's weather report. What mattered was what the weatherman said today.

"Look at that meringue, precious." She had put the egg custard on a cooling rack. "Give it ten minutes and you can have a piece."

I didn't share my mother's indifference to the past, but her lack of emotional engagement showed me another way to deal with what had happened to me. She had gone through the same events, and despite her disclaimer of any great investment, she had to worry about the safety of her children and her husband and thus she had everything at stake in 1965, whereas I only had to worry about myself.

In one of my first AA meetings, an old guy called Dave G. concluded an emotional meeting full of self-revelation with a declaration: "I'm not much—but I'm all I think about."

Maybe, Mama would say, we could choose what we think about in our self-absorption, and we might as well choose things that make us look forward.

27

DIXIE

My heart raced and my stomach churned as Daddy parked the station wagon in front of the Yancey County courthouse, a squat attempt at Greek Revival architecture that looked like a square silo had hooked on at the back. Marvin told me to stand close to the car. We would wait for Junior and Sam before we went into the courthouse. He assembled the group quickly, putting Junior, dressed in a dark-blue suit and tie and glowing with sweat in the morning heat, on my right. Daddy, also dressed for church, stood on the left. They ignored each other.

"I walk directly in front of Tom," Marvin instructed. "Sam, you stay close behind him." He looked at Mama and Cathy. "Ladies, y'all follow." As we approached the courthouse, a gang of reporters and photographers rushed over. It felt like a football team was charging me, and I had to steel myself.

"Tom, what are you going to tell the jury?"

"Why did he shoot Jackie?" As per Joe Black's orders, I said nothing.

"How 'bout you, Judge?"

Daddy's jaw was hard. "No comment." All the while, the photographers took pictures.

A large crowd of people, most of them black, covered the courthouse steps. Hundreds of eyes watched me as our group edged through the throng. I kept my eyes locked on the back of Marvin's head.

"'Scuse me. 'Scuse us." Marvin was polite but very firm. The crowd parted and grew quiet as we went through.

"God bless you, son."

It was a familiar voice, and when I looked in that direction, Reverend

Banks was nodding soberly at me. He was holding Orene's hand. She looked worried but then she smiled sweetly. My throat tightened and water filled my eyes. I just couldn't start to cry. I clenched my teeth and smiled at her through blurred vision.

The crowd was just as thick inside the courthouse, and we moved very slowly toward the stairs leading to the courtroom.

"Y'all let the nigger lover through."

The words slashed through the air, coming from a loud male voice in a clutch of whites standing to the side of the stairway on our right. I glanced that way and turned back to see Marvin glare at them. His right hand had slipped behind, up under his black jacket. He looked over his shoulder at Junior.

"Tighten in."

The man who had yelled stepped forward, in front of his group. "Look at the nigger lover and his niggers." The people behind him roared in laughter.

"Goddamn rednecks." It was Daddy.

"Be quiet, Buddy." Marvin kept his eyes locked on the white group as we moved past.

Joe Black was waiting on the landing of the second floor. When we got there, he reported that the lawyers were almost finished striking the jury. "So far, all white men—farmers, truck drivers, an insurance man, coupla retired guys. 'Bout what we expected."

I would have to wait outside the courtroom until I was called. There would be a witness before me. Marvin and I sat on a hard oak bench that looked like it might have been a church pew at one time. We watched Reverend Banks, Orene, and a contingent of colored people from Ruffin County enter the courtroom.

When anyone walked toward us down the tiled hall, all three black men fixed stares on him to see whether he represented a threat. To my surprise, Bill and Virginia McKee arrived. I imagined they were no happier than I was to be there. I guessed that Bebe might have commanded their presence. Bill shook my hand—and Marvin's. As they moved away, Marvin mugged at me in surprise.

"You're his only first cousin, Marvin," I said.

Over the next, interminable two hours, I almost continuously felt like I had to pee, and Marvin and I went to the men's room three times. Shortly before ten, a bailiff went down the hall to where a black man was sitting on another bench—the doctor who had examined me that night at St. Jude's.

"He'll tell how Jackie died," I said to Marvin, as the sick feeling of that night returned.

Sam offered me gum. "Junior, them folk down there on the first floor here for the trial?"

"Naw, they got them federal registrars here too. Saw a guy I know from the Masons, and he said they been running more than a hundred a day gettin' registered in this county. We registered more than a thousand colored in Ruffin County by last Friday."

"I was one of 'em," Sam said evenly as he unwrapped another stick of Juicy Fruit.

"What difference that going to make?" Marvin was looking at Junior.

"Lotta difference, pretty soon. This time next year, most voters around here be black."

"Y'all going to get a nigger sheriff?"

"Maybe. Or probate judge. County commissioner."

"What about you, Junior?" I said. "You going to run for something?" Bebe had gotten me thinking about blacks in office.

"I might. What you think about it?"

"Well, I think you'd be good. You're smart. People like you, look up to you."

"Ain't no whites look up to me."

"You might be surprised. You may not need any white votes to get elected if enough colored get registered. But I bet you'd get some."

"If the whites don't cheat on election day." Sam remained the skeptic.

"Going to be harder to steal elections now the government so involved in this registering," Junior said.

"They going to be doing whatever they can to hold power," Sam said. Junior nodded. "Sho', I know that."

Marvin blew a smoke ring. "You know something else. This time next year, shouldn't be no all-white juries in these counties. Jury gets picked off the vote list."

"Ain't no colored man on a jury going to vote to let this sonuvabitch"— Junior nodded toward the courtroom—"go free."

We sat silently for a while, but Junior didn't like the quiet. "Y'all see the pictures of all that shit in Los Angeles?"

A riot had been blazing for several days in the Watts section of Los Angeles. Huge fires had had been set, looting was rampant, and several had died. Riots seemed like something that should happen only in another country.

"You see how they thumbed they nose at King when he went out there?" Junior was looking at Marvin.

"Didn't surprise me," Marvin said. "Lotta folk in the ghetto think that nonviolence stuff is bullshit."

"Reckon that could happen in Chicago?" Junior looked worried.

"Could and probably will," Marvin said.

It was eleven o'clock when I heard a man and a woman approaching. I kept my eyes cast down, as usual, to avoid the stares of curiosity. But the woman's clicking heels stopped near me. I looked up.

"Hey, Dixie."

She said it very softly with a tentative smile on her face. She addressed the disbelief on my face by holding out her hand. When I extended mine, she pulled me off the bench. It was a long, tight hug with her shock of frizzy hair pressed hard against my chest. I didn't want to let go. She finally leaned her head back to look up at me.

"Geez, I hope you're glad to see me."

I looked at her wet eyes and then surveyed her face. She was wearing more make-up than I had ever seen on her. She tilted her head to the side. "You should say something now."

"I'm shocked you're here."

"Shocked. But you are—pleased? Angry?"

"Very pleased." I pulled her back to me and kissed the top of her head. I wanted to kiss more of her.

She let out a big sigh. "Right. Let's make some introductions. Tom, this is Mr. Hirschfeld, from the Anti-Defamation League of B'nai B'rith in Montgomery. He put me up last night." Mr. Hirschfeld, tall and solemn in black-framed glasses, shook my hand. I introduced everyone else to him and to Beth. She went around and shook each man's hand. "I've heard about all you guys." She pointed at Marvin. "Well, he had the most to say about you, Cousin Marvin."

"I believe I've heard about you, too, Miss Kaplan."

She arched her brow and turned to me. "You may have some explaining to do." When we sat down, she took my right hand and held it in both hers.

I was still amazed. "I can't believe you're here."

She laughed and shivered a little at the strangeness of it. "I can't either. It just happened. I asked Dad what he thought about me coming down on Friday, and he got on the phone and arranged the whole thing." When I asked Beth how Arthur knew Hirschfeld, she said, "Dad lends him money."

I was slow on the uptake and she stuck an elbow in my side to remind me to have a sense of humor. "He didn't, but Dad just called him up and explained the situation, and Mr. Hirschfeld offered to help. He's followed the case."

"Well, what do you think of Alabama so far?"

"The truth? It seems like a foreign country."

We gazed at each other for a long moment. "You look terrific," she said, "tanned and blonder than ever. *Very* handsome. How do you really feel?"

"Scared shitless."

"It's okay to be scared if you don't look like it." She kissed me on the cheek.

The courtroom door opened and the doctor emerged. He walked straight to me. "Mr. McKee, my prayers are with you."

I was about to reply when the bailiff appeared, looking stern. "Thomas McKee."

Panic rushed over me. Marvin leaned in to me very close and gripped my shoulder.

"You tough, and you going to go in there *be* tough."

Every seat in the small courtroom was filled, and people stood along the back walls. Low murmurs quickly died so that the sound of my dress shoes on the hardwood floors echoed around the room. The high windows were topped with arches. A chandelier hung near the center of the room. The tables and chairs were all of old wood, indifferently polished except for the oiled paneling around the judge's high perch. The abundance of bodies accounted for the stuffy air and the multiple smells—sweat and perfumes—that I inhaled as the bailiff led me to the front of the courtroom. Every pair of eyes settled on me as the bailiff swore me to tell the truth.

My family was gathered in the first row of public seating. Marvin sat on the aisle, his eyelids at half mast as he studied the whites directly across the aisle. Next to him, my parents looked frozen in their frontward stares. Cathy and Joe Black were more relaxed, each scanning the room. At the other end of the row, with William at her side, Bebe smiled at me from her wheelchair.

The jury sat within a wooden rail to my left, but I didn't let my eyes rest on them. Judge Saffold McKinley nodded down to me with a slight smile. He was about seventy, with thick white hair and tortoise-shell half-glasses and a distracted expression. On the far right of the room sat two rows of men in ties with reporters' notebooks. Sweat glistened on Cal Taliaferro's full face, and his hair positively shined from the abundance of hair cream.

At the defense table, Buford Kyle hardly resembled the man I remembered. He wore a suit, was freshly shaved, and had his hair slicked down. Crutches were propped against the table. Behind Kyle sat two young men with sunburnt faces and no ties, alongside three large women, all looking very resentful and uncomfortable in tight, flowered dresses. Kyle's family, I guessed.

"Mr. McKee, I'm Cal Taliaferro, and I'm going to ask you a few questions this morning. If the question isn't clear, just say so and I'll rephrase it, okay?" He asked for vital information and then about my education. "Valedictorian of your high school class, right?"

"Yes, sir."

"Captain of the basketball team, correct?"

"My senior year, yes, sir."

"You worked on your daddy's farm from the time you were a boy, didn't you?"

"Yes, sir."

"Belonged to the Future Farmers of America?"

"Yes, sir."

At this point, Kyle's lawyer stood. "Your honor, I'm going to object to this kind of questioning. It's not relevant to why we're here today."

Hubert Brophy stood very erect and well above six feet. I had to admire his carriage because he sported a substantial potbelly, enveloped that day in a blue-striped seersucker suit supported by red suspenders. My attention was drawn toward his large jowls by a bright red bow-tie. His tanned face was accented by half glasses. His hair receded, but on the sides was thick and silver, combed back.

Judge McKinley looked at Taliaferro. "Let's move it along, Cal."

"Tom, how'd you know Jackie Herndon?" I told the circuit solicitor how we had met playing basketball. "Would you say your relationship with him was similar to others you had with boys at college?"

Brophy rose swiftly to his feet, startling me. "OB-jection. He's leadin'." The judge overruled, without looking up.

"It was about the same except that we shared a special interest in basketball. Jackie was a fantastic basketball player. So we played a lotta ball together."

As I finished, I thought I sounded mealy-mouthed. Taliaferro was about to move to another question when I interrupted. "But we were true friends. He was my best friend."

My answer caused Kyle's family members to smirk and whisper. They were all shaking their heads toward one another. I guessed it was the very idea that your best friend might be colored that bothered them. I looked at Beth, who stood along the back wall. She was smiling.

"All right, now tell us how you came to drive Jackie Herndon to Alabama last May twenty-fourth."

I gave the "lean truth," omitting any details of Alma's behavior on the drive.

"So you stopped at the defendant's store to go the bathroom and get gas. Did you have a conversation with the defendant?" Taliaferro said.

I recounted what Kyle said about "goddamn freedom riders" and what I heard once Alma had entered the store. He took me through a move-by-move account of the shooting. He raised Kyle's shotgun high and asked why, after I had taken it, I had thrown it away.

"I thought if the police stopped me with it they would hold us. I needed to get Jackie to the hospital."

"Just to remind the jury, why did you drive through Yancey County on May the twenty-fourth?"

"Well, my friend needed a ride and I was going that way."

"Were either you or Jackie Herndon freedom riders?"

I said no. Taliaferro looked up at the judge. "Your honor, that's all. Reserve the right to re-direct."

The judge announced a break for lunch. My throat was dry and my head throbbed from the tension. Joe Black was immediately at my side. "You did good, son. Real good."

"But we haven't gotten to the hard part."

"Naw, you haven't. Remember, son, the lean truth."

28

NEGRO HISTORY

"Mr. McKee, I'm Herbert Brophy. You didn't tell us much about this colored girl, Alma Jones, who you also brought to Yancey County that day. Did you?" Taliaferro had not asked anything about her.

"No, sir."

"You describe yourself as the best of friends with Jackie Herndon. Were you also the best of friends with Alma Jones?"

"Well, no. I knew her just a little bit."

"But you knew she was the head of Snick, the Student Nonviolent Coordinating Committee, at your college?"

"Yes."

"You *did* know this SNCC does much of the outside agitation here in Alabama?"

"I knew it was a civil rights organization."

"I'll take that as a yes. Of course they're outside agitators." Brophy swept by the jury box, then turned back to me. "This Jones woman is from California, correct? 'Bout as far from Alabama as you can get and still be in the United States, right?"

"Almost."

"All the newspapers reported that you're a member of SNCC, didn't they?"

"Some did write that, but I wasn't."

"So you say *now*, Mr. McKee. Jackie Herndon was a member."

"I don't think so, but I don't know for sure."

"Well, sir, you may have been and he may have been, we just don't know, do we?

"I never was and I don't think he was."

"Y'all best friends and you don't know whether he belongs to a agitator organization? But it didn't make any difference to you, did it, if your best friend thought it was a good idea for radical blacks from all over the United States to come to your home state and start riots just so they can get their pictures in the *New York Times* or *Life* magazine?"

All the reporters were shaking their heads and whispering to one another. Taliaferro was on his feet. "Your honor, he's badgering the witness."

Judge McKinley looked at the jury. "Gentleman, disregard Mr. Brophy's speech right there." Then he looked at Brophy. "Counselor, questions, not speeches."

"Yes, your honor. Mr. McKee, this colored girl, was she your girlfriend or Herndon's, or did y'all share?"

"Irrelevant, your honor!" Taliaferro shouted.

"Answer the question, if you understand it, Mr. McKee."

"She wasn't my girlfriend or Jackie's."

"Was she a good-looking wench, well-built?"

I looked toward the judge, who shook his head at me. "Don't answer that question. Move on, counselor."

"But it is true, isn't it, that in these so-called civil rights organizations, the niggers and whites all fornicate together? We found that out during the Selma march. Didn't you and Herndon plan on making Alma y'all's girlfriend once you got her down to Camden?"

Taliaferro threw his hands up in the air. Joe Black leaned over the rail and whispered in the circuit solicitor's ear. He had seen the smiles among the jurors as Brophy baited me. Constant objections just belabored the discussion of sex.

"No, sir, I was going to drop her off and go on to Eden Rise. I was just giving her a ride."

"You and Herndon didn't have plans to bed her down when you got to Camden?" He shook his big head in a great show of disbelief. "You under oath, son."

The courtroom seemed to be getting hotter by the minute. "No, sir."

He smirked. "Well, what do you say they were going to do in Camden?"

I explained about the Freedom School, keeping it lean.

"Freedom School! You mean you agitators didn't think that the state of Alabama and the good people of Wilcox County weren't providing enough *freedom* in the public schools?"

"Well, I think that was just the name of the school. I think they were just going to provide some classes in subjects like Negro history. Jackie was going to teach science."

In 1965, the very act of pronouncing the word Negro correctly was taken as a challenge to segregation. I had pronounced the word correctly.

"*Knee-grow* history?" He pirouetted in front of the jurors. "Well, I'll be a monkey's uncle, *Knee-grow* history. The very idea." There was laughter from the jury box. "Tell us about *Knee-grow* history, Mr. McKee. And, hey, don't be shy either. Begin back over there in Africa when the *Knee-grows* were running around naked, eatin' each other, worshipin' thunder."

"I was told that's what they were going to do. I didn't know any more about it than that."

Brophy had leaned against the jury box and wiped his sweaty forehead with a red bandana. "*Knee-grow* history," he said in a low tone to the jurors, a confidential derision of me and all that I represented.

"Well, I guess I'm just confused, Mr. McKee." He put on a sarcastic smile. "You and Jackie Herndon were the best of friends, but you hardly knew this agitator woman and you didn't know anything about SNCC. How do you explain this?" He was holding up a newspaper clipping, the story on the Selma sympathy march in Durham.

I could feel sweat running from my armpits down my ribs as I told the lean truth about that. As I spoke, a thin smile arose on Buford Kyle's face.

"Well, did y'all succeed in agitating up a lot of violence at your college like SNCC does here in Alabama? That's the whole point, isn't it?"

"No, sir. We didn't want any trouble, and there wasn't any trouble. We didn't bother anybody, and nobody bothered us."

"I guess that made it a failure then. What was your SNCC group sympathetic to?"

"Like I said, I wasn't a member of SNCC. But these people marching, we were sympathetic to the colored people in Selma who got beat up on the bridge." I had to say that much, and I was glad to say it.

Brophy moved to the witness box and and put a foot on it, so close to me that I smelled his Old Spice and a sweet pipe tobacco. "So you are sympathetic to *thousands of niggers* and their *outside agitator* friends demanding immediate voter registration so they can *take over* any county in Alabama they want to?"

Having thrown that incendiary bomb from close range, he moved back to the jury box.

I finally faced the twelve men directly. Several sunburned faces, only one circled by a tie, and they all fixed me with hard stares.

Taliaferro was on his feet. "Objection, your honor. He's trying to do the testifying."

"Sustained. Move on, Mr. Brophy."

"Well, let me put it to you this way, Mr. McKee: What about the situation in Selma were you sympathetic to?"

The full truth was this: I went on the sympathy march because I was furious at the bigoted Sigma Nus who tried to tell me what to think. But how could I say in court that I protested because I was catching shit from some other fraternity boys? That was so convoluted, and it would sound so lame. Finally, it came to me.

"I was sympathetic to colored people voting if they met the qualifications. I knew that a lot of them could meet the requirements if whites would let them try."

A couple of jurors shook their heads. Brophy picked up on that and shook his too. "How do you know that whites wouldn't let them try, when you're off up there in North Carolina with your SNCC friends?"

I looked up at the judge. "I hadn't finished answering the other question when he asked me that one."

"All right, son, finish your answer."

"I was sympathetic to the Selma people because they got beat to the ground and trampled by horses just because they wanted to walk down a highway in the state they lived in. All white people in Alabama aren't thugs. I thought I oughta be ready to say I disapproved of treating anybody that way, black or white."

"Well, you're quite the bleeding heart, Mr. McKee."

Brophy was back close to me when he said it, and then he quickly turned and started walking away.

"I'm not—"

Brophy looked back over his shoulder and pointed at me. "I didn't ask a question."

The gavel hit the judge's desk so hard it made me jump. Judge McKinley raised it again and pointed it at Brophy. "Counselor, one more speech and you're in contempt. It'll be $500 and tonight in jail. You hear me?"

He didn't look up when he said, "Yes, your honor." Judge McKinley asked if I wanted to respond to Brophy's bleeding heart comment. My adrenaline had surged.

"I'm not a bleeding heart. I just was taught that bullies shouldn't win. I thought if people in Selma were willing to treat folks like that, they had asked for trouble and they got it."

"Did you go on the Selma march?" Brophy shouted it from his table.

"No." Watch out. Brophy might know something. "But I watched the end of it at the capitol."

"Oh, you did? You were one of the marchers?" The smirk badly disguised his joy.

"No, I didn't march. I just heard the speech at the end."

"You mean the speech given by Martin Luther Coon—excuse me, King?" All the jurors laughed. It was the most common of all racist jokes in Alabama. "Well, what'd you think?"

"It was a good speech."

"You thought King gave a good speech?"

"Yes, that's what I thought."

Brophy smiled, believing, I knew, that the jury would hate me for what I had just said.

"Let's go back to my earlier question: How do you know that whites wouldn't let the niggers try to get registered to vote, when you were off up there in North Carolina?"

"I knew from personal experience that whites in the Black Belt counties kept colored people from getting registered."

"And just what personal experience made you know that?" I immediately knew I shouldn't have said it, but it was too late to take it back. "I know that in Ruffin County there have been only a handful of colored people who are registered to vote. And the county is way more than half colored."

"You didn't consider that most niggers in your county are ignorant or criminal or both?"

I looked at Brophy and suddenly felt very tired. I was losing the energy I needed to control the repulsion, and all that was left was just anger.

"I didn't consider that because it's not true. Most of the colored people I've ever known in Ruffin County are good people and good citizens. They've been kept from voting so the whites could have complete control."

"That's your opinion, boy. Yours and Lyndon Johnson's."

I did not take that bait. Brophy shook his head in disgust. "I guess you approve of the way these federal registrars are here in this county today, in this very courthouse, registering ignorant niggers as fast as they can make an X on a sheet of paper, so the niggers can go to the polls in a herd and take over Yancey County. That's perfectly fine with you, isn't it?"

Taliaferro stayed silent in his seat.

"Mr. Brophy, I don't know anything about politics in this county. I do know that in Ruffin County, there are a lot of colored people registering to vote for the first time, because this is the first time they thought they had a realistic chance to do it. I don't know what they intend to do with their votes, but knowing a good many of them, I'm not too worried. They've got good sense."

At that point, I looked away from Brophy and over at the jury. Several jurors displayed pure hostility, but others held my gaze blankly. What were they thinking?

Orene was dabbing her eyes with a handkerchief, and when she saw me looking, she waved the hanky at me. My throat swelled tight. I reached for the glass of water on the rail but my hand was shaking so bad I was afraid I'd drop the glass. I tucked my hand back in my lap.

Brophy flipped his legal pad on the table in front of his chair and moved behind Buford Kyle. He put his hand on Kyle's shoulder. "Mr.

McKee, you've got all kinds of sympathy for every nigger in Alabama but you think it's okay to kill Buford Kyle."

"No, sir, that's not true."

"But you did shoot to kill Buford Kyle, didn't you?"

"I shot at Mr. Kyle to try to keep him from killing all of us." I struggled not to scream my answer at Brophy. "As it was, he did kill Jackie. He was aiming at me when I shot him."

"Well, that's your story. We'll get the real story in a while. Let's talk about this gun." He picked up the pistol I had used and walked toward me holding it. "You intentionally brought this gun with you to Yancey County that day, didn't you?"

"Well, not intentionally."

"Well, did one of these other agitators sneak it into your car?"

"No, sir. The gun was in the car when my grandmother gave it to me after my grandfather died. But nobody knew that he had kept the gun under the seat of the car. I didn't know it was there until I discovered it by accident one day up at school."

"But you left it there, didn't you, so you would have it handy when you went on your little nigger-agitation joyride through Alabama?"

"No, sir. I didn't have anyplace else to put it, so I left it under the seat, and then I pretty much forgot about it."

"Forgot about it? *Forgot about it?* Yeah, you forgot about it until you needed to shoot somebody who got in your way in Ruffin County."

"No, sir, that's not right. It just happened to be there."

"Nobody just forgets about a loaded pistol in his car, Mr. McKee. Don't treat the good people of Yancey County like they're stupid."

Taliaferro stood up. "He's badgering the witness and testifying too, your honor."

"Move on, Mr. Brophy."

"You meant to kill Buford Kyle, didn't you?" Brophy said. "You went to his store, gun in hand, to teach Mr. Kyle a little lesson in nigger-loving, didn't you?"

"No, sir. We just happened to stop at his store, and he got enraged about us being there and turned his shotgun on us."

"You went in the store with your pistol drawn to show this man that the agitators are the bosses now, didn't you?"

"No, sir, I never had the gun inside the store. I only got the gun out *after* he had shot at us twice, *after* he had fired the shots that killed Jackie Herndon. I got out the pistol only to stop him from shooting at us anymore." I paused to calm myself. "And I did. I stopped him from shooting us anymore. I'm sorry I had to shoot him to make him stop. But he didn't leave me any choice."

"But nevertheless, he's the one crippled on crutches today, isn't he?"

"I'm sorry about that, but Jackie Herndon is dead today, Mr. Brophy."

"And you drove him to the place where he got killed, didn't you?"

I looked down at my trembling hands. "Yes, I did."

Brophy paused a long moment. "That's all I have, your honor."

The judge looked down at me with either curiosity or sympathy, I didn't know which. "Any re-direct, Mr. Taliaferro?"

"Yes, sir, just a couple of questions. Tom, could you in fact have killed Mr. Kyle?"

"Yes, I guess I could have."

"Why didn't you? He had tried to kill you and did kill Jackie Herndon."

"I didn't want to. I needed to get Jackie to the hospital."

"No more questions, Judge."

"Mr. McKee, you're excused."

I was startled that it was over. I rose slowly, not knowing where I should go. I walked past the two lawyers' tables and toward the back of the courtroom. But suddenly the anguish and tension I felt erupted deep within me, and I knew exactly where I needed to go.

29

Damn Champion

I trotted down the hall with Marvin in close pursuit and went straight to the toilet. I dropped to my knees and threw up. Marvin stood over me and held my necktie back. When I finally stopped dry-heaving, I began to gasp for breath. He pulled me to my feet and jerked a long strand of toilet paper off the roll. He had begun to wipe the puke off when I started to sob.

"It's going to be all right, Tommy. You going to be fine."

"I'm sorry. Shit. I'm a mess. I don't know what's wrong with me."

"Built-up tension, baby, that's all." He was gently wiping the tears from around my eyes. "You was a damn *champion* in there. You kept control when you had to but that tension had to get out. Now take some deep breaths and use this paper to blow your nose."

He led me to the sink and instructed me to wash out my mouth and gargle.

Just then Junior's voice came in through the door. "Marvin, y'all all right?"

"Yeah, we good. See if Sam got more that gum and bring it here, okay?"

Junior returned with the pack and Marvin put three pieces of Juicy Fruit in my mouth.

"Yo' eyes real red." He reached in his pocket and put his sunglasses on me. He stepped back and looked, and then he plucked them off. "Naw, makes you look like mafia."

I let out a half-sob, half-chuckle.

He put his hands on my shoulders. "You all right. You strong. Ever' *damn* body knows it. Keep yo' head up, don't look at nobody, don't say nothin.'"

Somehow my brain focused on Marvin's gentle ministrations in the courthouse bathroom, holding the sweetness of that moment so I could ignore the pain and ugliness of what happened in the courtroom and what had happened to put me there.

Joe Black met me in the hall. "Son, you did a great job."

"I probably said too much about the march."

"Naw. It didn't matter. Didn't matter. Once Brophy confronted you, you stayed strong. He ever thought he could run over you, it woulda been a lot worse. Everybody in that courtroom saw for a fact you tellin' the truth, whether they agree or not. I'm tellin' you—a *beautiful* damn job. Couldna been better if I'da testified myself."

That was an ironic observation, given how I parroted his answers.

Cathy had discovered Beth and invited her to stay with us. Mama told Beth she wished she could have visited under less stressful circumstances.

"You mean you guys don't do this every day?" Beth said.

William rolled Bebe up to me. "Come here, sweet boy," she said weakly, "and let me kiss you. I am *so* proud of you."

As we left the courthouse, I was peppered with questions from reporters waiting outside. Joe Black stopped and told them that I couldn't talk, but he would answer a few questions. I wondered where the reporters were from, and as we got in the car Mama said she'd overheard someone say they were from New York and Washington and Los Angeles.

Beth sat in the backseat between Marvin and me. "I'm sure the ones from New York are real gentlemen." Daddy mumbled something. "I'm sorry but I didn't hear that, Judge McKee."

Mama looked over the backseat and winked. "He said he thought you were right, Beth."

We rode along in exhausted silence for a few minutes, but Beth wanted to chat. She looked at Marvin. "Tom tells me you are a very dangerous guy. Is that true?"

Marvin's eyes danced. "Very, very dangerous."

"Do you expect to have to kill anybody today?"

"Could be. It's still early."

"Do you have any particular hostility to short Jewish women with New York accents?"

"I don't like 'em."

She stared at him a moment. "Me neither. In fact, I hate 'em."

Marvin started laughing. "How'd you know that man who brought you here?"

"All Jews know each other. It's like one big happy family."

"Niggers are like that too."

"The word is *Knee-grow*. Didn't you hear the nice man in the courtroom lecturing about *Knee-grow* history?" She looked at me. "You told me Cousin Marvin was dangerous but you didn't tell me how good-looking he is. I guess it runs in the family."

She turned back to Marvin. "You got lots of women, huh?"

"More than I can deal with."

"That was always Tom's problem, too."

I rolled my eyes at her. "You're treading on thin ice." She leaned into me and looped her arm through mine.

"Come on, we all need a laugh to relieve a tense day. That and a lot of whiskey, I'd say."

And, in an uncharacteristic gesture, Mama offered everyone Jack Daniels when we got to Eden Rise. Daddy didn't say much, but he did smile at several of Beth's cracks.

Out on the patio, Marvin, Beth, and I were having a second drink—and our last one, Mama assured us—when Beth fixed me with a studious gaze.

"You look so much older than you did this time last year. Five years older—out of the eyes. Last year you had these innocent, open, *big* eyes. Now, they're still blue and pretty, but somehow they're more hooded, or squinty. They cut and dart more."

After Mama and Daddy went to bed, we slipped a radio out on the patio. Cathy and Marvin started dancing. At midnight, Marvin announced to Cathy that Beth and I needed some time alone. Sitting under the stars, we necked vigorously, but she stopped us from going further; she would be mortified, she said, if we got caught doing it.

"Tom, after all this is over, what's going to happen to Marvin?" Marvin had told me he didn't want to go back to the old neighborhood, but he'd not brought up any other plan—other than a tentative willingness to go on the run with me. I took a deep breath and told Beth about that. She'd come all this way to see me; she needed to know.

She frowned. She understood my fear of prison but worried about what becoming a fugitive would do to me. "But then I guess I would worry more what prison would do to you. Shitty choices. Maybe I'll go with you on the road—sell beads in San Francisco or something."

"Yeah, right," I said. "And I'll explain to your parents that their brilliant future-doctor gave up college to hang with hippies and fugitives." Secretly, at that moment, it was what I wanted.

She looked up at the scattered stars, then turned back to me and gave me her wide, white smile. "Let's think positive. Assume you don't have to go to prison *or* on the lam. Will Marvin just drift away from you?"

I suddenly knew that I wanted Marvin to stay connected to us. I was sure Cathy would want that, and Mama saw the best in him. "He feels to me like I imagine having an older brother would feel. I mean, he can be so violent, but I think he's basically a good person."

"Well, he doesn't have to be a good person to belong to your family."

"Daddy will be very uncomfortable with it. Maybe worse than that."

"I think you guys could use a little variety in this family."

"What do you mean? A dose of color, African blood?"

"No, some new names. One Thomas McKee after another. Geez, it gets boring."

30

Surprise Witness

An even bigger crowd thronged the courthouse the next morning: More blacks, more whites, more reporters and photographers. Two television cameras patrolled the front steps. Marvin led us to the courthouse in the same formation as the day before, and I steeled myself for an assault from the press. But my self-protection was unnecessary, because reporters were focused on a young black man speaking into a half-dozen microphones. Marvin was advancing past the speaker when I tugged the hem of his coat. "Slow down."

"The Student Nonviolent Coordinating Committee is here," the young man was saying, "to protest the murder of another Negro taking a stand for Negro rights. Jackie Herndon did *not* deserve to die, and we are here to see that he did not die in vain."

"No, he did not!"

"Yeah!"

"That's right!"

The shouts came from a crowd of perhaps a hundred blacks standing around him, many younger than the black people at the trial the day before. The speaker was tall and thin and spoke with an accent that originated outside the South.

"We expect Jackie's murder to be avenged. We ain't going to accept no cracker justice in Yancey County!"

"Hell, no!"

"We going to make our feelings known, right?"

"Yes!"

"The Student Nonviolent Coordinating Committee wants everybody here to show solidarity by puttin' on a black armband for the rest of the trial." Two young men moved through the crowd handing out armbands. "It's important to sit through this trial. We gotta support our sister who will testify today." I thought he meant one of the nurses from St. Jude's.

"And then you got to wait for the verdict, so we can demonstrate our concern about whether this man will be punished for killing our brother." Someone came up and whispered in his ear, and the young man nodded. "We have already run out of arm bands. If you didn't get one, here's what do: Get you a handkerchief and tie it around your arm or your neck to let everybody know you care about what is going down around here."

Marvin resumed our advance into the courthouse at that point. Inside we passed a group of white onlookers. "Over here, nigger lover." I looked in the direction of the voice and saw a young white man giving me the finger. Junior saw it and growled. "Pick it up, Marvin."

Outside the courtroom, Joe Black waited for us, typically gregarious in his greeting, but turning serious as he pulled our group into a corner. "Circuit solicitor tells me he's callin' Alma Jones."

Shit. "How did that happen?"

"Taliaferro got a call saying she wanted to testify. Said she was in his office yesterday after court. He thinks it's part of a publicity stunt by SNCC, and he doesn't want to put her on, but Brophy knew about it somehow, and he let Taliaferro know he would call her if Cal didn't."

"Brophy wants to show the jury a troublemaker, doesn't he?"

"That's right, Tommy. She's the face of the outside agitator, and her face is black. It's cynical as hell, but in his place I'd probably do the same thing."

"And why is Taliaferro going along?"

"He just can't ignore a material witness. Be way more criticism than Cal can take."

Because I was done testifying, I was allowed to sit in the courtroom today, but I couldn't face it again, nor could I bear to see Alma again. The last time I was with her, I wanted to beat the hell out of her. "Joe Black, I don't think I can go in there."

"Yeah, you can, son. Can't let anybody down here think you got anything to be ashamed of. Everybody will notice if you not there. Go on in. She ain't going to say nothin' to hurt you."

We found seats near the front. Every black person wore an armband or a handkerchief. When the jurors were seated, all of them eyeing the crowd and the menacing armbands, Taliaferro called Alma. My stomach fluttered as she strode to the front in black silk pants and a black blouse. She towered over the man administering the oath.

Marvin nodded. "Uh-hunh. All right. I see what you sayin' 'bout the sister."

Cathy leaned in. "She's not your type, remember?"

As soon as Taliaferro greeted Alma, Brophy was on his feet. "I object to the witness wearing that armband. If she's a witness here to tell the truth, she doesn't need to be making any agitator protest with her dress." I hated Brophy, but I had to appreciate how he had figured out a way to turn the jury against her before she opened her mouth.

Judge McKinley studied Brophy and then turned to the witness. "Young lady, would you mind taking that off?"

She looked up at the judge and studied him as long as he had gazed at Brophy. Finally she nodded. She slowly pulled the band off her arm. The courtroom was buzzing by the time she finished. But while Taliaferro was getting her name and address, she had pulled out a white handkerchief, which she used first to dab her forehead, and then she looped it around her neck.

Brophy was back on his feet. "She's still doing it, now with that handkerchief." There were giggles and twitters around the courtroom. The judge swung his head around and looked down at Alma again. Then he returned his gaze to the legal pad on the desk in front of him.

"Overruled."

I asked Joe Black if he knew what she was going to say. "I ain't sure Cal knows," he said.

Taliaferro asked her if Jackie was a member SNCC, and she said no. Was I a member?

"No. Tom wasn't in SNCC. He was just giving us a ride."

Taliaferro got her to tell what happened at the store. "I asked him"—she pointed at Kyle—"where the toilet was, and he said they didn't have one, which I knew was a lie." Every gas station she had ever been in had restrooms. She and Kyle had argued about that, and then he got his gun. She was leaving the store when he started shooting.

Taliaferro asked her what Jackie was doing.

"He was leading me to the car." Leading? Pulling her was more accurate.

"Did Jackie Herndon attack Mr. Kyle?"

"No. I don't think he said a word to him."

"Did Tom McKee attack Mr. Kyle?"

"No."

"But he shot Mr. Kyle?"

"Tom McKee shot the man after he had hit us at close range with two blasts from a shotgun—and after he was shooting at us again."

"Tom McKee did not shoot first?"

"No. Absolutely not. Only after that man had already hit us."

She looked down at her lap for a moment. "Tom was very brave. He saved my life and he tried to save Jackie's."

It hadn't occurred to me that I would get any acknowledgment from Alma.

Taliaferro turned Alma over to Brophy.

"Well, I'm glad you and your good friend Tom got your stories straight," he began.

She looked startled. "I didn't—we didn't—"

Joe Black leaned over my shoulder. "I knew Cal should have cleared it up that y'all hadn't talked since the shooting. Blunder."

"Tell me 'bout this so-called freedom school. What kinda freedom were y'all going to be teachin' down there? Free love? Free welfare? Free run of the courthouse?"

"Objection."

"I'll rephrase."

He looked at his legal pad. "You from California, right, Alma?" He moved over to the jury box. "There's a lot of freedom out in California, right?"

Alma kept her face tight. "I don't know what you mean."

"Well, now, girlie, don't play dumb just 'cause you in Alabama. They's all kinda freedom out there in California we ain't got here Alabama. You got your movie stars—they always marryin' and divorcin' and swappin' wives. Freedom to sleep with whoever you want."

Several jurors were smiling.

"Again, I don't know what you mean."

"Take that nigger singer, Sammy Davis, Jr. He's got a white wife, hasn't he?"

Alma rolled her eyes. "Yes."

"These movie stars, they like comin' down here to the South tellin' us how we oughta live, don't they?"

"I don't know what you are referring to."

"Now, honey, remember you under oath to tell the truth."

Alma turned at that point and looked up at the judge. "I don't appreciate being called 'girlie' and 'honey.' He should address me with respect."

The judge looked at her for a moment and sighed. He turned to Brophy. "Counselor, address the witness as Miz Jones or ma'am and leave off the pet names, you understand?"

Brophy didn't look at the judge. "Is it not true that your major nigger movie stars like Harry Belafonte and Sidney Poitier have come from California to tell Southerners how to live?"

"I know that those men have participated in the civil rights movement."

"Agitators, they agitators, just like you."

"Not agitators, activists."

"When a California nigger comes to Alabama to stir up trouble, they become agitators."

"I don't think so." Alma was trying hard to sound reasonable, unprovoked. It was almost working, but I could hear the anger edging through and guessed the jury heard it too. I knew exactly how she felt. "Now, are you from the part of California they call Watts?"

"No, I'm from northern California."

"But you know where Watts is, a little to the south, right?"

"About four hundred miles away."

"But close enough to home for you to be aware of what's been happening there, right?"

"There have been civil disturbances."

"*Civil disturbances.* Is that what you said? Civil disturbances. The niggers in Los Angeles been trying to burn down the city and kill any whites who get in the way."

"Mr. Brophy, either ask a question or move on." The judge said it while looking at Taliaferro, whose failure to protect his witness was glaring by this time.

"Your honor," Alma said before Brophy had a chance to go on, "I object to his use of the word nigger. He should refer to my race correctly." You had to admire her guts.

"Mr. Brophy, refrain henceforth from the use of that word in this courtroom."

Brophy looked at the judge but said nothing. He turned back to Alma. "My question is this: Why does somebody from California need to come to Alabama to stir up trouble when you got all the trouble you need right there at home?"

Alma was shaking her head, looking up at the judge, and smiling incredulously. "I can't believe this." When the judge did nothing, she turned back to face Brophy.

"People from around the country come to Alabama to protest attitudes like yours, because your racial hatred is a sickness that has to be stopped."

Alma had been a good witness up to that point, but Brophy had now goaded her into making a sweeping statement that would surely inflame the jurors. It was exactly what he wanted. They jousted back and forth in much the same way for the rest of the day. Alma, having lost her cool, played the part that Brophy wanted her to—the angry, intolerant, anti-Southern black agitator. It got boring and ridiculous, and none of it had anything to do with May 24 and the death of Jackie Herndon.

Court was adjourned when her testimony finally ended. As Alma was headed out of the courtroom, she paused at my seat. "Are you okay, Tom?" She looked tentative, even nervous, whereas she had seemed self-confident while under attack from Hubert Brophy.

I didn't know what to say. We shouldn't be enemies—should never have been. It was just a day that went horribly wrong. I could have said, "No. I'm not okay. My life is completely fucked up. My future is ruined, and my family is all but destroyed over this." But we both had to live with what had happened, and I doubted that she had done much more than I had to figure out how to do that. So I said, "Yeah. Pretty good. You?"

A deep crease marked her brow. "I'm really sorry about what happened."

"Me, too."

"I guess I won't be seeing you again. I'm transferring to Berkeley this fall."

"Well, I hope you like it there. Good luck."

She smiled faintly and nodded, and then she moved on, to be enveloped by the SNCC people as she left the courtroom, all of whom had helped us lose this battle in the name of winning the war. But it meant a lot to me that she said what she did. I'd needed to release my anger at her, and after that day, just by exchanging a few words with her, my fury was gone. I still knew that through her headstrong lack of common sense, she had precipitated Jackie's death, but I didn't blame her so much after that. As lousy a witness as she was, I was glad she had been there to say that one thing about me, that I had saved her life—and tried to save Jackie's.

My parents and Marvin were escorting me out of the courtroom when I ran straight into the reporter from the *Washington Post* whom I had met in Daddy's office. Two other reporter-types stood beside him. "What did you think of Alma Jones's testimony?" he said.

Joe Black moved in. "We thought her testimony fully corroborated what Tom said about the shooting. As for her views on people and politics in Alabama, we don't have any comment."

"What do *you* say, Tom?"

Again I didn't answer immediately, which then gave Beth the opportunity to tag-team with Joe Black. "Hey, aren't you from New York?" she said to the *Post* reporter. "You sure sound like it. So am I." She held out her hand. "Beth Kaplan, from Wantagh on Long Island. College friend of Tom's. Man, this is some amazing stuff down here, isn't it?"

As Marvin herded us out of the courthouse and into the car, I watched her banter with the three reporters. She gave them her full analysis of race relations in the South, based on one day of observation. "That's

Kaplan with a K," she said as I reached over and shut the car door. "I'll be looking for what you guys say about me."

There would be editorials from Atlanta, New York, and Los Angeles that were vitriolic in their condemnation of the Yancey County jury—and of "Alabama justice" in general. Herbert Brophy's racist remarks were quoted at length and made to represent the dominant opinion in Alabama, though all the editors noted that I defended Jackie. Many newspapers carried cartoons lampooning Alabama's bigoted lawyers and Negro-hating jurors. We had it coming. We flout all notions of justice, and they scorn us.

THE NEXT DAY BUFORD Kyle took the witness stand.

"Never said nothin' 'bout no freedom riders." Buford Kyle shook his head at Brophy.

"You didn't say whites shoulda killed all these agitators when they came to Alabama?"

"Naw. That boy just made all that up. He's a liar."

"Well, what made you use the shotgun?"

"That nigger girl tried to git it and kill me, but I helt on to it."

"How did this boy Herndon get involved?"

"He come at me to git the gun and he was so big I had to shoot at him to protect myself."

"What did the white boy do—McKee?"

"He was wavin' that pistol at me, threatening to kill me, and I had to shoot to stop that."

"Did you mean to kill the nigger boy?"

"No, I didn't want to, but hit was three of 'em. Had to shoot to protect myself."

I leaned over to Joe Black. "You know these are all damned lies."

He shook his head. "Some them jurors know it, but we see if they'll stand up and say so."

In his cross-examination, Taliaferro suggested some skepticism about Kyle's account but didn't go after him point by point. When I complained about Taliaferro, Joe Black shrugged.

"Cal pulled his punches," he said in a low voice. "He lives here, these people elected him. He doesn't think they going to convict Kyle. He ain't going to scrape any skin off his ass."

Taliaferro's short closing argument barely summarized the evidence against Brophy. He read it from a legal pad to signal, it seemed to me, that he was only going through the motions.

Hubert Brophy, on the other hand, used a full hour to re-tell the history of Northern aggression against the South since 1830. How, I wondered, did Wilson's raid through Alabama in 1865 have anything to do with this case except to stir the jurors with images of Yankees' setting fires to Alabama property? He went on and on about "carpetbaggers and scalawags abusing loyal white men" during Reconstruction, but then he did connect those troublemakers to the latter-day carpetbaggers Jackie Herndon and Alma Jones, who were on their way to stir up trouble among "the peaceable niggers in this state." I was a scalawag and maybe the worst of the lot because I had grown up here and should have known better than to get involved in this outside agitation. "Don't blame his mama and daddy," Brophy said. "I'm sure they did their dead-level best with the boy. He went up North and fell in with the wrong bunch. But he's old enough to know better, and we can't excuse it if he comes back down home fulla lies and *hate*."

I glanced at Mama and saw her eyes locked on Brophy. If ever I'd seen *hate*, there it was on her face. Her twitch was jumping to double-quick time.

Brophy then concluded with a long recounting of the atrocities perpetrated by outside agitators during the past few years. The jury looked transfigured, as if a tent-revival evangelist had just given them their first description of hell.

Later, outside the courtroom waiting for the verdict, Joe shook his head when I ranted about Brophy. "That's the system, Tommy my man. Freedom of speech is also the freedom to propound pure, stinkin' shit. And you might think that it don't work, but it does, I'm afraid—when you're a George Wallace demagogue, people listen, and they heed. Wallace, he'll soap it up with some code words, but ol' Brophy can't afford to soft-sell. Gotta spread that race shit out there pure to save his client."

Daddy paced at the other end of the hall, smoking one Pall Mall after another. I figured he wanted Kyle acquitted because he thought it would mean I wouldn't go on trial. Mama saw him and shook her head sadly.

After three hours, Joe Black stood up and rubbed his hands together. "Well, they been going long enough now for me to know that somebody on the jury isn't comfortable with turnin' Kyle loose. I'll be shocked, but stranger things have happened."

Mama shrugged. "Justice for a dead colored boy would be a strange thing here."

About an hour later, we were told that the jury was coming back, and we returned to the courtroom. None of jurors looked my direction. The judge looked over his half-glasses at Kyle. "The defendant will rise." Kyle took a crutch and slowly hoisted himself up. "Mr. Foreman." The lone juror wearing a tie rose. "What say you in the matter of the charge of manslaughter against Buford Kyle for the death of Jackie Herndon?"

The foreman glanced at Kyle and then turned toward the judge. "Not guilty."

Kyle's family burst into shrieks and tears. They were hugging and laughing. The sound was loud static in my ears, provoking a surge in my blood pressure and sending pain through my temple. Their feelings didn't look like regret or relief or quiet thankfulness at their good luck in having an equally racist jury, but joy at having killed somebody and gotten off scot-free. Now, with the clamor breaking around me, I was enraged all over again at what had happened to Jackie, and I felt a new horror at the realization I was next to be prosecuted in a place devoid of any notion of justice. Poor Jackie. Dead, gone, and probably soon forgotten.

We hurried out into a wall of press people, all shouting questions about the jury's decision. "No comment, no comment," Daddy said over and over. We had almost made it to the car when a photographer kneeled directly in front of us and took a picture pointing up at me.

"*Goddamn it.*" Daddy took a quick step forward and kicked the camera hard, knocking it back into the photographer's face and toppling him over backward. "Get outa the way!" He was almost on the photographer when Marvin grabbed his arm and held him back. The photographer scrambled out of the way, blood on his forehead above his broken glasses.

"I'm so sick of this shit, I really am," he yelled, as Mama led him to the car.

Daddy had said almost nothing during the trial. I had expected him to be happy, or at least relieved, with the verdict. But looking at him then, he seemed only distraught.

BETH STAYED ANOTHER DAY after the trial. She never stopped trying to comfort me, continuously talking to me about courage as an end in itself even when it didn't overcome injustice. I appreciated it, but finally told her we needed to talk of something else. So in the morning, I showed her the green expanses of crops, their leaves shining from the dew just before it evaporated. We walked out into a field of cotton, and I pointed out the scarlet blooms that would turn into hard green bolls. I made her take off her shoes and bury her feet in the soil deep enough to feel the cool. We examined a field of soybeans, their dense stems and leaves making them even more verdant than cotton.

"I don't get this, Tommy. You must have enough bean plants out here to feed the whole United States, and I've never eaten a single soybean." I explained to her about cooking oil, food processing, and a billion hungry Asians.

"You really love all this farming stuff, don't you? Where I grew up, the only nature we really appreciate is the ocean." She was playing with an immature bean pod as a warm wind blew her frizzy hair eastward. "But in defense of suburbia, I think we treat each other better."

Cathy made a picnic for the four of us, and we went to the Warrior River and ate it on a blanket. Marvin said he and Cathy were going for a long walk and he'd whistle when they were almost back. Beth and I made sweet—and hot—love in the 90-degree shade of a willow grove, and it brought back a flood of memories and emotions that I had felt the previous fall. Afterward we lay naked and sweaty, alternately caressing one another and swatting away flies and mosquitoes. She saw me smile when a bird sang from a nearby branch, and asked what was funny. I told her what Bebe had taught us to sing with the sparrow.

She raised her head. "Loovvve, Tommy, Tommy. Tommy."

It took my breath but it also sent a flash of anxiety through me. "Can you really use that word about me?" I managed. "After you dumped me?"

She rolled over on her stomach and then climbed partly on top of me. "Tommy, I am sorry. You are the most admirable guy I've ever met, and I should have known it before now. But I didn't, and I'm amazingly lucky you would see me again." She kissed me wetly with her sweaty torso sliding up and down mine. "If you'll really forgive me, I promise to treat you right." She wriggled against me. "Oooh. I believe something is happening. Colonel McKee, is the South about to rise again?" But just then we heard Marvin whistling.

The next day the three of us drove Beth to the Montgomery airport. She looked at me very seriously. "You're my man, Dixie. I won't forget that again."

31

Latin and Celtic

Two days after the trial, Joe Black and Daddy met with Taliaferro to argue that with Kyle free it wouldn't be right to try me when I had clearly acted in self-defense. Afterward Joe Black came straight to Bebe's, and she called me over to hear a report. Taliaferro had said his "ass was in a crack" because the people in Yancey County had made it clear I had to be tried, because Kyle had been tried. Daddy said a jury might send me to prison out of spite. When Taliaferro said juries in Yancey almost always did the right thing, Daddy had cussed, and then Taliaferro claimed if there was any prejudice in my trial it would be because people had seen him kicking the reporter and took it as his anger about the acquittal of one of their neighbors.

"Buddy was so mad then he was about to pop, Brigid. He'd been sure Taliaferro wouldn't try Tommy when it got down to it." Joe Black shook his head. "But look at who has put Taliaferro in office over the years—Yancey is the hard core of segregationist Alabama. Their days are numbered but the whites are still in control. People don't give up power. It's gotta be snatched from 'em. The nigras are provin' that."

Bebe nodded solemnly. "What about our little plan, Joe?"

Joe Black brightened. "I already kicked it in motion, honey."

I didn't know what they were talking about, and they wouldn't tell me then, but about a week later, after various events had transpired, they came across with the story. Bebe had asked Joe Black to figure out what it would take to get Taliaferro to drop the charges against me. When the circuit solicitor wouldn't listen to reason, Joe Black put his investigators on Taliaferro, and they came back with stories about his high living and free spending, which didn't make sense because circuit solicitors were not well paid. Bebe told Joe Black to find out if Taliaferro was in debt.

There were liens on his house, a farm he had inherited, a beach house, and a big boat. Joe Black said it was all worth about $200,000 but most banks would lend no more than $150,000 on it. Bebe had asked Joe Black to find out exactly what Taliaferro owed the bank, but he came back to her embarrassed.

"Joe said, 'I'm ashamed to say that, while I have been known to bribe a bank examiner, I currently don't have that kind of relationship with those responsible for the Yancey County bank. This is a humiliating failure on my part, Brigid.'"

Bebe chuckled. "Dear, there should be *some* limit on what you will do in the name of gallantry."

At that point in the narration, Joe Black leaned over and kissed Bebe on the forehead. "Well, we hit a brick wall there, but this smart little rascal figured it out. 'Let's buy the bank,' she said. See, we had been discussing selling y'all's bank. So she says to me, 'go buy the bank and find out what the man owes.' Just like that. I said there was an easier way than buying the bank flat out. An option to buy it would allow them to examine the books, which would reveal what Taliaferro owed. So I got this boy at Biloxi—a lawyer who's been with me on some suits against some corporations—to go up to Birmingham and get a business broker to offer the owners of the Yancey County bank an option to buy."

"Wait a minute," I said. "Why did you bring in this man from Biloxi?"

"Well, if I showed the interest, this whole little scheme could be traced back to y'all."

Marvin leaned in. "Been a lot less complicated if you'd just let me go down there and shoot that red-faced, greasy-headed cracker."

"The direct approach," William said.

Joe Black pointed his cigar approvingly at Marvin. "So it works fine. Brigid paid a hundred thousand for a thirty-day option to buy Yancey National, owned by the Trotter family. We get the bank records and find that Taliaferro has borrowed right at four hundred thousand, half of it in the last five years." He gave us the smile of the cat with a bellyful of canary. "Now why in the cowboy hell would a bank lend twice or more what the collateral was worth? Only one reason. Got sumpin on 'em.

My investigators go back down there, look at this Trotter family that owns the bank and they found"—he snapped his fingers twice—"what we were looking for."

John Trotter, the banker, had a son who in 1959 had been in an accident driving drunk, killing his girlfriend. Taliaferro didn't prosecute him, and soon after that Taliaferro bought a beach house and a boat, divorced the second wife, and married number three, and started going to Las Vegas four or five times a year. "Wife number two filled us in on this."

Bebe pursed her lips. "Hell hath no fury."

On the Monday after Daddy and Joe Black had been to Yancey County to beg Taliaferro one last time, Joe Black sent this friend from Biloxi to see the circuit solicitor. Joe Black said it had probably happened about like this:

A man walked out of the Yancey County bank, headed down to the courthouse to Cal Taliaferro's office, and asked for a moment of the circuit solicitor's time.

"How you doin', sir?" Taliaferro had said it with his big smile, shaking the man's hand as he glanced down at the business card. "Mr. Thibodeaux." He pronounced it "Thigh-buh-dex."

"Tib-eh-dough. Felix Thibodeaux."

"What brings you up here from Biloxi? The cool weather?" The widest possible smile.

"Well, I'm here to do some business." Thibodeaux's face was perfectly blank.

"What kind of business, may I ask?"

"Banking business." Thibodeaux said it slowly.

Taliaferro's grin held. "You going to give the boys across the square some competition?"

"Well, not really. I represent a group of investors who have bought Yancey National."

"Bought it? I didn't know it was for sale."

"Well, Mr. Taliaferro, you know what they say, ever'thing's for sale at the right price. You mind I smoke?"

"Sure, sure, go ahead. Yancey National's my bank. I'll be one of your good customers. Say, tell me, who are the new owners?"

Thibodeaux had taken out a large cigar and a cigar knife, and he spent a full minute preparing it for lighting. All the while Taliaferro kept the smile pasted on.

"We know you are one of our biggest borrowers." Thibodeaux was veiled in smoke.

"Well, I don't know about that. I believe I'm pretty much caught up on my payments."

"Not quite, Taliaferro." There was no accommodation on his tanned, fleshy face.

"Well, let me have to the end of the day and I'll get it current," Taliaferro said.

"That be good, but the real problem is yo' collateral."

The circuit solicitor shrugged. "Well, the bank's got liens on everything."

"We figured that, but it ain't sufficient to support, let's see here"—he pulled a piece of paper from his pocket—"the $408,000 you owe the bank."

Taliaferro sputtered. "Well, Mr. Trotter knows I'm good for the whole amount, even if my property doesn't appraise quite up to that."

"It's not close, Taliaferro, and the new owners don't know you from Adam's house cat." Thibodeaux let that sink in. "They take over Yancey National on September first. That's a week from Wednesday. You have a cashier's check for"—he looked down again—"$408,629.12 ready by the close of bidness that day. All right? You un'erstan'?"

Joe Black gave me a mischievous grin. "Now, Tommy, ol' Taliaferro's smile was gone. 'Look, uh, can't we work this out? Going to need, you know, more time. Cain't, cain't y'all work with me on this?'" Joe Black mugged his delight. "Thibodeaux, he studied his cigar for a minute, and he says, 'Let me talk to the new owners. How 'bout I send one our accountants 'round in the mornin' to talk to you 'bout it? That make you feel better, son?'"

He had acted out Thibodeaux's response with his own cigar. As soon as Felix left, Taliaferro made a beeline to Trotter's office. "You figure Trotter ain't too smart to let hisself get blackmailed," Joe Black said, "but he's smart enough to know if word got out about how he had financed Cal, and the new owners could easily put it out, he was in big trouble. Paying a bribe is a crime, too."

When Thibodeaux got back to Biloxi that afternoon, Trotter was on the phone to say he didn't want to sell his bank after all. Thibodeaux refused to withdraw, and Trotter tried to talk tough. Joe Black had foreseen this, which was why he involved Thibodeaux, rather than some easy-going fellow, as his go-between in the first place.

"So at that point Thibodeaux—who, I have to tell you, Tommy, has some associates that even *I* wouldn't meet with on Easter Sunday in St. Peter's Square—got a little rough. 'Boy,' he said, 'you did sell, and if you try to welsh on this, you best be ready because I'll turn your miserable life to pure shit. You un'erstan'?'"

Joe Black had looked at Bebe. "Brigid, I apologize—I just get carried away telling these stories." She smiled and waved her hand. Trotter had begged for an extension to get "a loan or two straightened out," but Thibodeaux again refused. When Trotter hung up, Felix called Joe Black.

"So, Tommy, Felix is the kinda fella doesn't say hello or how you or nothin'. He just starts talkin' in that Coonass accent. 'Hey, Blackie, you must be the only sumbitch up there in Alabama who don't scare easy. That circuit solicitor put out a foul smell when I dropped the word on him in his office this morning. And you know smells don't travel too good over the telephone, Blackie, but I'd say that banker was in much the same hygienic condition when he called me a minute ago.'" Bebe was laughing, despite all her Victorian virtue.

"So they all real scared when the man drops in on Cal the next day. Actually, it wadn't an accountant, just an investigator watching Cal for us. Secretary shows him in. Cal says, 'Surely we going to be able to work this out, aren't we?' Our boy sorta nods. Then Taliaferro says, 'How about y'all givin' me a little while so I can get some things arranged?' This other boy studies Cal a little bit and then holds up two fingers and nods. You figure Cal is hoping for a month at least. He's kinda in shock. Cal ain't exactly for sure, but he prob'ly reckons the man means two days. Then the guy just gets up out of his chair and turns to the door. He ain't said a word yet. But before he leaves he reaches in his coat pocket and puts an envelope on the chair."

Joe Black paused a long moment for dramatic effect. "There's a piece of paper inside that envelope with three words on it. Y'all wanta guess what it says?" We all shook our heads. "I'll give you a hint. Two words are Latin and one is Celtic."

I looked at Bebe. "Do you know?" She was delighted by the intrigue. "No, this is the first I've heard of how this scheme worked in the details."

"*Nolle prosequi* McKee." William had said it quietly.

Joe Black bowed toward William. "Well, we have a scholar here."

Marvin frowned. "What's that mean?"

"'Don't prosecute McKee.'"

Bebe looked at Joe Black. "Does that mean Taliaferro will drop the charges?"

"We hope so, darling. We'll see." He kissed her forehead and gazed down at her. Their old eyes held each other with the kind of affection I had only known briefly in the afterglow of making love with Beth. Indeed, I wouldn't have known otherwise what I was seeing.

I was astonished at the Byzantine plan my grandmother and her childhood playmate had concocted to liberate me. I could just imagine them as two eight-year-olds perched in a magnolia tree on McDonough Street in Montgomery in 1902 making up an adventure of knights and damsels plotting how to free their friend from their enemy's clutches.

Now, sixty-three years later, neither seemed to have any compunction about the deceptions they had promoted or any care at all about the huge amount of money they had risked, so sure were they of the rightness of their purpose.

But, Lord help me, I hoped it worked.

32

GOD KNOWS

Cathy, Marvin, and I were playing gin rummy on Monday night after supper when the phone rang, which I quickly prayed would bring news of *nolle prosequi* McKee. We heard Mama answer it in the kitchen. "You're *where*?" A pause. "*Why?*" A longer pause. "We'll be there as soon as possible."

We met her at the door of the den. "I need y'all to go with me. Your Daddy's in the Montgomery jail." She saw our looks of disbelief. "Arrested for DWI."

For the past week Daddy had seemed to be drinking all the time, and he said very little. I heard him typing something in his little office at home on Sunday. At supper, Cathy said he had gone to Montgomery. We presumed it was to see Bebe. Dr. Hill had put her in the hospital.

On the way to the jail, Mama started talking, thinking out loud about what had been happening with Daddy. She said he hadn't come to bed the last two nights. He had wandered around the house, drinking and smoking. When she had asked him about the meeting with the circuit solicitor, he got real agitated, cussing under his breath, but he wouldn't talk about it.

"I think he's finally realized that there's a real chance you'll be sent to prison." I didn't like to hear those words, but if they pierced me, then I knew how much they would wound my father. I prayed again that Bebe's bank intrigue would work.

In the barren, linoleumed waiting area at the Montgomery city jail, Mama was off writing a check to post bail and the rest of us were waiting for them to bring Daddy to us when a short, middle-aged man approached me. "Tom McKee, right?" I nodded. "Dwayne Capshaw from the *Advertiser*." I flinched. "You comment on what has happened to your daddy?" I said I didn't know what had happened.

"The city police arrested Judge McKee for drunk driving and resisting arrest. Hit an officer. He drank a whole lot this afternoon at the Governor's House Motel bar. The bartender tried to get him to take a room and when the judge wouldn't, the bartender called the police. They arrested him 'bout as soon as he got on the by-pass."

I didn't know what to say, so I stayed silent. "Judge McKee got a drinking problem?"

"No." I turned my back on him to let him know I was answering no more questions.

When they brought Daddy out, I could tell something was wrong, more than just being drunk or hung over. He was holding his left arm and grimacing in pain. The muscles in his forehead and around his mouth were knotted. Mama went to him. "Honey, are you all right?"

At that moment, Daddy dropped like dead weight to the floor. His big body began to convulse violently and his eyes rolled back in his head. Mama screamed. I fell to my knees trying to hold him still. The spasms stopped. I felt for a pulse in his wrist and couldn't find one. I held my hand on his chest. Nothing.

I held up his torso and told Mama to put her folded sweater under his neck. Then I lay him back down and held his nose and fit my mouth over Daddy's and blew as hard as I could—three, four, five, six times. I'd seen demonstrations of this in tenth grade but never done it.

Still no breath. I could taste the Pall Malls and the bourbon.

"Come on, Daddy." I straddled his chest on my knees, tugged loose his tie, and placed the heel of my right hand over his heart. I jammed my hand into his chest a half dozen times. Marvin squatted beside me. "Harder. Harder." I did it again several times, and then I ripped his shirt open to listen for a heartbeat. I thought I heard something. Just then I felt a firm grip on my shoulder, and when I looked back there was a broad-shouldered man in horn-rimmed glasses and a white uniform, with another man in the same uniform standing by a gurney.

"Son, let me have a try." He pulled me to the side and repeated what I had just done, only harder. Then he dropped an ear on Daddy's chest. He leaped to his feet. "We got one. Let's go."

They hoisted Daddy on the gurney and rushed it out door. I ran beside and asked where they were going. St. Margaret's.

In my adolescent anger, I'd sometimes wished Daddy dead. But now I knew better how final and awful death was; I felt it now, a terror in every molecule of my body. And maybe there wasn't a God, or there was and he didn't give a shit, but I pleaded now to God Almighty to save my daddy.

"How are you doing, Mama?" I had taken her hand and was tracing the veins on the back with my index finger. It was 3 a.m. and Daddy was holding on, though the doctor said he had a dangerous arrhythmia. Another heart attack was very possible and probably deadly.

She sighed. "He just had it in his mind this trouble would be over when Kyle's trial was done. When he saw it wasn't, that the circuit solicitor was really going to try you, he just broke down, and started all that drinking and then he broke down physically."

She started to cry. I put my arms around her and she fell against me. "I'm so afraid."

"I know you are, Mama, but you've also been so brave, and you've held us together."

At five o'clock Marvin went for coffee and donuts, and by six the rush of sugar and caffeine had started my brain working. I went to the hospital lobby for the morning *Advertiser*.

There on the front page was a mug shot of Daddy with a story about his arrest, complete with several quotes from the bartender about Daddy's alcohol consumption. It recounted all of my own troubles as well as Daddy's "attack" on the photographer outside the courthouse. A separate story was news to me: Daddy had resigned as probate judge, which explained why he was in Montgomery the previous day, to deliver a letter to the governor's office. The story quoted Governor Wallace's aide Walter Fagan, who "assumed McKee's resignation was the result of his embarrassment over his and his son's behavior." That redneck shitheel.

"The governor's boys are behind those stories." Joe Black was shaking his head, an unlit cigar in his mouth, as he approached me in the lobby. "I already been on the phone this morning. State troopers monitored the first call to the Montgomery police and told somebody higher-up, who called the governor's office. Somebody there called the newspaper. Bastards never miss a chance to go after somebody who don't stand tall for segregation."

We rode up the elevator together. "How is he?"

"Not good, but thanks for coming."

Joe Black reached up and put his hand on my shoulder. "Y'all my people now."

Cathy was asleep, her head in Marvin's lap. Mama came out of the ward, and I handed her the newspaper. She read it, shaking her head. When she saw the part about the resignation, she started to cry. I asked her how he was doing.

"Doctor said vital signs were a little better. When they've been stable twenty-four hours, we'll be out of the woods, he thinks. But we aren't there now."

Just then Dwayne Capshaw got off the elevator. He veered away from me toward Mama. "Miz McKee, remember me? I'm from the newspaper." I asked what he wanted to know. "About Judge McKee's condition."

"Stable. We expect a full recovery." I took a step closer to Capshaw. "I wanta comment on a couple of things in the paper this morning. You got your pencil ready?" He nodded.

"What Walter Fagan said about my father's reasons for resigning was wrong. Nobody in my family is ashamed of what I did. I'm not going to apologize for defending myself against a man trying to kill me. The photographer got kicked because he was trying to trip us."

The reporter looked up at me skeptically. No doubt the photographer was a buddy of his.

"Mr. Fagan's comments just show what loyal Wallace supporters like my father can expect from the governor's people when the going gets tough—they turn on you like a rabid dog. Daddy resigned as probate judge because his work was done. In the past few weeks he oversaw a big change in the voting situation, and it took place peacefully. We hope other counties live up to Ruffin's good example."

I waited for a moment. "You get all that?" He wrote for another half minute and then looked up with another question on his tongue. I shook my head. "No more questions. Nobody else has a comment." Then I locked a stare on him until he headed back to the elevator.

Joe Black slapped me on the back. "Mighty fine, boy. Mighty *damn* fine."

"They won't put that in the paper, I bet," Marvin said.

Joe Black shook his head. "Hell they won't. Part 'bout the rabid dog be in the headline."

THERE WAS NOTHING TO do but wait and hope, and that we did, as we sat in the small intensive-care waiting room. At eight o'clock that first morning, William came over from Baptist Hospital to gather information for Bebe, who, he admitted, was "worried to death." About once an hour, Mama would get another report from the doctor, and it stayed the same—an unstable heartbeat that indicated continuing trauma in my father's system. At mid-morning, Cathy and I were admitted to see him. He had tubes up his nose and many machines hooked to him. He was sedated, not conscious, but I told Cathy he knew we were there and wanted him to live. She nodded tearfully.

At noon Orene and Sam arrived with lunch. "Orene, this potato salad is so delicious," I told her, glad for real food. Worry occupied her face, but she mustered a smile at me. "Good."

Orene was present in virtually all of my memories of Bebe's and Granddaddy's big house on the hill. She had been in the kitchen since Daddy was a teenager, and she had always doted on Daddy and me, something she proudly acknowledged and attributed to the fact that she only had daughters. She looked down the hall and slowly shook her head. "Buddy always loved my food." We had already lapsed into talking about Daddy in the past tense. I wanted to talk about something besides death so I asked Orene how she came to work for Bebe.

"Well, the reason I did wadn't 'cause I was all that unhappy working for Miz Collins—she was all right—but William had asked me to come by and talk to Miz McKee, and she sat me down right there in the kitchen and served me a cup of coffee and a little bowl of banana pudding, and she sat right there across from me with the same coffee and puddin', and she say, 'Orene, now tell me what wrong with this puddin', and I say, 'Well, Miss Brigid,' and she say, 'please jus' call me Brigid,' and I just liked her from then on. 'Co'se, she always paid better than anybody else would, never fussed 'bout nothin' 'cept my sugar—she always fussin' 'bout my sugar bein' too high. But I been real happy in her house and I hate to think about her passing."

Death reared its ugly head again. I turned to Sam. "Anything you need me to do on the farm right now?"

Sam shook his head. "We fine for a while. But we may need you to help run things."

"Aw, Sam, you and Junior can run things better'n I ever could."

"We gettin' ol'. 'Sides, we don't know nothin' 'bout that bankin', all them gov'ment progums. Buddy always took care of that."

I frowned. The various subsidy programs amounted to a lot of money, but tending to them took work and patience. "Hell, we just farmin' the government," Daddy would say.

"Good chance I'm going to be in prison, Sam. Can't do much farmin' in prison."

"You may have to go a little while, but we'll need you when you get out."

I was taken aback at this and intrigued. Maybe that's what I should do, prison or not. My life didn't have any other purpose now. Even if he pulled through, Daddy would be sick a long while. If I got out of this trouble, I would need to help with the farm. If I got sentenced, it was going to be lot harder to run off if my mama was widowed and left to run the farming.

At two that afternoon Junior and his wife Mattie came in. She talked quietly with Mama. Junior was not his usual self. He kept looking over at me but he didn't say anything. Finally I said I needed some fresh air and asked Junior if he wanted to come. I gave Marvin a signal to stay behind. We rode silently down the elevator and then walked outside where we found a little shade under a big crepe myrtle on the side of the hospital.

"How's it look for your daddy, Tommy?"

"He had a bad heart attack. He's probably got some long-term damage to his heart."

"What do they say caused this heart attack?"

"Doubt if it was one thing. Your arteries get blocked. Granddaddy had a bad heart. Runs in the family. Smoking's bad. Plus, Daddy was real upset about all my problems."

"Tommy, me and Buddy had that argument the other day at the courthouse—I just got carried away. I didn't mean all that, and God knows, I wish I could take it back. That probably caused some his attack."

I pondered for a long moment what to say. "Naw, I don't think so. Daddy needed to hear that. He respects you more than anybody, and if it worried him, that was because he knew deep down you were right. I've caused most of Daddy's aggravation, and he's caused the rest of it himself, thinking he could stop all these changes."

Doubt covered Junior's fleshy face, but he said no more. I put a hand on his massive shoulder. "Come on let's get out of this heat. How the crops looking?"

On the way back up to the waiting room, I picked up the afternoon paper. There on the bottom of the front page was a report that Wallace had appointed McCallister probate judge. Clem Brown would replace McCallister as sheriff. The triumph of the rednecks. All the class prejudices that I had caught from Granddaddy suddenly surged within me. Those weren't the people who were supposed to lead our society—we are. They lack altogether the character to do the honest thing, to see the common good, to care for the less fortunate. They were greedy to raise their own shitty status at our expense. And events were conspiring to let them do just that.

I showed the paper to Junior. He shook his head. "Going to mean trouble. They dang'ous men to colored folk." Anger began to cloud his face. "Here we are, everybody just gettin' to vote, and Wallace put McCallister in charge. Two steps forward, one step back. Politics real tricky business. God knows."

He looked down toward Daddy's room. "Buddy always said that, and look where he now." He shrugged. "We just going to have to get organized and beat him. That the only way."

"You gotta think about running for probate judge."

"It don't really matter who it is, long as it ain't McCallister or somebody like him. But, you know, if we just get the colored registered, we going to start changing things for the better. I really believe that."

Now didn't seem the time to be negative. "It should, Junior. We going to count on that."

33

New Politics

"We shoulda heard from Taliaferro by now," Joe Black Pell was saying. "I'm worried, Tommy, that this little trick ain't going to work." Marvin and I had come to Joe Black's office from the hospital on Thursday morning to discuss my trial, scheduled to begin the following Monday. "We going to give it one more shot," he said.

I found out what he meant when his secretary showed a portly, dark-haired man in his late fifties into Joe's office. He wore a yellow linen suit, a starched white shirt with French cuffs, a royal blue silk tie, and two-toned shoes. I knew before he took off his white straw hat and Joe introduced him that he was Felix Thibodeaux of Biloxi, Mississippi.

"Blackie, gimme the phone. Let's see what I can do." He dialed. "Trotter, the people here in Birmin'ham gettin' real nervous 'bout the situation down there," he said without preamble into the phone. "Bidness people don't like nigger trouble. Y'all got all your niggers real stirred up down there with this trial. Paper this mornin' says y'all fixin' to have another trial, and my clients are talkin' bout gittin' outa the deal."

I found myself holding my breath as he listened a minute. "Naw, they don't wanta cancel the option to buy yo' bank." He raised his eyebrows at Joe Black. "They think it's worth more'n they payin' for it, but ya nigger trouble has got 'em antsy, and they've got somebody they going to sell the option to. Say they can make some good money by just rollin' it over."

I had to admire this man's ability to make up an outlandish lie, one that would top another outlandish lie, in a matter of seconds. Such skill could only have come from long years of practice.

Apparently Trotter asked who the other buyer was, and Thibodeaux happily obliged with another instantaneous whopper. "It's a bunch headed up by the lawyer here who worked so long with Sparkman up there on the Senate banking committee. Real tight with the FDIC. Knows all them feds real good."

Joe Black smiled and shook his head at this man, the Michelangelo of liars.

"'Course I'm tellin' em they can make more money if they keep your bank. But Trotter, you going to have to put a stop to this nigger trouble. You have another trial down there, boy, yo' bank's going to be in the hands of a buncha ol' fed'ral bureaucrats."

He paused, in the manner you would imagine Homer or Chaucer or Mark Twain would have done it, so as to let the next line have maximum effect.

"Hope yo' nose is clean."

Thibodeaux looked at Joe Black and nodded. "Naw, I'll call *you* back in a hour and see if you done any good."

We had to wait for Trotter to rush to Taliaferro's office and try to persuade him to halt my prosecution for attempted murder. In the meantime, Thibodeaux asked Joe if he had any whiskey—notwithstanding the fact that it was 11 A.M.—and if he wanted to go to Las Vegas with him. "Lotta good-looking showgirls out there, Blackie," he declared. "My buddy Carlos Marcellus, he always fixes me up." Joe Black turned a bright shade of pink. Marvin, it turned out, knew who Marcellus was—a New Orleans Mafia kingpin.

"Naw, I be too busy for that, Felix," Joe Black said in a faltering voice. He was shaking his head at me as Thibodeaux reached for the phone.

"Uh-hunh. Yeah." Thibodeaux said into the phone, and scowled. "Too bad, Trotter. Glad I ain't in yo' shoes." He hung up, and his purplish blue eyes fell with abrupt gravity on the rest of us. "No go. He's scared, but the circuit solicitor just too stupid to understand."

Joe Black's face was hard. "Damn right he's stupid, and I guess I gotta smear his face in *shit* for him to admit it."

There was a malice in his voice I had heard only once before—when, as a matter of fact, he had also been talking about Taliaferro. Perhaps he reserved his real animus for other lawyers. I soon found out the kind of people Joe Black Pell most detested.

That afternoon at the hospital, Junior and Mattie were visiting us in the waiting area when Reverend Banks joined us. He prayed, and once again I thought the elegance alone of his appeal should have won God's mercy for my father—that is, of course, if he was paying any attention at all. Junior asked what the minister thought of the governor's appointments.

"Mr. Jackson, they trouble me. I don't think they are in the best interests of Negroes in Ruffin County. What do you think?"

"I agree. What you going to do about it?" Junior seemed to be more respectful of Banks.

"Well, I'm hoping we can organize the Negroes in our county, and those in other counties where our vote is surging, to replace some of these public officials opposed to any change."

With Banks's words, suddenly a light went on inside me. I remembered the conversation Joe Black and I had when we were returning from our first meeting with Cal Taliaferro. We'd been talking about Taliaferro's dismissal of his likely challenger in the next election, and Joe Black had sworn to me that he'd oppose the circuit solicitor politically if he went ahead with my trial. But the election wasn't until 1966, more than a year away, and we needed a positive response in the next seventy-two hours. As I put this together while I half-listened to Reverend Banks and Junior Jackson plan black political action in Ruffin County, it came to me what I should do. I told them I needed a cup of coffee. I didn't want Mama to hear what I was thinking. She wouldn't want me to do it. Junior, Banks, Marvin, and I went to the coffee shop where I pitched my idea.

"Taliaferro could choose not to try me, but despite all kinds of begging, he's going ahead." They all nodded at me. "Y'all know the circuit solicitor is elected to serve a four-county area, and that Ruffin is in his district, along with Yancey, Dallas, and Lowndes?" Staring at me, perplexed, Junior and Banks shook their heads, but the smile on Marvin's face told me he had figured out where I was going. "What I wanta ask is if y'all will help me by putting some pressure on the circuit solicitor. Just go to him and say: 'We wish you wouldn't try McKee. He was just protecting Jackie, and we going to be payin' attention 'cause we going to be advising a lot of colored voters about your race next year.'"

Junior's eyes narrowed. "Sound like a threat, Tommy."

"Oh, no, Mr. Jackson." Banks was grave. "That's not a threat. That's just a statement of fact." For the first time in my experience, the preacher smiled.

Junior shrugged. "Let's go on down there then."

Marvin leaned in. "Be better if there was some folk from them other counties. Junior, don't I remember you know a nigger down there in Yancey County?" Junior nodded. "Why don't you call them and tell him to meet us at the Yancey courthouse in an hour?"

Banks was nodding. "Well, there are two *Negroes*"—I don't think he approved of Marvin's habitual "nigger"—"in Selma who work with the Southern Christian Leadership Conference. I believe I'll go call them."

Junior's friend and the two men from Selma showed up just as we arrived at the Yancey courthouse. After introductions all around, Junior and Banks explained what was up to the new guys, and then Junior looked at me. "How we going to do this, Tommy? It was yo' idea."

"I shouldn't say a word," I told them. "Junior, Taliaferro's going to remember you as one of my guards at the trial and he may think you're just my mouthpiece. I believe Reverend Banks should do the talking. Reverend, I know that you can be nice and friendly but clear that, if the trial goes forward, every Negro vote goes elsewhere. If the charges are dropped, good chance Taliaferro'll get all those votes."

Both Junior and Banks nodded solemnly, and the new men agreed. Banks led us to Taliaferro's office, but just before he opened the door, he took out his handkerchief and asked Junior to tie it around his upper arm. The other men did the same except for Marvin, who didn't carry a handkerchief. I handed him mine. Banks strode up to the secretary and asked to see Taliaferro. She very suspiciously picked up the phone, buzzed his office, and whispered into the receiver. Still distrustful of us, she said we could go in.

Cal Taliaferro's smile was pasted on like a Halloween mask when the seven of us crowded into his office. He invited us to sit down, but there were only two chairs and Banks said we wouldn't be long anyway. Taliaferro looked relieved at that.

"What can I do for you boys?"

Boys. Taliaferro could piss me off just as fast as he did Joe Black.

But Banks stayed cool. He made the pitch exactly as I had suggested, except it came with enough of the preacher's pontification to make it sound like it was from one of the Major Prophets and not from some Machiavellian, horsetrading politico. While he was speaking to Taliaferro, Banks took off his handkerchief and wiped his forehead. Then he very gently waived his right index finger, wrapped in his handkerchief, toward Taliaferro.

"Mr. District Attorney, a lot of folk think Jackie Herndon didn't get justice. Sir, we going to be much in prayer 'bout yo' decision, as we know you will be." Taliaferro had to be getting tired of people dropping in, asking the same thing.

"Rev, you oughta pray right now," Marvin said.

Only I recognized the total absurdity of Marvin Whitfield's invoking Christian authority in the Yancey County courthouse. But Taliaferro scrambled to his feet as Banks began a long entreaty for mercy that alluded not just to the wrongs done lately but also to those that mocked any notion of justice over the last century or two. If Taliaferro didn't feel some twinge guilt after that, he truly had no conscience. When Banks finally brought it to a close, all seven of us chimed in "Amens." Marvin's was the loudest.

On the way back to Montgomery, Junior leaned over the front seat and placed his huge hand on Marvin's shoulder. "I got only two things to say. You going to make a helluva preacher, Marvin, and I want you to stop at the state sto'. Politics make me thirsty."

Banks declined the third swig off the bottle of Scotch, although he admitted he enjoyed the first two. "Mr. Jackson, I hope that liquor isn't going to interfere with *yo'* prayers for mercy."

That day, I think, was the real beginning of black politics in Ruffin County, because Junior and Banks never looked back. They wouldn't win all the time, or even a fair share of the time, but they would never flag in their commitment.

On Sunday afternoon, Bebe came over from Baptist Hospital to check on Daddy, whose vital signs had finally stabilized. She was desperate to see him and talk to him. It hurt me to see how afraid she was that he would die before she did. I asked how she was doing.

"Great. Full of liquids, bad hospital food, and dope."

I had waited since Thursday night for Taliaferro to tell Joe that he had dropped the case. I'd told Joe what Banks and Junior and I had done, and he'd been impressed. "Shoulda thought of that myself. I was just so sure this other plan would work. I bet this'n going to do it."

When Joe Black entered waiting room, I looked at him with great anticipation. He gave me a long look and shook his head. No call had ever come. Tomorrow my trial would begin.

"If a fella's going to commit political and financial suicide, and risk goin' to jail to boot, not much you can do but let him." Bebe looked crestfallen for a moment, but she recovered and forced a big smile. "Well, I'm ready to go back to Yancey County in the morning."

Joe Black looked at me and then he turned to Bebe. "Naw, honey, you can't go to this one."

"Why? I feel fine."

"Naw, it's just not a good idea."

"But, Joe, Abner Hill said I could go. I think Tommy will need my moral support."

"No, Brigid, I don't think you should be there." He sounded vague, even distracted.

Then he somehow reached down deep inside for a believable lie. "Won't be good for Tommy's defense. The judge knows who Tommy is since you were at the other trial, but he also knows you're sick—I told him that—and it might make us look desperate, bringing a sick woman to try to get the jury's sympathy. Sweetie, you go home and rest until this is over."

I didn't understand it any more than she did at the time, and she would never understand because she would never know, except in its vague outline, what happened the next day. But Joe Black Pell knew what was going to happen, and he didn't want the woman he loved above all others to see what he was going to do. It was like Marvin's not wanting Cathy to know what he did to Jimmy Oliver, or me not telling people how I had hated Alma Jones and that I wanted to beat her senseless. We just do things and think things we are so ashamed of, that we know are wrong, and we have to try to hide them from people we love because we don't want them to know what we're capable of.

Joe Black feared that if she saw what he did, she would go to her grave with the image of his cruelty, and he simply couldn't have that. But I did find out why Joe Black couldn't have her at that trial, because I saw what he did.

34

THE WHITE-HAIRED GIRL

In the courtroom the next morning, Joe Black cast a long, hard look at Taliaferro, no doubt willing him to drop the charges at the eleventh, even twelfth hour. But Taliaferro refused to look his way. My group of supporters was much reduced. Even Mama had stayed at the hospital with Daddy; I insisted she could do more good there. Orene and Reverend Banks were sitting with Marvin, Cathy, and Junior just behind me. They all looked as nervous as I felt.

I sat there sweating in my suit, feeling stunned but somehow hardened to it all, as if I'd witnessed all this before; the only difference now was that I was sitting at a table closer to the jury than I had three weeks before. Joe Black used his juror challenges to keep the first seven rural white men off the jury, but he saved one to eliminate a salesman who admitted he had been in court several times over a child support issue. It didn't make sense to me.

Joe explained none of his method, though I noticed he had all the females on the jury list circled, and he was particularly deferential to the three women who were approved for service. And he did say this: "I like number four a lot." I figured out that "number four" was a sixtyish, white-haired woman who was a retired teacher and enthusiastic Baptist. She had been married forty years and had five children.

Once the jury was seated and the opening statements made, Buford Kyle limped on his crutches to the stand and told essentially the same story to Cal Taliaferro that he had given Hubert Brophy in his own trial: Alma tried to take his shotgun, I had come at him with a pistol, Jackie had attacked him too, and he had only defended himself. It took only about forty-five minutes before Taliaferro turned Kyle over to Joe Black.

"Now Mr. Kyle, how's that leg doing these days? Well, I hope."

"It bothers me all the time."

"I'm sho' sorry to hear that. You let me know if the pain gets out of hand and we'll get you a aspirin."

Joe Black's sweet smile faded as he consulted a notepad. "Now, Mr. Kyle, you have told the jury in a previous trial that my client here, Tom McKee, is lying completely about his account of what happened at this store in Yancey on May the twenty-fourth. Isn't that right?"

"Yeah."

"Well, you were pretty emphatic, weren't you?"

"What do you mean?"

"Well, I mean you said, under oath—you were under oath, weren't you?"

"Yeah."

"Sure, you had sworn to tell the truth. You said, and I'm quoting you: 'That boy just made all that up. He's a liar.' You said that about my client, Tom McKee, didn't you?"

"I guess I did."

"You have a high regard for the truth, don't you, Mr. Kyle?"

"Yes, I do."

"You're an honorable man, aren't you, Mr. Kyle?"

"I don't know what you mean."

"Well, you tell the truth, look after your family, treat your neighbors right, pay your debts—that's what I mean by an honorable man. You all those things, wouldn't you say?"

Joe Black was smiling in his most accommodating way. Judge McKinley looked at Taliaferro for an objection about relevance of the questions, but the circuit solicitor was studying his blank legal pad.

"I guess so," Kyle finally said, almost meekly.

"All right then. Judge, let me submit as exhibits A through H, there are eight of them, eight photographs, and an affidavit signed by Richard Thompson, a photographer from Montgomery, in which Thompson declares that he took these photographs on July Fourth at Jake's Fish Camp near Autaugaville, Alabama. That going to be all right, Judge?"

"So entered." Kyle's face clouded.

Joe Black reached behind his chair. "Judge, I took the little liberty of having the pictures blown up so we can see a little better what's in 'em. May I publish them to the jury?"

Joe Black opened up an easel and placed on it a two-foot-by-three-foot picture of Kyle taking a long stride with his arm swinging upward, a horseshoe in his hand.

"Mr. Kyle, is that you throwing that horseshoe at Jake's Fish Camp on July Fourth, 'bout six weeks ago?"

Kyle frowned and looked at Joe's big smile. He nodded.

"Mr. Kyle, you need to answer so the reporter can git it down. Is that you taking that big step—I bet you th'owed a ringer that time—that is you throwing that horseshoe? Correct?"

"Yes."

"I got a few more pictures, Mr. Kyle."

Kyle had started to look pale. I was on the edge of my seat. Joe Black made him admit that it was indeed he who was throwing, bending over, and picking up horseshoes.

"Now, Mr. Kyle, I'm going to show you this picture here, also taken at Jake's Fish Camp, that shows a man standing up in a fishin' boat, casting out into some water. Can you identify the man th'owing that line?"

Kyle shrugged.

"You mean you can't see who that is? Let me pull this easel over here a little closer to the jury box and see can any of your neighbors from Yancey County identify the man with good enough balance to stand up in a little-bitty fourteen-foot boat, cast a rod, and *not* fall in the river." Joe Black almost succeeded in suppressing his overt contempt. He then loudly dragged the heavy wooden easel across the hard wood floor and placed it directly in front of the jury.

Cal Taliaferro spoke, finally. "Judge, I think counsel has made his point."

Joe Black almost leaped toward the judge's bench. His voice was suddenly louder. "Naw, sir, Judge. I ain't finished making my point. Not even close."

"Overruled." Judge McKinley gazed over his glasses at Joe Black with what might have been the faintest indication of bemusement.

Joe Black then walked slowly over to the witness stand. "So, Mr. Kyle, you hobbled in here, swore on the Bible, told us what bad shape yo' leg is in, and you called *my client* a liar."

He walked just as deliberately over to the jury box, put both hands on the rail, and swept his eyes over the jurors. "*That* is my point."

He turned and walked away four steps, only to pivot and point his right index finger at the jury. "Only I ain't *through* makin' my point."

The white-haired lady on the jury raised her eyebrows at me.

"Judge, I got a exhibit here, an official disposition, notarized by the circuit clerk of Yancey County, about a ruling with regard to Mr. Kyle." Joe Black handed copies of the paper around.

Taliaferro rose, reading it. "Judge, I fail to see how a matter from 1945 has any relevance to this proceeding."

"Goes to the veracity of the witness, Judge," Joe Black said.

"I'll allow you a little leeway, counselor, but you gotta tie it up."

Joe Black put a blown-up document on his easel. "Mr. Kyle, this document concerns a child named Carl Kyle, who in 1945 was seven years old, and according to the court, had suffered neglect and malnutrition because you had failed to provide support that the same court had ordered three years before. Isn't that what this document says?"

"I don't know what it says."

"Oh, I'm sorry, Mr. Kyle, let's just go over it."

Kyle had a child with a young girl, had abandoned the mother and the child in 1941, and when a court had attempted to enforce a support order, Kyle had hidden the fact that he owned a car, furniture, and some farm equipment, declaring himself indigent and unable to provide for the child. The court had confiscated all the property and sold it for the benefit of the mother and child.

"Now, is all that correct, Mr. Kyle, all that's in this document about the court findings with regard to your abandoned child?"

Kyle shook his head, looking down in his lap. "I don't know."

"You don't know? Are saying that Judge McKinley's predecessor here in Yancey County in 1945, he was a liar, too, like you say my client is a liar?"

"I don't know."

"You don't know? You don't know?"

Suddenly the pace of Joe Black's speech accelerated. "Well, when I asked you a little while ago if you are an honorable fella, truthful, a man who supports his family, you said you are. I heard you say it, not a minute after you said my client is a liar. Now I'm going to ask you again, Mr. Kyle, is it true what's in this document that you told the court you didn't have *nothin'* and therefore couldn't provide *nothin'* to feed your own flesh and blood?"

Taliaferro rose. "Your honor, counsel is badgering the witness."

Judge McKinley didn't look at the circuit solicitor. "Naw, he's not. Mr. Kyle, answer the question. Is the court document accurate as far as you know?"

"I reckon."

"Go on, Mr. Pell."

"Your honor, exhibits J and K."

The first was the transcript of a proceeding in which Kyle was tried and convicted in 1952 of stealing six head of cattle from another Yancey County farmer. He had spent three months in the county jail. The second exhibit was an affidavit from the farmer in which he explained how Kyle had found out about the cattle under the pretense of buying them, how he had loaded them on a truck in the middle of the night and kept them on the truck without water for two days, and how he had sworn to two different sheriff's investigators that they were his cows before the rightful owner showed up at Kyle's house and identified them.

"Now, Mr. Kyle, I'm going to hand you a copy of this affidavit, and I'm going to ask you to read the last line of it for the jury."

Kyle looked up at the judge and shook his head. "Please do as counsel requests, Mr. Kyle," the judge said. Kyle took out reading glasses and put his finger on the part where Joe Black was pointing.

"'Kyle is a thief, a man who will abuse animals, and a—'" Kyle paused.

"That word is *habitual*, Mr. Kyle."

"Habitual liar."

Joe Black went to the jury box and again gripped the railing, his arms far apart. He stared at the white-haired woman directly in front of him. She had worn an ugly scowl throughout the discussion of Kyle's failure to support the child.

"Mr. Kyle, do you know the meaning of 'habitual liar'?" Joe Black never took his eyes off the woman.

"Yeah."

"Mr. Kyle, do you know the meaning of the word 'abuse'?"

Taliaferro was standing again. "Judge, this is a trial, not a vocabulary test."

"Move it along, Mr. Pell."

"Thank you, Judge." Joe Black held up a small stack of paper. "Exhibit L. Last one, Judge."

He distributed copies, put the blown-up document on the easel, and then walked across the courtroom to stand behind Cal Taliaferro and directly in front of the same group of people who had been seated there three weeks before. Kyle's family.

"Mr. Kyle, we talked a little bit earlier about being an honorable man. That put me in mind of my wedding vows. I promised to love and honor and cherish my wife. Did you make something like that kind of a promise when you got married?"

Joe Black never looked at, or otherwise acknowledged, that he was within three feet of the woman who I felt sure was Mrs. Kyle. She was vastly overweight, and she wore an air of sadness, or defeat. Her arms were crossed in front of her, as if she were under attack, and indeed what Joe Black was doing amounted to a massive indirect assault on her, because, after all, she was married to the man he was systematically ripping apart.

Kyle looked confused at Joe Black's question. If he was truly perplexed, he was the only person in the room who didn't anticipate that Joe Black was about to lower the boom.

"Yeah, I guess."

"I'm sure you did promise to love and cherish yo' wife, but according to Exhibit L, you have fallen *a little short* at times."

The document told the sordid story of the sheriff's repeated visits to the Kyle home to stop his beating of Gertrude Kyle. She had been periodically hospitalized with bruises, broken bones, and internal bleeding. He had been arrested seven times, and she had refused seven times to press charges. Joe Black put the document on the easel and read it verbatim, his voice getting slower but louder around the descriptions of Mrs. Kyle's injuries. At the end of the report of the fourth injury, one of Kyle's daughters rushed out of the courtroom. Joe Black, still standing close against the rail within touching distance of Mrs. Kyle, turned his gaze to follow her daughter's exit. Every single juror did the same. When he finished the description of the last injury, Joe Black looked up at the jury and then over to the witness.

"Mr. Kyle, my question is this—"

But he didn't ask his question then. Instead he walked slowly over and put the document he had read on the table where I sat. Then he took the blown-up document off the easel and put it on the floor. He folded the easel and laid it loudly on the floor. All this took at least a minute, during which every eye and every ear in the courtroom was trained on every single movement of Joe Black Pell.

Finally he went to the witness box and stood to the side so that Kyle had to turn almost all the way around to see Joe Black, who looked not at the witness but at the jury.

"Mr. Kyle, you swore on the Bible that you are an honorable man. Now, were you tellin' us the truth?"

I didn't know then, but I have since learned, that it was one of the oldest tricks of lawyering, which was to change the testimony of a witness just enough that nobody noticed the lie in your retelling but plenty enough to outrage the listener at the subject's hypocrisy.

"*Objection.*"

"Withdrawn."

Joe Black walked to his table and said to Judge McKinley that he thought now might be a good place to stop for lunch before he began "the next phase" of his examination of Kyle.

"Both counsel, in my chambers." McKinley was frowning at Taliaferro.

I looked at Joe Black, hoping for a tip about what was happening, but he just looked at me and jerked his head toward the judge, signaling me to follow. I did, feeling wary. The judge had taken off his robe and was sitting at a desk in a small office. He didn't invite anybody to sit.

"Joe Black, how much more you got for the witness?"

Joe Black was licking a cigar. "I be done by noon tomorrow, Judge."

"Noon tomorrow!" Taliaferro's mouth suddenly changed from his usual pasted-on smile to a wide gape. "How?" Joe Black was still wetting his cigar and said nothing.

"Cal, what else you got besides this witness?" The judge's face held an angry frown. Taliaferro shrugged, indicating he had nothing else. The judge shook his head in disgust.

Taliaferro turned to Joe Black. The smile of accommodation was back. "How 'bout if we reduce the charge to a misdemeanor, say disorderly conduct, y'all plead guilty, and we agree to a small fine and a suspended sentence."

My head was spinning. No jail. I liked that idea. I looked at Joe Black as he licked the cigar some more. I had used my tongue less on some of those big caramel-flavored Sugar Daddies than he had on that cigar. "Let me ask my client."

We stepped to the side. "Shouldn't take a plea," he said in a whisper. "Admits guilt. You going to get off completely. Trust me."

I wanted desperately for this to be over, but I wasn't guilty. I had defended myself that day at the store, tried to defend Jackie and Alma. I wanted everyone to know that; I wanted my father to know that. I shrugged my okay, and he turned back to the circuit solicitor.

"Naw."

"Pell, you gotta give me a way outa this."

Joe Black's eyes blazed. "You know, Cal, I been beggin' yo' fat ass all summer for some consideration, and you played politics all the way through, and then you made me go in there and humiliate that poor woman in order to expose the truth about Buford Kyle."

I wondered—did he really have to do that to the woman in order to save me? My best guess is this: Joe Black had calculated that an old, miserable life could be further and publicly degraded to save mine, which he believed, rightly or not, was more valuable. Bebe had said she knew of no limits on what Joe Black Pell would do to help somebody he cared about.

It was perfectly clear why Bebe couldn't be at the trial: she couldn't see what he did to Kyle's wife, an innocent victim of the man's brutality, just as Jackie had been. Even if she read about it in the newspapers, the reports would never capture how awful his evisceration really was.

Joe Black took two steps to get very close to Taliaferro. Now he had to look almost straight up to see the circuit solicitor. "You think any o' them three women on the jury going to vote to convict Tommy on the basis of anything said by that miserable sonuvabitch? Huh?" He turned and spit, so angry that he neglected to do it, as he always done in my experience, into his handkerchief.

"Shit. If I ever owned a jury in a Alabama courthouse—and by God I've owned a lot of 'em—I've got this one."

He spit again and sneered up at Taliaferro one more time. "You take that goddamn disorderly conduct plea and you cram it up yo' ass sideways."

"Mr. Pell, you been real polite through this. Let's not go ruinin' it now."

"I apologize to you, Judge." I noted that he was pointedly *not* apologizing to Taliaferro.

"Cal, buddy, you screwed up on this," the judge said.

Taliaferro bowed his greasy head to inspect his two-toned shoes. "I'm sorry, your honor."

"Y'all go on."

We filed out of the judge's office. I asked Joe Black if this meant that I would testify the following afternoon.

"Naw, you go on right after lunch." He shook his head. "I was lyin'. Call it bluffin' to put a nice shine on it. Right now the jury's got a firm picture of how sorry Kyle is and that's the one I want 'em to keep. You'll tell your story, and they going to believe you and they'll acquit."

He wasn't smiling like he had done so often over the summer to encourage me and buck up my spirits. His face was serious, because he was telling me what was going to happen because he knew it as surely as he knew his own name.

"Remember two things—'the lean truth' and that I'm not going to be sweet to you but you going to stay firm. You understan'?"

"Yes, sir."

"Actually, they's one more thing. When I ask if you tellin' the truth, you look at that white-haired girl on the jury. You hear me?"

All women, regardless of age, race, or national origin, were girls to Joe Black.

"We in good shape, but if eleven vote to convict, she'll hang it."

At 1:30 P.M., Joe Black and I were sitting at the table when a sheepish Cal Taliaferro came in the courtroom. Joe Black looked at him intently but didn't speak. He leaned close to me. "Cal went to the office and had a few nips. Sonuvabitch had two good offers made to him and he managed to turn 'em both down. Now the only thing going for him is his Jack Daniels, and after today it probably going to be Four Roses."

Joe Black reserved his cruelest streak for those who wouldn't admit that he had bested them: They deserved only the cheapest, rot-gut alcohol available.

When the jury was seated, the judge nodded at Joe Black. "That's all I've got for Mr. Kyle." The judge smiled at Joe, whose wiles he obviously appreciated. He nodded at Taliaferro.

It took the circuit solicitor a moment to realize what had happened. "No more witnesses," he said.

"Mr. Pell, go ahead."

Joe Black took me through the events of May 24, and I repeated what I had said in the first trial as nearly verbatim as I could remember.

"Son, you ever been charged with any other crime beside this one?"

"No, sir."

"You beat anybody up, stole anybody's property, or pretended you something you not?"

"No, sir."

"The way you told us 'bout what happened at the store, have you told that the *right way*?"

"Yes, sir."

"The way it *really* happened?"

I locked eyes with the white-haired lady. "Yes, sir."

"You sure about that, boy? Are you *real* sure?"

He was standing with his feet apart in front of the jury box, facing the jury, but pointing at me with his outstretched left hand. The white-haired woman wore a stern look.

"Yes, sir, I'm *real* sure that's what happened."

"Boy, you *sure* you ain't just makin' this stuff up to *save* yo'self?"

"No, sir, I'm telling the truth."

She looked convinced, finally.

"Yo' witness."

Cal Taliaferro was studying his legal pad. He looked tired, perhaps even sleepy.

"No questions."

Judge McKinley looked at Taliaferro for a long moment, and then he turned to me. "You're excused, Mr. McKee."

The adrenaline drained from me like air from a tire. It had taken less than an hour. It was completely anti-climactic, hardly worth the untold hours of worry I had put in about it. What was Taliaferro up to? Why hadn't he cross-examined me, tried to save his self-respect if not the case against me?

I sat down beside Joe Black, who was staring intently at the judge. A tiny smile crept onto my lawyer's wrinkly face as he figured out what was about to happen. He took out a cigar and began to prepare it for a smoke—never, however, removing his gaze from the judge.

Finally Judge McKinley looked up from his desk.

"The state has shown no credible evidence that the accused did other than defend himself." He turned to the jury. "I'm going to direct the jury to acquit. The case isn't proved. Ladies and gentlemen, thank you for your service. You can go."

I looked at Joe Black in astonishment. "What does that mean?"

He smiled wickedly. "That means Judge McKinley ain't running for re-election, and he has done the right thing. He ain't going to take a chance on the jury, even though I know I'm right 'bout what they woulda done."

He struck a match and twice sucked hard on his cigar. Finally Joe Black's sweet smile returned. "It's over, son."

In the clamor of the adjourned courtroom, I hugged Cathy and Marvin and Orene, but I was diverted by the exit of Buford Kyle from the courtroom, his face blank as if he wasn't really cognizant of what had just happened. Five feet behind him trudged Gertrude Kyle, her head bowed.

I would soon feel the relief that the summer of 1965 was over, but what I was feeling at that moment was horror. When Kyle waved his gun that May afternoon, I'd seen only one, momentary instance of his capacity for brutality. Others knew it day in and day out. I turned my sight away from Gertrude Kyle because I had to.

35

Leaving

The doctor had told Mama that afternoon that he thought the immediate danger of further attacks had passed, and so it was a double celebration when we arrived at the hospital from the trial. Daddy asked to see me. His face was as white as a cigarette, which made his blue eyes seem brighter. He was sitting up, and gestured me to the chair by his bed. "B. J. won't let me see the newspaper, but she told me what you said to the *Advertiser* reporter, Scoot." His voice was thin, coming from his throat, not his chest, but his words were clear. "You lie real well when you want to. Won't lie for yourself but you will for me." But then his look softened and he winked at me. "I appreciate you taking up for me."

I needed to change the subject so I asked how he was feeling. "Like hell. Weak. But lucky to be alive, I hear."

"Oh, Daddy, we are so thankful." I meant it. He smiled weakly.

Joe Black came by the hospital that night, went in to see Daddy, and came out smiling.

"Your daddy was real appreciative, Tommy. Means a lot. He didn't want me to be your lawyer, but he didn't really know me. All he knew, he'd heard from his daddy, and your granddaddy thought I was the devil's best friend." He nodded solemnly at me. "'Course I didn't like him, either."

"Was that because of Bebe?"

"Yeah, mainly. No man's going to be too crazy 'bout his wife's old boyfriend." He shrugged. "'Course, no man's going to be too crazy about the fella that got the one he really wanted."

"Joe Black, I don't understand how you knew you had that jury."

He smiled and nodded, happy to hold forth on his expertise. "Well, Tommy, you know, you go into enough courtrooms, argue before enough juries, you get a feel for what people thinkin', what they going to do and ain't going to do. You get a sense of how the evidence is soundin' and you watch folks' faces. They tell you a lot."

His became positively triumphant. "But, hey, after court today, I hightailed it over there and talked to six of those jurors, three of the men and the three women. The men and two of the women said flat out they woulda acquitted, but the other woman wouldn't say."

He nodded. "Know which one it was? The white-haired girl. Said she didn't think it was right to say. But she said to tell you that she was sorry for all that had happened to you."

He shook his head. "She'da hung it, sure as hell, if she'd had to."

"But how did you *know* that about her?"

He frowned and thought a moment, and then it came to him. "'Bout twenty years ago, I had client who got treated real bad by a insurance company that didn't pay as they should've. An agent forged a document. Actual damages 'bout two hundred thousand, and we asked for a lot of punitives because they were really pretty insensitive to her predicament. We gave it to the jury, and the way I heard it was that a girl on the jury quoted my closing argument two or three times in their deliberations that first afternoon. And some man on there gave her some hell about listening to only one side of it, and it made this girl mad, and she looked at the fella and said, 'well, anybody expects to get home by Saturday'— this was on a *Tuesday* afternoon—'they better start payin' attention to what Mr. Pell said.' Jury came back the next morning. That girl held open that insurance company's pocket and I reached in there and got *four million dollars*."

He nodded. "That girl looked just like the one on the jury today. Wadn't her, but looked just like her."

It was as scientific as that—a person's ability to observe a human being and imagine what she was feeling, thanks to her body language and from what you know or guessed about her life circumstances. It was an art, and Joe Black was one of its Old Masters.

"What's going to happen to Taliaferro?"

"Ah, hell, nothin' really. Ol' Felix has already sold the option back to Trotter for two hundred thousand, a hundred percent profit. He's as greedy a sonuvabitch as ever walked the earth, but I don't begrudge that hundred. He did what I asked him to do. But now that the bank ain't going to be sold, their little bribery ain't going to be discovered. I'm goin' down to Selma tomorrow to introduce that boy runnin' against Cal to his new best friend. I 'spect with my money and the nigras' votes he'll retire Cal next year. My hunch is then ol' Cal will drink hisself into oblivion."

I GOT THE IDEA that Joe Black many times in his day had witnessed such a demise. It wasn't callousness or pleasure on his part that Taliaferro was headed for a fall—Joe Black knew that everybody had witnessed how he had whipped Cal's ass on his own turf. But he also knew that such men had an impulse for self-destruction, because they so doubted their own worthiness. They knew somehow they were fraudulent, undeserving of the place where society had put them, and inevitably destined for a fall. I knew this because it was true of at least some of the men who have had my name.

I thought about that several times during my visits over the next few days with Bebe. "I'm so disappointed in the way the local situation has turned out," I told her. "With Daddy out of office and sick, we've got a bunch of mean and lowdown men running everything."

She shrugged. "My whole idea was that, with Buddy in the courthouse, the old guard could oversee change without conflict. But Buddy resisted that."

"I'm not sure Daddy could have managed it even if he wanted to. It's just too much change to come that easily."

She nodded. "I've come to think that may be right, dear. Plus, the federal government sort of took control of the situation anyway." A bright smile spread over her ever-thinner face. "But it was a nice idea I had, wasn't it?"

I pondered a moment whether to say that all her good intentions didn't cancel out the fact that she had railroaded Daddy into a role he didn't want, which caused the stress that helped make him sick. Should the fact Bebe was dying and had good intentions mean I have to excuse her from the responsibility for what happened to Daddy? No. I thought it, believed it, but I couldn't say it.

"It was a good idea. But Daddy did good in the end. Things went smoothly at the courthouse because he accepted that the change was inevitable."

"I'm real proud of him for that," she said. "I'm going to tell him that when he's stronger."

Given her health and Daddy's, I wondered if that would happen. She looked weaker every day. It was like she could read my mind.

"Tommy, when I'm gone, I hope you'll help Junior and Reverend Banks in local politics. It'll be important for some whites, even if only a few, to join hands." I promised I would.

She asked me to read poetry and stories to her. I did that for a couple of days. Then, already visibly fainter, she said, "I want you to read some particular parts of the Bible to me, Tommy. Do you mind?"

She asked me to read from the King James version. "It's the Bible of my youth." A twinkle flickered from her sunken eyes. "It had just been translated when I was confirmed."

She wanted only to hear Isaiah. I finally asked her, after I'd read the fortieth chapter to her for the third time, why she liked that so much.

"Justice, Tommy. Sometimes it's hard to believe it can happen. It's been hard this year." Then she turned on a big smile, which stretched her thin, almost transparent skin. "But now I have renewed faith. How about you, Tommy? Do you have faith now?"

"More than I did a few days ago."

"Faith in what?"

"That somebody, maybe the Almighty, was looking after me."

She seemed pleased, less interested in what I believed than *that* I believed in *something*.

"But what I really believe in is the love that all this trouble brought out. Your support, Cathy's, Mama's. And Marvin and Joe Black, they protected me, got me out of trouble." I thought for a moment. "Of course, you were behind what they did."

She studied me. "Well, things worked out like they did because they should have. I choose to believe that a higher power took care of that."

Within hours of my acquittal, it had dawned on me that the end of my crisis meant that Bebe could stop struggling to live. Cathy had been thinking it already. "There's some bad with the good," she said, "and good with the bad."

DADDY CAME HOME FROM the hospital moving slowly. He was under strict orders to quit smoking and drinking and to avoid stressful situations. He was on a new diet. He didn't say much. He ate little, read the paper, sat in the shade outdoors, dozing.

I asked Mama about Daddy's long silences. "The doctor says sadness is usually a problem after people have a heart attack. They're pessimistic, afraid about their future."

I awakened before dawn one morning and heard clattering in the kitchen. Daddy was making coffee. I was alarmed and asked if he was okay.

"Yeah. Couldn't sleep. Why you up?"

"'Bout the same." I fetched the *Advertiser* from the driveway, and we shared the newspaper with our coffee. I looked up from the paper after a while to see him staring out the kitchen window. The larks were chirping and the daylight was creeping in.

"How 'bout we go have a look at the crops?" I said. His face looked like he had to return from a thousand miles away to hear what I said, but then he nodded.

The rising sun blinded us if we looked eastward, but going any other direction, as we did, it threw a powerful yellow light on the massive green vegetation that seemed to choke the fields. A heavy dew on the waist-high plants wet us both as Daddy waded into the fields. He bent plants back and checked their fruit, looking for the boll weevil in the cotton and assessing how heavily the beans were bearing. After each inspection, he would raise up and squint across the field for a long moment.

His skin was gray and dark circles framed his eyes. His hair was grayer and it needed cutting. He had lost at least fifteen pounds in the last two weeks. He kept reaching up to his shirt pocket and then jerking his hand away, and it was only after I saw this for the third time that I realized he was reaching involuntarily for the cigarettes the doctors had banned. The poor guy was not only weak and scared but in the throes of nicotine withdrawal.

He said almost nothing, but I could tell he was pleased with the absence of insects and the heaviness of the bean pods.

"Look all right?"

He nodded. "Real good. No thanks to me. I'm a damn lucky farmer this year."

"Well, Daddy, you deserved some good luck."

He glanced over at me quickly and then looked ahead. "You think?"

"Sure. We all do. It was our turn."

When we got through examining the last field, I sensed his sadness, and I imagined that it was borne of the realization that we had done all the farming he could do that day, or any day, for a while.

"Daddy, I been thinking I might stick around and help with the farming this fall." It was partly an offer and partly a question to see where I stood with him. But I was sincere in wanting to be in Eden Rise, at least for a while longer.

He didn't say anything. In a couple of minutes, he directed me to drive to the warehouse. When I parked the truck, he didn't open the door but turned to face me.

"Thanks, Scoot, but I think we'll be okay with the farming. You need to go on back to school." He stared at me and grimaced a little, but said it: "Back to North Carolina."

Then he got out of the truck, went into the warehouse, and started talking to Junior and Sam and the other guys. Everybody greeted Daddy warmly and pretended like we hadn't been to hell and back.

As I stood there and felt the morning heat come down on me like the blazing breath of God, realizing I didn't have to be absorbed with the threats to my own fate, a feeling began to creep up my back and take over my body like a low-level fever—not hot enough to put me to bed but warm enough to make me feel shitty all the time.

It was guilt and the accompanying depression. I had been responsible for the death of Jackie Herndon and the destruction of my father's world. I knew all the reasons it wasn't my fault that Jackie was dead or that Daddy's health and future lay around him like the ruins of a tornado, but reason only went so far toward accepting the consequences of what I had done.

Later that morning I found Mama in her garden with a slingblade, slaying vegetable plants that had quit producing or had dried up from neglect. I made the same proposal to her about staying through the fall. I thought she might want the help.

"Absolutely not. You must go. All this has to be put behind you. I can handle the farming until Buddy is up to it."

"But you'll be in Birmingham, won't you?"

"Yeah, but I can get down here enough to keep an eye on everything." She gave me her kindest look. "You gotta go on back to Duke. Up there you'll know the score and know what you're supposed to do—get an education."

Marvin had made plans to return to Chicago. A few days before he was to leave, I got an idea. I asked if he would drive to Durham with me and fly from there. I was still too wary of the world to relinquish my protector.

"Yeah, man, I'd like to see what it looks like up there."

The morning we left, Marvin and I had breakfast with Bebe. She was light and witty, tolerating no morbid or teary good-bye.

"Now, boys," she said once our plates were empty of Orene's pie, which she insisted we have even if it was breakfast. "I want y'all to promise me that y'all will take care of the family. Y'all and Cathy are going to be the leaders now. Buddy is weak, Bill is moving away, I'm going to be gone soon. Y'all will have to work together, looking after each other. This is your family now, Marvin. I think y'all love each other."

Marvin and I both nodded at her but didn't dare look at each other.

"Come kiss me, Tommy." I did as instructed, holding my breath the whole time.

Marvin was standing across the room, studying his shoes. "Marvin, dear, you come here and kiss me too." Marvin obeyed.

We both hugged William and Orene good-bye and walked quickly to the red Ford. Marvin slid behind the wheel. His sunglasses masked his eyes as he steered down the bending driveway, between the parallel rows of pecan trees that shaded our way.

There was a little wet trail darkening Marvin's cheek. "Damn, that was hard," he said.

"Yeah. No kidding." I looked over and caught his eye. "It would have been a lot harder by myself."

We headed east into the morning sun, by fields of cotton now showing spots of white as bolls began to open. An airplane buzzed along the northern horizon. The hot air carried the bitter odor of defoliant. To the south, a sudden burst of breeze sent a wave through a big field of soybeans, turning the dark green leaves over and exposing their pale undersides. The wind propelled a cloud over the field, its shadow leading the leaf wave eastward, in front of us. I guess it was still the most beautiful place on earth.

36

THE SPARROW

At Duke I was haunted by Jackie's ghost. I drank too much and slept either not at all or for a dozen hours at a time. Beth told me I was depressed, and she talked with me about my "trauma" to the point that I bored the shit out of myself. She thought I should go to a shrink, and I did eventually. Everyone on campus treated me strangely, either with elaborate courtesy or with subtle avoidance; after all, I'd been party to a death, and had shot a man. Nobody else had done those things. I was as exotic as a paratrooper returning from Vietnam, and just as bothersome. I tried to play basketball a couple of times, but it just made me mad that I was doing it without Jackie. The court was empty without him, no matter who else played. I started running the campus paths and playing fields, and that helped some.

I was, of course, waiting for a conclusion to one important matter. I was taking notes in European history class in early October when I was given a message to call home. Mama answered. "Bebe died this morning. She went peacefully in her sleep."

Cathy met me at the Birmingham airport that evening, and we spent the night in the bungalow she and my parents had moved to in late August, on the city's southern border. Mama and Daddy were already in Eden Rise preparing for the funeral. It seemed so strange to be in a house with my sister that wasn't the one we grew up in. And yet Cathy seemed comfortable. Her new school was more challenging, the kids smarter and more worldly. She had even met some Birmingham boys she liked and one she had been out with three times.

I asked how Mama and Daddy were bearing up with all the changes. She smiled widely. "Mama is doing great. She's loved fixing up this little house, even though she knows they're going to buy something bigger pretty soon. She likes the shopping and the parks." She paused. "Daddy is calmer but he's still wrestling with it all. He's got no idea what he's going to do."

"Are they getting along?"

"Better. They don't argue. They spend a lot of time together, walking and reading. Mama says it's a little eerie how quiet he is, but then she was ready for peace."

THE NEXT MORNING THE air in Eden Rise held the dry, dusty smell of autumn. The cotton fields had been stripped of most of their whiteness, but every field looked mauled and messy because the mechanical cottonpickers had littered strings of lint across the mostly naked stalks. The once-green expanses of soybeans now were endless parallel rows of stubble cut off near the ground, to be picked over by starlings. The nearly black soil was dry and gray.

I was bothered by how much Daddy had aged in just the past month. His hair was silver in places, and the skin around his face seemed to sag, mainly from loss of weight. He moved slowly when he came over to greet me. He shook my hand and then pulled me close for a hug, something he hadn't done in a long time.

"You look good, Daddy," I said, lying. "How you feeling?" He was fine, he said, though low on energy. He asked me about school, but then our conversation stalled. I wanted to talk more, but I didn't know how without going into dangerous territory. Worse things than silence, I decided.

Mama was better—pretty and bouncy, with new clothes and a new haircut and a happier countenance.

William came for lunch and, to my surprise, brought along Marvin. "I spent two weeks in Chicago, and I realized I'd rather be down here. Y'all ruined the Windy City for me with all this slow-assed livin'."

"Wasn't all that slow this summer."

Mama shook her head slightly. Marvin saw her signal and subtly changed directions. "I'm going to be a pallbearer. Bebe appreciated all that baby-sitting I did."

Bebe. That was nice that he thought of her in familiar terms.

William had handled the funeral arrangements. "Tommy, as per your grandmother's instructions, we'll receive friends tonight at home, like we did for your grandfather. The funeral will be tomorrow at two. At Bethel Baptist."

It made sense when I thought about it. "Reverend Banks is a fine fellow." Mama nodded. "He came and prayed with 'Sister Brigid' every day near the end." Cathy grinned. "Bebe loved being called 'Sister Brigid.' It reminded her of being Catholic."

Mama and Cathy looked at William, who finally spoke again. "Tom, your grandmother asked that you give a eulogy tomorrow. Do you think you could do that?"

I looked at Daddy. "Why me?" He smiled sadly but didn't respond.

"She thought you understood her life better than anybody else," Cathy said. "Well, except for me, and she said speaking at funerals was men's work."

The next afternoon, a fresh breeze from the west brought the feeling of fall to those of us assembling outside the brand-new red-brick Bethel Baptist, which sparkled in the soft fall light. I could easily look up to examine the little white steeple above the front of the church and note the swaying boughs of the surrounding oak and poplar trees whose leaves were just leaning toward one new bright color or other.

Six pallbearers assembled at Bebe's casket at the steps of the church. Junior and Marvin were in the front, Joe Black and Dr. Hill behind them, Sam and William bringing up the rear. All these men were either dear to her personally or close to her larger family but none had any recognized social standing in the white community she had lived in for the last fifty years. Granddaddy's pallbearers, by contrast, had been a who's who of the county's powerful men.

At five minutes after two, a piano inside began to play a familiar melody. The harmony became so complex that I realized in fact there were two pianos and an organ at work in the little church. Soon a choir began to sing. Robert Addison, William's undertaker brother, signaled to Junior to move forward. Reverend Banks and Sister Carol from St. Jude followed the pallbearers. Then came the family.

The little church smelled of fresh paint and varnish. It was crowded, mostly with black people except for a row of elderly white women I didn't know. Bebe's Montgomery friends, I guessed.

In the choir loft at the front of the church, forty singers, gowned in powder blue, were swaying as they offered "Swing Low, Sweet Chariot" with multiple parts of both melody and harmony. Reverend Banks then welcomed the people to "our service of celebration and farewell to our beloved Sister Brigid." Sister Carol talked about her appreciation for "Brigid's good works" and read the Twenty-third Psalm. Then the choir rose and sang "His Eye is on the Sparrow," a hymn that I had never heard but which would, after this day, always linger in my mind. This time the two women soloists shared the melody with a booming baritone.

> *Why should I feel discouraged,*
> *Why should shadows come,*
> *Why should my heart be lonely*
> *And long for Heav'n and home,*
> *When Jesus is my portion?*
> *My constant Friend is He.*

Then the whole choir:
> *His eye is on the sparrow,*
> *And I know He watches me;*
> *His eye is on the sparrow,*
> *And I know he watches me.*

Then the three soloists, alternately on successive verses.
> *I sing because I'm happy,*
> *I sing because I'm free*
> *For His eye is on the sparrow,*
> *And I know He watches me.*

They ended with several repetitions of the chorus sung in rounds, with each of the soloists executing an individual offering of "I sing because I'm happy" while the other two were still in the midst of their own.

Music is, next to sex and the fear of death, the most powerful inducement to my emotions. The hymn enveloped me, until all my senses except hearing were suspended.

"Thomas McKee will now offer a eulogy," Reverend Banks announced. Cathy patted my knee, and I looked over at her, her encouraging smile prompting me to rise. I took a deep breath and walked up to the pulpit.

For a moment I inspected the audience. Mama was smiling, and Marvin was nodding, as if to say, "Do yo' thang." Daddy looked too drained to show what he was feeling, and Joe Black and William wore their sadness on their old faces. The congregation was still.

I recounted the major events of Bebe's life, noted surviving family and friends, and then paused.

"My grandmother always wanted our world and our community to be better than it is, and she did what she could to make it better. Some of you out there know that well." I felt a collective sigh of relief from the gathering.

"*I sho' know it.*"

"*Uh-huh.*"

"*That's right, son.*"

"*Bless her soul.*"

"*Say on.*"

Their calls eased my tension, and I proceeded more confidently.

"In my last times with my grandmother, she was mostly thinking about justice, about how we achieve righteousness and fairness in our time. And about whether God finally delivers justice on this earth. Frankly, she had her doubts, as we all do from time to time. Some of those doubts, I know, came from my experience the past few months—the senseless death of my college friend Jackie Herndon and the acquittal of his murderer."

The church had returned to absolute quiet.

"She took comfort from the prophet Isaiah, who promised that God was both all-powerful and just, and she was particularly helped by the fortieth chapter of Isaiah." I read the first eleven verses. When I finished the prophecy that "every valley shall be exalted and every mountain and hill brought low," there were shouts, and even more at "the crooked places shall be made straight and the rough places smooth."

"Yes, Yes, Yes! Yes!" from a woman who stood in her pew halfway back.

"My grandmother grasped the faith that a higher power does rule, even if we lowly humans can't understand it. It is purely and simply an act of faith to believe something good is in control, especially when we see so much hatefulness in this world. But she did believe that truth pressed to earth would rise again. That no lie could live forever."

"Uh-hunh!"

"Yes, sir!"

"That's right, McKee."

"In my darkest hours this summer, when I couldn't imagine how a just God could let my friend die, I thought of those words. It was hard to believe they were true."

"Don't you know it!"

"But I had the example of my grandmother's faith that she was God's instrument on this earth. Her life is a testament to the faith that we can do something, that we must love justice, that we are put here not to help ourselves but to be instruments of God's justice."

"Amen. Amen." An elderly voice from the back.

As I sat down amid shouts of affirmation, Cathy took my hand and leaned over and kissed my wet cheek.

Banks raised his arms for quiet. "Choir, give us something to soothe our spirits." They sang "Beautiful River." He commended Sister Brigid's soul to the Lord, saying she was near the throne now. To the refrain of "His Eye is on the Sparrow," the pallbearers carried the casket out of the church. The family followed and everyone drove to Oak Hill cemetery, where the three soloists from the choir sang, *a capella*, "We are Climbing Jacob's Ladder" as the pallbearers carried the casket up a rise to the family plot. She was buried next to Granddaddy. There were two brief prayers and a benediction, and it was over.

THE FAMILY, THE MINISTERS, and the pallbearers gathered at our house after the burial. We all spent the late afternoon talking and eating and laughing. It was as if there had been a signed contract among the two dozen people that our crying was over.

Joe Black led me outside so he could smoke his cigar. "Tommy, I'm going to tell you something important. You go on to college and think about law school, and if you decide you wanta go, you call me and we'll get you in and then you come down to Montgomery and in a few years I'll put a sharp edge on you, make you into the best and richest damn lawyer in this state, you hear?" He handed me his card—and a cigar.

I went back inside and sat with Marvin and Cathy at the dining room table. I looked at Daddy, who was talking with Junior and Sam about farming. He looked so old.

"You think Daddy's okay with what I said?"

Cathy nodded. "He won't say anything to you, but he liked it. He knows you said exactly what Bebe wanted you to say."

I asked Marvin about his plans. "William wants me to stay with him at your grandmother's. You know, Bebe added me into her will, so I'm going to have some money to start something good with." I wasn't surprised to hear that Bebe had seen fit for Marvin to inherit some of Big Tom's money. I'm sure, too, that she was taking care of William by encouraging Marvin's presence in his life. "I'm going to go back to school. But you know what Joe Black said? Said he'd train me to be his investigator. I kinda liked that idea."

"Negro detection, right? Should come natural to you."

Marvin nodded. "Be kinda fun sneaking around, finding out shit."

Cathy was shaking her head. "Marvin, you going to do that so you'll find out every woman in Alabama who's cheating on her husband and then you can sleep with them all yourself."

"That's right, Baby Sister. It would be a fringe benefit."

She turned to me. "Church did him absolutely no good at all."

The next morning my family had a quiet breakfast before Cathy took me to the airport. I said my good-byes to Mama and Daddy without tears, though it was hard not to cry at the sight of Daddy's bereft face.

As Cathy pointed the Ford northward out of the town, I looked left and right at Eden Rise, a little plantation town on a high place in the middle of a prairie—a rich land of dark soil now mostly colored yellow and brown but with occasional shimmers from the light on heavy dew. An old black man walked toward us on the other side of the road, a hoe resting on his shoulder, a cigarette dangling from his lips. I waved at him and he returned it, but he was actually looking over toward the soybean field encircled by a fence row, a line thick with little cedar trees that had been planted by roosting birds. A flock of a thousand starlings was executing maneuvers above the field, whipping with great precision left and right, up and down, according to directions that came from an unknown commander.

I realized that the days were about over when you would see an old Negro carrying a hoe down an Eden Rise road. But I guessed the blackbirds would always fly there on cool, sunny fall days.

I wondered that October day if this would be my last such departure—if, in fact, I would ever go back to Eden Rise, if I would have a reason to return, or the courage. But it was still my place, and it always will be.

Postlude

SPRING 1994

As we came through the cut on the Red Mountain Expressway, I watched the morning light bounce off the fifty-foot burnt-orange stacks and the silver water tower of the Sloss Furnace, a nineteenth-century iron works and the city's masterpiece of industrial art. I appreciated the sun, because it suggested some optimism about a day I dreaded.

Marvin, masked by sunglasses, steered his BMW off the big highway and onto a westbound avenue leading to the federal courthouse.

"Aw right, Baby Sister, who's going to do the talkin', you or me?" he said. I noted that he didn't even consider me for the role of spokesman to the media who would swarm us, just as they had at another courthouse almost twenty-nine years before.

"I'll talk," Cathy said, "and you give the nasty looks to the ones who ask the bad questions."

Cathy took Marvin's car phone and punched in a number. "This is Cathy McKee. What's happening?" She listened a moment. "How soon will you need him?" Another momentary pause. "We'll be there."

She swiveled to face me in the back seat. "Defense is making its opening statement right now. Fifteen, twenty minutes, and you're up." She smiled. "Showtime."

I rolled my eyes. I had been so apprehensive about this day so long that I was relieved that the anxiety of anticipation could only last a few more minutes. We parked in a deck and walked the block to the courthouse. Marvin, still shaded and wearing a black suit, was on my left. Equally powerful in her equally black suit and pumps, Cathy strode briskly on the right. I was half a step behind them.

The reporters and cameramen saw us from half a block away and came running.

"Mr. McKee, what will you tell the jury?"

"Tom, are you happy about testifying?"

"How do you feel now about Buford Kyle?"

I said nothing but when we got to the steps of the courthouse Cathy stopped and turned toward the reporters. She called several by name as she greeted the assembly.

"My brother is doing his civic duty today, giving evidence about tragic events that occurred a long time ago. He is not happy to be here, but of course he is perfectly willing to be here. He has no comment about Mr. Kyle. The evidence he gives will speak for itself."

A television reporter pushed a microphone toward Marvin. "Mr. Whitfield, are you representing Tom McKee?"

"No, he's a witness. He doesn't need a lawyer. I'm here as Tom's friend and a family member." Then Marvin flashed a smile. "Plus, hell, I'm just as curious as everybody else."

"That's it. We gotta go." Cathy pivoted and quickly climbed the steps. At the courtroom door, we stopped to wait for the bailiff.

Cathy turned to face me. She reached up and tugged my necktie gently a fraction around my collar. "I like the tie." She smiled. "You look great. How ya feel?"

"How ya think?"

She just smiled faintly and nodded.

The bailiff, an old acquaintance from trials gone by, opened the door and nodded at me.

Marvin put his hand on my elbow and leaned in close. "You tough and you going to go in there and *be* tough."

I almost choked up over the *déjà vu*. It was amazing that he remembered.

I WAS LED TO the front of the courtroom and sworn in. When I sat in the witness box, I looked around for Mama, and there she was sitting on the front row, behind the U.S. attorney and next to a white-haired black woman, Mrs. Herndon, with whom my mother had stayed in contact all these years, and whom she was now hosting for this sad occasion. Again my throat swelled. These two friends, now old, were joined by a horrible accident that had brought them together only twice, for the saddest occasions you could imagine.

It was a new and prosperous courtroom, beautifully appointed with polished dark paneling and clean green carpeting. Still I kept going back to the Yancey County courtroom, seeing the faces of people who were there then and who would have been here now except their time had run out. For some, it had expired long ago, but I still missed them, and I missed them even when I didn't have some major media event like this to remind me of them.

And finally, inevitably, I looked at Buford Kyle. I wouldn't have recognized him on the street. I had been surprised to learn that he had only been forty-nine in 1965. Now he was wrinkled and bent over the table before him, and his eyes seemed not to focus on anything. I would watch him for the next few hours, and his gaze remained unrecognizing. I wondered if he knew where he was.

But credit the physical durability of those too mean to die. To my great relief, there was no one sitting behind him that resembled the family I remembered. I had prayed that Gertrude had been liberated, somehow, some way, and now I had the circumstantial evidence to confirm that she had been. But surely some of the children were still alive. Why were they not here to lend him support? Had the intervening years defeated or destroyed them? Or had three decades led them finally to reject and scorn their father?

I hoped that they hadn't spent those three decades salting the wounds of the past. I knew the jeopardy of that, and I couldn't wish it on even my worst enemy.

Randy Russell spent an hour eliciting from me what happened on May 24, 1965. He even spent a few minutes examining my motives for being in Yancey County that day. It all went pretty smoothly. I had studied the transcript from back then and had my story straight.

The lean truth.

A couple of times Russell drifted over toward the jury box so I would look that way. Eight women and six men, including the two alternates. Nine blacks and five whites. I reckoned that almost half weren't even born in 1965. I couldn't imagine how they would understand what this was all about.

The court had appointed a well-known Birmingham criminal defense lawyer to represent the indigent Kyle. I knew him slightly, had heard he was a decent fellow, and didn't take any umbrage as he exploited the fact that I had such good command of events so long ago but couldn't summon information about my life from very recent times.

"Mr. McKee, what did you have for breakfast Tuesday a week ago?"

He asked several such questions, and then, being the good lawyer he was, sensed that he was annoying some of the jurors by belaboring the point.

"Did black and white children go to school together in Alabama in 1965?" "How long had blacks and whites been eating in the same restaurants in the South in 1965?" "How many blacks were holding public office in 1965?"

With those questions, he made the point that those were different times, that people thought and acted differently from how we do today. It was a good point, one I would have made in his place.

But he and I both knew that it didn't matter whether my memory was all that reliable or if the times were different in 1965. People judge others pretty quickly by what they do or did, and they judge them by the moral standards of today. When I finally had realized that fact in the run-up to the trial, I had relaxed somewhat about its likely outcome.

It didn't much matter what his lawyer did. Buford Kyle was going to be convicted. As it turned out, the jury deliberated only a couple of hours. A few weeks later the judge sentenced the old man to twenty years and suspended half of it. He would die in prison, and the rest of us could decide for ourselves whether that amounted to justice.

When Wayne, my AA sponsor, asked me over coffee if I thought justice had indeed been rendered, I answered, "I'm not sure."

"Hell, McKee, the older you get the more like yourself you become."
But Wayne was wrong about that.

I never knew if it was Kyle's long-after-the-fact second trial, or just the forced middle-aged acceptance of mortality, but I did turn over most of the guilt about Jackie Herndon's death and the destruction of my daddy's life.

To be sure, the past is never over. But something has made it easier to find the place inside me where hope resides.